ABOUT TH

Joseph Maitland Cardwell joined the Royal Navy in April 1974. After completion of initial training at HMS *Raleigh* in Torpoint, Cornwall, he volunteered for submarine service, qualifying for his golden Dolphins in October 1974. He became part of the crew of HMS/M *Churchill*, a fleet hunter-killer nuclear submarine, in November 1974 at the age of seventeen. He served on board as a marine engineer until joining his second boat, HMS/M *Conqueror*, in September 1981. Deciding on a complete career change in March 1983, he qualified as a clearance diver in October 1983, serving on several single- and multi-role mine sweepers and diving teams all over Great Britain. In 1988 he qualified to plan and supervise all Royal Navy diving, demolition and explosive ordnance disposal operations.

Other duties included reporting to the commanding officer for maintaining discipline, the provision of victuals, regulating military law and medical services. He also holds qualifications as a Health and Safety Commercial Diver (Part 1), Health and Safety Diver Medical Technician, Health and Safety Emergency Medical Technician, Explosive Range Supervisor and Recompression Chamber Operator.

During his time in the Navy he also volunteered and qualified in civilian examinations as RYA Yachtmaster Offshore, RYA Power Boat Instructor and BSAC Open Water Diver. He left the Royal Navy in 1997, and now lives in the Peak District.

THE BLACK CIGAR

By

JOSEPH MAITLAND CARDWELL

FOREWORD

The Cold War had continued its passive-aggressive progression since the end of the Second World War. Russia and America, along with their allies, had been keeping a close eye on each other. Britain had been playing a major part in this tenuous spying game, with the nuclear threat ever present.

The fear of global destruction was the only thing stopping these two superpowers from going head-to-head. It was a time for patience, deliberation and tactics ... but for some it was a time of boredom and monotony.

This all-out focus and concentration, however, was a distraction from other lesser threats which, if not dealt with, could have the same deadly consequences.

Although no bullets were fired in anger, this war still had its casualties.

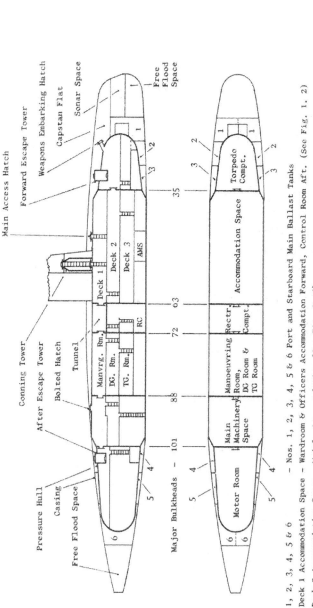

Main Access Hatch

Forward Escape Tower

Weapons Embarking Hatch

Capstan Flat

Sonar Space

Free Flood Space

Conning Tower

After Escape Tower

Bolted Hatch

Tunnel

Pressure Hull

Casing

Free Flood Space

Deck 1
Deck 2
Deck 3
AMS

Manvrg. Rm.
DG. Rm.
TG. Rm.
RC

Main Machinery Space

Motor Room

Major Bulkheads — 101   88   72   o3   35

6   5   4

Torpedo Compt.

Accommodation Space

Rectr. Compt.

Manoeuvring Room, DG Room & TG Room

Motor Room

6   5   4

1, 2, 3, 4, 5 & 6   – Nos. 1, 2, 3, 4, 5 & 6 Port and Starboard Main Ballast Tanks

Deck 1 Accommodation Space – Wardroom & Officers Accommodation Forward, Control Room Aft. (See Fig. 1. 2)

Deck 2 Accommodation Space – Mainly Accommodation (See Fig. 1. 3)

Deck 3 Accommodation Space – Miscellaneous Spaces (See Fig. 1. 4)

AMS – Auxiliary Machinery Space.   RC – Reactor Compt.   DG – Diesel Generator.   TG – Turbo Generator.

CHAPTER ONE

The freezing water numbed her brain. She fought the urge to breathe as her body pleaded for oxygen. Fear began to set in quickly. *I've been down too long*, she thought. *I'll not make it back. The entrance pool is too far away. How long was this tunnel?* After losing her grip on the torch and now in total darkness, she became disorientated. Half-swimming, half-crawling, she scrambled her way along the flooded narrow sump tunnel at the lowest point of the cave. Her fingers had gone numb with the cold, blood oozed from the scratched tips and she could no longer feel the guide-rope that ran the length of the underwater tunnel. She prayed she was heading in the right direction. *How am I going to explain this to my mam. I wish I was with her now, in her warm, safe arms or in my bed at home in Ireland. I only agreed to come on this expedition to break the boredom, something to do. My brother Liam is going to be in so much trouble.* The rocks were sharp and jagged as she banged into them. Her body stopped abruptly when she hit one with her shoulder; it should have hurt, but she felt no pain. Suddenly, her head was pulled back and her face banged hard against the dark solid rock that formed the roof of the narrow underwater stretch of water. Panic was now overwhelming her as she tried frantically to release her hair that had become snagged in the jagged rock. Small bubbles began to escape from her mouth and she could hold her breath no longer. She screamed silently, and felt the coldness of the acrid water as it ran down her throat, large bubbles now emerging as she finally gave in to the need to breathe. Her long slender fingers frantically scratched at the rock where her hair was caught, and she could just make out the bubbles – her life-maintaining bubbles – disappearing through a small crack. With her strength deteriorating rapidly, she drifted into unconsciousness.

CHAPTER TWO

The whole moor grew darker; the gorse and heather lost their colour as black clouds rolled in from the west. The wind had started its long journey from Greenland, crossing the vast expanse of North Atlantic water before cooling again as it travelled over Iceland, picking up more moisture from the sea again on its way south-east across mainland Britain and depositing rain here on the Derbyshire Peak District. Even for winter, this wind was particularly cold. From a distance, he moved with ease like a floating black spectre gliding quickly across the terrain; looking closer, however, he was jumping across leats, leaping athletically from one boulder to another, and when needed trudging through marshland. His sturdy leather boots kept the water out and his gaiters parted the heather and bracken as he moved stealthily across the ankle-breaking tuffs of grass. The rocks glistened jet black and purple and some with a green tinge from moss and lichen. He sidestepped through narrow gaps between the bigger ones, his rapid pace never faltering. The rain was repelled from him by his waterproof clothing, causing it to fall from his body in torrents, his full hood and peak allowing him to see by keeping the horizontal downpour from his eyes. Ben Taylor's earpiece, connected via a small wire to a radio hidden deep inside his rucksack, crackled to life. Normally he would keep to the high ground to avoid boggy areas and maintain vigilance for approaching bad weather, but now he descended rapidly into the valley that ran down to his right. He bulldozed his way through the wetlands at the bottom and began pumping his legs to gather height up the other side, all the time listening to the person talking in his ear. It had been raining in Derbyshire for three days, but now it was a storm. The weather forecast did not show any let-up. Taylor had checked the weather forecast twice in the space of a few hours with the Castleton potholing rescue team to see if there was any change. He was trying to descend Oxlow Cavern, trying to find the longest natural underground tunnel in the world, and needed the ground to be reasonably dry. It was not going to happen. This was Taylor's version of escapism, getting away from the confines of a submarine – and to a lesser extent, its crew. Taylor was used to walking in these uninhabited places, and had spent a lot of his free time in the Royal Navy doing just that. From Scotland to the Lake District or Exmoor and Dartmoor in Devon, he liked the solitude and quietness that these areas provided. He liked to give himself a challenge rather than just walk, but this quest was rapidly becoming a wash-out: just too risky. The volume of water on the surface was extreme, so the amount soaking through to the underground would be incalculable but immense. Taylor was due, the day after tomorrow, back on board his submarine HMS/M *Covert*, which was berthed in Faslane Scotland and undergoing routine maintenance. He was about to call it a day, when the emergency radio in his backpack crackled to life. He was listening intently through his earpiece to a policeman who was reporting an incident to the local potholing rescue service. A Female in her early twenties had been missing for over three hours in an underground cave system known as 'Giant's Hole'. Another member of her team had returned to the surface and raised the alarm. Taylor was not far from the scene and was making his way there fast.

It was twenty minutes later when Taylor arrived at the entrance to the hole. He watched as the rescue team came out of a hole in the ground into the pouring rain, exhausted and shaking their heads. There seemed to be some confusion as to the exact whereabouts of the girl. One of the four in the original team of three men and one girl became agitated. Taylor noticed how poorly the man was dressed for the conditions up on the moor – trainers, jeans and a thin green jacket. Green Jacket began to shout.

'She's got to be there, I watched her go into the sump and she didn't come out the other side. She's got to be in there!' The man made a dash for the entrance hole but was grabbed by one of the rescue team.

'Hold on, pal, we don't want two people getting lost down there.' They struggled with each other and Taylor stepped in to help the rescuer keep the man from entering the hole.

'He's right, buddy, let's not go off half-cocked. Charging in there like a bull will only make things worse.' Taylor turned to the police officer. 'Do you know where we can get some diving gear?'

'And you are?' His officious reply startled Taylor, which was unfortunately reflected in his answer.

'Chief Petty Officer Diver Ben Taylor of Her Majesty's Royal Navy. Now, do you know where we can get some diving gear? A local sub-aqua club, maybe?'

The policeman, now flustered, answered straight away. 'There's a club in Castleton, but I doubt if we can get hold of anyone. They only meet on certain weekends and I wouldn't—'

'OK, leave it with me,' Taylor cut him off. 'Would you be kind enough to get your station sergeant on the radio? I wish to speak to him.'

'Now wait just a minute,' the policeman started to complain. Again, Taylor cut him off.

'Please, let's not argue: there's a young woman down there who needs our help. The water level is rising and any delay could cost her life.' The police officer took out his radio and turned his back to Taylor.

Taylor shook hands with the leader of the rescue team. 'Hi, I'm Ben.'

'Hi; nice to meet you, Ben. My name is Sid, Sid Cawthorne.'

Taylor began gathering information. 'Let's say, Sid, that the guy is right and the girl is where he says she is. What depth of water can we expect with all this rain we're having?'

'If he's right, she's in the east tributary canal. The deepest part of that is twenty-four metres in a drought, but now I would say nearer to thirty metres.'

The police officer interrupted and held out his radio for Taylor.

'Excuse me, Sid.' Taylor took the radio, and brought the sergeant up to speed with who he was and the latest developments with the missing girl. Then he asked, 'Sergeant would you be kind enough to patch me through to the Portsmouth area bomb disposal team? I'd like to speak with the operations officer.' The radio went dead for a while.

'We'll need to rig up a guide-line straight to the entry pool where the girl went in.' Taylor spoke out loud to the rescue leader while Green Jacket was led away from the entrance hole. 'And we'd better rig some lights, so we'll need a generator up here as well.' The rescue team came to life and rushed off.

'It looks like you've put yourself in charge; what would you like me to do?' the police officer said quietly.

Taylor ignored his remark but was glad to have another willing helper. 'Better get these people somewhere warm, we're going to be a while. And discreetly arrange some medical support up here, fill them in with the details.' Taylor spoke to one of the original potholing team before they were led away. The radio crackled and Taylor pressed the transmit button.

'Hello, boss, Chief Taylor here from the submarine *Covert*. Have you got a diving team on the road near Castleton in Derby? We've got a bit of a situation in a pothole called the Giant's Hole.' Taylor went on to describe in detail to his superior what exactly was going on and what he needed. After hearing his story, the operations officer came back at once.

'Let's take a look, shall we. Nothing from Faslane or Rosyth, but I think the Portsmouth EOD[1] team are up that way somewhere, there always gallivanting around the east coast.' The radio went quiet for a moment. 'Yes, we have a Land Rover in King's Lynn, Chief …
just been sorting out an unexploded Second World War mine trawled up by a fishing boat. I'll get in touch with them straight away and see how long it'll be before they're with you.'

'Thank you, boss; can you talk to the police sergeant and get an escort for them as well, we're pretty remote here I would hate for them to come all this way to get lost at the final mile.'

'Leave that with me, Chief; you concentrate on getting that girl home safe. I hope we're not going to be too late. Oh, by the way, the leader of the diving team in King's Lynn is a good friend of yours, I believe: Tim Sherwin?'

'A very good friend, sir; haven't seen him for a while, though. Thanks again.' Taylor smiled to himself. *Tadpole* the name he had given Tim when they'd first met five years ago at the Navy's diver training section on Horsea Island in Portsmouth. Tim was relatively new to diving, hence the nickname 'Tadpole': he was not a fully grown frog-man. Taylor had chanced his arm a bit calling him Tadpole, as Tim, although new to diving, was a seasoned Royal Marine and could easily have taken it the wrong way. Taylor was glad he took it with good humour, and as their friendship grew the name stuck.

---

[1] EOD: explosive ordnance disposal.

The rescue team leader appeared as Taylor handed the radio back to the policeman.

'Ready to rig the guide-line, Ben.'

'OK, Sid, I'll be right with you.' Taylor pulled on a thin diver's dry suit he took from his backpack, checked his underwater torch and slid it into his leg pocket. As an afterthought, he placed a small ice axe he used for climbing into a loop on his belt, then closed the bag and threw it at the policeman.

'Look after that, there's a good chap.' He then joined Sid at the entrance hole.

'We'll need a good man up here to organise lights and communicate with us down at the sump in case we need medical backup,' Taylor said to him. 'The radio is no good, it won't work down there. We can organise a chain of men to pass messages back and forth. My second-in-command will sort that.' Both men then descended into the cold darkness of Giant's Hole.

CHAPTER THREE

Their first obstacle was a twenty-foot drop down a waterfall that was in full flood. The narrow wire ladder twisted and turned as they climbed down through the torrent. Once clear of the last rung they scrambled on their bellies through a narrow hole leading to a larger chamber, enabling both men to stand and walk. Then they came to a narrow ledge with a drop-off on one side, which narrowed into a black hole as it disappeared far below. They crept along the ledge, this time on their backs, keeping their balance with their hands on the low roof above them, the camber on the slippery rock trying to ease them towards the edge. Taylor could now see his own breath as the temperature plummeted. They followed the flow of water down another slightly smaller waterfall, this time without the assistance of a ladder.

Sid turned to Taylor. 'We have to leave the watercourse here and climb over a hard face; we pick it up again on the other side.' Taylor pointed on. They climbed up a rock face and passed through a narrow hole, then slid down the other side, which was as smooth as glass. Taylor hoped they didn't have to get her out on a stretcher. Both men continued for another half-hour, Taylor following the light on Sid's helmet. Finally, walking waist-high down a narrow tunnel, bent over double so as not to bang their heads on the rocks above, the roof went up and a cave opened up enough for them to stand upright again. Taylor noticed a large pool of water in the corner of the cave. Sid stopped in his tracks and Taylor saw he was shaking.

'What is it, mate?'

'The water level is much higher than I thought … we're not even in the right chamber yet. Down through that hole and in the corner of the next chamber is the sump. There's a stake driven into the ground and a rope leading from it down into the sump, it's the guide-line that takes you to the other side.' Sid paused for a moment to take it all in, then he turned and faced Taylor with eyes as big as dinner plates. 'And that's probably flooded as well, anybody going down there won't have a clue where they're going or where to get out.'

'We'll see about that.' Taylor took off his helmet and slipped into the pool of water. He'd been in cold water before but this was exceptional. He knew he would not have long. His ability to hold his breath was not the problem here; it was hypothermia, and being so far underground he would not be able to warm up. Taylor found the stake, scratched around the base and found the rope, then pulled himself down into the sump tunnel. It was going to be a tight squeeze with a cylinder strapped to his back. The rocks were jagged above and to the sides, but the floor of the tunnel was clear and smooth where hundreds of bodies had scraped their way across it over the years.

Taylor turned back and explored the entrance to the cave, which was now underwater. He went as high as he could and found what he was looking for: a small air pocket in the corner, just enough for his head. Taylor rested for a moment and gathered his thoughts. When he was ready, he pushed himself back down and re-entered the sump tunnel.

Crawling slowly he carefully inspected the tunnel floor and walls, and spinning on his back, the jagged roof. The strong beam of light from his torch revealed a thin layer of green slime covering the rocks. As he moved on he noted a large boulder protruding from the side of the tunnel, and raised his shoulder so as to miss it. Something caught his eye: a change, different … what was it? Taylor was lying on his back looking up at the roof of the tunnel. He raised his head so he could look closer. The green slime had been removed, scratched away. He probed with his fingers and found a broken fingernail lodged in the stone. A crack appeared. He followed it with his fingers as it widened. Coming from this direction no hole could be seen, but from the other direction a lip turned into a ledge that turned into a hole … could it be possible? Taylor had to contort his body and wriggle into the gap. His head grew heavy as the water ran off his face. He was in a black rocky hole, clear of water from the chest up; the smell was nauseating and the beam of his torch had stopped dead on what appeared to be a person. The sight of it made him jolt back, hitting his head on the rock behind him. Then he froze. He stared at it, as it stared back at him. He had never seen such terror. It was a female. Her hair was matted and wet, hanging down like string; a clump was making an 'S' shape around her nose. Mixed with the green slime from the rocks was blood from … where? Taylor couldn't see. Her green eyes burned right through him. Wisps of steam puffed out from her flared nostrils as she breathed in short gasps. Taylor realised she was in an agitated state. He didn't move for fear of making her panic.

He didn't know how she would react. Taylor needed to keep her calm ... what she needed was reassurance.

He simply said: 'Hi.'

Her cheek muscles tightened as she bit down on her teeth.

'OK, my name is Ben; I've come to get you out of here. Everything is going to be fine, we have help from outside as well.'

There was no reply, no movement ... just those piercing, alert eyes that pinned him to the wall.

'Are you hurt?'

No response.

'Can you move?'

No response.

'Can you speak?'

No response.

'What's your name?'

He didn't expect a response.

'You must be very cold.'

Taylor raised his hand and moved it towards her head. She flinched back and then became rigid as her breathing increased.

'I just want to take a look at your head, see where the bleeding is coming from.' He moved his hand closer and this time she let him touch her head. He gently brushed her hair away from her forehead with the tips of his fingers and examined the small cuts he could now see. She began to lightly push her head against his fingers and her eyes reduced from the size of planets. He let his palm caress her head, and as he stroked her, her eyes took on a more distinctive shape.

He wanted to hold her, to make her warm, to make her feel safe. First he had to get her out. He went through the escape route in his head.

Duck down, enter the sump tunnel facing the right way for the exit to the first cave. Swim to the top, find air pocket for breather, back down, swim to exit and Sid.

But it wasn't going to happen, not that way. She wasn't going to give up the security of this hole very easily. Perhaps he could drag her out and sort out the mess once they were clear of the water. Nah, was he crazy? He watched her shallow breathing and decided.

'I'm going to have to leave you.' She immediately braced and her eyes widened. 'It's OK, I'll come back for you but I must go for help.' She flew across the short gap that separated them, splashing water into Taylor's face as she clung to him like a limpet. He could feel her trembling and hear her wispy breath rasping in his ear. Taylor moved his head slightly and kissed her full on the lips. He was surprised how quickly she responded to his advances and soon they were kissing passionately. Like lovers reunited. As much as he was enjoying it, he pulled away and whispered.

'I must go for help. I promise I'll come back for you.' She slowly released her hold on him, staring pleadingly into his eyes as he slid beneath the water, leaving her alone once again in the cold and the dark.

While squeezing through the narrow slit in the roof of the tunnel he tore a hole in his dry suit and cursed as the cold water crept down from his shoulder, over his ribs and down past his waist to his right leg. He made his way quickly back to where Sid stood staring down at the surface of the water.

When Taylor emerged, Sid breathed a big sigh of relief. 'I was beginning to worry whether I would see you again. Are you OK?'

'Yeah I'm fine, just a little cold.'

'I'll get some blankets sent down. Did you find her?'

'She's in the smallest of holes, I was lucky to find her. She's in a bit of a state, though, mate.'

'I can't imagine what that girl is going through.' Sid shook his head. 'But at least you found her.'

Both men turned to look at the myriad of torch lights flicking from side to side as the clatter of the Navy divers arriving became louder and louder. Taylor stood at the water's edge and noticed the startled look on Tim's face when he saw him.

'Thanks for coming so quickly, guys. I need to get back in there as soon as I can.' Taylor realised he must look quite a state, but knew that Tim was too professional to say anything; he would save it for later. 'I need just one cylinder but with a second DV. I'll leave Sid to fill you in with all the details.'

Within minutes, Taylor was back in the water. He carried the air cylinder under his arm, with one of the demand valves in his mouth the other dangling at his side. Wearing a mask made the trip back to the hole a lot easier.

He pushed the cylinder in the hole and climbed in after it. Taylor stopped breathing, let the DV slip from his mouth and removed the mask before his head came clear of the water. She was pressed tightly against the back wall, her eyes closing slightly as she recognised Taylor. He thought for a moment he saw the faintest of smiles. Her features blended in with the dark, craggy, moist rocks behind her head.

'Have you ever used diving equipment before?' She shook her head.

'Would you like to?'

There was no response.

'OK, we'll take this real slowly.' Taylor helped her put on the mask and eventually got the spare DV into her mouth. However, when it came to putting her head under the water, she was having none of it. She breathed so deeply the DV struggled to supply her with that amount of air. He had to get her to calm down. He tried distraction, asking her where she was from, was she married, boyfriend – anything to get her mind away from this place. She answered him in grunts and slight gestures with her head. He let her keep the DV in her mouth, allowing her to become comfortable with it. He then told her about his diving courses at Horsea Island near Portsmouth, his deepest saturation dive to one thousand feet off the coast of Canada and some of his more exotic dives in Belize. He noticed the air in the cylinder was beginning to reach a critically low pressure; they had to go now. He stopped talking. She tensed.

'Look at me, look directly into my eyes.' He was stern; he put as much severity into his voice as he could. 'There is no compromise, we must go now.'

Taylor gripped her arms and lowered himself into the cold water. She struggled against him slightly but then gave in to his increasing strength. Taylor squeezed through the gap first and she followed close behind him. They were now clear of the hole and in the tunnel again. She clung to his arm, both her hands looking small as she gripped his strong bicep. They moved off towards the surface.

CHAPTER FOUR

The rain continued to lash down and the light was fading into twilight. Thick banks of fog and mist rolled over the ground, reducing visibility even further. Taylor watched as the potholing rescue team carried the girl away on a stretcher. She was wrapped in so many clothes and blankets it was hard to distinguish what they were carrying. Taylor thought about the first time he had seen her: she had been petrified, scared out of her wits, and he would never forget the fear in her eyes. She had also shown fortitude to put her trust in him and force herself to slip back under the freezing-cold water to escape. The woman under the mound of wool whom he'd met for such a short but immensely intimate period of time was indeed a very brave and lucky young lady. The blue Royal Navy Land Rover with its red-painted wings pulled up alongside him.

'You want a lift, Jack?' Taylor would normally refuse, but this time he didn't. He climbed into the V8 and it rolled off the mountain, slightly top-heavy due to the inflatable Gemini boat slung onto the roof rack. The driver, a young able seaman, handled the four-by-four expertly; beside him another fresh-faced seaman watched his every move. Taylor sat with Tim in the back two seats, the diving equipment behind them.

'This is Able Seaman Cross – 'Jumper', and Morgan 'Rattler.' Taylor acknowledged the two young lads in the front. 'Where are you staying?' Tim asked Taylor.

'Checked out of my digs last night … I didn't know where I was going to end up today. I was hoping maybe to find a cave.'

'Well, as much as you would've probably enjoyed a night in a cold, damp and lonely cave, I cordially invite you, old boy, to spend the night with us – that is, of course, if you could stand some company?'

'It's always a pleasure to spend time with an old friend, especially one so refined as yourself.' Tim was an educated man with a degree in History and Sociology. 'You can be a tasteful, sophisticated person when you want to be, Tadpole, but you choose not to be?' Taylor asked.

Tim ignored the question totally. 'Are you still incarcerating yourself in those obscene submarines?'

'I am.'

'They can't be good for you, Ben; all that time cooked up, missing what's going on in the real world. It's not natural, my friend. What the blazes do you do with yourself?' Taylor began to wonder where he was going with this. Tim threw him another question. 'How long do you stay down for?'

Ben grabbed the seat in front of him as the Land Rover went over a particularly large pothole. 'It depends what we've been tasked to do. The longest I've been down is eighty-four days. That's why I like coming to places like this, it makes me feel alive,' answered Ben with a smile on his face.

Tim was quiet while he thought about this, ending the conversation with a shake of his head.

The driver dropped them and their personnel gear off at what appeared to be a modest hotel, and then parked the 'red wing' Land Rover in the local police station compound before rejoining his colleagues back in the hotel.

Tim had telephoned his superior to inform him of the outcome of the rescue and their location for the evening. 'And I'll phone again before we leave in the morning, sir. Thanks again, yes, sir; I'll certainly give him your regards. Have a good night, sir.' Tim joined his friends in the reception. It was dimly lit inside the seventeenth-century century hotel with solid oak beams and a red-coloured carpet that strained the eyes. Ben booked into a single room, and after changing into dry clothing met his friends in the bar. The two young seamen wanted to know all about the day's events and pumped Ben with an avalanche of questions. After drinking several rounds of beer, Ben eventually changed the subject, and after chatting about the new diving facilities at Horsea Island, Jumper and Rattler excused themselves and headed off to play a game of darts.

'Tell me about what's been happening," Taylor said to Tim. 'What on earth is a Royal Marine Commando doing driving round the country in a red wing?'

'Well, firstly let me congratulate you on a good day's work.' Both men raised their glasses. 'Now, as you know, on completion of our course I went back to Four-Two in Plymouth.

Although there were some, the opportunities for using my newfound underwater skills were just not enough, so when I came back from my last tour in

Norway and asked to transfer to the—'

Taylor couldn't resist the lead. 'The Royal Navy's finest front-line NATO attack frog force.'

'No you imbecile, the SBS[2].'

One of the young seamen brought over a couple pints. 'Here you go, Sarge … and yours, Chief.'

'Ah, very kind; very kind, young man. But please, while we're among civvies and off duty, as it were, no rank, OK? You never know who's listening.'

'Sorry, Tim.' The young lad rejoined his friend at the dartboard.

'Got them well trained I see. So, what's all this with the PACDU[3]?'

'Volunteered; you know me, never one to let anyone struggle. The PACDU needed a hand; I provided it for them.'

Taylor looked at his friend's eyes and his facial features and thought for a moment. 'Now, what's the real reason?'

Tim smiled. 'They requested I obtain more experience, and so I grovelled to the boss. Three weeks later I was seconded to PACDU and they threw me straight into the mêlée. I'd only been with them for two months when they packed me off to Alaska – nice little job, recovering practice torpedoes from under the ice … you boys are changing the theatre.'

---

[2] Special Boat Squadron.
[3] Portsmouth Area Clearance Diving Unit.

Taylor nodded in agreement. 'The Cold War is a psychological war. It was inevitable that submarines would begin to play a major role in it. Ever since the Second World War, East and West have been using propaganda and espionage as a tool to gain the upper hand, and submarines under the ice is just another area to take control of.'

Tim acknowledged what Taylor said and continued. 'A lot of people think the Cold War is entering a new phase. I spent a good month up there.' Taylor was intrigued by the topic of Tim's conversation and wanted to know what he knew. 'There have been many "proxy wars" – the Berlin Blockade and Chinese Civil War, the Korean War ... even the Hungarian Revolution and Suez Crisis have played a part, but the big change came after the Cuban Missile Crisis in '62, mate ... so what's changed now in 1981?' Tim asked.

'The Strategic Arms Limitations Talks have fallen through and Brezhnev is trying to take Afghanistan. The mujahideen are putting up a fight, but the outcome is inevitable.'

'And what do you think, Tadpole ... will we have a nuclear holocaust?'

'No, not unless the Red Chinese enter the battlefield; they're crazy enough to press the button.'

'Or the Koreans.'

'Well, yeah. So what, then? More spying, more war games?'

'More proxy wars for sure.'

'What's troubling you, mate?' Taylor asked.

'We're missing something.'

Taylor could see real worry on Tim's face and decided to lighten the mood. 'Only the big boys know what's going on with this game of chess. It won't be a decision for us to make, Tadpole. How long have you been with PACDU?'

'Nearly eight months now. Love it. You Navy boys have an easy life, you know.'

'Yeah I know, but don't tell anyone. And how long before the call to Poole?'

'I'm expecting it at any time now.'

Both men turned and watched the two others playing darts.

'They seem like good lads?'

'Yes, good lads, but I'm afraid it's the same old problem: profuse potential that will neither been seen nor fulfilled through a lack of qualified nurturing.'

'And why is that, dare I ask?'

'Because everybody is too busy; too busy to impart the finer points of this life. Now that they've completed their sixteen-week diver training, they're thrown into the real world where they're left to discover its perilous menaces all by themselves. These boys are so delirious with having the diver badge sewn on their arm they think they're indestructible and above the realms of failure. I was told to keep quiet and let them have their five minutes of fulfilment. But it's not five minutes: it never happens. Someone needs to let them in on the big picture; they need to realise that they're not infallible and can make mistakes … and what those mistakes could cost.' Tim sat back in his seat.

'Now, if I know you, that will not happen,' replied Taylor.

'Even I grow fatigued, my friend, with the endless red tape they're piling on us. Cutbacks, budgeting, everything has to be scrutinised … and eventually it will cost us. If we're lucky, one life – if not, then many – will be lost, mark my words. ' Tim paused for a moment to take a mouthful of beer. Then he grimaced. 'Can't even get a good pint of real ale in these hovels they put us up in.'

'If you had joined as an officer you would have been in a place to do something about it.'

'Don't get me started. This navy is not run by officers, it's run by politicians and bureaucrats, as well you know. I do believe in a higher power and therefore a mandate of heaven, although I've confessed to believing in Confucianism as well.'

'That reminds me, how is your father?'

'You're a rascal, Ben Taylor.'

'I know, but seriously, how is he?'

'Rich.' Taylor was expecting this, as Tim was the son of a retired brigadier general and could have stepped straight into a commission at Sandhurst if it had not been for this rebellious attitude he had towards his father. It was the main reason he had joined the Marines as a 'normal' soldier. He continued: 'The last time I went home, which was some time ago now, I got the taxi to stop outside the gates—'

Taylor interrupted him: 'A taxi, is that not a bit—'

Now it was Tim's turn to interrupt him: 'The plan was to let my father see me get off the local bus and walk up the drive, but I went for a couple of brews at the local pub in the village and ended up missing the dammed thing anyway. So I got a taxi, got dropped off outside the gates and walked up the drive. Entered by the servants' quarters and had a lovely chat with Janet my old nanny. Whom he was going to sack when I left home so I pleaded with my mother to keep her on and she got her a job in the kitchen. They were going to throw her out like a used rag.'

'So what happened then? I can't think for one minute you got away scot-free?'

'I was summoned, pilloried in front of my mother who was just as embarrassed as I was. I loathe him. Janet was always the one to look after me – he never had the time. We were always packing and moving to a different posting. We've lived in fourteen different countries.'

There was a long silence before Taylor asked: 'Would you like another beer, mate?'

'Yes, why not, let's get pissed,' said Tim. Taylor bought a round and took two pints over to the dart board before returning to his table. The atmosphere was slightly better.

'Do excuse my rantings, Ben. I get carried away sometimes. Now, how are your family?'

'They're all fine, although I must admit I too haven't been home for a while. I phone when I can.

Dad's keeping active with his sailing; mum has her gardening. They often ask about you … we must arrange a weekend leave together, they would love to see you again.'

'Mmm, definitely, love the hospitality your parents show,' Tim said as he sipped his drink. 'Sorry, it wasn't a dig at my parents, I really mean it. Your parents are great – they're normal people.' Then he decided to change the subject. 'I still don't know how you manage to keep yourself sane cooped up in one of those tin cans for such a long time. Is it not boring?'

'It can be sometimes, but you can't let your guard down. When something happens down there it happens quickly … it can be exciting.' He paused. 'And we're doing a very necessary job.'

'There's a big old world out there, and money is not everything, my friend.' *Twice now he'd brought this subject up. What's he up too?* Taylor thought to himself. 'You be very careful down there, we don't want anything happening to you.' Tim leaned forward slightly as he finished his sentence.

'What are you getting at, Tadpole?'

'We've been friends for some time now, Ben … I know I can trust you.'

'And me you. What's on your mind, pal?'

'Do you remember 1961, the Portland Spy Ring?'

'Sure, go on.'

'Well, I was thinking how, not only the USSR but any country with communist interests – and in some cases not even communist but monetary interests – could gather information on the ever-increasing

technology of the hunter-killer submarines that you're on.'

'How it could be done, you mean?'

'Well, not so much how it could be done, but how easy it would be. I mean, considering all the trouble and how deep Houghton was at Portland … then gathering information from Faslane would be child's play. The pubs and restaurants of Helensburgh must be crawling with Russian spies, and they would gather information of sailing times and sub movements with no trouble.'

'All submariners are given a security lecture on joining and regular briefs on any amendments. I'm sure they're on top of it.'

'Well I'm not. The Cold War has been going on for some time now and some say it may well be over soon, but the Russians have always found it easier to gather information through espionage rather than develop their own ideas. So even if the Cold War does end, they will still be sniffing around. After the Second World War we gave them all the information we had on the German U-boats, but instead of using the information to progress, they copied it exactly and spied on the West for improvements.'

'I don't think we'll be dropping our guard on espionage for any reason, Tadpole.'

'It's a threat that's taken too lightly I think. More should be done to protect our technology and our men.'

'Heavy thoughts, mate. Are you keeping them to yourself or have you voiced them to the hierarchy?'

'Oh, I've made my voice heard all right.'

'I'll bet you have. Did telling people they're not doing their job get you into trouble?'

'Some of the people dealing with counter-espionage and intelligence gathering are so old and set in their ways even a Neanderthal could gather what information he wanted. They need to be brought up to date.'

'Is funding a problem, do you think?'

'One of the problems, yes, but the main one is the "old school tie" mentality. How much money would it take for you to give information?'

'I don't know anything secret; I'm a very small cog.'

'You'd be surprised what you know. That little bit of information that you may think is worthless may be the last piece in a large jigsaw.'

The two seamen finished their game of darts and came over to the table.

'Who won, lads?' asked Taylor. He gestured for them to sit and join them.

'He did,' said the disgruntled younger of the two as he slumped into a chair.

'It's only a game of darts.'

'Failure is not an option,' he spat back quickly. Taylor was slightly startled by his reply.

'Sometimes you learn more by losing than you do by winning. Showing grace in losing can on occasion prove you are a better man than your opponent. Letting someone win can have a far better outcome.' Taylor didn't like to preach like this but was glad when he saw the youngster digest the information and raise his eyebrows as he realised the truth of what had been said.

Tim decided it was a good time for a story. 'Let me tell you about an incident we had at Horsea while we were on our senior's course,' he said as he gestured towards Taylor. He paused to take a drink. 'Taylor and I were always buddied up together. We had an understanding, the ability to communicate underwater without talking – I'm sure you've experienced it yourselves.' The two lads nodded. 'We arrived at the huts at the end of the lake one morning to find the booster pump completely stripped down and the individual components laid out on the concrete. The task we had been set was to rebuild the pump, pressurise our diving sets with a mixture of sixty-forty nitrogen and oxygen and swim down the lake to the loch gates at the bottom end – which, as you know, are three-quarters of a mile away. But instead of turning around and swimming back up the right bank, as you normally do, we were ordered to continue round and swim back up the left bank, which you probably don't know is full of debris, old discarded wires and other obstacles that would slow you down. Normal protocol applied when the main gas supply was expired: we would switch to emergency and surface at the correct rate, swim to the bank, get out, collect all our gear and run back to the huts to recharge and go again.

We both knew that it was a long way and we would have to swim quickly or our gas supply would run out. We were determined to do it, as nobody enjoys running with a set on their backs and all the rest of the equipment you have to carry. Our first attempt was abysmal. We swam down the right side of the lake without any problems because we knew it like the backs of our hands, but once we turned the corner it became a nightmare. Snag after snag underwater, and we were also up and down in depth to clear the float line on the surface from snags on wires. Needless to say, we were about halfway back up the left bank when I ran out of main. The second attempt was slightly better as we had over-pressurised the sets a little …'

'I don't think it's a good idea to tell these young lads this,' Taylor interrupted quickly.

'No, no. I'm sure these lads have already done it.' Tim was beginning to feel the effects of the beer. 'The second attempt, I ran out of air by the tool hut. Almost there; three-quarters of the way, around a hundred metres away from the end, and we were running again.

I normally used the booster pump by myself while Taylor prepped the sets with soda lime, but on this third attempt we shared the pumping as we were both getting very tired.'

Tim began slurring the occasional word. 'Down the right-hand bank we swam, round the end of the lake, clearing obstacles that now we knew were coming.

Back up the left side, and I saw the shadow of the tool hut go overhead. So it was because of our previous failures that we were now able to do this.' Tim stopped abruptly, let out a big sigh, placed his glass to his lips and finished is drink. 'My round, I think.' With that he stood up and walked to the bar.

The two young lads turned to Taylor. 'So you did it, then?'

Taylor smiled. 'Of course we did.' When Tim returned, Taylor suggested that it was getting late and maybe it was time to eat.

After dinner Taylor helped Tim to his room and watched as he tried to open the door. Tim eventually opened it, and turned to face Taylor.

'You didn't have to nursemaid me to my room, friend.' He leaned against the door-jamb.

'I know, but what are friends for?'

Tim beckoned Ben closer. 'When I was in Alaska I overheard the support team talking.' He paused for a moment to let out a quiet burp. 'Excuse me. They were saying that the Russians where churning out submarines like cars off a production line.' He slowly entered the room, still talking. 'It's becoming like the M25 down there, one day and very soon there's likely to be an almighty collision. You ought to get off those bloody subs mate, far too dangerous, eh?

Remember when we jumped from that bloody helicopter into the Solent, dam near broke my legs? You want to do like I'm doing, travel around blowing things up on beaches and having a great time.'

He took a deep breath. 'Breathing fresh air. Get it organised for me to come home with you.' The door slammed shut.

CHAPTER FIVE

The train smelled dusty. The seat Taylor sat on felt like it had collapsed and he was sitting on the boards of the floor. He wanted to sleep but every now and then the train jolted him awake. He held on to the flimsy cup of coffee as firmly as he could, a fine line between crushing it and letting it slip out of his fingers. He looked out the window not seeing what was beyond the glass. A smile crept across his broad chin as he reflected on the previous night. Tim could be a real idiot; what a waste. How someone so intelligent could put himself through these hardships because of a feud with his father. Taylor shook his head. It was great to see him again, although a little painful on the kidneys. He was glad Tim hadn't finished the Horsea story, as he had used not only his main supply but all his emergency as well. Ben had had to drag him the last five yards without any gas in his set at all, semi-conscious, to the end of the lake, were he'd brought him to the surface and removed his face mask so he could breathe. Luckily the instructor hadn't seen it. As for the helicopter incident, Taylor supposed it had been his fault, in a way. The brief had been that the Sea King would hover at a hundred feet. Taylor and Tim would stand in the doorway with their diving sets on and fins under their arms. The aircrew man would tap them both on the shoulder and they were to sit down ready to jump. The helicopter would then descend to twenty feet, when the aircrew man would tap them both again and they would jump. As the Sea King came in to hover at a hundred feet, the aircrew man tapped Tim on the shoulder and he immediately sat down. Taylor followed his lead. The aircrew man, realising he had not tapped Taylor on the shoulder, decided to do it while he was sitting in the doorway. So Taylor jumped; Tim saw him go and followed. The Sea King was at an altitude of around ninety feet. The water felt like concrete when they hit it; they lost their fins, smashed the sets and ended up in Haslar Hospital for a few days.There was a particularly heavy jolt when the clattering wheels bounced over multiple line crossings as the train neared Helensburgh station. Taylor began to think he should have gone home and seen his parents instead of charging around Derbyshire in the rain. He hadn't seen them now for over six months and didn't usually leave it that long between visits. He knew he was in for a telling off from his mother Elizabeth, affectionately nicknamed 'Elli' by his father, for leaving it too long, but then in the next breath she would forgive him and start piling his clothes into the washing machine while asking about food. His father Mathew, on the other hand, was quite laid back. He was born in Vancouver, British Columbia, Canada. His parents Tom and Sally became successful in the twenties starting with a single gas station, progressing to fifteen in and around the Vancouver area. Restaurants and eventually motels built adjacent to their gas stations increased their equity. Taylor especially remembered his grandfather for being involved with the setting up of the mechanical engineering apprenticeships in the province and becoming a founding member of the Automotive Retailers Association. The business survived the Great Depression in the thirties when mining, logging and farming were hit hard and a lot of businesses went under. A high percentage of people were out of work. Mathew and his younger brother Thomas helped run the family business, but Mathew grew restless. He wanted his own business and all its related challenges. After Tom died in a car accident and Sally died shortly after from cancer, Mathew immigrated to England, thinking there were more opportunities, but landed straight into World War Two. While serving as a colonel in the British Eighth Army under the command of Lieutenant General B. L. Montgomery, Mathew was flown home after being injured in Tripoli, just prior to his regiment moving up to the Mareth Line, southern Tunisia in 1943. Taylor remembered him complaining about 'the sand getting everywhere – in your tea, in your food – everywhere'. Mathew met Elizabeth, a young accountant who was nursing at Withington Hospital, Manchester, where he eventually ended up. They married in the hospital grounds. Once the war was over Mathew had no problem purchasing garages, and soon became owner of a large chain of them. Ben Taylor was born in 1954 in a small rural town called Winsford in Cheshire. He attended the local grammar school. Ben adored his parents but recognised how sad and sometimes lonely his mother had become over the years because his father was too busy working. Perhaps he could get them together with Tim's parents – it might help. Ben and his mother regularly confided in each other; she worried about Mathew's health and wished he would slow down. Elizabeth had her friends with whom she went shopping, but Ben knew she put on a brave face and denied that she was in any way upset or unhappy with the life she was living. Ben felt guilty for not taking over some of the work from his father and felt that he had run away from his responsibilities. He had wanted to make his own decisions in life and his father had understood that, but there still loomed this nagging guilt in the back of his mind. He joined the Royal Navy in 1972 as a marine mechanic and was offered a technician path at HMS *Sultan*, but he chose to stay with the rank and file and build his way up through hard work and merit to gain experience. He hadn't thought it would be this hard and often wished he'd not been so noble and had taken the fast track. He choose to sub-qualify as a diver with the sole intention that it would help his career advancement, but like Tim had fallen in love with it, and it was fast overtaking his mechanical path. Now, ten years on, he was looking for a change but wasn't quite sure what. Perhaps Tim was right: he needed to get out of submarines.

He stepped down onto the Helensburgh station platform and into the cold night air. The wind blew through the wrought iron girders that held up the roof. Graffiti claiming Scottish independence was daubed onto the red ceramic tiles that formed the walls of this Victorian building, which was erected to allow people from Glasgow to travel the twenty-five miles and experience the spectacular views and breathe the fresh air around Gare Loch. The popular route was then to return to Glasgow down the Clyde on the paddle steamer *Waverley*.

Now the peace and tranquillity had been replaced with drinking bars, curry houses and betting shops all cashing in on the overindulgence of the sailors based at the submarine base. The rain began to fall as Taylor climbed into the taxicab. He exchanged pleasantries with the driver, and without being told was taken off on the five-mile trip straight to the submarine base. Ben wondered if he was a spy?

CHAPTER SIX

The morning air was still damp from the previous night's rain, but now the sun was breaking out and drying the freshly cut grass surrounding the outside of the building that housed the Olympic-size swimming pool. Taylor had risen at 6 a.m., run down to the pool and completed his morning workout. Now he was showered, dressed in clean No. 8 working clothes and headed towards the main building of HMS *Neptune*, hungry for his breakfast. *HMS Neptune* was the ashore establishment housing accommodation and recreation for the sailors not on duty aboard the submarines. Only a skeleton crew needed to be on duty while the submarines were alongside. HMS *Neptune* also provided support for maintenance and repairs to the submarines.

The chefs as usual paid no attention to him from behind the heated counters. After choosing a self-service breakfast of bacon and eggs he sat in his favourite position by the window that overlooked the loch and the submarines moored at the high-security jetty area. Over to his left the large floating dock used to raise and lower the submarines out of the water partially hid the view of the hills on the far side of the water. Looking straight ahead gave him unobstructed views of Scotland at its best. The loch was almost black, and this morning calm as a mill pond. The slight rippling of the reflection of the hills on the water merged with the solid image of the real slopes as his eye followed the stony beach up the tree line with all its spring season colours and eventually reached the craggy ridge at the top and beyond into endless blue sky.

'There you are! I was looking for you last night, where were you? I thought we had arranged to meet in the bar?'

'Ah – sorry mate.' Taylor was brought abruptly from his daydream back into the dining hall by his Welsh friend Sion Williams, nicknamed 'Taff' after the river in Wales, banging his plate down on the table and slopping beans off his plate. Sion Williams was a spindly chap in his early twenties, but had powerful arms and legs that he had attained through his hobby of rock climbing, mostly in Wales. Sion now lived near the Llanberis Pass with his wife Enfys and his two-year-old baby girl Sara. 'Please, join me.' Taylor said sarcastically. 'I got back really late. The pubs where kicking out as I got into Helensburgh so I jumped into a taxi before they all went,' he lied.

'Well, you missed all the action on Saturday night: a stoker off the *Courageous* was beaten to a pulp by some civvies while he was walking back on Saturday night. The whole crew of the *Courageous* were out last night looking for them.'

'Did they find them?'

'No, but God help them when they do, and they will: they won't give up till they do. Anyway, see you down the boat.' Sion left Ben's table and walked over to another. 'Hey pal, how're doing? Listen, did you hear about Saturday night?'

Somehow the view out of the window didn't seem the same. Taylor wished he was back in Derbyshire.

Although a good friend, Taylor didn't like Sion's attitude to women. He wouldn't pass up any opportunity to flirt with the opposite sex even though he was married to Enfys and had a daughter.

Sion was born in Wales and spent most of his leave periods rock climbing. He also got on Taylor's nerves by talking constantly. But he was a hard worker and Taylor trusted him on board the submarine. Taylor ate his poached eggs quickly.

After breakfast Taylor walked silently through the corridors and down the stairs leading out of the dinning and recreation block. For the past few days he'd been thinking about the debrief he was due to give the captain at 0900 hours. Sion walked beside him talking the whole time but Taylor wasn't listening. After the captain, he was to meet with his divisional officer – no specified time for this as it was an informal chat about the submarines programme and any other pressing matters.

They walked through the first of two security gates, showing a green-coloured pass to the Ministry of Defence police officer while behind him stood a Royal Marine with a self-loading rifle slung over his shoulder. They emerged onto an area of the main jetty that housed the maintenance and repair sections, then they walked through the second security gate, identical to the first, but this time they showed a red pass. Surveillance cameras left no section of this high-security red area uncovered, and now they walked onto the finger jetties that berthed the nuclear submarines.

Taylor noticed there were only three submarines at the base and wondered where the others were. The quartermaster seaman stood on the gangway wearing a submachine gun slung on his chest. He recognised the two senior rates and summoned them on board without delay.

They climbed through the narrow hatch and down the metal vertical steps into the control room. Taylor told his mate he would see him later but was glad to leave Tam, who had been talking continuously about his weekend leave.

Taylor knocked on the wooden side frame; the captain immediately answered with 'come'. Taylor slid back the privacy curtain and stepped into the eight-by-six-foot cramped cabin. One wall taken up by a desk, which the captain was sat at, the other taken up by his bed. The captain shared the hardships of a submarine like all the rest; his privilege was the fact that he did not have to share his cabin. He indicated for Taylor to sit on the stool placed awkwardly at the end of the desk and got straight to the point.

'We had a brand-new lad join us on Saturday, Ben. Straight out of the box he passed his Part 1 at HMS *Dolphin* and Part 2 at his relevant trade establishment, and now he's ready for his final Part 3 training, which the powers that be have decided will be on *Covert*.' The captain continued speaking as he picked up a file in front of him. 'He's a bright lad; Martin Thompson, came top of his engineering class at *Sultan* but didn't perform so well in his basic submarine design and layout at *Dolphin*.

I think he's going to make a good engineer, and I'd like you to make him a good submariner engineer. Volunteers are few on the ground at the moment, nobody wants to join submarines, so we need to tread carefully and not frighten him off until he finds out what we're about. Will you do it?' This was not a request, but the captain being polite.

'Of course, sir, I would love to.' Taylor thought of all the extra work he would have to do.

'Good. You're now officially the sea daddy for a brand-new baby stoker.' The captain scribbled a quick note on top of the file and handed it to Taylor.

'Where is he now, sir?'

'He's in the mess probably drinking all our supplies of tea. Now, tell me all about your leave.' Taylor talked his way through the events of the weekend, the captain making a note to dispatch a message of thanks to Portsmouth.

'You did a fine job, not just for yourself but for *Covert* as well. I'll make sure it's put on your record,' the captain said as he scribbled a note on a pad on his desk. 'Now, one last thing: on completion of the next voyage, and the dates have yet to be confirmed, I've been asked by our American friends to attend a meeting in San Diego. Admiralty want me to look at their new "Tigerfish" torpedo with the hope of incorporating it into our arsenal. I'd like you come along as they also have an updated version of the rebreathing diving equipment and your knowledge will be useful as I know bugger all about it. Your DO will fill you in on the details as and when we know. I know I can rely on your discretion – no one is to know about this outing until nearer the time.'

Taylor confirmed his captain's wishes. When he left the captain, he passed through the control room and greeted every one of the crew he passed. Word had got around quickly: they were eager to find out what had happened in the cave … but that would have to wait. He walked down the few steps to the accommodation level and flattened himself against the Formica wall as a dockyard worker passed with a large metal bar.

It was always hectic when in port with all the extra people on board, and just something that they had to endure. Taylor popped his head into the junior rates' mess to find his new stoker, but saw that Sion had found him first. The new recruit was captivated by Sion's story. Even with his back to Taylor the new stoker was instantly recognisable. The fresh, clean-cut, unfaded blue of new No. 8s, along with the unscuffed, polished, steel toe-capped steaming boots, a special boot worn only in the machinery spaces in the aft section of the submarine, were a dead giveaway.

'It slammed into the port side of the conning tower, sending the submarine over to an almost unrecoverable, dangerous angle. With a slight flick of its enormous tail it continued to push, the conning tower slipping from its nose down under its chin and eventually onto the more blubberous part of its underside. Inside the submarine the captain was thrown across the control room, his fall stopped abruptly by his chest hitting the chart table. He slumped to the floor, struggling for breath.'

Taylor shook his head and decided to leave them to it as he went to see his divisional officer. Sion continued: 'The fore-planes man steering the submarine fought to keep the boat from slewing around, and the after-planes man, almost thrown from his seat, struggled to maintain the correct depth. One of the torpedoes in the fore-ends came loose from a restraining strap and swung across the compartment, hitting one of the crew on the back and sending him into the bilge before it collided into one of the other torpedoes on the other side, causing a flash of sparks to fly. In the galley, two huge pans, one containing hot water and cabbage, flew off the range and scalded the killick chef before knocking him out completely. Back aft, the engines oversped and began to shut down. Alarms sounded everywhere – the noise was deafening – and the smell from the oily bilges mixed with spilt battery acid was putrid. In the electrolyser compartment the machine producing oxygen from seawater began to heat up to an enormous temperature, followed closely by a rise in pressure. It quickly reached a critical state and was in danger of blowing a hole through the submarine's hull. A first-aid locker door flew open and discharged its contents all over the deck. Bandages, plasters, an eye patch, glass bottles and safety pins lay strewn across the deck, themselves becoming a hazard. One of the crew lost his grip going down the accommodation ladder and fell on other crew members coming up. Drinking cups flew across the mess inches from people's heads and smashed into the bulkhead, causing shards of knife-sharp ceramics to whiz around the place.'

Sion, now with his arms flailing, became a lot more animated. His voice rising an octave, he pointed to one of the walls at the back of the mess. 'There's still marks on it, see?' In the junior rates' mess his captivated audience of one submariner trainee, now joined by a dockyard worker, sat across the table with their mouths gaping. One of them plucked up the courage to ask a question.

'Did you have any notice it was going to happen?'

The young Welshman glared at the interrupter. 'It had been following us for days, boyo! Most of the crew had been sneaking into the sonar room to listen to the whale singing. Normally, nobody is allowed in there, see, but everyone wanted a listen. Wow, it was some noise, I'll tell you! Out of this world, but somehow intelligent – you know, you could tell it was trying to communicate. There'd be deep groans that sounded so far behind us you would think it could never catch us up. Then all of a sudden, higher screeches getting louder and louder, so loud you had to rip the earphones right off your head. Boy, he was close. Then it happened.'

'Where were you when it hit?' stammered the trainee, forgetting himself. Sion was now too carried away with telling the story to worry about being interrupted.

'I was in the mess at the time. The sub began to roll over, slowly at first.' Sion bent his body over to one side, and felt slightly elated when the two onlookers followed his actions.

He continued: 'I'll tell you boys – I've never been so frightened in all my life. Although we didn't know it at the time, we later learned the angle was fifty-two degrees.' He placed great emphasis on the number fifty-two. 'Well, you can imagine what it was like in here.'

'Why did it attack?' the trainee bravely asked.

Sion was now angry and shouted: 'Will you stop butting in while I'm talking!' He composed himself before going on. 'We were fortunate nobody was killed. A fire extinguisher broke off its bracket and rolled down the accommodation deck, hitting my mate "Jumper" Cross on the back of the legs and shattering one of his knees. He was later casevaced off by helicopter. We were quite lucky in here because it's kept quite clean and stuff is put away after we've used it, right?' Sion pointed to the trainee, who nodded intently back at him, understanding the lesson. 'It was back aft we suffered the most turmoil. And I'm telling you one thing, boys: if it hadn't been for my best mate Ben Taylor, this submarine would not be here now. We would all be "brown bread".' Sion paused for a moment to let him figure out the slang. 'Anyway, as I was saying, machinery tripped, turbines oversped and the smell from the bilges was knocking people out.' Sion glanced away from the trainee and looked at one of the other experienced crew members who sat close by reading a book. When he lowered the book and shook his head, Sion quickly turned back and continued in a louder voice.

'Steam was everywhere. The stokers came running up from the machinery spaces with their skin red and hanging off – they were literally being cooked alive.' Seeing that the trainee was turning paler than he already was, the experienced crew member put his book down.

'That's enough, Taff. You'll give him nightmares, for Christ's sake,' he said firmly. The mess was quiet for moment. Sion fought hard to resist the temptation to carry on; he could see that the trainee wanted to know more.

Eventually Sion addressed him calmly: 'We'll continue some other time, lad.'

'I still don't understand why the whale attacked the submarine?' the confused trainee enquired.

Sion stood up slowly. 'It wasn't an attack – oh no, nothing of the sort. It had apparently become a bit amorous and tried to mount the conning tower. Wanted a bit of rubbing, you see. The rounded hull provided no resistance so it rolled the sub easily. Right, well I'm off to work.' He said nothing more as he walked to the mess door, but he knew his listeners were watching his every move. At the door he suddenly stopped, turned and, staring at the young trainee, winked his eye. 'Same time tomorrow,' he said softly.

CHAPTER SEVEN

Gallymore cautiously approached the deserted farmhouse. The night sky was overcast, blanking out the moon and making it difficult to see the outbuildings. He could vaguely make out the black silhouette of the main house, which he watched for a while from a distance. There was no smell of animals or manure, as this farm had not been worked for some time. Off to his left was a small copse of trees and a light breeze rustled the leaves in the branches. He was careful where he placed his feet, trying not to make any noise but more importantly trying to keep the mud off his new, soft-leather Italian shoes. Although his body didn't burn off the calories quite as fast as it used too, he still kept himself in good physical shape. His high cheek bones accentuated his sunken cheeks and he had a good head of hair, thick and black. Gallymore had parked the car off the road among the trees a few hundred yards further on past the drive and had walked back. The previous evening while sleeping in the Gresham Hotel on O'Connell Street in the centre of Dublin he had received a wakening telephone call from Shamus McCann. The message was clear: he was to drive three miles north of Sligo, on the north-west coast of Ireland, and turn left off the N15 onto the coast road until he came to the farm entrance. Gallymore did not like being summoned; he knew it would be bad news. But he had come, even though it had taken him all day. He was careful not to be followed, driving ten miles north and then turning back to the coast road where he waited for a while, watching for other cars, before eventually continuing on the coast road. Gallymore was nervous of McCann; he still wasn't sure whether he could be trusted. He tried to keep these meetings to a minimum to avoid being associated with him, but McCann sounded desperate. There were no lights on inside the farm as Gallymore quietly stepped up to the front door.

Then suddenly: 'Gallymore.' The voice was soft but gripping.

'Fecking hell, McCann, what the feck's up with you, man?' Gallymore's heart was racing.

'You're jumpy tonight ya Irish git,' said McCann, Gallymore's countryman appearing from the shadows by the side of the building.

'Unlike your ma and da, I'm going to teach you some manners one day.' The two men where close enough to stare into each other's eyes, the smell of stale cigarettes and cheap cologne filling Gallymore's nostrils. He narrowed his eyes and broke the silence.

'Why have you dragged me all the way out here, McCann?'

'We need to talk.'

'We could have done that on the phone.'

'Not about this we couldn't.' McCann looked nervous. 'Let's talk in here.' He turned and unlocked the door and the two men went inside. Gallymore's heart rate was returning to normal. Taking an oil lamp from the mantelpiece above the huge open fireplace, McCann lit it with a match, and in the warm glow Gallymore could see that nobody had lived here for a very long time.

'This your old place?' Gallymore smirked as he looked round the room. McCann's lips tightened but he didn't answer. The smell inside was stale and musky from the damp.
Spiders were beginning to fill the corners with their webs, making the room seem smaller. The whitewashed walls were peeling badly. Gallymore noticed cups, plates and other stained crockery lying about the kitchen … the last occupants must have left in a hurry. Gallymore moved a piece of old wall paper from a seat and brushed off the dust before sitting down at the faded dining table.

'Right, get on with it,' he barked. 'I don't want to stay here any longer than I have to.'

The dour-faced McCann sat down opposite him and began scratching the back of his head.

'You ought to have a bath.' Gallymore spoke in a quiet, soft voice while never letting his eyes stray from McCann.

There was a short pause while McCann gathered his thoughts. He shook his head at Gallymore and breathed out heavily. Eventually he began.

'We've upset the lads.'

'And what lads would that be?'

'Jesus, Gallymore, I'm sick and tired of your pathetic piss-taking. Do you want me to spell it out for you?'

'Well, I think you're going to have to because I've got no idea what you're talking about.'

'We've upset the fecking IRA. Big style.'

'Now, correct me if I'm wrong, but how can we upset them if they don't exist anymore?'

'This isn't a time for jokes, Gallymore. They may not exist in the eyes of the law, they may well be lying dormant, but everybody knows the heart's still there … and we've bloody well stirred them up … just given them one of those fecking "stand clear" electric shock things.'

'Calm yourself down, man. Tell me the full story.'

'They paid a visit to Paul Kennet.' McCann dropped his head while he composed himself.

'Kennet is a vet, living a normal life with his wife in the sticks. They smashed their way in through the back door, tied up his wife and gave him a slapping. I went to see him in the hospital this morning.' McCann lit a cigarette and continued. 'He's never going to walk again, not on his own pins anyway. They told his wife that freeing Ireland was their job and that if we kept interfering, we too would become their enemy.' McCann's eyes narrowed. He sucked hard on his cigarette and blew the smoke into Gallymore's face.

'Feck you, Shamus, the fecking IRA are soft, you're getting soft. When we started this splinter group every one of us knew what we'd be up against.' Gallymore spread his hands out on the table in front of him. 'All people want to do is talk, talk and fecking talk. You knew this sort of thing would happen, that's why we have to be careful and stop having these secret meetings in the back of nowhere. Ireland needs us to show these Brit bastards we don't …' Gallymore was slightly startled as McCann sprang up, knocking his chair over. He stood facing the fire place.

'For Christ's sake, Gallymore, Kennet will never walk again.' McCann turned to face Gallymore and leaned over the table, staring straight into his eyes. Gallymore, however, was the first to speak.

'I think you're fecking losing your bottle.'

McCann broke off from the stare and began pacing around the room. Gallymore turned sideways in his chair and spoke with composure.

'What did you have Kennet do anyway, to upset the IRA so much?'

'He was team leader for robbing the post office van getting funds for us.'

Gallymore turned his hands up. 'So?'

'When Kennet blew the van he killed a kid who was in the back. He had just started working for the post office, his first job.'

'Shit happens. What's one more dead kid?'

'You're a heartless twat.' McCann sat back down. 'The IRA denied having anything to do with it straight away.'

'Well they would, wouldn't they?'

'They're putting the word out that this action would not do their cause any good and that they don't like any "Tom, Dick or Harry blowing kids up".'

Gallymore produced a hip flask and took a slug of whisky before passing it to McCann. 'What do you mean, their fecking cause? They don't like! I think we've got to step things up; show these feckers we mean business. These fecking IRA pussies need to see that we're not a bunch of amateurs and they haven't got the sole rights to this war.'

'Gallymore, we've got tourists pouring into Dublin. Young men trust it here to get steaming drunk before their wedding day. We've got more Chinese Nippon cameras in Ireland these days than we have pints of Guinness.' McCann threw his arms down by his side. 'What do you think we should do?'

'I left you in charge for five minutes.'

'Five minutes!' McCann was back on his feet. 'You left me here while you went swanning off to fucking Libya. I'm doing all the work here, I take the flack.'

'I don't have to justify what I've been doing, especially to you. Now, in the future I want to know before we do any more jobs. You personally discuss any ideas you've got with me, you piece of shit … nobody does anything without my say-so.'

'Since when have you been in charge?'

Now it was Gallymore's turn to jump up from his chair. Leaning right over the table he grabbed McCann by the collar and pushed his head down hard onto the wooden tabletop. Gallymore's eyes bulged from their sockets; the blood went from his lips as he pressed them tightly together and began to shake.

'You piece of scum, I was the one who started this outfit; if you can't handle it I'll get someone who can.'

McCann's head was flat on the table, it was hard for him to breathe. 'We're all on the same side … Christ … we have friends in the IRA … I know them … we know them.' McCann blurted out between heavy breaths.

Gallymore raised McCann's head a few inches and slammed it down again. 'They're not doing enough, we need to keep pushing.' Gallymore's heart was racing again. He gripped McCann's hair tighter. The head went up and down on the table again; a trickle of blood flowed from above Gallymore's eye down over his nose and into his mouth. 'There's only two things that people see in the IRA: what they want to see, and what they want to show us. Like you they can't be trusted. From now on, things are going to be different – you're either with me or against me.'

Gallymore pushed McCann away, who fell backwards hitting his spine on the hearth, causing him to whimper slightly as a searing pain shot up his shoulder and gave him pins and needles in his right arm. Between gasps for breath, he spoke in a whisper.

'You've lost your mind, Gallymore … you don't know what we're up against here.' He stopped speaking while he spat some blood from the back of his throat. 'We'll have the English on one side and the IRA on the other and we'll be fecking stuck in the middle.'

Gallymore headed slowly for the door, turned and looked down at the now pathetic-looking McCann. *It's a good job I still need you*, he thought.

'We've both lost family and good friends to these English bastards … we can't let them walk over us anymore. They treat us like shit.'

'I know.' McCann tried to wipe the blood from his mouth but only succeeded in smearing it across his cheek. 'I know that; but we must be realistic. The IRA have been trying for years now to make a difference, but nothing has changed.'

Gallymore walked back to McCann, who flinched as he approached. He bent down and put his arm around McCann's shoulders.

'We have a chance to change things. To do things differently. All the IRA want to do is talk and gain political power. They've lost the plot – all they want now is power and money. I – we – want to free Ireland, which was the fight in the first place.' Gallymore stood up and slipped his hand round the back of his trousers and onto the butt of a Browning handgun without McCann seeing. 'You've been a friend for a long time … are you with me?'

McCann slumped staggered from the floor and slumped into the chair. 'Yes, I'm with you.'

Gallymore was glad he hadn't had to kill his friend. *It's going to get a lot tougher and we'll have more enemies than just the IRA and the English before I'm finished*, he thought.

'*Tiocfaidh àr là*,' Gallymore said quietly. When McCann didn't answer, he shouted it: '*Tiocfaidh àr là*!'

McCann grimaced. 'Yes, all right. Our day will come.'

Gallymore left the room and closed the door quietly behind him. He paused outside for a moment while his eyes adjusted to the dark, listening intently for any movement. McCann would have to go, but at the moment he needed him. He moved off into the night and disappeared into the shadows.

CHAPTER EIGHT

Taylor had received good news from his divisional officer. On completion of the next voyage he was to take some leave, and after a short trip to Portsmouth the captain, his DO and Taylor would fly to San Diego. He began to mentally plan what he would do while at home, but first he had to rescue his stoker from the mess.

'Hi. I'm Chief Taylor, get your overalls on and meet me in the fore-ends in five minutes.' The boy's frightened face peered up at Taylor. He wanted to tell him not to worry and that this was going to be an easy ride, but that wouldn't happen in the junior rates' mess surrounded by others. The full brief would come later; right now all he wanted to do was get him on his own. Taylor left the mess, ducked his head below the serving counter and said hi to the chef in the galley before making his way to the forward torpedo compartment. Taylor checked out the compartment to see if he would be disturbing anyone else, but he was alone. A few moments later he was joined by the trainee.

'Good to see you, young man. Come.' Taylor gestured for him to follow and took the trainee to a torpedo tube used by the watch-keeper. Taylor sat down and the trainee perched himself on the side rail of a torpedo rack. There was no Formica in here – all the pipework and valves were exposed for ease of operation and maintenance.

'When did you leave *Dolphin*, Martin?'

'Last Friday.'

Taylor paused waiting for more information but it was not forthcoming, so he probed deeper.

'Did you manage to get home at the weekend?

'Yes.' Martin looked around the compartment as he spoke.

'Live with your parents?'

'Yeah.'

This was going to be hard work. The lad was obviously apprehensive. At least he had managed to see his parents, which probably wouldn't happen again for a while.

'And where is home, buddy?'

'Brixham in Devon, Chief.'

'Nice part of the country down there. What does your father do?'

'He was a fisherman first before joining the lifeboat as permanent crew.'

'Nice to hear; they do a fantastic job – hard but a very rewarding job. And that's your connection with the sea … but Plymouth's your nearest base port, isn't it? Why have you chosen to come up here?'

'Plymouth was my first choice but they sent me here, Chief.'

'Typical. Well, that's going to make your trips home long and difficult, but we'll worry about that when the time comes. So, let's start right at the beginning: you went to HMS *Raleigh* first for your basic training – how was that? Get on all right?'

'Yeah, it was fine.'

Taylor wanted him to talk rather than answer yes or no. 'How long did you spend there?'

'I was there for ten weeks, Chief.'

'We're going to get to know each other really well while you're on *Covert*, Martin. So, when there's officers around, call me Ben.' Martin raised his head slightly. Taylor continued. 'You're out of formal training now and in the real world, as it were. I'll try and teach you everything you need to know but we'll do it the easy way, my way. Have you had a cup of tea this morning?'

'Yes, I had one in the mess just before you came for me.'

'Well, I need one. Nip down to the senior rates' mess – you'll find my cup hanging above the kettle; it's got a picture of a submarine shaped black cigar on it. Milk, no sugar … and if the mess man says anything, just tell him it's for me.'

The young man stood up timidly and slowly walked to the other end of the torpedo compartment. Taylor sat back to think.

Martin Thompson gingerly pulled back the curtain of the senior rates' mess and peered inside. It was the first time he had seen inside this compartment, and he was shocked to see it was even smaller than the junior rates' mess.

There was a junior rate cleaning the tables with a cloth. 'What do you want?' His voice was over-authoritative as he moved towards Thompson.

Thompson assumed this was the mess man. 'I've to make a tea for Chief Taylor; he said I was to use his cup.'

'They use this place like a bloody café … there are set times for making tea, you know, and it's not stand-easy yet,' the mess man said loudly, pointing at the clock on the bulkhead.

Thompson didn't know what to do. 'Well you'll have to do it, I'm too busy.' The mess man took down a mug with a black cigar printed on it and passed it to Thompson. 'Here's his cup.'

Thompson said thanks and quickly made a cup of tea.

'Ah lovely, just what the doctor ordered,' Taylor said, reaching out for the steaming-hot mug of tea. 'Mossman all right, was he?' he asked knowingly. Thompson lowered his head and made a noise that Taylor couldn't make out. 'That's your first task passed with flying colours. Getting past the mess man before stand-easy – he must like you.'

'I don't think he does.'

'Don't worry, it'll get easier. You'll get to know all the crew's little quirky ways before long. You'll see behaviour that will astound and surprise you, and sometimes you'll ask yourself difficult questions. But it's all part of submarine life, and it stays on board the submarine.' Ben paused to make sure Thompson had understood what he had just said. Satisfied, he carried on. 'You mustn't forget that all the crew – the permanent crew, that is – know each other very well … you could say "warts and all". They've been cooped up in this metal can on many patrols, and unfortunately they don't know you at the moment … don't know if they can trust you, rely on you … you're not part of the team – yet.'

Taylor smiled as he sipped the tea. 'By the way, a word of warning about Taff: don't be led astray by him; take what he says with a pinch of salt and try to avoid him ashore or he'll get you into all sorts of trouble. Now, where were we? When we're in harbour we all turn to at eight.

You come and find me and I'll give you your jobs to do. Don't be late – five past eight gets you a black mark. Stand-easy in the morning is at ten and dinner is from twelve till one. Afternoon stand-easy is at three and we secure at five if you're not part of the duty watch.'

Taylor talked to Thompson about his initial training at the shore establishment of HMS *Raleigh*, where he would have received his basic military training, before going on to talk about his engineering training at HMS *Sultan*.

'I felt more relaxed at *Sultan*,' Thompson explained. 'I enjoyed the routine and loved working in the engineering workshops. We had a really good instructor and it was … well, there was a better atmosphere, not as strict. The knowledge they taught us about how engines worked in the classroom was enjoyable too.'

Taylor let the young man, who was now feeling more at ease, ramble on about his time at *Sultan*, before eventually getting onto HMS *Dolphin* to undergo his submarine training.

'How did you find your training at *Dolphin*?'

'It was all right, but I found it hard. How a submarine works is very difficult to grasp – all the different systems from fresh water to high-pressure air, electrics and torpedo … it was all very confusing.'

Taylor tried to put his mind at ease. 'Learning how a submarine works is difficult for anyone, especially when they're teaching you in a classroom on a chalkboard. You'll find it easier on here, actually – seeing the systems work. When you separate the systems and break them down into bight-sized chunks, as it were, you'll grasp it a lot easier. I'll take you through them one at a time and it'll all become clear. Let's start with a quick history lesson. The first submarine used in combat was in 1776. Unfortunately it was an American boat, the Turtle, trying to sink the British ship, Eagle.

Britain's first nuclear-powered submarine, HMS/M *Dreadnought*, had her keel laid at Vickers shipyard in Barrow-in-Furness in June 1959. The Queen herself launched her in October 1960. She underwent extensive sea trials before being commissioned in 1963. This first nuclear-powered submarine came to be after an agreement between Great Britain and America to combine their efforts and technology, which had begun shortly after the Second World War. *Dreadnought* actually used an American nuclear reactor for propulsion. Three short years after dreadnought saw the arrival of the first full British nuclear-powered submarine: HMS/M *Valiant*. HMS/M *Warspite* completed a threesome of this ambitious, technologically ground-breaking class of submarine. 1970 saw the introduction of the *Churchill*-class, which was built primarily to detect and destroy other submarines and led to it being called the 'hunter-killer'. By the end of 1971 we had three hunter-killers – can you name them?' Taylor was checking to see if the lad was still awake.

'*Churchill* … *Courageous* … and uh … I can't remember.'

'*Conqueror*,' Taylor helped out. 'Then two years ago we launched, along with *Splendid* and *Spartan*, the Navy's most up-to-date and finest submarines, *Covert* being the best of the three, obviously. *Covert* is a Fleet-class hunter-killer submarine – she displaces around four thousand nine hundred tonnes and has a top speed of about twenty-eight knots. Now, let's see what you know about my submarine. What do you know about the hull?'

'The pressure hull is approximately two hundred and twenty feet long, surrounded by a casing for streamlining, making the total length about two hundred and eighty-five feet. Five major bulkheads split the submarine into six major watertight compartments, and each of these bulkheads has a hydraulic door on the centre line.'

'How many ballast tanks?

'Six.'

'How many torpedo tubes?'

'Six.'

'What else have we got in this compartment?'

Thompson showed Taylor round the compartment, pointing out the equipment as he went.

'Oxygen candle burner.'

'And what does it do?'

Thompson went into auto: 'Insert a candle, ignition by firing pin and the chemical reaction between, I think, its chlorate and potassium.' Thompson looked at Taylor quizzically.

'Yeah, correct. Carry on.'

'Escape tower.'

'Where is the other one?'

'It's right back aft in the motor room.'

'OK. Next.'

'Submerged signal ejector.'

'What's this used for?'

'It's used to signal the surface … uses flares and various pyrotechnics.'

After fifteen minutes …

'OK, I've seen enough in here, take me on a tour of the rest,' Taylor said.

'You want me to take you right through?'

'Yep. Not too much detail though – we'll come to that later. Right now I want to know what you know.'

They walked slowly through the submarine, Taylor asking questions as they went.

They passed the O_2 candle store, above them the dry provisions store and on their right the ship's office and cupboard canteen.

'What's down here?' asked Taylor.

'It's the electrolyser, which uses a chemical called lye in a pressurised vessel to split water into its basic elements of oxygen and hydrogen by passing an electric current through it.' They went on and Thompson continued: 'Below us the main battery, sonar console space and health physics lab … then comes the junior rates' bathroom, auxiliary machinery space and walk-in refrigerator. Next is the senior rates' bathroom and laundry containing one washing machine and one dryer for the whole ship's company.

In there the senior rates' bunk space, eighteen bunks; this is the junior rates' bunk space, thirty-three bunks … then the senior rates' mess, galley, junior rates' mess.'

'Where's the garbage ejector?'

'Just before you enter the galley on the left.'

'Good. Go on.'

'This is the radar office and wireless transmission office … below us now, the carbon monoxide scrubbers and air conditioning space.'

'We'll probably be in the way if we go into the control room, so talk me through what's above us.'

Martin thought for a moment.

'The conning tower—'

Taylor interrupted him. 'What's in that?'

'The search and attack periscopes, diesel exhaust and induction masts, radar and communications mast and shuff-duff mast, which houses the aerial for the interception and warning system.' Thompson paused.

'Is that it?' asked Taylor.

'I think so,' Thompson answered unsurely.

'One more, mate: the fixed ventilation exhaust mast gets rid of stale air and battery gases using the LP blower. Not to worry, you did very well to remember the ones you did. What's special about the conning tower?'

'Oh, it's reinforced at the top for ice-breaking.'

'Good. Now talk me through the compartments.'

'The main entrance hatch comes down from the casing up there, and we also have an eight-berth cabin, wardroom, captain's cabin, officers' bathroom and pantry. Then the sonar room and the main control room, which has the steering and helm position, the chart and navigation table, the two periscopes and the systems console that controls ballast blowing, ventilation and operation of all the masts.'

They climbed the short steps that took them off the accommodation deck and brought them to a small space with two exits: left took them into the control room, and to the right and forward brought them up against the forward tunnel hydraulic door. The two of them stood in the confined space and Taylor spoke.

'Between you and me, that's the hotel end of the submarine and through here is the business end. Have you been back aft on a nuclear submarine before?'

'Once, Chief – we went on HMS *Churchill* while she was refitting in Chatham.'

'Be honest – did you learn anything?'

'Not really. It was very busy.'

'Workers everywhere, equipment ripped out. I know. Not the best way to see systems and the layout. By the time I've finished with you, you'll know everything back here.' They had to squeeze together to let an electrician through and down the ladder. 'Have you got your film badge on?'

'Yeah, it's right here.' Martin pointed to the little blue badge pinned to his No. 8 shirt.

'Right, follow me.' Taylor looked through the small round glass viewing porthole in the door checking the other door was shut before pressing down on a lever at the side. The heavy tunnel door swung slowly open. They stepped through and into the tunnel.

Taylor pressed down on the lever on the inside of the door and it closed behind them with a thud. It was like stepping into another world. Quietness surrounded them; unlike the other parts of the submarine, no machinery could be heard. The Formica walls in the forward section where replaced by stainless-steel pipes and valves. 'We're now in the "tunnel". Six feet wide and twenty feet long, and in some places you can't stand up straight without banging your head. It sits on top of the reactor compartment and is the only way from the rear section of the submarine to the forward section.

Because of the different ventilation set-ups and watertight integrity, only one door should be open at a time; check through the glass porthole before you operate the door. Many systems pass straight through here, important systems, so later we'll go through them one at a time. There is a fail-safe system incorporated called "containment".

In the case of a massive radiation leak, major flood or accumulation of four alarms going off in the manoeuvring room, it will cause the system to automatically shut off the hydraulics to both doors and neither can be opened. Think about the consequences of that for a moment. It can only be reset from the control room and the manoeuvring room simultaneously, not from one or the other. Containment can be initiated another way, but I'll go into that later. Right, let's move on.'

Taylor walked to the after tunnel hydraulic door and pressed down on the lever. As the door opened, machinery noise swarmed into the tunnel and filled their ears.

Heat hit them full in the face and the smell of oil and bilge lined their noses as they stepped through into the machinery spaces of the submarine.

Taylor took Martin to the manoeuvring room and introduced him to the marine engineering officer. He then walked with him back to the tunnel door.

'Always report to the senior man in the manoeuvring room when you come aft, Martin, so they know who's back here, and they'll tell you if anything untoward is happening in the machinery – things to watch out for, ladders removed for access, et cetera. Right, then, let's continue our tour.'

They went down to the turbo generator room and back up to the diesel generator room, which also contained the hydraulic plant, then up to the manoeuvring flat and along to the main machinery space where the main turbine engines lived along with other ancillaries like freshwater-making distillers. These spaces were very cramped; getting around them sometimes required a contortion act.

The possibility of hurting yourself was immense, and Taylor explained that the sooner Thompson learned where all the dangers were and how to avoid them the better. They went back up to the manoeuvring room flat through the last watertight door and into the electric motor room, which doubled up as the aft escape compartment. Taylor was happy with his trainee's basic knowledge.

'We're sailing tomorrow at 1000 hours; it takes about eight hours to warm through the steam systems. If we opened up the steam directly onto cold pipework and turbines, they would quickly expand with the heat and cause leaks and possibly cracks, so everything has to be done slowly, gradually raising the temperature to avoid sudden shock. I'll arrange it with the MEO[4] and I would like you to be here to see the start of it, say around midnight. You can hold on to the shirt tails of the on-watch stoker. Follow him around, see what he does and ask as many questions as you want – but think about the question before you ask it, don't make yourself look a fool.

Get involved with the valve line-up and preps. Stay for a couple of hours, because once the steam is flowing it's a slow process of temperature monitoring and I'm sure you know how to read a temperature gauge. Get your head down about 0200-ish and then be back at 0600 hours – by then the steam systems will be warmed through and you can witness the engines being flashed up. Arrange a shake with the quartermaster, he'll come and wake you up. In the meantime, the first system I want you to familiarise yourself with is the main steam system. Follow it from the TG[5] room, right through to MMS[6] and main turbines. Anything you want to ask me now?'

The young lad's head was spinning as he thought for a moment. He eventually shook it from side to side.

'OK. They'll probably be carrying out a vacuum test later today to see if the pressure hull is tight, so listen to the main broadcast. I also arranged for you to do a casing crawl between the casing and the pressure hull – it has to be done sometimes

---

[4] Marine Engineering Officer.
[5] Turbo generator.
[6] Main machinery space.

prior to sailing to check for tools and rubbish left by dockies, but not required this time,' Taylor continued: 'If you need me, check with the QM,[7] he'll know my whereabouts. Right, then, see you later. Oh, there's one other thing …' Taylor made sure he had Martin's attention. 'There are seasoned characters on this boat that will find it funny to try and impress you and even lead you astray – don't get involved with them. There's a fine line between becoming a good shipmate and part of the team and being led into the pub every night and getting into trouble. I'm not saying don't go ashore with your crewmates; just think about what you have to do the next day and the consequences that may come of it. Trust your instincts and be yourself. If you have any problems on board, come to me first.' Taylor shook Thompson's hand and began to exit the motor room, before adding: 'Anytime, my cabin door is always open. Welcome to the real world.'

---

[7] Quartermaster.

CHAPTER NINE

It was raining hard; so hard the windscreen wipers hardly had any effect on clearing the water from the windshield. Gallymore drove like a maniac, not caring about the treacherous road conditions and the consequences it could have. Sitting beside him, McCann was trying his best not to look afraid as he clung to the handle above his door and the edge of his seat. Both men were silent and wide-eyed as they concentrated on the road ahead, particularly on the white lines that Gallymore was using as his guide to keep the car on the road and to stop it from crashing off into the trees that lined the road. Inside the Ford, they were being thrown from one side of the car to the other as Gallymore negotiated the twisting corners. The noise from the tyres skidding on the road, the rain and the engine roaring was deafening. Even if they wanted to speak, neither of them would be heard above the cacophony that was going on around them. They were lucky no one else had decided to travel that same route tonight. Finally they arrived at the safe house.

McCann opened the large wooden gate and waved Gallymore through onto the potholed muddy drive leading up to the farmhouse. McCann left the gate open and jumped back into the car.

'When will the others be here?' asked Gallymore.

'Should be about fifteen … no, wait … the way you were driving, make that thirty minutes.' McCann smiled.

Gallymore checked around the outside of the rented farmhouse, the moon providing all the light he needed. All seemed in order: the brambles growing around the barn, the planks missing from the side, the hole in the roof … He looked down the drive and listened for a while. McCann went inside. The farmhouse had been empty for some time and smelled musty and damp. The whitewashed walls had streaks where water had trickled down. The lounge was quite large but the only furniture in there was a stained sofa that could seat at least four and an old television that stood in front of it. The low ceilings looked down on an open fire place and a wooden floor. Old newspapers and crockery lay where they had been left on the large dining table. Gallymore entered the house as McCann walked into the kitchen, which was almost the same size as the lounge. The work surfaces were covered in dust and the footprints of small animals that had run across the top. One of the cupboard doors hung off its hinges and pots and pans lay unwashed in the ceramic sink. McCann checked the cupboards: tinned potatoes and carrots were in one cupboard while another had stewing steak and a jar of something he didn't recognise. The glass in the back door was broken and there was a strange smell – which he also couldn't recognise – coming from outside.

Forty minutes later both men heard the sound of the van approaching. Gallymore quickly switched the lights off and they crouched looking out of the window, watching their four colleagues exit the van and cross the muddy yard to the house.

When they entered, Gallymore told Mickey Kelly to go back out and keep watch by the main road leading up to the farm.

'Why the feck me?'

'Because I say so, d'ya hear me, Mickey?' Gallymore was in no mood to be questioned.

Mickey Kelly was the oldest in the group; his hair had started to turn grey at the edges. A big gentle giant of a man, he had told Gallymore the whereabouts of the IRA man bragging in the pub about killing Paul Kennet. Mickey left immediately; he had questioned Gallymore before so he knew about the man's bad temper. There was an air of trepidation as the rest of the gang turned on the television set and the five men sat in front of the screen waiting for the evening news to come on.

'Sean, how about rustling up some food, I'm starving,' snapped Gallymore.

'Anything you say, boss. How does Irish stew sound?' Sean O'Brean raised his tall, slim and athletic body from the arm of the sofa where he had been perched, tied his long, tight red curls back behind his head and headed for the kitchen.

'Stew will be fine. At last, someone who respects me enough not to answer back.'

'I respect ya, boss,' answered Michael Mullen almost too quickly. He too was a giant of a man, with a broken nose and scars above both eyes.

'Good, I'm glad to hear it, Michael. Go get Mickey from the road, will you … it'll be clear now. If anyone was following us, they would be here by now.'

Michael Mullen was not the cleverest of the group and struggled to raise his massive frame to the upright position.

They were all eating when the television presenter reported on the bombing of an English military Land Rover on the A3 between Armagh and Craigavon. They cheered and slapped each other on the back as they listened, and discovered that one soldier had been killed in the blast.

'That's brilliant, just brilliant.' Andy McDowell, the sixth member of this newly formed splinter group, was the smallest and probably the toughest man in the room. 'That'll make 'em sit up and take notice.'

'They'll soon learn who they're dealing with,' added Sean.

Andy went upstairs. After checking the four bedrooms, a long landing and a bathroom, he descended the stairs back to the lounge. 'Four bedrooms up there, but the wooden floorboards are a death trap: most of them are rotten, and in some places you can see the room down here.'

After the remains of the stew had been eaten and the plates thrown into the kitchen sink with the others, it didn't take long for the whisky to appear. Three hours later, although a little worse for wear, Gallymore and McCann where the only two still awake.

'Why did you split from the IRA, Gallymore?'

'It's a long story, Shamus.'

'I've got all the time in the world.'

Gallymore realised that McCann was not going to give in until he got an answer.

'Well, where shall a start? I'd been a member of the IRA since I left school, even running errands for them. They meant everything to me, everything my family stood for.

Christ, my father told me some stories, I'll tell you. My da used to say, "A good Englishman is a …" Ah, well … he was very clever my da. We never had much money and we lived in a hovel, but we made it by. His only enjoyment came from playing snooker once a week.' There was a long pause while Gallymore reminisced. 'He also used to say, "Just because a man is born in a stable is no reason to treat him like a horse." Yeah, very clever was my da.'

There was another long pause. McCann topped up their tumblers from the whisky bottle.

After taking a gulp, Gallymore continued. 'He was coming out of the pub when an English bastard shot him. He'd walked out right in the middle of a street fight. The squaddie later said in his defence that my da was carrying a gun. How he could mistake a snooker cue case for a rifle is beyond me. I asked the IRA for revenge but they turned me down flat … said the time wasn't right.' The tumblers where filled again. 'I formed the Irish Free Fighters the next day, the IRA fuckers dictating to me who we'll hit and who we won't. Pillocks! I'll show 'em, I'll make my own decisions. I won't rest till all those English bastards are back across the sea in their own country, and if anyone else gets in my way I'll sort them out too!'

'So that's what all this about. Not fighting to free Ireland and the people, not about years of suppression and rule … it's about your personal revenge!'

Gallymore sat up straight and looked at McCann. 'Don't let anyone light a fire in that hearth, the smoke will be seen for miles …
and I want blankets put up at the windows at night. Oh, and McCann?' Gallymore drank the last drop from his tumbler. 'Get this placed rigged in case we get unwanted visitors.'

CHAPTER TEN

Faslane was shrouded in cloud and a light drizzle was falling. It was surprisingly warm for April in Scotland. Three submarines lay docked alongside the jetty; two had dockyard workers and crew busily scurrying on and off the gangway but one, HMS/M *Covert*, lay quiet with all her hatches closed. On board, the crew members were busy at their stations; the engines were running at maximum temperatures and pressures but no revolutions were rung on; drills were being performed as if at sea and emergency procedures were being carried out. *Covert* was carrying out a 'fast cruise' – a routine check of all systems before proceeding to sea. The last thing to do was reverse the ventilation and pull a small vacuum inside the submarine. If the vacuum held, the pressure hull was intact and the submarine had no leaks. The previous day, a seaman had crawled between the pressure hull and the casing, checking for loose items and any tools or equipment that had been lost or discarded and that could cause a noise short or rattle detectable by another vessel once the submarine was submerged.

Cranes moved into position, hatches were opened to allow crew members on the casing to release the submarines tethers, the gangway was lifted off and the captain and first lieutenant where peering over the top of the conning tower, barking orders at the men below.

The submarine eased away from the jetty with the aid of tugs, and eventually free from all her ties the massive propeller began to turn slowly and the black hull pushed the water aside with ease as she slid forward through the waves. The captain gave the helmsman a course to steer and picked up his binoculars. He was looking down the loch at Rhu Narrows, the narrowest point at the mouth of the loch before immerging out into the broad river Clyde.

Down below, the crew were already settling into their routines. In the forward torpedo room the watch-keeper sat in his seat sipping tea and reading a book. In the galley two chefs cooked lunch and at the same time began the prep for the evening meal. The control room was a calm place with crewmen watching radar screens and helmsmen watching compasses while the navigator charted their course on a large paper chart. In the manoeuvring room quiet chat between the watch-keepers did not distract them from their routines, while in the machinery spaces the watch-keepers went about the non-stop tasks of keeping the machinery turning. Once clear of the restraints of shallow water in the Clyde, and at 1100 hours precisely, *Covert* slowly and deliberately disappeared beneath the waves.

The hulking, bulbous nose of the ship pushed its way steadily through the roughening sea, the cold black steel hull becoming colder and blacker as it heaved the freezing Atlantic waters aside at her bow before allowing them to glide effortlessly down the sheer sides of the bulk container ship. The water changed colour again at the stern of the vessel where it quickened, slid across the stern and collided with the water coming down the other side.

The confused, white frothy foam that formed soon disappeared back down into the darkness and regained its composure as the ship rolled on.

On board, two sailors glanced at each other from either side of the wheelhouse, their faces unemotional and haggard-looking, only their tired eyes giving away their true feelings. They were worried because the earlier weather forecast had given out gale warnings in this area. Neither man revealed any sign of weakness to the other. The red lighting made them look even more morose.

They did not speak. The hum of the cooling fans inside the radar and global positioning machines was the only sound to be heard on the warm bridge. They returned their gaze out of the bridge windows with eyes that squinted as they pierced the darkness,

looking out past the rain-soaked decks, over the cold steel 'V' shape of the bow and out into the endless night. The sea and the sky had merged into one and no distinction could be made between the two. This blackness had been engulfing them for the last hour. Now it was on them. It gripped the ship and made it feel small and even more lifeless.

Their experienced eyes searched for the smallest of lights that would indicate the presence of another ship. Radar alone could not be relied on – they had to keep a good lookout as well. Through the thick glass the muffled noise of the wind increased and became almost banshee-like. From out of nowhere the wind screeched across the deck and quickly removed anything that had not been lashed down.

Out of the corner of his eye one of the sailors saw a grey shape rise up, twist and fly off into the darkness. He presumed it was a piece of tarpaulin sheet that had torn free – not important enough to report to the officer of the watch, who was sat at the back of the wheelhouse studying charts intently. He was in charge of the vessel while the captain took a rare opportunity for sleep, and who had left orders to wake him as soon as the storm worsened.

The OOW clung onto the chart table as he peered out of the wheelhouse window when the ship began to yaw around. He decided to leave it a while longer before disturbing the captain.

The two lookouts knew they would lose many more objects off the deck before the storm released them from its grip. Surprisingly, the sea was still relatively flat. The squall hadn't had time to stir it up, but the two sailors knew what was to come. Nobody on board would sleep all the way through tonight. The vessel steamed on into the darkness. The large white painted letters on the stern read '*Czar of Prussia*', and underneath the name of the vessel was the port of registration: 'St Petersburg.'

Unbeknown to the Russian merchant vessel, and a half-mile behind them at eight hundred feet below the surface in the freezing, murky waters of the North Atlantic, travelled *Covert*, stealthily sliding through the water with ease, her speed of ten knots by order of the captain far below the maximum speed she was capable of.

On board, Taylor was getting ready to hand over his watch in the MMS.

He pulled the zip of his blue overalls down to his groin, slipped the top half of them off his broad shoulders and pulled them down to his waist. The muscles in his strong arms rippled as he pulled off the white t-shirt he was wearing. His flat stomach glistened with the sweat that covered him. Taylor twisted his t-shirt and rang the fluids out of it into a plastic bucket. He then pulled a new clean t-shirt over his short, dark hair and was dressed again in seconds. This process he had repeated many times while on watch in the steaming-hot engine room. He stood on the top plates with Martin Thompson at his side. A red-faced stoker appeared up through a hole from the lower level. Dougie Milne, the most experienced stoker and ready for promotion, was a burly Scotsman from Stirling who superstitiously always carried a piece of tartan about his person. Whether it was the colour of his handkerchief or his socks, Dougie always had a reminder of his clan on him somewhere. They all wore ear defenders to protect them from the noise of the giant steam turbines that filled most of the available space in the engine room.

All the other machinery had been squashed in around these gigantic propulsion units. Wisps of steam occasionally spat from some of the valves that surrounded the three men and condensation dripped from the pipes. Taylor sat down in his makeshift seat, a cushion that had been tied on top of a metal toolbox, the only place in the engine room where he could sit down comfortably but with only room enough for one. From this strategic position he could instantly see all the turbine speed, pressure, temperature and oil gauges that were vital in keeping the engines spinning. Taylor tapped Dougie on the arm; Dougie immediately turned to face him, watching Taylor's lips.

'Turbine speed increasing,' he told the stoker. Taylor swivelled round and tried to open a valve that was behind him. 'Damn thing's jammed shut.' He quickly reached into his overall pocket, took out a spanner and calmly freed the valve. He swivelled back to face Dougie.

'I wonder where we're going in such a hurry?' Taylor mouthed to his colleague. Although Dougie couldn't actually hear him, months of watch-keeping in constant machinery noise had taught both men how to lip-read; it was a talent learned by everyone who worked in the noisy rear section of the submarine.

Taylor moved off his seat, tapped one of the gauges in front of him and tweaked another valve, then faced Dougie. 'Where's your relief?' he said, pointing at the clock and wiping the sweat of his brow with a rag.

'Looks like Taff's late again,' he answered. 'I can't wait to get out of these wet overalls, Chief.'

Dougie's overalls were soaking wet with sweat from his body and condensed steam that dripped on him from the pipes and cables above his head.

Suddenly there was a loud noise from above. Another man came sliding down the ladder, his feet not touching the rungs, hands clenched loosely on the rails. He landed with a thud on the deck plates next to Dougie.

'You're a noise short, Sion … they'll hear that in the control room,' shouted Taylor, annoyed at the Welshman. 'Sort him out will you, Dougie?'

Dougie shook his head at his watch relief. 'You're going to get that so wrong one day, Taff, and really bang yourself up. Where have you been anyway? You're late.'

'Sorry, mate, overslept. Stayed up a little longer than I thought I would, winding up the trainees in the mess,' he said proudly.

'I hope I do get it wrong, that way I'll get to see Enfys and my little Sara; these trips are getting longer and longer. We've been at sea for three weeks and it already feels like we've been away for months.' While talking to Dougie, Sion acknowledged the chief. 'Anyway, do you want to get out of here?' he continued grumpily. Taylor knew Sion very well – knew that he would be grumpy like this for at least half an hour longer while he woke up properly.

Taylor immediately felt concern for Sion. 'We'll soon be back, mate,' he told him, trying to console him. *It was strange*, Taylor thought. *When you were on board you wanted to be at home, and when you were at home for a few weeks you started to miss the sea and couldn't wait to get back on board.*

Dougie started with the watch handover to Sion.

Taylor spoke to Martin. 'Don't bother with any system tracing tonight, Martin. You could do with a rest; shower and straight to bed, my lad. See you in eight hours.'

Martin thanked his crewmates and climbed the ladder out of the MMS.

Dougie had finished the handover, and finally he said to Sion: 'Is my bunk still warm?'

'Yeah, and I've turned back the top sheet and fluffed up your pillow,' Sion answered sarcastically. Dougie and Sion shared a bunk to save space, known as 'hot bunking'.

Dougie had now lost patience with him. 'Anything happening up front?'

'Not much. Eat – sleep – watch-keep … usual stuff. I've just been telling the trainees about the time we were hit by that randy whale.'

'They're on board to learn, Sion, not to be frightened out of their minds. Give them a chance, some of them are quite switched on. We all had to start at the beginning once. I'll see you later.' Dougie faced Taylor again. 'OK with you, Chief?'

'Yep, see you in eight hours' time. Thanks, Dougie.' Taylor would be relieved at quarter past the hour. This staggered the handover, as the aluminium walkways in the MMS were narrow and space was limited. It would get rather crowded with four people trying to hand over the watch at the same time. It also meant you didn't have two people on watch that were possibly still waking from a deep sleep. At least one would be fully awake.

Taylor's relief, Tam, arrived on time, and as Taylor climbed the ladder he heard Sion still complaining: 'Eat, sleep, watch-keep …' He emerged out of the hatch and into the slightly cooler passageway that led him through the manoeuvring room, the nerve centre of the engineering department. Taylor removed his ear defenders and hung them on a peg.

He raised his hand to acknowledge the three panel watch-keepers sat at their respective panels: propulsion, electrical and reactor. Sat behind them and slightly above were the engineering officer of the watch and finally the chief engineer. The manoeuvring watch-keepers returned Ben's greeting as he took a drink of ice-cold water from the drinking fountain.

As the hydraulic door closed behind him, he breathed a sigh of relief in the eerie silence. The noise of the engines and equipment in the after section immediately stopped. It took a while for his ears to adjust to the silence.

As he walked through the tunnel, Taylor stooped to avoid the pipes and valves, which were manufactured from stainless steel, giving them an almost clinical look. He disliked going through the tunnel and always tried to do it as quickly as possible. Although he knew he was safely shielded by solid-lead sheeting from the deadly radiation beneath his feet, he still worried about this invisible killer. Taylor walked to the for'd door and pressed down the handle. He opened it just enough to slide through, and could immediately hear the low murmur of people talking in the control room.

In front of him were eight steps leading down to the accommodation deck, but he sidestepped them and entered the control room. It was dark in here, the red lighting illuminating just enough for the watch-keepers to see their panels. It took a while for Taylor's eyes to adjust to the darkness after coming from the bright lights that were on constantly in the rear section of the submarine.

Taylor would often come into the control room when he came off watch; he would stand at the back and observe what was going on.

The control room was the only compartment on board the submarine that switched to red lighting when it was dark in the real world far above them on the surface. It was the only way to distinguish between night and day on the boat. It was also done so as not to hinder vision when looking through the periscopes at night. The quiet hum of the electrics behind the panels and the softly spoken orders from the officers made him quite envious. It must be nice to go on and come off watch wearing the same clean, dry No. 8 working uniform. On his left in a small broom-type cupboard room sat the sonar operator wearing earphones and staring at the large, round orange screen with its spider's web continuously pulsing from the centre. In front of him were two men, one controlling the rudder for steerage and the other controlling the fore-planes for changes in depth. Across the room was the navigation table where a yeoman sat continuously plotting the submarine's progress above the seabed. In the centre of the control room stood the officer of the watch, in overall command while the captain was not on duty.

'There's a nasty storm brewing up top,' he said to no one in particular. 'Not that it'll have any effect on us.'

Taylor lowered his head and spoke quietly into the ear of the systems console operator.

'What's happening, buddy?' he enquired.

'We're following a Russian freighter, going up to take some photos of the prop later if the weather improves,' he replied in Taylor's ear.

Taylor suddenly felt tired; the lack of noise and the darkness made his eyes heavy. He left the control room and descended the ladder to the accommodation deck. About halfway along the passageway was the ladder down to the washrooms, which like most vessels that put to sea were called 'the heads'. He passed the etched brass plaque that read: 'The use of deodorants, aftershave, talcum powder or anything else that might contaminate the atmosphere with odours and dust particles is absolutely forbidden.' Taylor pulled back the curtain that allowed him access to his mess; there was a solid wooden door fitted, but it was rarely used. Some of the crew had been trapped in the mess when the door was shut at periscope depth; the submarine had then dived deep, causing the pressure hull to contract, squeezing in on the doorframe and jamming the door shut. Consequently, it was now usually left open. When Ben walked in there were two people sat on opposite sides of the mess, the space between them still not more than six feet, but obviously trying to get as much privacy as possible. The senior rates' mess catered for around fifteen people, but fortunately not all at the same time due to people sleeping or on watch. Meal times were the busiest. Overalls were banned from the mess but it was an unwritten rule you could come in as long as you didn't sit on the cushions.

The person nearest the door was reading a book and the other was playing solitaire with a pack of cards. Taylor made himself a cup of tea quietly, not wanting to break the silence. Had he wanted sugar he would not have been able, due to it becoming contaminated with moisture in the store and turning into sweet blocks of concrete. The only milk that was left was UHT, which he had become accustomed to. He would have made himself a sandwich but all the butter had been used a few days ago. He went without. Due to the fact that no radio or TV signals could be picked up when 'dived', the mess was without television or radio. There was, however, a music cassette player on a shelf in the corner, but it wasn't used because it had a nasty habit of chewing the tape, the owner losing his favourite tunes forever. Taylor had a Walkman by his bunk which he used sparingly due to the lack of batteries. No pictures were hung on the walls as these would be a hazard if fire broke out or if the submarine were to turn or dive violently. The mess was made even drabber by the dull seat covers supplied by the MOD.

'Fancy a game of crib, Ben?' the card player asked.

'No, not tonight, I've got to have a shower before I climb into my scratcher,' Taylor told the card player while looking at the book reader. Then he continued: 'That must be a very good book he's reading ... if you get the chance to communicate with him, ask him if I can borrow it, would you?'

'Yeah, sure, Ben ... see you later, goodnight.'

Taylor said goodnight, washed his cup in the galley, and after taking a shower entered the sleeping berth compartment. Completely in darkness, he walked quietly in the narrow gap that separated the three-tier bunks on either side of him. The smell of body odours and the sound of snoring filled his senses, but he had become accustomed to this and it didn't bother him anymore. It was sometimes very warm in here, depending on what part of the world they were in and the water temperature around them. The sleeping berth compartment was far better than the for'd torpedo compartment where the trainees slept on empty torpedo racks. It was good incentive for the Part 3s to become fully qualified submariners.

Although in total darkness, he instinctively found his own bunk, pulled back the curtain that provided him with the only privacy from the other fifteen people that shared his bedroom and climbed onto what he called his 'shelf'. Taylor immediately fell asleep.

Three hours later he was awoken by the tannoy: 'Assume the ultra-quiet state, assume the ultra-quiet state.' All non-essential equipment was turned off. The cool air coming through the small punkah louvre vent by his head stopped abruptly. All personnel stopped moving around the submarine, unless it was absolutely necessary. Even the snoring stopped, as everyone was now (probably) awake. An eerie silence fell around the submarine. He tried in vain to go back to sleep but knew he would not.

Someone came into the bunk space and brushed slowly past Taylor's bunk. Taylor pulled back the curtain and could just make out the man's features.

'What's happening, Charlie?'

'There's a Russian ship up above; we're going to take some photos of her hull.'

Taylor slid the curtain shut and tried harder to sleep. Then he heard the far-off sound of a hydraulic motor, and the angle of the submarine altered. His feet became higher than his head as the bow started to rise. He could hear the voice of the fore-planes operator, through the now redundant ventilation system, calling out the depth as the submarine moved slowly upwards towards the surface. Then came the sound he was listening for ... ever so quietly at first but getting louder all the time ... the whoosh-whoosh-whoosh of the large propellers slicing through the water above them. The submarine was so quiet Ben heard the order for the periscope to be raised. The submarine levelled out. He sensed fine adjustments being made to the trim of the submarine. Then it was obvious that something was going wrong. There was a loud bang and the whole boat shuddered. Shortly afterwards, with the sub at an odd angle listing heavily to port, the noise of the general alarm, adding to the cacophony, rang nauseatingly in his ears. The four-thousand-nine-hundred-tonne submarine swayed and bucked from side to side. The ear-piercing screech of metal on metal could be heard above his head, but louder than that was the general alarm that rang out through the whole submarine.

There was mayhem in the sleeping quarters. Someone shouted 'What the hell's happened?' Bodies were falling out of their bunks, the people in the top ones scampering over the ones below, the strange angle of the submarine not helping.

Sleeping bags and bedding were being thrown around causing people to stumble, and men were groping around in the darkness trying to get dressed in whatever clothing they could find.

Taylor shouted at the top of his voice: 'Get the lights on!' Almost instantly, the fluorescent lights blinked and popped into action. Initially they were all blinded by the brightness, but in seconds they could see. As Taylor slid into his overalls, the steward fell from the bunk opposite and hit him on the side of the face with an elbow. He didn't have time to apologise. A small torch flew past Ben's head and thudded into the chest of another man, causing him to whimper as he lost his breath.

The tannoy sparked into life again: 'Hands to emergency stations, hands to emergency stations, close all watertight doors and hatches.'

Taylor knew he had only a matter of minutes to get to his emergency station, which was through the tunnel and to the aft section, before the hydraulic valves would be shut, automatically rendering the doors inoperable. The submarine dropped suddenly, like an aircraft in turbulence, as Taylor ran through the door of the sleeping berth. The angle of the list came off and the submarine was upright again. He bounded up the accommodation ladder two steps at a time and instinctively dodged a valve that protruded from a pipe on his right. He thrust the lever on the for'd tunnel door down with all his might. The door opened and he and another engineer, who was still getting into his overalls, stepped inside.

Taylor cursed as the door closed slowly behind him and pushed the lever harder to try and make the door close faster, but he knew it would make no difference to the speed.

'Come on, come on,' he said aloud, and finally the door sealed. The other engineer had run to the aft door, and as soon as Taylor shouted 'OK', he was opening it. Sprinting now to the aft door, Taylor knew he didn't have long to go, instinctively ducking and swaying to avoid pipes and valves. He squeezed through the narrowest of gaps when the aft door opened, and breathed a big sigh of relief when the after tunnel door eventually closed behind him. A wave of apprehension passed through his body. He glanced at his hand still on the door-operating lever: was he imagining it, or was there complete silence for a split second? It was almost peaceful. And then his mind was racing again as he entered the manoeuvring room. Each of the three watch-keepers was busy cancelling alarms and one by one reporting to the EOOW[8]. Taylor waited for his orders.

'Engine room bilge is at high level and both distillers have high salinity alarms,' shouted the EOOW. Taylor knew that this was not too much of a problem: the distiller just heats up seawater to boiling temperature and condenses the rising steam into fresh cold water for drinking and so on, all the salt remaining at the bottom of the distilling plant. If the salt is churned up, the distiller automatically ditches everything into the bilge.

---

[8] Engineering officer of the watch.

'Main engine condensers are all over the place,' reported the chief engineer. This, however, Taylor knew was serious.

Once the steam hits the turbine blades it cools and condenses into water; if the level rises too high in the main engine condensers, water can hit the rotor blades on the turbine, and because they're revolving at such high speed they'll disintegrate immediately, causing the main engines to explode.

'Ben, go and help with the condenser levels down the engine room,' ordered the EOOW. This was the order Taylor had been waiting for, and with just a wave of his hand he was on his way to the engine room.

Once down the ladder he met Tam on the top plates. The noise in the engine room was louder than normal and Taylor, rather than try and listen, stared intently at Tam's mouth to read his lips.

'Taff's working on the port condenser; you go to the starboard one.' Again, Taylor didn't need to answer and disappeared down a hole in the deck plates. The main engine condensers were underneath the main engines, which meant going into the bilge ten feet below the walkway. Taylor had to open a suction valve on a second pump before it could be started to help the main pump remove the water from the condenser. He could see that the water level in the bilge was much higher than normal, probably due to the distilling plant going wrong and ditching all the water it was making into the bilge. As he stepped off the ladder he was up to his waist in freezing-cold water.

He shouted across to the other side of the engines to see if Sion was all right, but the noise was deafening down there and he received no reply. The water level in the bilge was rising quickly; Taylor knew exactly where the suction valve was and dived down. The shock of cold water on his head as he went under numbed his brain; the cold made it feel like his head was being crushed. Taylor felt giddy and nauseous; he had only been beneath the water for seconds but already he felt the extreme need to breathe. His head ached and his chest tightened as he fought to stay down. His hand found the valve but he struggled to move it. He lost all sensation in his fingers, and his hands were not doing what he asked them to. He could feel the strength in his arms seeping away. The submarine rocked to one side and Taylor was thrown from the valve and slipped under the condenser. He needed to breathe, and fought with all his might for the surface. He emerged into fresh air between the two condensers, a place he had never been before, inaccessible without the flooded water to get him there, but also a place where he would drown if he stayed. He gasped in three or four gulps of air and dived under again. He couldn't swim, and used anything he could get hold of to pull himself along and out from under the condensers. He hit his head on the suction valve, and with adrenaline-enhanced strength opened it quickly. He needed air again. Using all his training to resist the urge to suck in, he moved off slowly and surfaced a few minutes later gasping for air, but found he couldn't breathe properly. He was struggling to get enough air into his lungs, so he calmed himself and told himself that he was fine now, that he had done it. His breathing back under control, he was still up to his neck in freezing water. He couldn't feel his arms and legs and his head was pounding from inside. A strange feeling flashed through his thoughts: he could stay here … he was all right, he had air to breathe, he felt no pain. 'Sod this.' Taylor ducked under the oily water, the only thought in his mind to get to the ladder.

CHAPTER ELEVEN

Her Majesty's Submarine *Covert* had recovered an even keel. The accommodation deck in the for'd section of the submarine was strewn with clothing, broken crockery and the crew's personal belongings. A first-aid post had been set up in the officers' wardroom. One of the medical technicians tried tirelessly to stem the flow of blood from an open wound on a sailor's head. To reduce the risk of fire, the ventilation system had been shut down and the temperature on board had soared. There was also an acrid smell from the batteries in the stagnant air. All the unnecessary machinery had been stopped, which gave the submarine an unusual, eerie, quiet atmosphere. There was, however, a constant screeching noise followed occasionally by a large bang coming from the top of the conning tower. The noise heightened in the quietness, making it sound as if it was right above the crew's heads. One of the chefs had burned his hand while attempting to stop himself from falling over in the galley. He was now wading through a swamp of water and rags that had collected in a dip at the base of the accommodation ladder, his burned hand throbbing as he made his way to the first-aid post. The aft section of the submarine was in turmoil as well. The violent rolling motion of the submarine had caused the large amount of water in the bilges to wash from side to side and rise much higher than Taylor had ever seen.

Old oil and spilled battery acid had mixed together to make a mind-numbing concoction that smelled acrid and disgusting, making everyone feel nauseous. Neck-high in rising freezing water, Taylor heard the turbine blades of the main engines above his head slowing down, at first thinking it to be a reduction in speed, but he soon realised the engines were stopping. The submarine had to move forward to allow water into the inlets to cool the reactor, and it's easier to control the submarine's depth if it's moving through the water. If the propulsion was not restored, the submarine could slip uncontrollably down to the seabed, however far below that was. The manoeuvring room watch-keepers watched as the main engine revolution gauge fell towards zero. The row of one-inch-square Dowty alarm indicators flashed from green through to yellow and then to red, indicating a full alarm. The watch-keepers acted quickly to change from steam propulsion to battery-powered electric motor. Taylor had passed the shivering stage and knew his body would be shutting down blood flow to his extremities to maintain core temperature. He lunged for the ladder but missed, and his head went under again. He lay there face down in the bilge not able to move, his muscles not working, when suddenly his thoughts went to the young woman trapped in the cave. He could see her quite clearly looking at him, her hair wet and matted, her face dirty and blood-stained …

but there was no panic in her eyes this time – she was calm. A smile slowly spread across her whole face; she looked warm and joyful. Taylor reached for her outstretched hand and held it tight. She held out her other hand and Taylor heard the machinery tannoy blare out: 'Reactor scram, reactor scram, reactor scram.' Taylor didn't know how, but he was climbing the ladder, his body slowly emerging from the freezing water, his goal now the top plates – and quickly. The reactor had scrammed, causing the control rods to drop into the core and shut it down. The consequent loss of steam had caused the main engines, turbo-driven generators, distilling plants and major cooling pumps to shut down completely. The heat in the MMS was intense – Taylor went from freezing to boiling instantly. He struggled up the ladder one rung at a time, his legs not working as normal. Once clear of the water, his muscles still aching, he could feel the warmth coming back through his body as he got higher, and the pain in his feet and hands increased as the blood flow and warmth returned. When he eventually got to the top plates, he shouted to Tam.

'Start the pump!'

Tam started the second pump straight away.

Sion came over and shouted in Taylor's ear: 'What took you so long, Chief?'

Taylor smiled for a moment before the pain in his arms and legs became excruciating. Sion helped him off the ladder and held onto him for moment. The returning heat in his body eventually causing steam to rise from his wet clothing, he stood on the top plates of the engine room looking like a demon from hell.

The bilge pumps did their job. Condenser levels dropped and the main engines were prepared for restarting. With every movement, Taylor's muscles eased and he moved more freely. They waited for the word from the control room. After what seemed like an age, the throttles were opened and propulsion restored.

Taylor was impressed at the calmness of the watch-keepers when he entered the manoeuvring room and spoke to the engineering officer.

'Everything seems to be stable down there now, sir.'

'Well done, Ben. You look in a bit of a state … what happened to your eye?' Blood dripped down Taylor's cheek from a small cut above his blackening eye. Then he remembered the steward hitting him with his elbow in the bunk space.

'It's nothing, sir, I'm all right.'

'All the same, have the medical technician look at it – you may need a stitch to stop the blood flowing. It won't heal by itself.'

'What happened, sir?' Taylor enquired. 'Do we know what hit us?'

'Just give me a second and I'll be right with you.' The engineering officer picked up a machinery tannoy microphone. 'Second Engineer, manoeuvring.'

Taylor leaned on the side of one the electrical cabinets; the adrenaline was not pumping as fast as it had been and he was now feeling tired. He listened to the reply over the tannoy.

'Second here.'

'Give it one more turn, Mike.' The engineering officer looked closely at one of the gauges, and the Dowty flicked from red to yellow. He spoke again into the microphone: 'Hold it there.' Then he turned to Ben. 'Well, while we were under a Russian merchantman it would appear that we went through a change in seawater density, enough to alter our trim. The control room couldn't correct it in time and we hit the bottom of the ship with the conning tower, our search periscope taking most of the force. The damage is a big dent in the captain's reputation and a search periscope that's … well, in God knows what shape. All we know at the moment is it won't come down. There are two seals where it comes through the pressure hull, Ben – the top one is badly damaged and the bottom one is leaking slowly. But they're managing to contain the water with a portable pump, so we're staying at periscope depth to keep the outside seawater pressure to a minimum until we're well clear of the Russkie … then we'll surface and take a look. The situation back here is: one of the reactor coolant pumps tripped due to the acute angle we went to, and there was a short delay until the backup pump cut in. This caused a fluctuation in core temperature, which initiated the reactor scram and containment. We're about to reset the valves now.'

Climbing back down into the engine room, Taylor felt exhausted. *I'm getting too old for this*, he thought. He explained what had happened on the top plates.

'So what happens now, Chief?' Sion asked him.

'Well, it looks as if you're going to see your family sooner than you thought, Sion.'

Sion managed a rare smile. 'Bet it gave those Russians a scare. What damage will we have done to the merchant ship, Chief?'

'Hard to say, really. Probably not a lot. Their hull is a lot harder than our search periscope. We may have been given a swipe by their propeller, in which case they may not have felt anything and may be unaware of the turmoil down here. If that's the case, then their engineers will get a shock at their next dry docking.'

In *Covert*'s control room, the captain ordered a course that would take them directly to their base at Faslane on the Clyde.

The crew worked indefatigably to get the submarine ship-shape again. Repair work to machinery, as well as cleaning the whole boat to get rid of the foul stench that had engulfed its compartments, was undertaken with gusto.

Covert surfaced off the coast of Ireland away from prying eyes. The dawn was coming slowly, the sun rising and spreading its orange fingers across the sky. As soon as the conning tower was clear of the surface, the captain, closely followed by two lookouts, opened the top hatch and climbed out to inspect the damage.

The smell of fresh air filtered through the boat. In the junior rates' mess, a trainee complained.

'What the hell is that stink?'

Sion was always there to explain. 'When the boat is submerged, the air we breathe is so pure and clean it doesn't have any bacteria in it, which is what you're smelling at the moment. This does cause us a problem, though.''

'How come?' The young man enquired.

'Even the freshest of fresh air has bacteria in it. It's the bacteria which cause a scab to form over an open wound and help it to heal. This is a problem to us living in an atmosphere with no bacteria, because if we're unfortunate enough to cut ourselves on board, the wound will stay open for the rest of the time we're in this bacteria-free atmosphere. Long or deep cuts have to be stitched and bandaged straight away, to stem and hopefully stop the bleeding.' Sion smiled at him. 'That smell … is fresh air, my boy. Don't worry, you won't notice it in a little while.'

'My God, stinky fresh air; what next?' The young man shook his weary head.

No damage had occurred to the conning tower, but the search periscope was beyond repair. Like a giant porpoise with a bent harpoon sticking out of its back, HMS/M *Covert* slid silently up the river Clyde and a few hours later was back into Faslane. She was eventually secured alongside with the help of a tug. As soon as the gangway was across, the periscope maintainers were on board and the process of rectification began. A huge tarpaulin was draped over the conning tower to keep out prying eyes from the surrounding hills and the sky above.

The captain went ashore shortly afterwards, with all due ceremony. He looked official in his immaculately pressed uniform, the gold of his insignia and rank braiding gleaming in the daylight. With a pensive expression he walked briskly along the dockside carrying a bulging briefcase.

The captain headed towards the office of the commander-in-chief, his immediate boss and the officer in charge of the submarine fleet. This was the normal procedure after a sea patrol. The commander-in-chief would receive a debrief of the patrol from the captain of the submarine, but this particular debrief was going to be a long and intense one.

Taylor and Martin were working on the aft casing.

'I wouldn't like to be in his shoes right now,' Martin said to Taylor while they were attaching water-cooling hoses and a bilge connection through the pressure hull. Martin glanced out of the corner of his eye. 'I wonder what's in the case?' A crane beeped its way away along the metal tracks on the dockside and swung its jib over the conning tower as they worked.

'He'll have all the documents, reports, charts and tape recordings of everything said and done in the control room just prior to and during emergency stations,' Taylor answered him while opening a valve. High above them the bent periscope was removed from the conning tower and carried away.

Suddenly, Martin stood up straight. 'We were lucky, weren't we?'

Taylor looked at Martin and saw that his friend had gone pale.

'Yes mate, we were.'

When they had finished connecting the hoses, Taylor and Martin went back down to the engine room. It was still very hot on the top plates, but thankfully not as noisy. Taylor squeezed onto the cushion on top of the toolbox.

Sion came up from the lower plates complaining. 'Filthy, rotten stinking place!' He wiped his hands on a cloth from the rag bin.

Taylor ignored him, knowing it would be something trivial. Martin made the mistake of asking him what was wrong.

'Everything. This place. Being here. What I really don't like is the fact we have to stay on board and turn these engines until the turbine blades cool down, while the seamen get to go ashore straight away. That bloody steward is always the first off the boat, too,' he added as an angry afterthought.

Taylor suddenly thought of another job that needed to be done. He slipped off the cushion and went to the back of the engine room. When he returned some minutes later, Sion was still talking to Martin and becoming more and more animated.

'And when we're in a foreign port we have to come back on board earlier than those bastards. Just to warm the engines through.'

'The pipes would crack from the shock if we didn't, Sion.'

Sion leaped off the watch-keeping seat and tapped the glass on a gauge. 'That's another tankful.'

Taylor slid back onto his seat and was glad the subject had been changed. With the distillers shut down, the freshwater tanks were filled from shore via hoses.

It was uncommon for the senior rates and the juniors rates to go ashore together, but Taylor wanted to know more about Martin.

'I'll tell you what: Tam and I are going ashore tonight. So as soon as we've finished here, we'll get cleaned up, grab a bite to eat and all go for a few beers in Helensburgh.'

'Sounds like a splendid idea,' Sion answered, slightly happier.

CHAPTER TWELVE

The night air was chilled. Orla Brodie looked up at the clear, star-studded sky. She was sat outside the caravan with her mother, as she had done so many times before. Orla wondered how she would cope if she ever lost her. She worried about her mother's health. She had tried many times to get her to stop smoking. Orla also knew her mother drank too much whisky.

Mrs Brodie was happy here in Scotland. She had her routine, and although not a healthy one, it kept her busy. She had friends here at the camp and the cause was justified. The Faslane Peace Camp, as it was known, was one of a number of peace camps all over Europe set up to actively protest against nuclear missiles – at least, initially. But newcomers would bring their own views. They would add disproval of nuclear power, and protests against war, conflict and poverty. Protesters came and went, their individual protests coming and going with them, but the main theme that stayed with this camp was nuclear disarmament. The camp had a good relationship with the local council and the protesters rented the land from the regional council for a nominal fee of one pound a month. Peace camps set up in the south of England were being harassed and evicted from their sites while the Faslane camp was allowed to concentrate on campaigning against a nuclear-free world. The camp gave Mrs Brodie purpose and made her life worthwhile. On the whole it was a peaceful, subdued, passive protest camp, but every now and then they flexed their muscles and had a march with banners and placards, some of them dated saying 'Ban the bomb' but others depicting the end of the world in detailed, colourful artwork. Mrs Brodie enjoyed making the banners; they used almost anything they could find in and around the camp to make the elaborate signs with which they then marched down to the main gate at the Faslane submarine base, causing as much disruption to traffic as they could along the way. They would abandon the banners, placards and signs in a heap on the road and walk back to the camp, leaving the Navy to clear up the mess. Back at the camp the kettles would go on and more often than not, home-baked cake would be passed around with the tea as they reflected and rejoiced on the disruption caused.

There was nothing left for her back in Ireland, only bad memories. She had her daughter with her, Orla, born in Dublin twenty years ago, as well as her son Liam, who was older but not always wiser. Both lived with her in their caravan at this peace camp on the shores of the beautiful Gare Loch. The only blot on the landscape, so she thought, was the nuclear submarines moored at the Royal Naval base just down the road.

Mrs Brodie watched her daughter closely; she knew Orla was a strong-willed girl with strong views, but she also knew she was a hopeless romantic. Mrs Brodie realised that one day she would have to let her go, and she prayed it would be with the right man.

Liam, on the other hand, was a numbskull, as she often told him. If trouble was around he would find it. She knew it was not all his fault: he hadn't been the same ever since his father had passed away. Mrs Brodie knew Liam missed his father dearly … almost as much as she herself missed her husband.

They had lived at the peace camp for seven months, and had got themselves settled in. Their mail was delivered by the local postman from Helensburgh, and the camp's committee had appointed a 'milk monitor' whose job it was to find out how much milk and bread was required by the people at the camp. This was done on a rota system and changed from day to day, with people coming and going to attend to other jobs and commitments. The milkman was understanding and every morning left the required amount of milk and bread. They had tried to get him to deliver cheese, but he had told them not to push their luck. There was a core of about fifteen activists who lived permanently on the site. Freshwater standpipes provided drinking water to the fluctuating number of caravans on the site. The council had officially informed them that they could have no more than eight caravans on this site, but they rarely had under this amount and refused entry to no one. They were an ethnically diverse community and got on well; some of the older committee members had been living on and organising peace camps all over the world. Mrs Brodie had no enemies here and was particularly friendly with Mrs O'Brian from the other Irish family that lived at the camp. Mrs O'Brian shared her caravan with her three children and her husband. All had anti-nuclear feelings as their common bond.

Mrs Brodie broke the silence.

'Where's your brother, Orla?'

'He said he was going into town for a few hours. Probably in the pub; he's getting quite friendly with the locals in Helensburgh.'

'He needs a job.' Mrs Brodie pulled her shawl tighter over her shoulders.

'Are you warm enough, Ma? Would you like me to get a blanket?'

'I'm fine, thank you, Orla. I hope he's not getting into any trouble.'

'No, he wouldn't do any wrong, Ma. It's good for him to mix with lads of his own age.'

'And what about you, my dear?'

'What do you mean, Ma?'

'What about you mixing? It's not right for a young lady of your age to be stuck with her mother twenty-four hours a day.'

'Mam, don't be silly. I love being with you.'

'I wonder what that young man is doing ...'

Orla knew right away who her mother was talking about. Not a day had gone by without her thinking of the handsome young man who had come to her aid on that terrible day potholing. She secretly longed to meet him again. Orla didn't know who he was, what his name was or where he had gone, and didn't know if she would ever see him again.

Mrs Brodie knew her daughter better than Orla knew herself – the way only mothers can – and she played along. Mrs Brodie would not mention him for a few days, and then would drop him casually into the conversation.

'I pray for him and hope he's, safe you know.'

Orla looked at her mother and furrowed her brow.

'You know, Orla – the one who rescued you from that hole you were trapped in.'

'Oh, him. He's probably on the other side of the earth, with nothing to do but lie on a beach in the sun, enjoying himself.'

'I have a funny feeling he'll be back, though, Orla.'

Orla hoped he would, and soon.

CHAPTER THIRTEEN

The blood splattered over the whitewashed walls of the cottage. It landed like large red polka dots then trailed off into thin lines. Gallymore was amazed how the man in front of him had stayed on his feet so long; he hit out again, catching his adversary this time square on the chin. Brendon Forester fell backwards; his body was rigid as he collapsed to the floor like a felled tree, taking the whole force of his descending body weight on the back of his head. He remained motionless, and seconds later thick, dark red blood oozed from his ears and nostrils and began to soak into the rug that partially covered the stone floor.

Gallymore had discovered that Forester was the man behind the assault on Paul Kennet from a friend, Mickey Kelly, whom he had known since his school days at Denton secondary modern in Dublin. Mickey had told him that he had overheard two men talking in the local pub; both men had been drinking heavily and one was bragging about being given a job to take out a splinter group man who had stepped on the IRA's toes, and how the little wimp had howled with every kick he had delivered. He'd also said how much he was looking forward to going back and sorting out his slut of a wife.

Mickey had had no trouble finding out where the man lived, and had given all the information to Gallymore, wishing him good tidings to bad rubbish.

Gallymore opened a cupboard above the sink draining board, looked inside and closed it again; he opened the cupboard door to the right and found the glass he was looking for. Holding it up to the light, he inspected it for dirt before filling it with cold water from the tap. After drinking the water he washed the glass, wiped it dry with a tea towel and, being careful not to leave any fingerprints, replaced the glass in the cupboard. He then left the cottage silently through the back door.

CHAPTER FOURTEEN

The sky overhead was heavy and thunderous. It cast its blanket of greyness over everything, taking away the colour and making everything drab. The sharp wind blew off the tops of the hills across from the Faslane submarine base and swooped down across the loch and straight onto the jetty, where the submarines berthed. It was not a strong wind, but it was enough to make the sailors wear their work coats.

The submarines were totally different when alongside. They seemed to go into a dormant, sleep-like state, especially at night, when all the dockyard workers went home and, because of the cramped conditions on board, only a duty watch (roughly one person from every department) were allowed to be on the boat overnight. They were mainly there for security and first-hand firefighting, especially after welding or burning had been undertaken on board during the day. In the daytime, four thousand local civilians worked at the base and most of them had clearance to work on board the submarines.

While the duty watch suffered the arduous rigours of sleeping in their bunks on board overnight, the rest of the crew slept in the shoreside barracks. Sion had a cabin near the top of the naval establishment. It was a rectangular room measuring ten feet by fifteen.

Inside were a bed, a free-standing wardrobe, a small writing desk and a chair. Sion sat on his single bed and put on his shoes.

The curtains were drawn, covering the only window that was directly opposite the door. Sion got up and went immediately to the mirror on the front of the wardrobe. He stooped down and began straightening his hair.

'Flipping gorgeous,' he said to himself.

Taylor grabbed a scarf from the fitted wardrobe in his twenty-by-fifteen-foot cabin in the senior rates' block and went to meet Tam in the foyer. They left the accomadation block and walked down a small flight of steps and onto a narrow concrete pathway that led past a large glass wall that let the light in on one side of the swimming pool. The glass was reflective so he could not see anyone, but he could hear people splashing and shouting inside. He would normally be swimming or playing five-a-side football himself at this time of night, so he would work twice as hard tomorrow.

They were silently following the path through a shrubbery and flowerbeds on either side, and passed the vast brick wall of the gymnasium housing the squash, volleyball, five-a-side and basketball courts. Then came the weightlifting gym, followed closely by a gym with old-fashioned wall bars, vaulting horses, thick mats and wooden benches strewn about inside. The double fire doors were open and the light from inside came flooding out into the darkening sky that was descending on them quickly. Two Royal Marines in full camouflage gear came up the path towards them; they nodded acknowledgement as they walked past. One carried an SA80 rifle while the other carried a light support weapon close across his chest.

One of the Marines recognised Taylor.

'Hey, Ben … we're having a shoot tomorrow night at the range, coming along?' he enquired.

'Yes, mate, I'll be there.'

'They must be having another exercise.' Tam flicked his head back as he smiled at Taylor. 'I don't know why they bother, the SAS win every time.' The exercise would usually consist of the Royal Marines defending the base against the SAS soldiers, who would try to enter the base illegally and take control of a facility in the submarine base or even get on board one of the boats.

'They don't win every time,' Ben replied to his friend.

'They bloody do, mate.' Tam's voice rose as he spoke. Taylor knew the story that was coming next, but was prepared to listen anyway. 'What about the time that SAS bloke lived in a dustbin just inside the main gate for a week without anybody knowing he was there?' Tam was still relaying the story when they walked into the main amenities block on their way to the main gate. This eight-story block housed the NAAFI[9] store, the dining hall and six bars, ranging from the carpeted concert room on the top floor down to what was known as the 'Hooley bar' in the basement. Drinks were served in plastic tumblers, the chairs were also plastic and the tables were Formica.

---

[9] The Navy, Army and Air Force Institutes – the private company that operates the military stores and leisure services for the British Armed Forces around the world.

Submariners returning from a long patrol would use the Hooley bar on their first night out, although some people preferred to use it every night.

Taylor and Tam descended the wide staircase that led down to the ground floor and out past the administration block, where the path turned sharply to the left and led them to the main gate a hundred yards away. The MOD Police and Royal Marine soldiers manned this gate every minute of the day and every day of the year. Security was very tight, with different passes needed to get to different areas. This area was classed as 'accommodation' and required just the normal Royal Navy identity card. The clock on the wall in the security building read seven o'clock as Taylor and Tam emerged through the last security check and were greeted by Sion and Martin. The town of Helensburgh was the nearest town to the submarine base; a taxi ride would get you there before the flavour of toothpaste had dissolved from your mouth. The fare was always more expensive coming back to the base than going into the town, no matter what the time was. The submariners would pay any amount of money rather than walk back to the base late at night, mainly through laziness but more times than not due to consuming copious amounts of alcohol. A fact the taxi drivers knew and exploited to its full extent. Most of the local people didn't like the sailors; they crowded their bars and flirted with their women, transforming this normally quiet backwater of the Clyde into a place of iniquitous and sometimes immoral mayhem.

As much as the locals hated being overrun by the sailors, they also knew that they were a vital part of the economy and brought wealth and vitality to this small town. Mainly the two tolerated each other. The restaurants and bars were full nearly every night with British 'matelots', most of whom were trying to over-indulge with as much food and drink as they could in the shortest possible time – their way of relieving pent-up emotions that had built up after being incarcerated in a metal can for weeks on end. Inevitably some took it too far and this would lead to trouble. It was not uncommon to see whole crews falling over and staggering along the streets, or the police breaking up a fight. Not all of the submariners lived the 'rock star' lifestyle while ashore. Some of them did use the gymnasium regularly. Some were content to read in their cabins. Some found comfort in religion, music or painting … but true enough, the majority found alcohol to be their salvation. Whichever method was used, no matter how it was achieved, the end result was always the same. Their goal during this off time was to relieve themselves of the frustration and boredom they encountered on long monotonous routine deployments in their boats. They had to get it out of their system before the next trip, or they would be at risk of serious mental stress.

All four men made their way to the first car in the taxi rank. There was never a shortage of taxis outside the base. They didn't have to tell the driver where they wanted to go as they jumped into the back of the cab; he would drop them off in the centre of town, where he dropped everyone from the base.

Without a glance back, the driver sped off down the road. At the end of the base approach road the taxi turned right onto the main highway. They passed the peace camp that had been erected on the left-hand grass verge. Taylor had stopped to chat with the protesters on several occasions while out jogging, and he recognised one of the men standing by the side of a caravan. He waved through the window of the taxi. Taylor found them pleasant enough people, if a little naive. He had tried to explain, politely, that the Royal Navy submarines were a nuclear deterrent rather than a threat. They had listened to what he had to say but his words were in vain: it had not changed their views. Taylor enjoyed his brief chats with the protesters and found they had a wide variety of education levels and came from all walks of life. Although he would never join such an organisation, he somehow admired them. They were always polite, and would normally offer him a drink of tea or water, which he always accepted. It had not always been peaceful, however. When the protesters had first arrived on one Friday afternoon, a silly one had lain down in the road to stop a sailor driving home. The sailor hadn't stopped and had run over the man's legs. It had of course made a good story for the press. Taylor remembered the sailor being quickly drafted to Plymouth with a very bad report in tow.

'I see the tree huggers are still here,' Sion said openly.

'Yep.' The taxi driver let his gaze drift from the road for a moment as he looked at the caravans. 'You boys had a long trip?' he enquired.

'Long enough,' Taylor said, bringing the conversation to an end.

Moments later their taxi arrived in Helensburgh. They split the fare four ways.

'Right, which one first?' asked Sion. 'Let's see if any of the lads are in here,' he continued, pointing to the Imperial Hotel. It was quite strange that even when ashore you found that crews stayed together and didn't mix with other crews. However, idle banter between the crews was common, though the Navy discouraged it because it sometimes got out of hand, especially when heavy drinking was involved. The Navy warned: 'Friendly banter provokes violence' … but it happened all the same.

Taylor opened the door and was immediately hit with the smell of cigarette smoke, stale beer and sweat. The bar was brightly lit, plastic plants lined the booths on one side and a long, well-used, badly varnished wooden bar ran the length of the other. The jukebox played loud, so the level of talking was even louder. Groups of people stood around talking and Ben recognised the faces of at least three different boat crews.

'There's our lot over there,' Sion said over the din of the jukebox and gestured towards a group of six people sat in a booth halfway down the bar.

Taylor bought four pints of beer at the bar and they joined their colleagues, who were deep in conversation but stopped when they saw their crewmates.

'A-all right, l-lads?' stammered one of the seamen, whose eyes looked heavy and who was obviously well on his way to becoming drunk.

'You see what I mean about these people getting off early,' Sion said to Taylor, but loud enough for them all to hear his sarcastic comments.

'Yep, it looks as if they've wasted all their free time in here as well,' Taylor replied.

'You guys are just jealous,' shouted a baby-faced electrician.

Sion whispered to Taylor. 'He's only nineteen. There's no hope for us, mate; we're not going to get any sense out of this lot … come on, let's move over to the bar.'

'I'm right behind you,' Taylor answered. Tam and Martin followed them.

Taylor couldn't make out the profanities that were hurled at them as they got up and left for the bar, but he ignored them knowing that tomorrow his friends would be apologetic – if they remembered tonight's events at all. There were three barmen working, which was normal as this was a popular bar with both submariners and civilian people, and Taylor knew the bar would get fuller as the night wore on.

'Fancy going to the Highlander, Tam? It'll be a lot quieter …' Taylor still had to talk loudly to overcome the jukebox. Before Tam could answer, a large, bearded Scotsman that was standing next to him drank his double whisky in one swallow and belched loudly. Both Taylor and Tam looked at his matted ginger beard and grimaced.

'I think the Highlander sounds like a good idea,' Tam replied. All four men finished their drinks quickly, squeezed through the bodies that were now cluttering the bar area and walked out into the fast-chilling night air.

The smell of the sea filled their nostrils, and as Taylor looked across the loch he could just make out the darker outline of the hills that stood high in the sky, overlooking the deep water that now looked like ink in the darkness. Taylor sucked in heavily through his nose and filled his lungs with sweet-smelling albeit slightly damp fresh air.

'It's going to rain,' Taylor said as he pulled the large collar up on his jacket.

Sion chuckled, for he knew what was coming: 'If it's not raining in Scotland, it's about to,' they both said together, laughing.

The Highlander bar stood one street back from the Imperial Hotel, and a few minutes later they entered a quiet, dimly lit room with red leather seats. Taylor immediately thought someone smoking a pipe must have just left, as there was a smell of sweet pipe tobacco in the air. The barmaid gave them a welcoming smile as Tam ordered four pints of Tartan beer.

'Get a seat, I'll bring them over,' Tam said to Taylor.

'Ben, Dougie told me we're going to be alongside for a while,' Martin said as he waited for his drink.

'Yeah, he told me that too,' interrupted Sion. 'I think I'll slap in for two weeks' leave. I need to get some climbing in. It's been a long time.' Sion was lustfully eyeing the waitress.

Taylor saw what he was doing and brought him back to reality: 'And I have no doubt Enfys will be pleased to see you as well …' He then changed the subject. 'I'm off to San Diego soon.'

'With who?'

'The skipper and my DO.'

'What are you going out there for, Ben?' asked Sion.

'The Yanks want me to test a new diving set.' Taylor laughed as he saw Sion's brain working overtime. He let him stew on it for a while.

Eventually Sion spoke. '*Covert* needs more ship's divers, doesn't she?'

'We always need more divers, mate.'

'What does the diving course consist of, Ben?' asked Sion.

'Well, there are two roads you can go down. One is to change career completely and become a professional diver or "clearance diver". You'll do an initial sixteen weeks' training using mixed gases for breathing and may dive in excess of fifty metres. I don't think you're quite ready for that yet, but there's an easier route called a "ship's diver". You stay in the same trade, so you'll remain an engineer, but after the four-week course you'll be a qualified Navy compressed air breathing diver.'

'And with more pay,' added Sion.

'It won't only mean more pay, Sion; it'll be an additional qualification on your documents. What's brought this on all of a sudden? Are you thinking of becoming a diver?'

Sion shifted in his seat. 'I've been thinking about it for some time. I asked my DO to look into it for me.'

'You haven't just decided because I've told you I'm going to San Diego, then?'

'No, of course not … tell me more about the ship's diver course,' he said excitedly.

Tam brought the drinks from the bar and sat down. Taylor thanked him and took a sip from his drink before continuing to answer Sion.

'The course teaches you how to breathe from compressed air breathing apparatus down to a maximum depth of eighteen metres. It's quite an intense four weeks, at a place called Horsea Island on the outskirts of Portsmouth.'

'Will I get extra money?'

'Yeah, course you will, as long as you reach your quota of minutes under water per period.'

'The Navy doesn't give you extra money for nothing, Ben … there has to be many extra duties involved.'

'As I said, it's not an easy course to start with and yes, you'll have extra duties to get your head wet. The extra qualification on your documents will help with promotion when the time comes. Now's a good time to do it, buddy,' Taylor said, smiling at him. The pint glasses in front of them had been drained.

Sion strolled to the bar and gained the attention of the barmaid. 'Four more pints here, love.' When he returned to the table, Martin was talking to Tam.

'Are we allowed civilians on board, Tam?'

'On special, rare occasions the captain allows civilian visitors on board. On these occasions it's the job of the duty watch to guide the visitors round the for'd section of the submarine. No civilian visitors are allowed through the "tunnel" into the aft machinery sections.

Not just because of the top-secret nuclear equipment but because it's physically dangerous to be near the nuclear reactor. Other out-of-bounds rooms are the sonar room and the captain's quarters. Visitors also have to be clear of the submarine by 2100 hours. This then allows the crew time to clean up and perform any last-minute requirements before turning in. The control room remains manned all through the night.'

They finished with a nightcap of Glenmorangie single malt whisky, said goodnight to the barmaid and walked back to the taxi rank situated opposite the Imperial Hotel. Taylor let Sion contemplate his future. They had to wait, as there were eight people already queuing. The noise emitted from across the road in the bar was deafening, and drunks were beginning to pour out of the door and head for the late-night Indian restaurant, always a favourite eating place for the sailors after they've been drinking.

Taylor looked at Martin and shook his head in disgust – this sort of behaviour brought disrepute on the Royal Navy, and unfortunately the civilians tarred them all with the same brush, saying they were all drunken brawlers. Then, fleetingly, Taylor heard one of the chaps at the front of the queue mention the peace camp. The voice he heard came from a group of four people. One of them, wearing a denim jacket, was of medium build and average height, but had one of those stupid-looking flying birds tattooed on his hands between the thumb and forefinger. Another was wearing a sports jacket and was slightly taller and thicker set, almost athletic-looking.

The other two were wearing just pullover jumpers, one of which was patterned with Scottish tartan and the other plain blue. The two Pullovers were swaying heavily.

'Did you hear that, Tam?'

'Hear what, mate?' Tam was engrossed with the scene across the road. Taylor eventually dismissed what he had heard about the camp as being nothing.

Two taxis came and went, in the direction of the submarine base; another taxi arrived shortly after, and the four of them got in. The taxi sped away, the loch on the left and grey stone houses on the right, and in no time at all they were passing the peace camp. Taylor looked out of the car window ready to wave, as he always did, but this time something was wrong. Four men were standing on the grass verge alongside one of the trailers that the protesters used as their homes. Although it was dark, Taylor recognised the sports jacket one of them was wearing as being the same as the one he saw at the front of the taxi rank back in Helensburgh. There was an altercation going on between one of the four men and one of the male protesters … and then Taylor saw a fist fly.

'Stop the car!' he yelled. The startled taxi driver slammed the brakes and the cab slid to a halt. The three passengers didn't know what was going on, but before they could ask, Taylor was out the door and running across the road. As Taylor approached, he clearly saw Sports Jacket rolling on the grass with a protester. Denim Jacket and the two Pullovers were shouting and cheering, urging their bullying friend on. A young woman with long dark hair ran out of the trailer and tried to stop the two men fighting.

Taylor heard her scream as Tartan Pullover knocked her to the ground with a slap to the head. Taylor hated bullying ever since he'd been on the receiving end of it at school, but hitting woman he disliked even more. It made him fill with anger, and he was now travelling at speed. As he arrived on the grass verge, he dropped his shoulder and charged Tartan Pullover, knocking him flat against the side of the trailer. He followed up with a straight-arm punch to the lower-left side of the man's back and Tartan Pullover went down with a loud cry. Taylor turned, and with his right hand grabbed the back of the shirt collar of Sports Jacket; he twisted his vice-like grip and pulled him off the protester. This caused the collar to tighten at the front and partially block off Sports Jacket's air supply by compressing his windpipe … he could hear him start to choke. Taylor felt a sudden pain in his neck and his head was jerked back by his hair. His legs buckled slightly, but without loosening his grip on the collar he thrust his left elbow backwards and it connected with a chest. His head was freed and Taylor could now turn and face his adversary. Denim Jacket threw a slow punch aimed at Taylor's head but it was easily parried away and Taylor retaliated with a kick to Denim Jacket's right knee cap. The man squealed and immediately fell over, holding his injured knee. Ben released his right-handed grip on Sports Jacket's collar when he saw Blue Pullover being chased up the road by Sion. Taylor was confused and his body was shaking with anger as the adrenaline sped round his body. He heard voices behind him and turned to see more Greenpeace protesters coming from their caravans. They gathered round him, thanking him for his help and patting him on the back, when Sion appeared in front of him.

'You, OK, mate?'

'Yeah, I think so. Did you catch him, Sion?'

'No, he took off like a scolded cat along with Sports Jacket ... I can't blame them really, you scared the living daylights out of me, Ben.'

Tam and Martin stood by the taxi across the road.

'Thanks for your help ... I just saw red when the girl got hit.' Taylor suddenly remembered the girl with the long dark hair and looked across to where she had been. He saw two older ladies helping her through the doorway of the trailer. The sound of sirens could be heard in the distance. A male protester ushered Taylor and Sion out of the small crowd that had gathered around them.

'You two had better get out of here if you want to stay out of trouble,' he said with an Irish accent.

'But ... we didn't do anything wrong?' Sion replied quizzically.

'Some people might say your friend here used a little more than necessary force,' he replied.

'He's got a point, Sion ... come on, let's go. What's your name, mate?' Taylor asked the protester as they stepped off in the direction of the submarine base.

His reply came in a whisper: 'Liam, my friend. Liam.'

It then began to rain.

CHAPTER FIFTEEN

Showing their passes, they quickly entered through the main gate of HMS *Neptune.*

'Do you think they suspected anything, Ben?' Sion's voice was quiet and quivered slightly.

'Not a thing, mate. Most men come through that gate looking like they've done ten rounds with Muhammad Ali; we look like we've been to choir practice.' Taylor could see that Sion and Martin were worried. He continued: 'Tam, if you want to carry on I'll see you in the mess later. I've really got the urge for a coffee – do you fancy one, lads?' Taylor put the question to the junior rates.

'Yeah, OK,' they both replied.

Sion and Martin followed Taylor up to the all-night 'automat.' This place had a whole wall of vending machines containing sweets, cakes, pies and drinks. The coffee was just about bearable, and if that was all there was, well … Small change was required to operate these machines, and if the change machines on the wall were empty or out of order, obtaining change was never an issue as you could always find some on the floor, under the plastic chairs or under the Formica tables, which the sailors returning from ashore in their inebriated state had dropped and hadn't bothered (or were incapable of) retrieving.

Large glass double doors opened into an even larger room. Two stainless-steel bins stood at either end of the room and were so full of plastic cups, cartons and silver foil trays that their contents had begun to spill onto the floor.

There was only one other person in the automat; Taylor and Sion took their coffee to a table some distance from him for a little privacy and settled into their seats.

'I hate fighting,' Sion said with a big sigh.

'So do I, mate, but we couldn't just drive by and watch those people get harmed. They aren't hurting anyone. They come from all walks of life and really believe that nuclear energy is wrong. They don't deserve to be beaten for just having beliefs,' Taylor said, trying to make Sion feel better.

'They wouldn't be the first,' Sion said, his voice louder than he wanted.

'That's one of the cleverest things you've ever said, Sion.' There was a long pause as they drank their coffee. Sion's mind began racing again. Taylor watched both men as they contemplated their actions. Then Martin spoke his first words.

'I'm sorry I didn't help.'

'You did the right thing staying out of it, Martin; don't feel bad. Sion and I had it covered.'

It was Sion's turn to pipe up. 'How much trouble do you think we're in? One of those guys looked pretty bad. Do you think he'll have to go to hospital? They all know what we look like; if they tell the police we're in for it. Not only will the captain throw away the key, we'll get the consequential punishment and the civvies will do us as well. Beating up civilians is not taken, lightly, Ben … that's our careers over!'

'Calm down, Sion, you're blowing this all out of proportion. Listen … you're not in any trouble, all you did was chase someone up the road. Not one of those guys is going to say anything to the cops: they're thugs, Sion, bullies ... and bullies don't go around blathering to the cops. The peace camp people won't say anything. They want no trouble in case the police move them on. And if it all goes pear-shaped ... which it won't ... then we have numerous witnesses to say I was defending myself.'

'So what's the worst-case scenario?' Sion asked, looking right into Taylor's eyes. Just then, the glass doors flew open and a hoard of drunken sailors staggered into the automat. 'Fucking great, that's all we need.' Sion crunched his empty plastic cup and threw it on the floor.

Taylor leaned across the table so only Sion could hear him. 'Wrong, mate, that's a good thing. The police may obtain the time of the incident, and the more people that come through the gate around that time the better.' Taylor sat back down in his chair. He eyed Sion cautiously, looking for telltale signs that what he'd said had sunk in. Moments later he leaned back across the table. 'The worst thing that could happen of course is if they come looking for me themselves, or perhaps with their friends ... from Glasgow. So we say nothing and go ashore with the rest of the crew. We'll be fine. Now, I suggest you two get off to bed. I'll see you tomorrow.'

The following morning Taylor rose early, put on his sports kit and jogged out of the submarine base. Waving his security pass at the main gate staff, as he had done many times before in the morning, he noticed that the clock on the office wall read 0600 hours.

The sky was overcast and the air was heavy, which wasn't ideal for running but he wasn't going far. Ten minutes down the road he stopped outside the peace camp. Taylor was hoping there would be someone outside the caravans that were arranged neatly in the makeshift encampment. He briefly contemplated knocking on the door where the two older ladies had taken the younger woman the night before, but he dismissed the idea because he didn't want to wake anybody this early in the morning.

Taylor sat thoughtfully on the kerb by the roadside pondering what to do next. He found himself watching a rain cloud climb over the top of a mountain on the other side of the loch and begin to slowly engulf more and more of the summit. He was startled by the creaking of a door behind him. Taylor turned to see one of the older ladies from the previous evening, dressed in a nightdress, dressing gown and shawl. She was carrying a teapot and was surprised to see Taylor. He realised that he'd startled her and proceeded to reassure her straight away.

'Pleased, don't be alarmed – I came to see if everything was OK after last night …'

'Oh! You're the young gentleman that helped my daughter … yes, we're all fine thanks to you, but I can't say about those other people … don't think they'll be back for a while!' She gave a cheeky little chuckle.

'Yes, sorry about that, I'm afraid it got slightly out of hand; did the police get involved?'

'Don't you worry none; they were here, and asked a lot of questions too, kept us up quite late they did, but they got no information about you and your friend out of us … it was the least we could do after what you'd done for us. The most excitement we've had round here for a while, I'll tell you.' She emptied the teapot onto a pile of used tea leaves on the ground that had obviously been building up over a long period. The older lady saw Ben's brow wrinkle.

'Makes good compost for the plants,' she said, answering his unspoken question.

'Right,' he said, nodding his head in acknowledgement. 'Did you see what happened to the attackers?'

'They fled.' She pointed over her shoulder to a large group of trees growing near a brook. 'I don't think the police even saw them. If I were you, young man, I would just forget about the whole sordid incident.'

'Has this happened before?'

'Yes. They do it from time to time, when they get bored or just feel like it I suppose … no set pattern … They'll forget about us for a while, then all of a sudden they'll be back. I don't know what it is; we're just an easy target I suppose. We'll be all right for a while now, though.'

He saw the lady shiver slightly from the cold morning loch-side air. He wanted desperately to ask about the young woman, who was probably this lady's daughter, but he had kept her out in the cold too long already.

'Well, sorry to keep you from your tea; I'm glad to hear everyone here is OK. Cheerio, then.'

'Yes, cheerio.'

Taylor turned, ready to trot off down the road, but came to a halt suddenly and, holding one hand above his head, stopped the older lady just before she disappeared inside.

'How is the lady, Mrs …?'

'My name is Mrs Brodie, young man, and my daughter is just fine,' she replied, flashing the same cheeky smile Taylor had seen earlier. Taylor jogged back to the submarine base in high spirits. He also had an unexplainable tingling feeling in his stomach and a sense of overwhelming happiness. He put it down to being relieved and a lot less worried about the previous evening's escapade.

CHAPTER SIXTEEN

In the back room of a large house in Ballymena in the county of Antrim, members of the IRA where gathered in a meeting.

'Who is it, Frank?'

'It's a little upstart called Barry Gallymore. He was with us for a long time but now he's obviously decided to go it alone.'

'What else has he been up to?'

'We had to pay a visit to one of his men.' Frank flicked through a folder for more information. 'His name was Paul Kennet … he'd blown up an empty Land Rover in Armagh when he was told not to go it alone. Somehow Gallymore found out who our man was and paid him a visit. He was quite a mess when we found him.'

'And we've warned him?'

'Oh yes, several times.'

'This Gallymore doesn't seem to be listening. I need to know all there is to know about this man, Frank! What's his background?'

Frank continued reading from the file. 'He was born in Dublin, went to a local school, came to work with us part-time early on. In and out of jobs for a couple of years, then came to work for us full-time in 1976. There was a misunderstanding about the shooting of his father and he splintered shortly after.'

'We need to pay this Gallymore a visit in person. Find him, Frank. We don't need a loose cannon causing havoc out there. The government would love us to start a war between ourselves. Let's nip this one in the bud.'

CHAPTER SEVENTEEN

Taylor finished off packing his bag by placing his dirty clothes in a plastic bag and tucking it on top of his hold-all. He slipped his weekend pass into his wallet, checked his ID card was where it should be and closed the zip. He caught the train from Helensburgh to Glasgow, which passed through Dumbarton, Anniesland, Clydebank and a host of smaller towns before arriving about forty-five minutes later at Glasgow Queen Street. He walked across town to Glasgow Central station. The electronic departure board told Taylor that the train south was twenty minutes late, so he headed for the bar. From Glasgow Central he travelled south through Carlisle, and at York the train split: one half going to London and the other, which Taylor travelled on, going to Crewe. Eventually he was met outside Crewe station late in the evening by his father.

'How are you, my son?'

'I'm fine, Dad. That train journey doesn't get any shorter.'

'Have you thought about getting a car?'

'I have, but with the time we spend at sea, it would be sat in the car park at Faslane for long periods, and the weather being what it is up there the rust would soon take hold.'

'Well, let's get you home. Mum has food waiting for you.'

Taylor began to relax as he passed the familiar roads and buildings that he knew so well, and of course he especially loved the moment when he saw his family.

He felt like he was leading a double life. One part of his life consisted of professional non-stop alertness, constantly on the lookout for something that could go wrong. On a submarine, prevention is a better option than the cure. In complete contrast, his home life was relaxing, and his parents made sure he was comfortable. Home was the only place he could let his guard down. Both his mother and father were proud of him, and showed it through their love and attention whenever he was home, which was not all that often these days. He thought about the way his mum would pamper him all the time and how she couldn't do enough for him. There would always be food prepared, and his bag (which his mother knew would be full of washing) was whisked away to the washing machine almost before he could put it down. When it was time for him to go back she would become all emotional, and Taylor had to go through the same routine every time of calming her down and telling her he wouldn't be away long, that he would write and telephone when he could. It upset Taylor too; he wanted to show emotion but knew it would make his leaving harder for all the family. So he hid his feelings and put on a hard face. His father, on the other hand, was completely different: a smile and a firm handshake was his greeting, although Taylor knew that inside he was just as pleased as his mum to see him. Occasionally Taylor would coax a story out him from his time in the SAS during the Second World War. Once, while Taylor was at Earls Court for the Royal Tournament, he had managed to persuade an SAS soldier to part with his beret, which he'd duly given to his overwhelmed dad. He was obviously a lot older now, but had kept his body in good shape.

Ben loved the way nothing changed at home; it made him feel almost serene after the constant vigilance needed while on board the submarine. Taylor could smell the food that his mother was cooking in the kitchen as he walked through the door, and his younger sister Marie ran to his arms as soon as she saw him. He wished he could bottle up that moment and then bring it with him during the long trips at sea. After giving his mum the flowers he had bought for her from the station and the presents for his sister and his younger brother Peter, he spent the evening with his mum catching up with affairs at home and the gossip about the neighbours. Taylor was not really interested but enjoyed listening to the sound of his mother's voice. The house was a basic three-bedroom council house with gardens front and back. The garage for the car was at the bottom of the garden. Winsford had sprung up as a small town when rock salt was found under the ground and had been expanded now to house the overspill from Manchester and Liverpool.

Taylor found it difficult to sleep in his own bedroom. The curtains blocked out all the light and the silence was deafening. But eventually, with happy thoughts, he drifted off.

He awoke on Saturday morning to the smell of bacon and sausage cooking, and his brother burst into his bedroom loudly exclaiming that breakfast was almost ready.

'I'll be right down, Pete,' he said with a smile.

After breakfast, Taylor and his father drove to the small marina where the River Weaver widened into a flash. They boarded their yacht, a little twenty-two-foot Hurley called *Sea Spray*, and while his father started the engine Taylor let go of the lines and prepared the sails for hoisting. The two of them sat back in the cockpit as the sails filled and a light breeze swept across the water.

'How is it going up there, Son?'

'It's all ticking along fine. We had a slight accident with a Russian tanker and we're undergoing repairs alongside at the moment. We have a short trip under the ice before I fly to San Diego to trial a new underwater diving set.'

'How long will you be away?'

'The captain's going for other reasons; it'll depend on his progress. I'm sure he's just taking me so he doesn't have to spend all his time with my divisional officer.' They both laughed.

'Ready about,' Ben's father said calmly.

'Ready,' replied Ben just as calmly. As Ben's father pushed the tiller over, Ben loosened and tightened ropes and lines in the cockpit and the yacht swung gently around, not spilling any wind from the sails as she picked up speed again in the opposite direction.

'They don't get on, then?''

'He's young ... can be a little eager and difficult sometimes.' Small ripples could be seen coming towards the yacht at speed from across the flash.

'Hold on, Ben, there's a squall coming.'

The ripples hit the yacht and the sails went taught as the yacht strained against the sudden gust of wind, which sent it leaning over a few more degrees. As quickly as it had come, the squall passed and the yacht eased back into a gentle rhythm.

'So, what's been happening?'

'I helped a young lady that had gotten herself in a pickle down a pothole in Derbyshire. She's OK and the last I saw of her she was being carried off the moor in an ambulance. I never did find out who she was or even where she was from. It was a bit tense. Then after I had returned back to the submarine and we had sailed to our designated patrol area, we had an incident on board … *Covert* was taking photographs of a Russian tanker's propeller and we hit a dense salt layer, which sent the search periscope into her hull. I don't think they noticed, but we'll be alongside for a couple of weeks. Hence the weekend leave. Most of the chaps have gone home for the week, but I have to be back on Monday for a briefing on the San Diego trip.' The yacht was turned again and this time headed downriver. 'Sion's being his usual colourful self and chasing everything in a skirt ... we had four Part 3 trainees join the boat and I've been assigned one, Martin. He's a good lad, comes from Devon.' Taylor climbed over the cabin roof and freed a line that had caught on a cleat, and then sat back down next to his father.

'This girl on the moor … was there any press involved?'

'No, we were in a remote area. Just the local police and the rescue service at first, but I had to call in a favour from PACDU to borrow a couple of diving sets. Luckily they had a team on the road nearby and were able to get to us quite quickly.'

'Have you still got my old commanding officer's number?'

'Yes, but I've not had to use it yet.'

'Well, if you have to don't hesitate. He'll be only too pleased to help.'

'There *is* one thing I would like you to do for me …'

'Sure, what is it?'

'Do you remember Tim Sherwin? He's the Royal Marine I become close with on my clearance diving course at Horsea Island.'

'Yes, I think so. Why, what's wrong?'

'I'm not sure. He was in charge of the team that was on the road … apparently been loaned to PACDU to gain experience … but it just doesn't sound right. The last I heard, the Navy had enough supervisors. Don't get me wrong, I would trust him with my life, but something isn't ringing right. I wondered if you could find out what he's up to, what he's been doing.'

'I'll make some phone calls.' Taylor's father grimaced as he pushed on the tiller.

'Are you OK?'

'Yes, I'm fine. Have you had enough? Shall we start heading back?'

'Already? That's not like you.'

'Yeah, come on, Mother will be wondering where we are.'

The rest of Saturday Taylor spent with his siblings, and in the evening he met up with his old school mates at the local pub. Conversation about what he was doing was kept to a minimum – Taylor kept moving the subject back to school days.

Sunday morning, Ben was helping his mum prepare the customary Sunday roast.

'Are you getting time to get out in this Helensburgh place, Ben?'

'Yes. I was there just the other night, actually.'

'I'll bet there are lots of young women chasing the sailors up there.'

Taylor knew where this conversation was going. 'Well, not that I've noticed, Mum ... I'm a little too busy.'

'You're not getting any younger, Benjamin, and it's about time you found a nice girl to settle down with and had some fun.'

'Mother, please, there's plenty of time for that. I really am too busy.'

'All I'm saying is, spend a little of your time to start looking.'

'I will, Mum.'

'Promise?'

'Promise.' Taylor was shaking his head and smiling.

After a huge Sunday roast for lunch and once his bag was packed with clean washing it was time to go back to Crewe station. The whole family had come with him to see him off.

Taylor was slightly embarrassed, but realised that it was a nice gesture. His mum especially wanted to show her affection. He stood in the corridor with the window down as the train pulled slowly out of the station, the whole family waving as he waved back.

Eventually losing sight of them, he went to find a seat.

Taylor was back in Helensburgh for around 10 p.m. and went for a pint to reflect on the weekend. He passed by the Imperial on the seafront and walked into a quiet Highlander bar on the street behind. He sat at the bar, and from the corner staggered Liam, moving slowly to the end of the L-shaped bar. He stared at Taylor … and then finally realised who he was.

Liam ordered a single Jameson and drank it down quickly. He wobbled slightly as he left the bar, pulled his coat close around him and headed for the taxi rank. He struggled to find the door handle in the dark, but after concentrating hard the door flew open and he fell inside, laughing.

Back at the camp, his mother was fortunately in her bedroom and didn't see the state of him when he arrived. Orla, on the other hand was sitting in the kitchen and sighed heavily as her brother lay on the floor. By her feet.

'Liam, for heaven's sake, why do you do this to yourself?'

Liam rolled onto his back and said: 'I've seen him.'

Orla ignored his drunken nonsense. 'Come on, let's get you up before Mam sees you.'

'I'm telling you; I've seen him!'

'Liam, you're too heavy for me to lift you, get into the chair. I'll make some coffee.'

'Orla, listen to me.' He grabbed her cardigan. Orla could smell the whisky on his breath as he pulled her close. 'Your knight in shining armour – I've seen him in the Highlander.'

'Liam, what are you going on about?' She was losing her patience. Liam eventually sat himself upright on the floor.

'The sailor who pulled you out of the tunnel on the moor – and he's the same one who fought off these thugs that attacked us the other night. He's in the Highlander in Helensburgh right now.'

Orla felt her heart race. She couldn't think straight and found herself running to the bedroom to change her shoes.

Her mother came to the bedroom door. 'Are you going out, Orla?'

Orla turned in shock, like she'd been caught doing something wrong. 'Erh, yeah … I've got to go into Helensburgh.'

'But it's quite late, my dear … what could be so important for you to go all the way into town at this hour?'

From inside the kitchen Liam shouted: 'She's going to see her boyfriend!'

'What's this?' Mrs Brodie exclaimed.

'I can't explain now, Mam. I'll tell you when I get back.'

'Don't be too late, cherub. Take your shawl with you; it gets cold out there at nights now.'

'Mother, please, people don't wear shawls any more. I'll take this lovely warm fleece instead, see here?' Orla produced a dark green woollen fleece from behind her chair and waved it at her mother.

'Nice colour,' her mother shouted as Orla left the caravan.

'Liam, what's going on?' Mrs Brodie asked her son. When he didn't answer she raised her voice slightly. 'Liam, you waste of space, start talking.'

Liam recognised the sternness in his mother's voice. 'She's going to see that sailor that rescued from the moor,' he slurred.

Orla stood on the pavement outside the bar. She looked at the door and took a deep breath. She surveyed the empty street and thought about going back home, but then the street lit up as the bar door swung open.

Her mouth fell open and her legs felt as if they were going to give way. They stood looking at each other for a moment before Taylor smiled at the young woman who was stood rooted to the spot outside the bar. She felt herself smiling back at the man.

Taylor held the door open. 'Hi. Are you going in?'

She realised he didn't recognise her. 'No, erm …' She took a deep breath and told herself to get a grip. 'It's actually you I've come to see.' Her Irish accent was smooth and distinctive. She was back in control.

'Oh really? Do I know you?' Before him stood a young lady who was around five foot four in height, slim and plainly dressed. Her black hair was just below shoulder length, and although she wore no make-up her round face was very pretty.

'You should,' Orla replied. She felt herself getting hot, annoyed he hadn't recognised her. 'You rescued me from a pothole in Derbyshire.'

Taylor's face changed from a smile to a concentrated contortion as his mind raced. Then the smile came back. 'My God, how … what are you … how did you find me?' He held out his hand. Orla took his huge hand in hers and shook it slowly. Their hands stayed together longer than a usual greeting.

'My brother was in here earlier and recognised you. You also helped me with some idiots who attacked us at the peace camp a few days ago.'

'Really? I had no idea.' Taylor realised they were still holding hands and that they were standing in the street. He let go of her hand.

'Sounds like we should chat. Would you like to have a drink?'

'Sure,' she said, smiling again.

The barman was surprised to see Taylor re-enter the bar, especially with a woman in tow. Taylor bought some drinks, and they introduced themselves and settled into a booth.

'I can't believe this. So you live at the peace camp?'

'Yes, with my mam and my brother.' Orla had forgotten just how good-looking Taylor was and found herself talking too fast out of nervousness. 'I wanted you to know how much I appreciate what you did for me. I really didn't think I would see you again.' They talked for another couple of drinks, and although she didn't want to she eventually said that she should be getting back.

They stood up and shook hands again. Taylor noticed she had deep-green eyes.

'I'm going back to the camp; why don't we share a cab?'

'OK, sure … but I'm paying.' They walked to the taxi rank, Orla looking small and petite beside Taylor. Taylor opened the door to allow her to sit in the back of the cab and slipped in beside her. Orla looked out the window at the loch. 'It really is beautiful here, isn't it?'

Taylor agreed, but was looking at Orla, not out the window. At the peace camp he asked the taxi to wait and jumped out to open the door again for her.

'You don't have to do that, you know, I'm quite able to open a car door.'

'I know … I'm just being polite.' They stood by the rear of the taxi and she trembled as Taylor took her hand.

'Would you like to go for a meal sometime?'

'I would love to,' she replied.

Taylor kissed her gently on the cheek and said goodnight.

Orla was once again frozen to the spot as she watched the taxi drive away. Her heart was racing. She wanted to cry and scream; she wanted to shout 'Please come back'; she wanted to run into the caravan and tell her mother all about this man she had just met – again. Instead, she walked quietly inside. Orla's mother was still awake when she entered the trailer.

'Mam, I haven't kept you up, have I?'

'Of course you have,' her mother replied excitedly. 'I'll make us a cup of tea and then you can tell me all about this young man you've met.'

When her mother asked her how it had gone she calmly replied: 'It was all right.'

Her mother smiled. Orla told her mother every last detail from the moment she found Taylor.

'I only went to thank him, you know.'

'Yes, of course you did,' Mrs Brodie lied with a smile on her face.

CHAPTER EIGHTEEN

The following morning Taylor was up early, and after a short exercise run to Garelochhead he ate his breakfast alone. His thoughts were on his trip to San Diego: although he was eager to go, he hoped it would be delayed long enough for him to get to know Orla better. On board *Covert* later that morning Taylor was called over the engine room tannoy system to the manoeuvring room.

'Hi, Ben, thanks for coming up. Leave what you're doing down there, your DO wants a word with you,' the first engineering officer informed him. As Taylor turned to go forward, the officer had an afterthought: 'And Ben!'

'Yes, sir?'

'Don't sit on my bed.' He smiled.

'I hear you, sir.' Taylor smiled back.

Once through the 'tunnel', Taylor entered the control room and bumped into Sion.

'I've just heard you were seen leaving the Highlander last night with a girl, Chief.'

'It has nothing to do with you, and if you continue, I'll troop you for insubordination.'

'Whoops, touchy!'

'I'll speak to you later.' Taylor hurried to the engineering officer's cabin and was asked to come in.

'Hi, Ben, take a seat. I've just got to finish this and I'll be right with you. Pull the curtain too, there's a good chap.' Taylor did as he was asked. His DO sat at his desk writing on a piece of paper. Taylor looked at the small bed opposite but decided to remain standing. A short while later his DO turned to face him.

'You will no doubt be very happy with the news that we are definitely going to Point Loma Naval Base in San Diego. I received confirmation from them this morning.' Taylor thought the smile on his DO's face looked rather strange.

'When are we flying out, sir?'

'After the next trip. The coxswain has all the flight details and the itinerary for when we're out there.'

'What uniforms are we taking, sir?'

'Again, the coxswain has all the details … but the captain has told me that we'll be travelling in civvies. Pack your shorts and sunglasses because it's darn hot out there. Once there, working No. 8s will be required. No need for full uniform.' Taylor was pleased about that – his No. 1 uniform was clean but needed a good pressing, he hadn't worn it for so long. 'The captain and I will introduce you to the diving team out there and then leave you to it, pretty much, as we'll have plenty of meetings to attend. We'll hopefully be getting rid of the old Mk 8 torpedo and taking delivery of a brand-new Mk 24 Tigerfish.'

'What will I be required to do, sir?' Taylor asked.

'They have a rebreather update and a new joint for the old JIM suit, and we've been asked to see if it would benefit us. But prior to going out there you'll be going to Horsea Island in Portsmouth to see an update on the JIM suit that we have to give to them. How familiar are you with the JIM suit?'

'The JIM suit is a solid suit named after Jim Garrett, who did the test diving in it back in 1971. It maintains the occupant at atmospheric pressure thus eliminating decompression sickness and the bends. No need for special gas mixtures and therefore no nitrogen narcosis; the diver can come straight to the surface with no adverse effects. Invented by an English firm called Underwater Marine Equipment Limited in 1969, I believe. It has a depth limit of around three hundred metres, this being the limit of the weak spots like the joints at the wrists, elbows and knees. I believe the Oceaneering people have tried to replace the old oil-filled joints with a newer "O" ring type which will increase the depth limit. Its normal air supply is through an umbilical which also carries the comms, but this can be disconnected, allowing the on-board oxygen to supply the diver. Endurance of the cylinders is around three hours. With the umbilical disconnected, the diver can talk to the surface with 185 through water comms. In an emergency situation the diver is able to ditch the outside weights to bring him to the surface. Four portholes in the head unit allow the diver to see what he's doing.'

'Have you dived in one?'

'No, never had the chance. I hear it's a good suit as long as you don't get your arms and legs caught in them joints; it causes a nasty blood blister.'

'Well, I've arranged a dive for you at Horsea Island so you can get to know it better.'

'OK, sounds good … when am I going?'

'Monday. The coxswain will have all the details for you.'

Taylor smiled. His DO smiled back.

'Please tell me I'm flying down ... the train takes an age from here,' Taylor said.

'Yeah, the captain's given approval to fly.'

'Brilliant.'

'OK, that's it for now, I'll speak to you nearer the time.'

Taylor went straight to the coxswain's office, which was on the accommodation deck just before the for'd torpedo compartment. The coxswain was the policeman on board and the ship's general coordinator. He was a large man with a thick dark beard. His watch-keeping station was controlling the after hydroplanes, which vary the depth of the sub, and the rudder. The coxswain gave Taylor a large envelope. Taylor thanked him and went to the bunk space. He would read it later; right now he had to go back to work.

At lunchtime, Taylor was called to the captain's cabin. Once inside he decided to sit down on the small stool beside the CO's desk, as instructed.

'Your DO has briefed you on the San Diego trip, Ben, but I wanted to go over a few things that I want from you.' The captain pressed a button and a few moments later the steward appeared at the door. 'Is coffee all right for you?' he asked Taylor.

'Yes, sir, that will be fine.'

'Two coffees please, steward. Now, Ben, I don't need to tell you that you will be representing the Royal Navy out in San Diego. Their divers will be watching everything you do. What I want you to do is the same. They will be taking you into their inner sanctum, as it were, so keep your eyes and ears open.

Gather as much information as you can; I want to know their routines, maintenance, how much gear they have, how many personnel. They'll tell you most things but it's the stuff they don't tell you I want to know about.'

'Understood, sir.' Taylor drank his coffee.

'And of course, a full and detailed written report on your return. I suggest you write up notes after each day – in private, of course.' Then the captain finished by saying: 'Ben, be tactful – these are our allies. I don't want you to spy on them, but the more we know the better the relationship will be. Who knows, they might even teach us something … but I very much doubt that.' They chatted some more while finishing their coffee.

The steward reappeared at the door. 'Excuse me, sir, sorry to interrupt.'

'What is it, steward?'

'There's a shore call for Chief Taylor in the control room, sir.'

'OK, Chief, you'd better get that. We're about finished here. If you think of any questions or need anything, just let me know – my door is always open.'

Taylor excused himself and picked up the phone that connected him to the outside world. He recognised his father's voice.

'Hello, Dad, how are you?'

'I'm fine … still being nagged by your mother.'

'It's her job. What can I do for you?'

'I've some info on your pal Tim. Can I continue?'

'Yes, carry on, Dad.'

'OK … six years ago in 1976 he earned himself the green beret of the Royal Marine Corps. Two years after that he joined the Special Boat Service, and that's when you met him on the diving course at Hosea Island. Since then he's been training with the Intelligence Corps and has been loaned to the Army and the clearance diving of the Royal Navy at Portsmouth.'

'So he's with the Intelligence Corps at the moment, going round gathering who knows what info?'

'Yes, that's about it; information gathering.'

'OK, Dad, thanks for that. How are things at home?'

'Everything is fine, Son. When will we see you again?'

'I'm not sure; I'm going to be busy here for a while. I'll be sure to let you know.' Taylor replaced the receiver and went to find Martin.

That night he met Orla. As she came to the taxi by the side of the road, Taylor noticed how light she was on her feet: she almost glided across the short strip of grass that separated the road from the trailers. Her hair blew gently in the breeze and she had put on a small amount of make-up that enhanced her features. He thought how pretty she looked. Taylor held the door open for her.

'You look amazing, Orla. Thank you for coming at such short notice.'

'I've had to rearrange my hectic schedule for this,' she said jokingly with a smile.

They chatted quietly in the back seat of the taxi as it sped off into Helensburgh.

'It's nice to know you like seafood. I've booked a table at the Cattle & Creel … have you eaten there before?'

'Ben, when we met in the pub the other night that was the first time I'd been out in Helensburgh. I only go into town to shop. This is a special occasion for me … I'm looking forward to it.'

In the restaurant, they sat at a window seat overlooking the loch. They ordered a starter of scallops and where soon tucking in.

'These scallops are wonderful, Ben.'

'When I booked the table the owner told me they get them fresh every day. They're hand-caught by divers straight out of the loch.'

'I could eat a dozen of them, but it would spoil my main course. They're very filling.' Orla smiled at Taylor.

Taylor glanced out of the window. The sun was setting over the hills on the far side of the loch. The sky was deep orange, which made the few clouds that were around seem brilliant white. Orla noticed him staring out the window.

'Beautiful, isn't it?' The scene now enchanted Orla as well.

'Yes … we're very lucky to be here to witness it.' Taylor turned to face Orla. At that very moment the last of the sunrays came through the window and gave her face a coppery, hazy look. He realised how beautiful she was. The waiter came and topped up the wine glasses.

'How did you come to be living in a peace camp, Orla?'

'My mother decided to move from Dublin after my dad died from a heart attack. He was a schoolteacher for twenty-five years in a Protestant area of Dublin and dedicated his life to teaching mathematics. He became ill when threatened by the IRA after giving extra tuition to a Catholic boy, a friend of the family who was struggling with homework for an exam.

He wasn't a religious man, and often commented on how pathetic all this nonsense was. He felt it was holding the whole country back – all this cowardly bombing and killing of innocent life was keeping them in the Dark Ages. Progress, he thought, had been withheld from a nation of very talented people, due to prospective investors going elsewhere for fear of the IRA.'

She stopped her account self-consciously, realising she was saying more than she'd intended. But Taylor was sitting there calmly listening, and she suddenly felt like she could tell him anything. So she continued: 'It came to a head when he was stopped by two men in the car park outside school one evening. There were plenty of other people around to witness the incident, but no one helped. They took him by the arm as he was getting into his car and pinned him across the bonnet. He was told to stop extracurricular teaching to students not attending his school, or his own children would be taught a lesson they wouldn't forget. They then left him shaking uncontrollably in a heap by his car. He stayed like that until after dark.

When he did manage to get up and go home, it was after ten o'clock, and in what my Mam described as "a bloody state". Two weeks later he was taken into hospital, and three days after that he died.' Orla had not spoken about her father for some time, and felt better for telling Ben. 'It was a difficult time for all of us,' she went on, 'but Liam, my brother – who you've met – took it really bad. Now my life is boring compared to yours, but I do really believe we can make a difference to world peace.'

'Your father must have been a devoted man. No one should die like that. It's understandable how Liam must feel. Your whole family must have been devastated,' Taylor said, dodging the subject of world peace. 'How's your brother now?'

Orla realised that he had avoided her prompt, but played along. 'He wanted revenge at first. It's a good job he's not still in Ireland … goodness knows what he would have got himself into. Now he's drinking himself into oblivion at every possible opportunity.'

'And how are you?'

'Oh, I'm just stringing along. Taking care of things … you know …'

The waiter brought over the main course of sea bass.

'So, tell me about yourself, Ben – how did you become a deliverer of nuclear death?'

'I'm just a mechanic. All I do is keep the engines turning.'

'Yes, but those engines are driving the vessel that will rain destruction down on anyone who stands in its way,' Orla pressed.

'Well, I believe it's keeping evil at bay … the provider of peace and the deterrent that is stopping the destruction from "raining down", as you put it.'

'Well, you see I've got a big dilemma here: I want to thank you for saving my life and for this lovely meal … which I'm enjoying immensely, by the way … but I can't imagine for one minute that you believe you're keeping peace throughout the world. Surely the only way is to abolish the weapon before someone uses it.' She was pin-pointing nuclear bombs.

'I'd prefer not to talk politics. Can't we just go back to talking about ourselves and enjoying the evening?'

'Hmm … well, yes, I suppose we can for now … but this conversation isn't over yet.' She wagged her finger at him.

'That's fine with me. Would you like another glass of wine?'

After the meal, Taylor offered to pay but Orla insisted they split the bill.

'Did you have to get back, or shall we walk along the loch for a while?'

'Yes, that would nice; it's still early and I'm not expected home yet. Will you listen to me – I'm twenty-two years old and still not making decisions for myself!'

'Orla, while you're under your mum's roof it's best you abide by her rules – that's how it works. Besides, I believe with your strong will and principals, decision-making will come easy for you.'

It was still quite warm as they strolled along the loch, the small waves lapping at the shore. Taylor noticed that Orla was pulling her shawl tighter around her shoulders.

'Are you warm enough? You can have my jacket if you want.'

Orla smiled. 'No, I'm fine.' She looked at him closely, straight into his eyes, and she smiled again. 'Thank you.' It was Taylor's turn to smile. The conversation turned to the future and she asked him what he had planned.

'Well, my immediate plans are to go to Portsmouth for a few days and then on a spot of leave before going back to sea.' Of course he left out what he would be doing. Orla suddenly thought of him being away from Faslane for a long time and Taylor saw the look on her face change. Without thinking he found himself asking her: 'Well, I know you're the adventurous type because that's how we met. How would you like to do something with someone who knows what he's doing?'

'What were you thinking of?'

'Well, would you like a short break, say just for a weekend?' Both their minds were now speeding into overdrive.

'Why, where were you thinking? When?'

'I just thought maybe we could go sailing for a weekend. My father has a small sailing yacht which we use on a river in Winsford, my home town in Cheshire.'

'You want me to come home with you?'

'Yes, it'll be fun. Have you been sailing before?'

'No … but how much will it cost?'

'It'll cost nothing because I'm going home anyway.'

'Yes, but there's still the price of the rail journey?'

'Don't worry about that, we'll sort something out.'

'Well, I've never been sailing before. I'd have to ask my mam …' Orla thought what a ridiculous thing to say and then made a decision: *No – I'm a grown woman, I'll tell my mam I'm going sailing.* Orla's heart was thumping out of her chest. What had she just agreed to?

'Don't worry, the boats are moored on a flash, it doesn't get very rough. Not like it's on the open sea or anything.' They walked in silence for a while enjoying each other's company before Taylor realised he should say something. 'I'll have to go to Portsmouth for a few days, then I'll come back up here and you can introduce me to your mother formally, if that would make things easier.'

'It would. She's bound to ask me a load of questions. I'm not in the habit of disappearing off with complete strangers.'

'I'm hardly a stranger. You trusted me once and I didn't let you down, did I?'

'Well, that's true, and I'm very grateful for what you did … but this is different.'

'I promise you I'll be the perfect gentleman.'

'I'm sure you will be.' Orla felt at ease with Ben but knew she would need to be cautious when approaching her mother with this news ... though she was convinced she could persuade her mother to agree.

They walked further on and watched the loch grow darker as the light faded and the air got chilly, then Taylor took her home in a cab. They stood by the roadside at the peace camp.

'Ben, I do trust you … and I would love to see where you're from. I've not seen much of England, but I must check it's OK with my Mam.' She knew she would have to get approval from Liam as well, although he would be an easier prospect to get around.

'Yes, that's fine. Here's my number.' Taylor gave Orla the telephone number for the office in the senior rates' mess and gave her a kiss on the cheek as he said goodnight. Orla blushed slightly and went inside. Taylor eventually went back to the base.

In the trailer, Mrs Brodie was sitting in her favourite chair, sewing a pair of Liam's trousers.

She spoke with a slight smile playing across her lips. 'Make me a cup of tea, there's a good girl … then we can have a chat.'

CHAPTER NINETEEN

Monday morning found Taylor on the one-and-a-half-hour flight from Glasgow to Southampton. He was met at the airport by his old friend Tim Sherwin.

'Hey, buddy, how's it going?' Tim was in a good mood.

'Good, mate … how's the time on PACDU going?'

'Busy, my friend.' Tim pointed to the large car park. 'Come on, I've parked the red wings over here.' Taylor followed him through the exit.

Tim pulled onto the M27, gunned the V8 Land Rover and headed towards Portsmouth.

'So, what brings you down here?' he shouted above the roar of the engine.

'I'm having a dive in the JIM suit at Horsea before going to San Diego.' Taylor purposely left out all the details.

'What the 'eck are you going to San Diego for?'

'They have some sort of upgrade for it; I'm going to do some spying and bring some intelligence back with me.' He gave Tim a long stare.

'Oh. It's a nice job if you can get it.' Tim laughed. They talked about old times as Tim drove on. They eventually pulled off the motorway and headed towards Portchester and Horsea Island. They showed their ID cards to the civilian security guard at the entrance gate and drove onto the island as he lifted the barrier.

Tim drove along the three-quarter-mile-long lake dug out to a depth of thirty feet by Italian prisoners of war to initially do test firings on submarine torpedoes, and which was now the training place for the clearance diving branch. He drove past the dining hall halfway down the lake and headed towards the classrooms at the top end. He turned to face Tim as he parked by the thirty-foot-high jumping board.

'Ben, I wanted to talk to you about the potholing incident.'

'Sure, mate, fire away.'

'The press had a field day on reporting how you rescued that girl, and wanted to published photographs of you as well as mentioning the fact you're on a submarine. I'm worried that if the wrong people see it they could target you.'

'Target me? In what way?'

'I don't need to lecture you on terrorist practices, Ben.'

'Why are you so concerned about me? Everyone at the submarine base is a target. Blimey, Tadpole – *you're* a target. We all have to be careful.'

'I'm just looking out for an old friend. Who at the moment is bringing a lot of attention to himself and creating a good target for either a kidnapping or a bullet. I know it's good PR for the Navy, Ben, but you're putting yourself in the cross-hairs, pal.'

'OK, I hear what you're saying.'

Taylor said goodbye to his friend. Even though he knew Tim hadn't told him the whole truth, he wasn't going to push it, and would let him come clean in his own time. He probably had a good reason to keep quiet.

After Tim drove off the Island back to PACDU headquarters, Taylor stopped a sailor walking past.

'Hey, erh, excuse me, buddy – do you know where I can find Chief Stringer?'

'Yes; he's in Classroom 2 just there, mate.' The sailor didn't give proper respect to a superior officer, as Taylor was in civilian clothing. Taylor thanked him and knocked on the door before entering.

'Hey, Ben, come on in. How was the trip, matey?'

'Hi, Bill. Flight was good, thanks. I haven't seen you since our time on the Faslane team – how long has it been?'

'That was about four years ago, I think.'

The classroom was a wooden hut. Inside, work benches ran round the four walls and pieces of diving equipment lay strewn on them – some being stripped for cleaning and repair, some being rebuilt for testing before completion. Large windows allowed the light to flood in and Taylor could just make out the loch gates that opened up to Portsmouth harbour three-quarters of a mile away at the other end of the narrow straight-sided lake. At the front of the classroom stood a large instructor's desk, behind which was an old-fashioned chalkboard. In the corner on a stand was a complete JIM suit. Photographs of the JIM suit were pinned to the wall above and around the door through which Taylor had just entered.

'Take a seat, mate. Would you like a cup of tea? Coffee?'

'Yeah, I would love a tea, but you carry on, I'll make it. Do you want one?'

'No, I'm fine, just had one.' Taylor left his friend Bill to complete the rebuilding of a soda lime canister that absorbs the carbon monoxide from the diver's breath as he exhales, to prevent him from rebreathing the poisonous gas. Bill fitted it into the suit and clamped it in firmly.

'There … right, I'm all yours.' He moved round the big desk and sat down in his comfortable-looking chair. He put his feet up on the desk, crossed his legs and eased back into the chair.

'Itinerary for today, Ben, is informal. We'll have a chat about the suit, take in lunch down at the galley and dive later this afternoon. I'll have to borrow some second dickies to help us put you in the water and get one to be standby diver should you need help. Which of course you won't, but even here we have to abide by the rules. OK?'

'Sounds good. What have the Yanks got, Bill, that we haven't?' Taylor asked.

'I'll come to that.'

Taylor waved his hand for his friend to continue. 'I won't bore you with all the legal stuff that's been going on between Oceaneering and the construction people, not to mention the government department that is partly funding the project. Basically, the joints are useless, and we've tried moving and adding more 'O' seals to improve water tightness and manoeuvrability.

The Yanks have come up with a clever little device which does this. Don't know what it is … they've put some sort of confidential restriction on it, so you'll be the first outsider to see it.

They're also using a new acrylic dome to improve the diver's vision. It all boils down to money: we struggle to get enough money for tea bags in here, and they throw money at this shit like it was growing on trees.'

'That's OK, they can do the trials, we make the finished article; let them make the mistakes, we'll get a suit that works.'

Bill raised his eyebrows and removed his legs from the desk. 'OK, let me show you around this baby. They both stood up and moved closer to the completed suit on the stand. An hour later they both walked down the side road by the lake towards the galley.

'What's new round here, Bill?'

'The Plymouth team are coming over tomorrow. They're working on a quicker fixing and detachment arrangement for the towed array sonar to submarines. If it works then the time it takes a diver to attach it to the submarine will be massively reduced and he can unhook in seconds. Better for the diver, and it means the submarine spends less time stopped on the surface.'

'The towed array … top-secret stuff.'

'Yes, but everybody knows it allows the submarine to hear what's behind it as well as in front.' Bill held the door open for Taylor to enter the dining hall. Inside, the high vaulted ceilings made the sound of clattering utensils and crockery echo around the large room. The Formica tables and plastic stairs were arranged neatly into rows in the centre of the room, with the serving hatches and hot plates along one wall.

The chefs were hard at work sweating in the heat of the open galley and Taylor recognised one from when he was there last, some three years ago.

'What do you fancy, Ben?'

Taylor took a plate from the end of the serving bar. Laid out before him was a soup terrine, then a selection of roast chicken, beef and pork. Further on there was a salad bar with fresh vegetables. Then came the desert section, and finally fresh fruit was on display.

'I see the food in here is still good. Plenty of it, too.'

'Got to keep these young studs fed; you know yourself how much energy you burn out there in the lake … it has to be replaced.'

'Indeed. The beef looks extremely nice.' Taylor said hello to the chef he had recognised. 'You still here, Chef?' he said with a smile. The chef recognised him and smiled back. A class of young divers came in through the main door and the noise level went up. Taylor and Bill sat a table near the back of the hall.

'Tell me more about the JIM suit, Bill.'

'Well, I heard that Slingsby Engineering are developing a glass-reinforced plastic to make the torsos on the latest suit.'

'Really? The ex-clearance diver Norman?'

'Yeah … they reckon that combined with the new joints and stuff it'll be able to go to two thousand feet!'

'Rather you than me.'

'The suit used by the Yanks is made from aluminium and is much smaller than ours.'

'Nice. What depth have they achieved in that?'

'One thousand feet. When are you going?'

'A couple of weeks. Got one more patrol first.'

The two men finished their lunch and Taylor held up his hand to the chef before they left the dining hall. After another cup of tea in the JIM suit classroom they were ready to dive. Taylor stripped and slipped on his woollen undersuit. The JIM suit he would dive in was winched up by the side of the lake. A second winch lifted him into the suit before the air was turned on and the helmet secured on his head. The whole suit with Taylor inside was then hoisted and slowly lowered into the lake. Inside, Taylor tested the comms with the surface and talked to Bill from inside the hard suit.

'Topside, this is diver.'

'Topside.'

'It feels so weird not having any water pressure on your body.'

'That's what it's all about, buddy. No decompression needed.'

'These pincers feel good. A lot easier to use than I had thought.'

'Yeah, there has been a lot of modifications done to them, they're a lot easier to move and pick things up with. How's your air supply, Ben?'

'Good supply and smells fresh.'

'OK, just get used to moving around and enjoy your dive; topside out.'

Forty minutes later Taylor was winched out of the lake, and once back in the classroom he carried out a debrief with Bill.

'How was it, mate? Did you achieve everything you wanted to?'

'It was just as amazing. It took me longer than I'd thought to get used to it, though. You're certainly restricted in movement. The pincers are definitely easy to use … picking up things was a doddle, and they're surprisingly dextrous.'

'It adds to our armoury of equipment. Horses for courses – it would be no good for underwater bomb disposal but would be great for crash-site investigation.'

'Yeah, and at depth too, without the decompression restrictions.'

'So, is there anything else I can help with?'

'No thanks, Bill, I've done everything I wanted to do. Thanks for your time again, I really appreciate your help.'

'No problem, Ben – anytime, buddy. If you think of anything else you need to know, just give me a bell.'

'Thanks, Bill.'

'When are you going back? Have you time for a beer?'

'I'm sorry, mate, I'm going back later today.'

Taylor walked off Horsea Island and took a cab to PACDU. He showed his ID card and went to the office of the officer in charge. He knocked on the door.

'Come.'

Taylor walked in smiling. 'Hi boss, sorry for not announcing my arrival.'

'Nonsense, Ben. Come in, sit down. You know you're always welcome here. What can I do for you?'

'Sir, I've been over at Hosea, diving in a JIM suit, and my flight back to Scotland is later today. I have a small problem and need a quick word with the admiralty intelligence officer, and I was hoping you could arrange for me to see him.'

'Let me ring his secretary.' The officer in charge picked up the phone on his desk and Taylor took the opportunity to look round the PACDU office. Display cabinets where full of defused ammunitions – everything from small arms bullets to hand grenades, with the larger ammunition on display outside in the enclosed secure yard. Framed certificates hung on the walls behind the officer's desk, and a large window on the outside wall gave a view of the entrance to Portsmouth harbour.

'OK, I'll send him over.' The officer in charge spoke into the phone and replaced the receiver. 'Right, you can go straight over to his office: it's in the admiralty building in the dockyard. The security men will tell you exactly where it is.'

'Thank you, sir. I'm sorry to disturb you, I know you're busy.'

'You probably haven't got much time as well – I'll get someone to drive you.'

'Thanks, Boss, I really appreciate that.'

'OK, good luck over there. Hope you get it sorted. It's always good to see you, Ben.'

Ben went outside and climbed into the Land Rover. A young diver seaman greeted Taylor with enthusiasm but drove in silence to the admiralty building in the dockyard.

Taylor jumped out of the vehicle and entered the old stone-built building. After showing his ID again, the security guard gave him directions to the second floor. He knocked on the office door with the sign 'Admiralty Naval Intelligence'. A young female officer told him to take a seat and disappeared into the inner office. Moments later she reappeared and told him to go in. Taylor entered a spacious oak-panelled room with large windows. The royal family were framed on the walls, along with erstwhile admirals Taylor didn't recognise.

'Thank you for seeing me at such short notice, sir.' Taylor noticed the three rings of a commander on the sleeves of the officer's uniform, who stood up when he entered. The two men shook hands.

'No problem. How can I help?' He ushered Taylor to a seat.

'Well, sir, I'm currently serving on board HMS/M *Covert* based in Faslane and I was wondering if I could talk to you about the threat of terrorism?'

The commander sat back down in his oversized leather chair. Taylor half expected him to put his feet on the desk, but he simply leaned back with a grin on his face.

'You've come to the right place … but can you be more specific? I could talk all day about the terrorists …'

'Well, sir, it's difficult to pin-point an actual question as I've not had any dealings with it, but can we start with why they do it?'

'OK, sure. Terrorists are striving for a perfect world. Their own perfect world. They're trying to achieve what politicians are trying to do with laws and regulations for the good of all the people, not just individuals. Politicians struggle with trying to please the majority in a debate about education, unemployment and health. Terrorists haven't even thought about these problems. They terrorise to gain territory that doesn't belong to them, they fight over religious beliefs, idealism and morals … or they cause havoc simply because of the way someone does something. Instead of using the democratic process and votes, they choose to use the bullet and explosives to get their rules or ideals implemented and into force. So, in its definition, terrorism is a means of getting something done, and not a cause. To get their message across the terrorist wants people to quickly take notice and listen to what they have to say. To do this they shock people. This they do by inflicting pain and misery upon the innocent. They must kill the child to make the adult pay attention. They obviously don't want to get caught, so the helpless are their main targets. The problem gets worse as time goes on. Some terrorist forget what the initial cause was, what they were fighting to achieve … hatred is passed from father to son, the son not knowing what the hatred is about. So sometimes you end up with a very professional, ruthless killer who meaninglessly takes innocent lives. Then it can turn into a power struggle.

Splinter groups form and gang warfare ensues. Funding becomes an issue, so associated problems arise like drugs, prostitution, arms deals and protection rackets, to name but a few. Young people are easy to recruit because it gives them a purpose in life and makes them feel like they belong to a team. They love the comradeship, the tribe-like membership: good mates fighting for the same – sometimes very vague – purpose. In the case of Ireland, your religion decides which side you're on. Terrorism is a worldwide problem, but it's closer to home in England than you think. In Wales, the Sons of Glendower are burning properties of English people crossing the border and buying cheap farms and houses. We're also keeping a close eye on the Scottish; in my opinion it's going to happen.'

'The Scottish National Liberation Army ...'

'Indeed.'

'Who's the biggest threat from abroad at the moment, sir?'

'Without a doubt Gaddafi; he's buying guns from the Russians and supplying them to the IRA ... and not just guns but training, explosives, interrogation techniques and refuge.' The commander threw his hands up in the air. 'It goes on and on, Chief.'

'So what does Gaddafi want, sir?'

'Money, power ... the same old thing.'

'Where do the IRA get their money, sir?'

'From supporters all over the world. The IRA are Marxist when dealing with socialists. Friends of Free Ireland in America are sending money and weapons.'

'Even the Yanks?'

'Oh yes, the IRA have supporters all over, even in England.' A knock on the door interrupted the commander.

'Excuse me, Chief … Yes?' He called through the door.

His secretary entered. 'May I remind you of your appointment with the captain of HMS *Amazon*, sir?'

'Oh, yes, thank you, Lieutenant.' He turned to Taylor as the secretary left and closed the door.

'Sorry, Chief … I hope that has answered just a few of your questions?'

'Yes, sir, very enlightening, it has certainly opened my eyes.'

'Well that's good … and keep your eyes open, because this problem isn't going to go away soon. Everyone can play their part against terrorism by knowing the threat and keeping vigilant. They'll strike indiscriminately and randomly.'

'Thanks again for seeing me, sir.' Taylor stood up.

'If you have any more questions, Chief, ask the intelligence officer at the Faslane base – he's a good man, I speak to him most days.' Taylor thanked the commander again and left his office. Outside, he was surprised to find the Land Rover still waiting for him.

'I'm to take you to the airport, Chief.' The young diver spoke with a bright smile.

'You're getting time off work, aren't you, young man?' Taylor looked him straight in the eye.

'Erh, yes, Chief.'

'Very good, carry on.' It was Taylor's turn to smile.

CHAPTER TWENTY

Gallymore woke first. He was still in the chair where he had fallen asleep the previous evening. The small coffee table in front of him was covered with empty bottles and glasses, cigarette ash was everywhere and the room stank of stale whisky, nicotine and human flatulence.

He shook his head. He went to the window and looked outside. The car and van were still where they had been left the night before. The rain had stopped and the sun was shining intermittently through the clouds and onto the muddy yard. When he was satisfied no one was around, he went into the kitchen and put the kettle on. McCann appeared behind him in the doorway.

'So, what now?'

'Now we open the window and get some fresh air in here. Didn't your mother—'

'I meant–'

'I know what you meant, I'm not stupid. Now we wait. We lay low for a week or so.' Gallymore pushed past McCann, and as soon as his nostrils sensed the smell in the lounge he pushed back past McCann and re-entered the kitchen. 'Wake those lazy bastards and get this place cleaned up. We're going to be here for a while so let's make this place a little bit habitable, shall we?'

'What we need is a cleaning woman.' McCann left the kitchen before Gallymore could argue with him.

Gallymore shouted after him.

'Get those vehicles under cover in the barn before someone sees 'em; I want this farm to look desolate like it was.'

The others were stirred from their alcohol-induced comas and an attempt to clean the house was made. One by one they slid off to nurse their aching heads. Michael Mullen was the last one and was left to clean by himself. McCann hid the vehicles in the barn, closed the rickety wooden door that nearly came off its hinges and decided not to bother trying to lock it. The smell of breakfast made the gang reappear from their hideaways. Michael became everyone's best friend that morning, and his breakfast went down extremely well.

After Michael's breakfast, Gallymore put on his coat.

'And where would you be going now?' McCann knew that this question would wind Gallymore up.

'I'm going out.'

'Oh, is that right?'

'Yes, that's right. I make the decisions round here … you do as I say, OK?'

'Christ, what did I say, no need to bite me 'ed off, boss.'

'Well, just remember who's the boss. You lot stay here; don't go outside and don't send any smoke signals up that chimney.' Gallymore pointed to the wood in the fireplace. 'I should be back before dark.' He drove out of the farm in a hurry.

The gang spent the rest of the day loafing in idle inactivity. As he had done such a good job, Michael was persuaded to cook the evening meal, and as soon as the dirty crockery was piled into the kitchen the whisky and cards came out. Everyone got involved in this pastime and the washing up was left for some other time.

Gallymore walked into the Victoria Hotel in Chichester Street, Belfast. Tom Jenks, a freelance journalist from the outskirts of Dublin, was sat at the hotel bar. A man who went by the name of Luke Stead, and who had said he was interested in more information on an article that he had written for the *Belfast Telegraph* the previous week, had contacted Tom. The meeting at the Victoria Hotel had been arranged for a large fee. Gallymore recognised Tom Jenks from his photograph in the paper.

'Mister Jenks?'

'Yes … and you must be Mister Stead?'

'That's right,' Gallymore lied. 'Thanks for coming, Mr Jenks, but please, call me Luke.'

The two men shook hands.

'My name is Tom. Would you like a drink, Luke?'

'That's kind, Tom … I'll take a small whisky with you.'

Tom ordered a round of drinks. When the drinks arrived, they took a quiet seat by the window. 'So, how can I help you, Luke?' Tom asked.

'I read with interest your article on this virus called "Ebola". I wondered when it was first discovered?'

'The first reported outbreak was in 1976, when it wiped out a whole village near a river in Zaire.'

'So it originates from Africa?'

'Yes. May I ask why you're interested, Luke?'

'Of course … no great mystery: I had a friend working in Dakar, West Africa, who I think may have died from Ebola.'

'There have been no reports of outbreaks anywhere other than Zaire, in Central Africa. Although, I have a theory that Ebola began its life in the Congo. It's just the fact that the Congo is not populated by as many humans as Zaire is.'

Gallymore sensed he had touched on a subject that Tom was obsessed with, and with a few well-chosen words he would get all the information he needed. He kept probing.

'What exactly is Ebola, Tom?'

'Do you have the money we agreed on?'

'Of course, it's right here.' Gallymore passed him an envelope.

'OK … Ebola isn't just one virus, it's a strain of five closely related ones. The worst being "Ebola Zaire". This one causes fever, massive haemorrhaging and death in a matter of days. "Ebola Bundibugyo" causes severe disease. "Ebola Sudan" is barely less dangerous, killing around two out of three of its victims. "Ebola Tai" has claimed the life of only one person – a Swedish scientist in 1995. The last member of this incredible virus, "Ebola Reston", seems to leave humans unharmed.'

'Exactly how does it kill?' Gallymore was getting genuinely interested.

'Studies have been carried out on the Zaire strain at the University of San Diego, and their findings have confirmed that it just wreaks havoc on the human body. Firstly it is somehow able to evade the body's immune system. It breaks into the cells that line the heart, blood and lymph systems and causes massive internal haemorrhaging and fluid loss, basically turning all the internal organs into mush.'

Even Gallymore was shocked, but he held his feelings back. 'Would you like another drink, Tom lad?'

'Yes please, Luke, that would be great.' While Gallymore was at the bar, Tom Jenks counted the contents of the envelope. He wasn't fooled by the story of a dead friend in Dakar. He didn't know why Luke Stead was asking all these questions, nor did he want to know. All he wanted was the money. He was satisfied with the contents of the envelope by the time Gallymore got back to the table.

'I wouldn't wish that kind of death on my worst enemy,' Gallymore lied again. 'How can this Ebola be contracted, Tom?'

'Through cuts, orally in food, water contamination or the use of dirty hypodermics, which is common in hard-pressed clinics in remote areas of Africa. But what's frightening is the fact that a Professor Davies in San Diego has discovered that this virus can mutate and can be caught by breathing it in through the air. That was the reason for the death of the Swedish scientist in 1995, and there are rumours that the Yanks have introduced a hybrid toxin that mixes snake venom with Ebola, with no antivirus … very potent, and of course, instant death.'

'Christ, how dreadful.' Gallymore could hardly control his excitement.

They talked for another half-hour before the journalist left. Gallymore stayed in the hotel bar for a full hour before he left. It was twilight outside when he drove indirectly back to the farmhouse. The gang were in the living room watching television. McCann and Gallymore went into the kitchen to be alone.

'I was beginning to worry about you, Gallymore – you've been gone for some time.' McCann was genuinely worried.

'You fecking woman, McCann, I'm a big boy now, I can take care of myself. How are things around here?'

'OK, I suppose. They're all getting a little restless. Being full-blooded Irishmen, it won't be long before they start getting pangs for the outdoors; we can't keep them caged up in here for much longer. We haven't even got a newspaper to read. Sean's already asked if he can go to the pub in the village.'

'No, definitely not. You must do your best to entertain them, Shamus. They have to remain indoors. There are people searching under rocks to find us, and I don't have to tell you what will happen if they do.' McCann was slightly shocked at Gallymore using his first name.

Gallymore reached down into a plastic carrier bag and pulled out a magazine. He threw it at McCann.

'What's this?'

'A present for you.'

McCann looked at the magazine.

'*Exchange & Mart* … is this some sort of joke?'

'Something for you to read while I'm a way.'

'Thanks very much,' McCann said sarcastically, and threw the magazine on the coffee table.

Gallymore changed the subject back. 'You do realise what they'll do to you if you're found here?'

'Yes, I do, but it's not going to be easy keeping this lot happy.' Gallymore gave McCann a look that would melt snow. McCann knew there was no point arguing. 'I'm sure I'll manage, once I explain the consequences. It's not going to help matters if you're going out all the time, though, Gallymore.'

'Well that's tough, I need to be going out. The fight must go on, McCann, and I can't do that from an armchair. I'm going out again in a few days, and I won't be back for a week. You'll be in charge while I'm gone … and I don't want any confrontations, you hear me, McCann?'

'Where are you off to?'

'America.'

'Fecking America, what the hell for?'

Gallymore ignored his question on purpose. 'I'll phone you now and then, to make sure everything's OK.'

'Tell me why are you going to the fecking USA, Gallymore?'

Gallymore pulled a .38 Smith & Wesson from inside his jacket and pointed it at McCann's head.

'I've told you before, McCann: I make the decisions around here and you're just my lackey. Do I make myself clear?'

'Yeah, OK, OK. You're a fecking nutter you are, Gallymore.' There was a long period of silence. Eventually McCann spoke. 'We'll have to get some

fresh supplies in, though.'
'Organise it.'

The broad, six-foot-four frame of Michael Mullen had difficulty entering the small village shop door. He smiled back at the young woman behind the counter, who had obviously noticed his awkward entrance. He began to flush as the embarrassment bubbled up inside, so he hid behind a stack of postcards. He eventually took out the extensive list that McCann had given him and, seeing that the young woman behind the counter was busy doing something, he picked up a basket. Michael Mullen had always been a shy man. He had turned to eating as an escape from the piercing eyes that followed him wherever he went. He heard people make unpleasant remarks, and it hurt him to ignore them. He had frightened himself once when, being tormented in a bar, he became so frustrated with himself for not retaliating that he smashed his fist down on a bar stool and watched it split it two and fall at his feet. The mocking had stopped as he had quietly walked out of the door.

Now he started to collect the items on his list. He was alone in the shop apart from the young woman, and Michael had the compulsion to steel glances at her. He was starting to become infatuated with her, with the way her hair curled under her neck and with the dimples in her cheeks when she smiled. He wanted to make her smile. Their eyes met on several glancing occasions. His basket was half-full when the bell above the door rang and a man entered the store. Neither man looked at the other directly.

Michael turned away and carried on placing things in his basket. The man looked around the store and chose a packet of biscuits from one of the shelves. Michael tried to hear what he was saying to the young woman but he was too far away.

The man left without giving Michael a glance, who tried to get a look at the man out of the window, but he was gone. He took his basket to the counter. Michael noticed the high cheekbones on the young woman's face and how her long dark hair was naturally curly. She wore a plain black dress with thin straps over her rounded shoulders and the dress showed off her curvaceous body. She was a lot shorter than Michael at around five foot four, and Michael flashed a glance at her large cleavage. He asked her for a carton of cigarettes, and when she turned around to get them he couldn't stop his eyes from staring at her bottom. Michael felt himself beginning to flush again and couldn't believe what he had just done. But he liked what he had seen.

'Do you live in the village?' he asked with a wide smile across his face.

'My father owns the store. We live upstairs.'

'What do you do for fun around here?'

'Fun? You must be joking. The only thing to do around here is go to that stinking pub.'

'Is it any good?'

'It's full of dirty old men who sit and get drunk every night.'

'Oh, I see. Can't be much fun for you, then?'

'No fun at all,' she said seductively.

Michael found himself getting hot; his hand went to his collar and he felt perspiration around his neck. 'What's your name?' he croaked.

'Maureen … what's yours?'

'Hi, I'm Michael.'

'Nice to meet you, Michael. I haven't seen you round here before; are you going to be around for a while?'

'I-I think, for a while anyway,' he stuttered. He regained his composure to ask: 'Did you know that man who just came in?'

'No. I thought at first he might be with you. Two new attractive young men in the village at the same time. Things could be looking up. Why do you ask?'

'Oh, nothing … I thought I recognised him from somewhere,' he lied. 'I don't suppose you get many strangers here in the village … it's a bit off the beaten track …'

'We don't get any.'

'I'll see you again, Maureen?'

'I really hope so … and please, call me Mo.'

They exchanged smiles as Michael went out into the street. He had mixed emotions. He felt like dancing a jig after talking to Maureen, but he was worried about this other stranger. It took him almost two hours to get back to the farm, and then he crouched in the bushes that lined the drive for a while before going inside.

'Where the fecking hell have you been, Michael?'

'I ran into a stranger in the store and decided to take the long way home.'

'Did you speak to him?' McCann was worried.

'No; I just thought it strange.'

'Don't worry, Michael, nobody will find us in this hole,' complained Sean as he went into the bathroom.

'Nobody in their right mind would come to a godforsaken place like this anyway,' Andy said as he slumped into a chair.

'Yeah, well, maybe you're right … I definitely wasn't followed back here anyway.' Michael said, trying to convince himself, and then dismissed the incident.

'Stick the kettle on, Michael.'

McCann was surprised by the relative quietness that had fallen over the small farmhouse. The four men he was keeping watch over had drifted into what he could only think was a slight depression. They were going about their daily lives with methodical routine. *Perhaps they've just run out of things to argue about*, he thought to himself. They were all sat round the television set at present, which was their favourite pastime.

McCann was slouched in a chair thinking about Gallymore. What was he up to in America? Probably trying to obtain funds from sympathisers … but why would he not tell him? McCann picked up the magazine that Gallymore had thrown at him before he left. He thumbed through the pages with no real interest, then suddenly stopped. Two large asterisks marked the top of one of the pages. He looked down the page and found a heading for an advertisement underlined. He began to read: 'Build your own burglar alarm. A quick and easy way to protect your home, the kit contains a photoelectric cell that reacts to light.' McCann sat up straight in the chair and read on. 'Imagine the shock a burglar will get when he shines his torch on this amazingly easy to build intruder alarm. ... The kit also contains a loud audible siren that will wake you from the deepest of sleeps.'

McCann now realised what Gallymore wanted him to do. He turned back to the beginning of the magazine and began to read it cover to cover. He found that Gallymore had asterisked all the items required to make not only passive alarms, but aggressive, active ones too. He had marked things like suppliers of garden fertiliser, weed killer, sugar, electrical components and even nails and ball bearings. From his earlier days with Gallymore, he knew these were all the things needed to make a bomb. His mind raced ... he began to get rather excited at the possibilities the items on the pages in front him presented. All on mail order too ... they wouldn't even have to go out to get them – they would be delivered by some unsuspecting postman right to their door. Without a word to the others he took a pen and a writing pad and climbed the stairs to his bedroom.

CHAPTER TWENTY-ONE

The quartermaster took Taylor's canvas bag from him as he descended down the main access ladder into the control room of HMS/M *Covert*. He thanked the QM and took hold of the bag as it was passed down to him. Immediately he noticed the signs of a submarine that was preparing for sea. The ambient temperature was a lot higher and the noise of running machinery could be heard in the background. Charts lay on the table in the navigation area of the control room … protection covers had been removed from sonar and radar screens … systems were being checked by radio operators … and electricians stuck probes into machinery. Taylor went directly to his bunk space and unpacked his bag into the small locker by his bed. He squashed the empty bag flat and placed it under his mattress. He quickly changed out of his No. 8 working dress into overalls and made his way back out of the bunk space along the accommodation corridor to the junior rates' mess. Taylor knocked on the side frame and slid back the curtain. He gestured to Martin to join him.

'Are you OK, buddy? Ready to go to sea?'

'Yes, I think so, Chief.'

'Good. Follow me, let's get to it.'

Martin followed Taylor up the accommodation ladder, who then took a slight right to the forward tunnel door. Taylor looked through the small round glass porthole to check that the after tunnel door was shut, and pressed the hydraulic lever to move the heavy tunnel door.

'Only one door open at a time, Martin. There's sometimes a pressure difference from back aft and for'd. The boat is basically in two halves, with the reactor compartment in the middle. This tunnel is the only access to either end.' The forward tunnel door shut heavily against the watertight seal and an eerie silence fell on the men. Taylor took advantage of the quietness.

'Been thinking of home much?'

'No, not really. Not had the time.'

'That's good. It'll only depress you. Everyone misses their family, but now isn't the time to be thinking of them … save it for when you're alone in your bunk. Keep yourself busy; try not to be distracted by your personal life. When you're on this boat, *we're* your family.'

'How do you cope?'

'It used to bother me, but I've trained my mind to forget them altogether when I'm on the boat. Don't put things like photographs up by your bunk; keep them inside your locker.' There was a long pause while Martin processed that information. Taylor didn't want him to go too deep. 'How's the training going?'

Martin's expression was of someone coming back from a far-off place. 'Slowly, I'm afraid,' he said hesitantly.

'Anything you're having particular problems with?'

'Tracing systems takes a long time, and I'm tired all the time …'

'Yeah, well, nothing I can do about your sleep, I'm afraid; just don't fall asleep when you're on duty.' Taylor took a rag from his pocket and wiped a bit of excess grease from a stainless-steel valve. 'Following systems can be difficult. Check the colour codes from your training manual ... all the systems have different colours. For example, the seawater system has all green valves; the high-pressure air system is light stone; main steam has blue valves; the pipes too in places are colour-coded, but not where they're lagged, of course. Another tip, matey: all the even-numbered valves will be on the port side and all the odd numbers on the starboard side. Don't forget the paperwork as well: get signatures in your training book by all the people in charge of the different sections; it's all the proof that the officers want to see. Don't worry about sleep, it'll get easier. You've been on duty in harbour and know the safety regulations governing that; now we'll be at sea and the rules change slightly. First off, read the captain's daily orders – you'll find new orders printed daily on each notice board. The safety regs that applied in harbour may be different at sea. What might have been safe to open in harbour may cause a catastrophe if opened when dived. Martin, you'll have to quickly learn what all the different alarms mean and how you act on them. Oh – one last word of advice: if you see something wrong, don't leave it to someone else to put it right; fix it yourself or report it to someone in that department, no matter how small or insignificant it may seem. Never think that because it's not in your department, someone will know about it and it has nothing to do with you. At sea the submarine as a whole is your department. No one will ridicule you for a mistake, and if they do, let me know and I'll sort it.'

'Thanks, Chief.'

'I know there's a lot to learn … come on, let's cram some more in.'

They walked to the after door and repeated the sequence of opening. As soon as the aft door opened they were hit by the heat and noise of machinery. Taylor lowered his head and spoke into Martin's ear.

'You'll also learn how to lip-read back here. We all do it, especially in the machinery spaces.' The first machinery space they passed was the TG room. 'Down there are the diesel generators and hydraulic plant, and down the second ladder takes you into the turbo generator room.' They walked a little farther along the plates, passing banks of electrical panels. 'This is the manoeuvring room.' Taylor popped his head round the corner and said good morning to the watch-keepers sat at their panels. 'The first panel is the reactor panel; it'll be at full power at the moment and Rob will be maintaining the reactor at critical. The next panel is the electrical panel and Steve will be supplying power to all necessary equipment. Next comes the propulsion panel; Dave will control the speed of the boat from those two throttle levers. Sat behind the three men are the marine engineering officer – the MEO – and the chief of the boat.' All the watch-keepers were busy adjusting the controls and relaying orders to the machinery spaces. Taylor turned around. 'This is probably the most important piece of equipment back here.' He pointed to the tea urn sat next to a small sink.

'We all have our own cups, so learn quickly.'

Taylor ducked through another hatch moving aft. 'Down there is the main engine room; two large freshwater distilling plants and four massive freshwater feed tanks that feed water to the reactor, which turns it into steam to drive the engines. Follow me ...' Taylor moved to the last compartment in the rear of the submarine. 'Hi, Geordie, how are you, mate?' he said in greeting to the watch-keeper. Geordie nodded his head and gave Taylor a wink. 'This is the motor room; we can disconnect the drive from the main engines and connect to the battery-driven electric motors normally used when the sub is in the ultra-quiet state, but also in an emergency to get us to the surface. Also back here is the aft escape tower.'

The main submarine tannoy system sounded throughout the boat: 'All hands to stations for leaving harbour. Close all watertight doors and hatches.'

Taylor looked at Martin. 'OK, end of the tour, let's go.' Taylor and Martin descended down the ladder into the main engine room. Two tugs slowly pulled *Covert* away from the jetty. The waters of the loch were still and black; the tethers were slipped and the submarine was free to go. Down below, the captain ordered 'slow ahead' and the order passed to the manoeuvring room via telegraph. Dave, the propulsion panel operator, pushed a small lever forward to the slow ahead position. Down in the engine room the revolutions came on instantly and giant turbines began to turn.

Taylor heard the steam valves open and the gentle hum of the turbine blades rise in pitch; he instinctively looked at the pressure gauges and checked all was within parameters. The black submarine pushed aside the loch water and quietly glided down towards Rhu Narrows, and then out from the river Clyde and into the Irish Sea. Moments later a plume of spray shot up from either side of the boat and four thousand nine hundred tonnes of metal slid slowly beneath the waves and disappeared, leaving no trace it was ever there on the surface. Taylor spent the rest of the watch telling Martin all about the freshwater distilling plants – their quirky adjustments and temperamental ways.

After four hours, Taylor's relief watch-keeper came down the ladder. 'Hey, Ben, how's it going?' he enquired groggily.

'All's well, buddy.'

Ben's relief checked around the gauges and knew through years of practice what was running and what was not. 'Anything I should know about?' He spoke without a sound coming from his lips. Taylor read his lips.

'No, mate, all good.'

'Where are we headed, do you know?' he enquired.

'I would say north – the outside water temperature is falling fast.'

'Oh good, under the ice again ... ah well.'

'If you're happy, mate, I'll shoot?' Taylor asked.

'Yes, Ben, I have the watch.'

'OK, have a good one.' Taylor nodded at Martin, who would be relieved in fifteen minutes, grabbed his cup from the ledge it was perched on and climbed the ladder, glad to be out of the heat and into the slightly cooler passageway. He waved to the manoeuvring room watch-keepers, placed his cup in its holder and went through the tunnel.

In the control room a voice came over the speaker: 'Captain, sir, sonar.'

The captain took hold of a microphone without lifting his eyes from the chart table and pressed the small button on the side.

'Captain.'

'Sir, I'm picking up a very faint noise from the boat's hull.'

'Where from?'

'It would appear to be from the aft casing – on the port side, low down near the stern.'

'Any ideas as to what it could be?'

The sonar operators where extensively trained and experienced operators – they would spend hours listening to pre-recorded tapes in sound booths both on board and while ashore in HMS *Neptune*.

'It sounds like a water vortex, sir … a definite noise short … I can't make it out. It's possibly something stuck on the hull.'

'Wait, I'll come in. Number One, take over for a second.' The captain ordered the first lieutenant to take control of the submarine and went into the sonar room.

'Let me have a listen.' The captain slipped on a pair of earphones.

'Yes, you're right … sounds like swirling water all right. What the blazes can that be? If we can hear it then the Russians will have no problem in tracking us.' The captain opened the door and summoned the steward from the wardroom. 'Ask the sonar chief to pop up, would you? Thanks.' The steward disappeared through the control room. The captain went back inside for another listen. A few moments later the chief sonar operator entered the sonar room.

'Sir.'

'Hi, Chief, sorry to disturb you – an unusual noise from our tail.' He handed the earphones to the chief, who looked puzzled at first, but then a dawning smirk came across his face.

'Sorry to tell you this, sir, but I've heard it before, and last time it was a mooring cleat that had been left in the up position.'

The captain went ballistic.

Ben Taylor was in a dark pool of water. Before him he could see the back of a woman; she had long dark hair swaying gently from side to side on her back and neck. He was cold and could see his breath gushing from his mouth as he breathed out. Very slowly she turned and he could see her face. The noise of the ventilation confused him and the gentle rubbing of a hand on his shoulder made the face of Orla Brodie disappear. He heard a voice, far off at first, then becoming a lot closer.

'Chief?' There was a pause. 'Chief, sorry to wake you.'

Taylor recognised the face of the steward stood beside his bunk. 'That's OK, Sam … what is it?'

'Chief, the captain would like to see you.'
Taylor was now fully awake. He dressed quickly in a
tracksuit and went to the captain's cabin.

'Sir,' he spoke as he entered the cabin after
being welcomed by the captain.

'Ben, we have a problem.' The captain spoke
informally, knowing that there was just the two of
them within earshot. 'I'll get straight to the point: one
of the mooring cleats has been left in the up position
instead of being folded down in the storage position.
Here's a drawing of the problem.' The captain
produced a blueprint plan of the hull with the cleat
highlighted. He went on. 'This is the cleat in its
working position.' He slid another blueprint over the
first. 'And this is it folded down in its stowed
position. It's an easy enough job, but made a little bit
harder because we're under a couple of metres of
solid ice and snow at the moment.'

Taylor thought that someone was in deep
trouble for forgetting to stow that away, but decided
not to enquire about it any further.

'Sounds like a job for a diver, sir.'

'That's right. I've just asked the diving officer
to join us; he should be here shortly.' The captain
looked at his watch and shook his head. Taylor
surmised he wasn't quite as fast as he had been to get
dressed. 'Do you think you can do it?'

'The nearest hatch is the after escape tower; I
could use that as my exit and my re-entry to the boat.'
Taylor had answered the captain's question. There
was a scuffle outside the cabin.

'Come in.'

The diving officer, Alistair Duncan, who was also Ben Taylor's divisional officer, entered the cabin immaculately dressed.

The captain explained the predicament they were in to the DO and continued: 'I'll put the submarine as close to the ice as I can to reduce the depth and hold her at a dead stop for as long as I can. The rest will be up to you two. Let me know when you're ready to go.'

An off-watch seaman helped the DO and Taylor move their diving equipment from the for'd torpedo compartment to the aft escape compartment. The small amount of diving equipment took up most of the space in the motor room. The DO would supervise the dive, Taylor would do the dive and Seaman First Class 'Muddy' Waters would be the standby diver, ready to go to Taylor's aid in case anything went wrong. Both divers checked that their self-contained breathing air cylinders were fully charged and sealed. A stout line would be tied around Taylor's waist, and the other end he would have to tie to the inside of the escape tower once inside. The motor room watch-keeper opened the lower lid on the escape tower and Taylor squeezed into the tower. He had to loosen the straps on the diving set and pull it up his back slightly to gain access through the narrow opening. Muddy passed him his fins and a pair of neoprene gloves. The lower hatch was closed and secured. The only light inside the tower came from a small round viewing porthole, and Taylor gave them the thumbs-up. The DO had a direct line to the captain in the control room via a sound-powered underwater telephone.

'Taylor's in the tower and ready to flood, sir.'

The captain acknowledged the report and brought the submarine to a dead stop using a small astern thrust to take all the way of the boat.

The helmsman reported: 'Boat stopped in the water, sir; depth: fifteen feet.'

The captain acknowledged the report and spoke to the DO. 'Depth is fifteen feet and the boat is stopped in the water; the diver is good to go.'

'Roger that, the diver is good to go.' The DO hit the side of tower once with a hammer. Taylor raised his thumb again and Muddy reported the message received. The motor room watch-keeper opened a valve and the tower began to flood.

Taylor felt the water at his feet and then moving quickly up his legs, the pressure growing all the time, and it was very cold. As it reached his chest, he slipped the demand valve into his mouth. The inside of the tower was now in complete darkness. A knock from inside the submarine told him that the pressure had equalised, and Taylor opened the upper hatch. He was surprised to find that it was slightly lighter above him. Carefully he crawled up the tower and out onto the casing of the outer hull. At first he thought the submarine was still moving, but realised the captain would be doing his best to keep it still in the water; this must be the effects of the tide. Gripping hold of the lip of the tower with one hand to stop himself being swept away, he tied his lifeline with the other hand onto the safety tow rail running along the casing.

He checked his air supply and looked around. The ice above him was light blue in patches, narrow shafts of light showing through the thinner parts and displaying odd-angled columns of different colours. It quickly turned to black as the light disappeared down the side of the submarine. Cold water streamed into Taylor's right glove as he pulled on his lifeline to check the knot. He looked forward along the casing and thought he could see the conning tower, but he was mistaken; the light faded into bluey darkness and all he could see was the casing disappearing ahead of him. Holding on with two hands now, he turned to look at the stern and could make out clearly the huge propeller aft of the rudder. He made a mental note to catch hold of the rudder to stop him colliding with the sharp blades of the prop should his lifeline snap. Taylor brought up the picture of the cleat in his head and crawled forward along the casing. The icy cold water was still annoying him in his glove. He arrived at the point where he thought the cleat should be, but found nothing. It was hard to move against the tidal stream that was trying to throw him off into the abyss of water below. He checked his air supply again and was using more than he normally would. He crawled on, the cold water now affecting his body. Taylor began to shiver and found it difficult to concentrate on the task. He stopped for a moment and gathered his thoughts. *It must be here – I've not passed it*, he thought; so he crawled on. There was a shift in the tidal stream; the submarine turned slightly and Taylor's lifeline went slack. His hand hit the cleat, that was causing the noise short that the sonar operators had heard.

Taylor secured his lifeline to the cleat with a couple of round turns and tried to find the cause of it going slack. The line went taught again as he pulled it; he was confused as to why it would go slack. It disappeared into the now darkness aft and he couldn't see if it was still attached near the escape tower. *I'm wasting time and air*, he thought. He untied the lifeline from the cleat and tried to force it into its stowage position, but it wouldn't budge and only resulted in Taylor being pushed backwards away from it. Taylor's breathing became hard and he sucked on the mouthpiece but nothing was coming through. He reached behind his back and equalised the two cylinders. His breathing became easier, and he now knew that he had only half the air he started with. Taylor tried to wrap his feet round the tow rail but realised it was too big, so he didn't hesitate to take one of his fins off and wrap his foot round the tow rail to brace his body and push the cleat. He swore to himself and pushed again. *I wonder if this is why it wasn't stowed.* His third attempt made the cleat move slightly and this spurred him on. After what seemed like an age, he had the cleat in the stowed position and the submarine's hull was again streamlined and noise-free. Taylor banged on the pressure hull twice as pre-arranged to let the captain know it was stowed.

With one hand and a now free foot, he slid along the tow rail back towards the escape tower. He found he could move easier without the hindrance of the fin. He was halfway back to the tower and could see the open hatch, when all of a sudden the lifeline stopped him.

He checked the line and found it heading back to the cleat. *What the fuck's going on!* Taylor's breathing again became hard. He reached behind his back and equalised the two cylinders again. He checked to see if air was escaping from a leak, but hindered as he was he couldn't see any escaping bubbles. Taylor had to act fast and untied the lifeline from his body. Now free from his tether he moved off again towards the open hatch. He was feeling very cold, which increased his breathing, and was glad to feel the rim of the escape tower. Realising the lifeline could flap on the casing and cause a noise short if he left it, he found the end he had tied it to the tow rail and pulled the loose rope back from the cleat. To his surprise and relief it was free, and soon he was coiling it around his arm. His breathing once more became hard. This time he opened the equalising valve behind his back and left it open, knowing that the next time his breathing became difficult he would have no reserve air to call on. Taylor climbed into the tower and closed the hatch, turning the locking wheel to seal it. He was now shivering uncontrollably. He reached down and found the hammer he had jammed behind a pipe when he'd left the tower, and banged twice on the side of the tower. Taylor's only thoughts were on the depleting air supply on his back as he waited for the water to drain from the tower. He waited and waited but could hear no movement from below him in the submarine. He banged again on the side of the tower. He was beginning to feel his breathing getting harder, and he tried to control it by breathing in and holding his breath bcfore breathing out.

Although his body was freezing-cold, he felt a drop of perspiration run down his forehead and sting as it entered his eye. *Come on, guys, get the water out of this tower, please.* Taylor couldn't see the water draining out of the tower because it was too dark, but he suddenly felt his head getting heavier. The muscles in his neck became taught as they automatically came into action to keep his head in the upright position. Taylor reached up, removed both his gloves and felt warmer air around his head; then he felt the water line on the inside of the tower. He followed it down his neck and eventually removed his face mask and demand valve when it was at his chest height. He gulped in several lungfuls of fresh air and eventually let out a big sigh.

'Thank fuck for that,' he said out loud.

He suddenly felt very cold and tired, and as the last of the water drained from the tower, found it difficult to stand. He leaned on the side of the tower and wedged himself up. He squinted his eyes against the glare of the light when the lower hatch was opened.

'You OK, Taylor?' he heard the diving officer call inside to him.

Taylor's voice was faint and strained. 'I'm, OK, sir.' Taylor somehow managed to prise himself from the tower and climbed into the motor room with the help of his crewmate Muddy. 'Wouldn't like to do that every day,' he said to his buddy.

'Sorry it took so long to drain the tower. We hadn't realised how much water was in that tower; it flooded the bilge and set off the Dowty alarm in manoeuvring.'

The DO informed the captain that Taylor was back on board and the submarine was free to manoeuvre. Taylor was taken forward by the medical technician, who was worried about his shivering.

'Let me take your temperature, Chief.'

'Sure, feel free.' Taylor opened his mouth to receive the thermometer.

'Oh, sorry, no: I mean your core temperature.'

'Oh, different opening, then?'

'Yes; I'm afraid you'll have to bend over.'

A few minutes later Taylor was told to take a hot shower before being stuffed into a sleeping bag with a hot-water bottle and a steaming bowl of soup, while the medical technician monitored his core temperature.

'Is it serious?' Taylor asked him. 'I mean ... I feel OK ... just a bit tired.'

'Well that's the problem: normal shivering stops because you no longer feel cold, and then other problems start – tiredness being one of them. Your core temperature is down slightly ... I want to bring it back up so you don't get hypothermia.'

Taylor finished drinking his hot soup and soon fell asleep.

In the control room, the captain ordered all stop on the engines. 'Make the submarine neutrally buoyant, Chief; maintain this depth,' he ordered the chief of the boat. Water was transferred from forward tanks to aft tanks to maintain trim.

'We've received intelligence that a Russian K-222-class submarine is in this area, so let's sit here and listen for her. Assume the ultra-quiet state.'

All non-essential equipment was shut down and movement of crew around the submarine kept to a minimum. 'I'll be in my day cabin.' The captain handed control of the submarine over to the navigation officer. In his cabin, he picked up the internal telephone and dialled the senior rates' mess.

'Petty Officer Med Tech, please,' he asked the person on the other end of the phone.

'I'll put him on, sir.'

'PO Med Tech, sir.'

'Hi, PO, how is Chief Taylor?'

'He's good, sir. Core temperature back to normal and he'll be fit to go back into the watch system in a few hours. In fact, he's sat opposite me.'

'Oh good, put him on, will you?'

'Hello, sir.'

'Hi, Chief … how are you feeling?'

'Fine, sir ... feeling a lot better, thanks. I've got the middle watch tonight; the heat in that engine room will keep me warm.'

'OK. Just keep it steady. If you need any more time to recover, just let me know.'

'No need, sir, thank you; I've had too much time off already. I'm keen to get back at it.'

'Roger that, Chief. Put the PO Med Tech back on, will you?'

'OK, sir, thanks again. Here he is.'

'Sir.'

'PO, keep an eye on him for me.'

'Will do, sir.'

The captain hung up.

There was a knock at the door. The PO Med Tech answered.

'It's for you, Ben.'

Martin Thompson stood outside the mess.

'Hi, Martin, you OK, buddy?'

'Hi, Chief ... sorry to disturb you but I have a few questions.'

'Sure, Martin, come in ... I'm just having a cup of tea. Would you like one?'

'Yes please, that'd be great.'

Taylor made him a mug of tea and they sat down. 'Now, how can I help?'

'Chief, I need to know about sonar but they're busy right now. I was hoping you could explain what we're doing at the moment?'

'Sure can, Martin, it'd be a pleasure.' Taylor took a drink from his cup. 'OK: we've been told that a Russian submarine is in this area and we're listening with passive sonar to locate it. Then we will follow it and positively ID it by its noise signature. Feel free to ask questions.'

'How did we know that a Russian submarine was in this particular part of the ocean?'

'Several years ago we placed sonar buoys on the seabed in this area, as we knew that the Russians patrolled in these waters. These buoys, known as "sonobuoys", can be dropped from planes or surface ships, but in the case of these sonobuoys under the ice they were dispatched from submarines. They sit on the seabed and listen passively for noise. There's a whole system of them called "Integrated Undersea Surveillance System" (or "IUSS") or "Acoustic Intelligence".

As you can imagine, there are hundreds of them on the seabed around the Clyde.'

'What's the difference between "active" and "passive"?'

'Active sonar sends out a signal wave, "a ping"; if it hits an object, the sound comes back and is picked up by the submarine. One of the pitfalls with active is it gives away the position of the submarine sending the signal, so we don't use it often and when we do, it's only in short bursts. But it'll provide us with a more accurate position, range, bearing and speed for the torpedo firing control. Another problem with active is if there's a lot of biomass around – that's fish to you and me ... it can have an effect called scattering, which in layman's terms is like your car headlights on full beam in fog. Are you still with me?'

'Yeah, no problem, all going in.'

'Good ... huh, what next ... oh yeah: we have active countermeasures, which we deploy if we're detected by the enemy. They can provide a false target which the enemy will hopefully fire at. It can also change the signature of the submarine and cause them to wrongly identify us.'

'What do you mean by "submarine signature", Chief?'

'Passive sonar, as the name suggests, doesn't send out a signal wave – the sonar just listens for sound. It detects and targets radiated noise, and we have a database of the different unique engine and propeller noises so that we can compare and confirm the classification or type of submarine we're listening to. This classification will tell us its top speed what depth it can go to, how many torpedoes it has, et cetera, et cetera. We always want to update these databases, and that's what we're doing here. The K-222 won't even know we've been tracking them. Passive countermeasures consist of mounting noise-short generators to confuse the enemy by sending out false signatures through the hull. And we have rubber tiles glued to the hull called "anechoic tiles", which absorb the active sonar beams and distort them.' Taylor noticed that Martin had finished his tea. 'Would you like another one?' He pointed to the cup.

'No thanks, Chief, I'd better be going soon.'

'OK ... I'll be quick, then. The forward-facing sonar array or nose-mounted sonar can detect objects a hundred and sixty degrees on either side of the bow. The towed array we tow behind us has three-hundred-and-sixty-degree capability. We initially listen on broadband scanner, then when something is detected we can zoom in for a better look on narrowband. Now, finally: Target Motion Analysis is a passive stealth listening sonar that can't be detected, and which provides solutions that give us the range, speed and course of the target.

There are thermal layers in the sea, layers of different temperatures and density that we can hide beneath to aid our non-detection from above. Torpedoes have active and passive sonar to detect and home in on the targets. The other sonar we have on board is the underwater communications 183 telephones in both escape compartments and the tunnel.

They can be heard in the control room and by other vessels that have the emergency frequency, for example rescue vessels. And that's it. Any more questions? Anything you're not sure of?'

'Thanks, Chief, I need to write it all down before I forget.'

'Well, if you think of anything in the meantime, just give me a shout.'

Martin washed his mug and left the senior rates' mess. Taylor settled back in his chair and began reading a novel.

Covert was under the ice for a further three weeks and had completed the task of intelligence gathering after covertly following the Russian K-222-class submarine, but she was now entering the river Clyde and the captain gave the order to bring the boat to periscope depth.
'Let me remind you, team: when we surface, I want everyone to be prepared to emergency-dive in case there's a ship up there that the sonar hasn't picked up. Up search periscope.'

He ordered. As soon as it poked through the surface he spun round three hundred and sixty degrees to check the surface was clear. 'All clear, surface the boat!' The angle came on the bow and the submarine slid elegantly onto the surface of the Clyde. The captain spun the search periscope again to double-check the surface was clear. 'Down scope. Bridge team to the conning tower.' The first lieutenant and two lookouts who were already dressed in foul-weather gear climbed the ladder to the conning tower.

Passing Gourock to the right and Kilcreggan to the left, the submarine turned left and passed through Rhu Narrows and then past Helensburgh, heading towards Garelochhead. Two tugs were standing by to manoeuvre *Covert* into the berth between two other submarines, *Conqueror* and *Courageous*.

CHAPTER TWENTY-TWO

Michael Mullen needed to go into town again for food supplies. He was also desperate to see Maureen again. He checked the cupboards in the kitchen and made a mental list of what was required. Then he went to McCann, who was sat at the table putting the finishing touches to an order form he was completing from the magazine in front of him.

'I need to go into town, Mac, to get some food.'

'OK, Michael, take the van; I'll just finish this order for you-know-what; take it with you when you go. Oh, and talk to the boys, will you? See what booze they want.'

Michael entered the living room and the rest of the gang were all in there. Mickey Kelly was reading pornography in a chair and the others were watching feuding neighbours on the television.

'I'm going into town, boys, what do you want?'

Mickey threw the porn mag across the room. 'Get me another couple of these, I've read this one from front to back three times and I'm getting bored.' He smiled at Michael.

'Whisky for me,' another one said.

This was repeated several times as the others all agreed on what they wanted. Michael wrote down there orders and went back to McCann.

'OK, I'm going.'

'Good. Don't forget: don't draw attention to yourself.' McCann waved his fist at him: 'Take this letter; you'll need to get a stamp for it. And Michael – don't forget to post it.'

Michael looked at the letter, saw it was addressed to the *Exchange & Mart* and scratched his head, not knowing why his boss was ordering things from a magazine. He reversed the van from the rickety shed and drove off towards town.

Michael smiled as he entered the shop and saw the dimples on the cheeks of Maureen behind the counter. He was pleased to see her face light up as he said hello and gave her a little wave while he picked up a basket.

The basket was nearly full by the time he went to the counter.

'Hi, Mo, how are you?'

'I'm very well, Michael, thank you. I see you have a lot of shopping ... I'm thinking that's not all for you?'

'Erm, no ... I'm staying with a few friends.' *Another lie*, he thought.

'Where are you staying?' she enquired innocently.

'At a farm on the outskirts of town,' he replied without thinking.

'Well, let's run this lot through the till and see what I can do for you.'

'Oh, thank you.' He smiled again.

The total was rung up, a discount deducted and then Maureen asked him shyly: 'I know it's forward of me, but I was wondering if you'd like to maybe come round for a meal one night?'

Michael Mullen went instantly into a panic. 'Oh, I don't know …'

Maureen saw his awkwardness. 'It would be just me, and you I can easily get rid of my dad for a night.'

Michael couldn't think fast enough and found himself agreeing to the offer. Outside the grocery shop, he stopped to contemplate what he'd just agreed to. *How am I going to get away from the farm? McCann will never agree to me going. But ... maybe he doesn't have to know. I'll make some excuse. Oh my God ...* Michael smiled to himself and chuckled as he put the supplies in the back of the van.

Across the road two men in a tawny Ford Escort wrote down the registration of Michael's van and followed him as he drove off.

CHAPTER TWENTY-THREE

Taylor pressed the button to call the lift. With the duty watch in place on board the submarine, he was now in the foyer of the senior rates' mess in the shoreside-established HMS *Neptune*. He carried with him a pile of washing that he wasn't looking forward to doing. *Needs must*, he told himself. On the second floor he put the key in the lock, entered the familiar surroundings of his shore cabin and threw his washing on the floor. Taylor looked out the window across the loch and admired the scenery. Tall workshop buildings obscured his view of the submarine berths, but he could see the other side of the loch and the hills beyond. The hazy sun was about to set, and spread its last remaining sparkle on the water. Taylor briefly thought of home ... when his thoughts were interrupted by the tannoy.

'Chief Taylor, telephone call, mess foyer.'

Taylor headed back to the lift, hoping the call would get him out of doing his laundry.

'Taylor,' he simply said down the mouthpiece.

'Ben, hi, it's Tim. I'm in Helensburgh again and I was wondering if I could come and speak to you?' Tim Sherwin was in a call box outside the Imperial Hotel.

'Tadpole, hi ... of course you can, buddy, I'm not doing much. Are you coming now?'

'Yes, mate, it's quite important.'

'Give me a call when you arrive.' Taylor hung up the phone. *It's about time we had a heart-to-heart. What's this guy up to?* he thought.

Taylor ran back upstairs, gathered his washing and placed it in the machine in the laundry room. He set the dial to 'long wash' and pressed the button. Half an hour later, the tannoy was calling for him again.

'Hi, Tadpole.' The two friends shook hands. 'Let's go in the bar. Tea, coffee or something stronger?'

'I can stretch to a beer.'

'Good choice.' Taylor ordered two beers and the two men sat down at a table in the corner.

'We'll not be bothered here. What's on your mind, buddy?' Taylor was intrigued.

'I … well ... we have a problem that I think you can help with.'

'OK. Why don't you start from the beginning and tell me who "we" are?'

'When I finished my diver training for 42 Commando, my CO approached me and asked if I'd like to be a part of the intelligence-gathering service.' Taylor showed no emotion. Tim continued. 'So, of course I agreed, and … you already know, don't you?'

'Yep.' Taylor replied after taking a sip of beer.

'How the hell did you find that out?'

'Not important.'

'Well it is, mate, because I'm supposed to be covert ops on this.'

'Listen, I suspected you were up to something, so I had a friend check you out. A friend who will remain secret, I must add.'

'Fuck me, Ben. This could mean I've been compromised.'

'My dad,' Taylor replied.

Tim thought a while. 'Who did he speak to?

'My dad still has a lot of friends in high places.'

'I'll have to report this.'

'Then you should have told me when we met.'

'I should have known you'd be suspicious of me turning up like that on the moor.'

'So come on, spill the beans, what's with this PACDU thing?'

'PACDU is just a cover to allow me to travel where and when I want.'

'Clever. So how can I help?'

Both men took long slugs of beer.

'I've been working with a large team for over a year now. I won't bore you with the details. After following up some leads, I've uncovered something that's got me worried.'

'Now you have my full attention.' Taylor leaned forward in his chair.

'As you know, the Russians are up to all kinds of stuff. Luckily, always one step behind. Their spies steal from us so we can dictate what they get. A lot of money is spent on intelligence gathering. But I think we have a new threat.'

'Who?'

'The Irish.'

'They've always been a threat.'

'I know, I know. But this is something else. Our guys across the water tell us a splinter group has been causing the IRA trouble. They apparently had a falling out and this so-called splinter group have been taking things into their own hands. It's becoming a big concern for the IRA – so much so that they've cancelled some actions to concentrate on catching them. This made me think that this splinter group is more than prepared or capable of doing something quite nasty.'

'I see. Do they have funds?'

'Not sure.'

'Do you know what this splinter group are planning?'

'No. They've gone deep and nobody can find them.'

'And you're telling me all this because …?'

'In the last four months, three new Irish families have moved into that peace camp down the road.' Taylor's mind jolted to Orla while Tim went on. 'Ben, I think they're putting operatives in that peace camp, and that would suggest an attack on either the base or a submarine.'

'Do you know who's running the show?'

'A man called Gallymore.'

'Christ … you don't have any proof. Tadpole, you have nothing.'

'I know it sounds bad, that's why I need your help.'

'I know nothing about spying, Tadpole.'

'I'll tell you everything you need to know. Your knowledge of submarines and diving will be invaluable to me.'

'Tadpole, I don't know about this … it could get very messy. Isn't there someone in the Intelligence Corps you can talk to? They'll have experts who deal with this shit …'

'Ben, I have no proof. Nothing to back up my theory. At the moment I'm flying solo on this.' Tim let his friend think this through for a moment.

'The Intelligence Corps is bogged down in red tape, Ben. They wait and wait; they waste time following people, chasing leads and gathering intel … until they have the bigwigs, the men in charge. It's a very slow process. In the meantime, buildings are destroyed, lives ruined and people killed. This guy Gallymore is a pawn, just a cog in a big wheel. They won't do anything to stop him: he's not big enough. I want to catch this lunatic and stop him from taking lives … the lives of people I might know.'

'Tadpole, you don't know who he is, where he is or even what he's planning to do?'

'Not yet, Ben.'

'Look, I've seen enough movies to know that you remove the cog, they replace it with another.'

'No, Ben. Don't you see: this guy won't be replaced. He's out on his own. The IRA want him off the streets.'

'Then it's easy: you give him to the IRA and they do the job for you.'

'I would really appreciate your help with this, Ben. All I'm asking is for you to keep your eyes and ears open and report anything unusual back to me.'

Taylor knew Tim well and realised it would be more than eyes and ears he would have to keep open. 'OK, but I don't know how helpful I'll be.'

CHAPTER TWENTY-FOUR

The inside of the Bedouin tent was cooler; a light breeze off the Mediterranean made the material flap. Gallymore hated the heat. A female bodyguard dressed in khaki fatigues adjusted the position of the AK47 slung over her shoulder and patted him down again, but this time with a lingering inspection of his groin. He watched her eyebrows rise as she smiled. Gallymore could have disarmed her easily. *Some other time, young lady*, he thought as she bent down to pull out a cushion for him. She gestured for him to sit.

'The Brother Leader will be here with you in a very short time,' she said in broken English.

Gallymore nodded at her, and she went outside to stand with the other four women who were on guard outside the tent. He heard them giggle. *So, he has another title now*, Gallymore thought. *Every time I come here he calls himself something different; what was it she said? 'The Brother Leader?' I wonder who dreams them up for him.* Gallymore looked around at the handmade, brightly coloured carpets that not only covered the floor but the walls as well. The silk drapes surrounding the gold-embroidered sofa made it look like a shrine. There were small iron tables with round tops made from solid gold, and on them burned large ornate brass lamps. Two dwarf palm trees stood either side of the entrance and cushions of gold, orange, red and blue were scattered everywhere. The smell of incense and whatever was being burned in the brass lamps filled the tent and made Gallymore's eyes smart slightly.

Then he was aware of a presence. Gallymore turned to see Muammar Muhammad Abu Minyar al-Gaddafi standing in the entrance. Gallymore stood up, Gaddafi put his hand on his heart and both men stepped forward. They hugged each other for a moment and touched noses three times before Gaddafi spoke.

'Ah, Gallymore, my friend, thank you for coming to see me.' He grabbed Gallymore's hands and held them for a long time, smiling at his Irish friend.

'I always have time for my brother Muammar.' Gallymore smiled back.

Gaddafi wasn't dressed in his usual refinery but had donned clothing that was quite casual for the flamboyant colonel. No medals, no gold bracelets and most strikingly, no hat – which revealed his receding hairline.

'Come, sit with me.' Gaddafi sat in the altar chair while Gallymore settled himself on a cushion to his right.

'You have come a long way; can I offer you some refreshment? Whisky perhaps?'

Gallymore stood and moved to a table with Jameson on it. He knew he would have to pour it – Gaddafi did nothing for himself. *Fat, useless blob.* He gestured to see if Gaddafi wanted one and the signal back was for a small one. When Gallymore had sat back down, he addressed the colonel attentively.

'Thank you for inviting me before the weather gets too hot.'

'This time of year the cool air from the Mediterranean loses the battle with the heat from the Sahara.'

Gallymore knew Gaddafi didn't like too much small talk, so got to the point. 'Now, how can I help my Libyan brother?'

The two men held eye contact as the colonel spoke.

'It's been three years since you last came to my training camp. I asked you then for your thoughts on how I could overcome the American ban on our military equipment sales. Your advice was good. As you suggested, I talked with them and made them promises, which they accepted, and in 1979 I bought three Boeing 747s and two 727s, to boost my country's commercial airline. It was as if I was winning their trust again. Now Reagan has said: "That oil imported from Libya is inimical to US national security." This I do not like. I have AWACS flying overhead and undercover CIA crawling around my country snooping into my private life. This I do not like.'

Gallymore wanted to keep the colonel happy, and keep him reminded of his advice. 'How are the Russians behaving?'

'Just as you said they would be: they are good allies. I have allowed them to use my ports and airfields for their military hardware; in return, I get an endless supply of weapons and …' he waved his hand, 'some training.' More whisky was poured. 'You have proved yourself to be a worthy ally and friend of Libya, so I ask your advice again. These Americans are again getting too close.'

Gallymore knew Gaddafi was planning something, but he would have to tread carefully: the colonel was no fool, and Gallymore needed his help.

'You're a great leader to your people. The Americans are stupid.' Gallymore didn't like blowing smoke, but knew this son of a goat herder liked it, and right now he needed his support. 'Let them snoop all they want but show them what you want them to see. Let them see you closing your training camps and tell them you're disassociating yourself from terrorist groups.'

'But my army is growing larger every day; I need to train my troops.'

Gallymore studied his glass. *What is he training his troops to do? Not my problem.* 'I'm glad to hear your numbers are increasing. Close the larger camps ... make a big thing of it, plenty of press, let them see what a peaceful man you are ... and then quietly open twice as many smaller ones. Streamline your training, open specialist camps well hidden from their eyes ... you have many hills and mountains to conceal your men.'

'You are a wise man, Gallymore.' Gaddafi held up his empty glass for Gallymore to attend to. The colonel seemed relaxed and sipped his refilled glass.

Gallymore had one more trick up his sleeve. 'When I received your invitation, brother, the only thing I could think of was bringing you a present. I pondered over what to bring a most astute and brave man who commands such a large army ... and then it came to me. It was obvious. Come, a moment of your time ...' Gallymore gestured his desire for Gaddafi to follow him outside.

Gaddafi paused a moment and was handed a cap with gold braid on the peak. He placed it on his head and gestured for Gallymore to carry on.

The sun's rays hit Gallymore's eyes like the blinding flash of a camera. Tiny particles of sand blew in the wind and stung his eyes like acid drops. He hated coming to the desert. Gallymore shielded his face with his hand as best he could.

Tribesmen stood in groups of three and four on large sand dunes off to his left, and crates of ammunition lay piled around the less flamboyant tents that made up this makeshift camp. Gaddafi's men walked around with rifles slung over their shoulders, tending to camels, the ones close by springing to attention when he appeared outside.

Gallymore signalled a small group of tribesmen standing under a single palm tree. One of the men waved his hand, and from behind a large mound of sand appeared a fuel tanker truck. It belched large amounts of black smoke from the exhaust as it accelerated towards them, and the squeal from the brakes hurt Gallymore's ears as it drew up to a halt in front of them. Two of the female bodyguards moved forward and raised their weapons as the driver got out and saluted Gaddafi.

'You have brought me fuel?' Gaddafi said with a puzzled look on his face.

Gallymore walked over to the tanker and slid the centre portion of a corrugated rubber fuel pipe running along the side of the truck back from its housing. It revealed a hiding place of approximately four feet of pipe, from which he produced a length of rolled cloth. He turned to face Gaddafi and unravelled the cloth from around the object. Eventually, Gallymore handed him a brand-new rifle.

'I give to you the Dragunov SVD sniper rifle, complete with modifications and high-powered scope,' Gallymore announced proudly. He could tell Gaddafi was pleased and excited by this gift, if slightly bemused at its potential. Gallymore tipped down the small piece of rubber pipe and out fell a box containing twenty-four rounds. 'With this you'll be able to shoot the flee off a camel at a thousand yards, my brother.'

Gaddafi smiled and held the rifle at arm's length, inspecting his new toy. He wanted to see it in action and gave it back to Gallymore as he whispered to one of the women by his side. She ran away quickly to another tent, and shortly after a man wearing only a cloth around his midriff fell from the opening and sat on the ground, hiding his face from the sun. The woman appeared and kicked him hard on the buttocks. He stood unsteadily at first, but when she aimed her rifle at him he began to walk away, eventually stumbling and running as fast as he could.

All the tribesmen lookouts on the surrounding dunes were watching as the man who had been held captive made his desperate escape.
Even Gaddafi was becoming concerned at the distance Gallymore had allowed the man to run before raising the SVD sniper rifle slowly to his shoulder. A quick look down the telescopic scope, a squeeze of the trigger, and the man fell into the sand and lay perfectly still. 'How many do you have?' said Gaddafi, amazed.

'How many do you want?' Gallymore asked with a stern face.

The two men went back inside for more whisky. It was time for Gallymore to reveal the true reason he had travelled to see the tribesman.

'I have some news from across the water, brother.'

'What news is this?'

'Margaret Thatcher is considering allowing US military aeroplanes to use UK airstrips.' He waited for this little bombshell to sink in before continuing. 'This would put them in striking distance of Libya.'

Gaddafi scratched his chin and sat forward in his seat.

'This I do not like.'

'I have a solution for you. These airfields are heavily guarded, but I think with a little help I can prevent them from operating.'

'After we have discussed how many rifles you can supply me with, I think we can come to an arrangement. Is it money you require?'

'Yes, my brother; I have the men to carry out the work but no funding – as yet.'

'Well then, let us talk more, for money is not a problem for me, and after all you are my friend, and if friends cannot help each other, the world would be a bad place.'

Gallymore smiled the biggest smile he had for quite some time.

'Is money the only thing I can help my good friend with?'

'Well ... I'm always looking for new ideas to cause havoc.' Gallymore broke into a grin. 'There is one other thing I was going to ask.'

'Ask me anything – if I can help, I will.'

'Your contacts in America: do you have someone I can trust to make me, let's call it, a unique explosive device?'

'Ah. You are stepping up your game, eh?' Gaddafi looked like he was contemplating the question for a while. Then he whispered to one of his women and she walked away briskly. 'I have a friend in California who is, shall we say, an expert in combustible gas munitions. Is this the sort of thing you are looking for?'

Gallymore's brain went into overdrive. 'Exactly.' His smile widened.

'Then I will give you his whereabouts and you can talk with him. He is a good friend and will help you because of me.'

CHAPTER TWENTY-FIVE

Orla Brodie was in a dilemma. She decided to confront her predicament head-on. The inside of the caravan at the peace camp was chilly, with the heat from the log-burning potbellied stove not radiating very far from the source. Her mother was sat in her comfortable chair reading yesterday's newspaper, and Liam was nursing a hangover in front of the small television set. Orla decided to put the kettle on.

'Anyone for tea?'

It was always a good idea to resolve any confrontation over a nice cup of tea. Her mother responded right away, but Liam was quiet.

'Liam!'

He slowly shifted his gaze from the screen to the kitchen and grunted his acknowledgement.

'That'll be a yes, then?' Orla raised her eyebrows. Steam from the kettle formed into spots of condensation on the roof of the caravan; Orla wiped it off as the tea brewed in the pot. 'Is that yesterday's paper, Mam?'

'Yes ... I haven't had time to read it yet.'

'You should make him do more of the chores around here to give you more time.' She nodded her head towards her brother.

'I'd rather do it myself.'

'I understand,' Orla agreed. She gave her mother her cup and placed Liam's on the table in front of him. Orla sat in the chair next her mother and sucked her teeth, fidgeting.

'What is it?' her mother asked, not looking up from the paper.

Orla hesitated, gathering her thoughts and trying to decide how she was going to do this. 'Well, I did need to talk to you.'

'Oh.'

'Yes. You know that I went to dinner with Ben the other night ...'

'Yes, of course I do. You said you had a nice meal, didn't you?' Then she added: 'He's a nice boy ...'

'He's hardly a boy, Mam ... and yes, I did.' There was a long pause.

'Well?'

'Well, we were talking, and he asked me to go sailing with him.' Orla waited for the reaction, but her mother remained silent. 'What do you think?'

'It's nothing to do with me, my love; it's how you feel that counts.'

This was not the reaction she had expected from her mother, and it caught her off guard slightly. It was, however, what Orla wanted to hear. So she continued.

'I know I've only been out with him once, but I feel as if I know him really well. When I was trapped in that awful cave ...' Orla gave a glancing, stern look towards her brother. 'I felt a true bond between us, and that's why I trusted him to get me out. There was just something about him that I ...' Orla raised her hands slightly and shook them. 'And when at the restaurant the other night, I felt it again.'

Orla's mother put down the paper. 'I'm glad that you want to get out of this camp, even for a while. As I've said in the past, this is no place for a young girl to spend her life.'

'But I want to be with you, Mam.'

'I can look after myself, dear. There's plenty of things here to keep me occupied, and I have friends.' Then her mother asked the question Orla was dreading. 'Where is he taking you sailing? On the loch?' Orla put her tea cup down on the table in front of her and drew a deep breath, then quickly spoke while she had the courage.

'He lives in Cheshire and he has his own yacht and he's invited me to his house and I've said … well, I haven't said yes, *yet* … but I think I would like to go.'

Liam suddenly sat up straight in his chair. 'Are you completely out of your mind?' he shouted. 'He's a fecking nuclear freak. Works for the fecking Navy, woman! Have you lost it completely?'

'Liam! Mind your language,' Mrs Brodie scolded.

'Mam, don't let him speak to me like that.' Orla's heart was now beating fast.

The volume of Liam's voice did not come down. 'The whole idea of being in a fecking peace camp is to protest against this nuclear shit, and you're fraternising with the enemy!'

'Liam, I won't tell you again,' Mrs Brodie warned.

'Mam!' Liam jumped up from his chair and stood in the middle of the room. 'She's only known this sailor for five minutes and she's jumping into bed with him!'

Orla began to shake with anguish. She didn't know what to say.

Liam began to pace the floor. 'Have you forgotten what these English have done to us?' He began to wave is hands aggressively.

Mrs Brodie took hold of her walking stick, and in one movement stood from her chair and cracked Liam over the shoulders with it.

'For feck's sake, Mam!'

'Get out of here, you; get out!' She hit him again.

Liam flung open the door and went outside. From the doorway he shouted back inside: 'She's nothing but a whore!'

Mrs Brodie slammed the door shut in his face and Orla began to cry uncontrollably. Mrs Brodie knelt down beside her chair and put her arms around her daughter.

'Pay no attention to him Orla; he didn't mean that.'

Orla tried to speak, but no words came out.

'He'll calm down when he's had a drink. Come on, now.' She held her daughter tight and started to stroke her back.

'I'm not a whore,' was all she could say, her voice quivering.

'I know, love, I know.' Mrs Brodie released her grip and stood up. She opened the door and checked to see if Liam had gone. Then she closed the door again and spoke in a determined voice. 'You tell this man of yours that you will go sailing with him ... and you will damn well enjoy yourself.' Mrs Brodie went into the kitchen and tore off some paper roll. 'Wipe your eyes with this,' she said soothingly.

Orla took the pieces of kitchen roll and held it to her eyes. 'I'm not a whore, Mam.'

Mrs Brodie switched off the television and sat down in her chair. 'When I first met your father I was seventeen and he was twenty-one. We used to spend our time hiding from other people, from our other friends. Nobody knew that we were seeing each other. I knew that I loved him right from the start and he treated me well. Like a man should treat a woman. But I felt guilty at the same time.' There was a short pause. Orla looked at her mother with red eyes. 'I hated sneaking around; all I wanted was to be with him. Then I made the mistake of telling my best friend. Within minutes the whole world knew I was seeing a man, and I was branded a whore.'

'Did your parents find out?'

'My mam did. I rightly convinced her that we were not having sex. We somehow kept it from my da, and three years later we married and had sex for the first time.'

'I had no idea. Why didn't you tell me this before?'

'There was reason to. So you see, you're older and wiser than I was back then, so go and enjoy yourself. Just take precautions,' she added as an afterthought.

'Mother!' Orla answered in a disgusted tone. 'Nothing like that is going to happen.' Both women smiled at each other. 'Where do you think he's gone?'

'Do you really have to ask?'

'There's probably going to be more shouting when he gets back?'

'He'll probably be drinking with his pal Jamie. I'll ask him to phone me when Liam's coming back. You pop out for a while and I'll calm him down.'

An hour later Orla walked to the nearest phone box and dialled the senior rates' mess in HMS *Neptune*. Taylor was in the shower after having been to the gym. The speaker on the tannoy system burst into life.

'Chief Taylor, shore telephone mess office.'

For crying out loud, he thought *what now?* Taylor quickly dried, threw on his tracksuit and ran for the lift. The young killick pointed to the receiver off the hook when he entered the office.

'Chief Taylor,' he answered in a quizzical voice.

'Ben, it's me, Orla. I hope I'm not disturbing you?' She spoke with a soft Irish lilt.

'Oh, hi, Orla … no, you're not disturbing me at all. I was just … uh … well ... is everything OK?' His voice was now mellow.

'Yes, everything's fine.' Orla felt her heart race slightly at the sound of his voice. 'I was wondering if we could talk.'

'Sure thing … and I was planning on going for a walk by Loch Lomond this afternoon. I could come by and pick you up if you like?'

'Yeah, that sounds great.' When Orla hung up she noticed her palms were sweating.

Taylor thanked the killick and ran back up the stairs. *This should be interesting*, he thought as he took his tracksuit off and climbed back into the shower.

The sun started to appear from behind a high cloud as Taylor paid the taxi driver. Orla was standing admiring the beautiful Loch Lomond.

'You've been here before, haven't you?' Taylor asked.

'Yes. I come here with my mam quite often, but it never ceases to amaze me.'

The taxi drove away and they both began to walk along the shoreline from the café car park towards the Bear Park. Taylor was wearing a woollen jacket and was starting to get hot. He removed the jacket to reveal just a white t-shirt. Orla found herself looking at the huge muscles of his arms and chest. When he spoke, she diverted her stare.

'How are things at the peace camp?' he enquired.

'Oh, you know … quiet. Well, they would be if it wasn't for my stupid brother.'

'Why, what has he been up to?'

'The usual … the things men do in Helensburgh.'

'Yeah, I know.' Taylor knew what she was talking about. 'They say it relieves stress, but I think that's just an excuse. I don't know when it'll stop, because the young lads coming through see the older ones doing it and think it's clever.'

'My brother doesn't know what stress is.'

'A different kind of stress, maybe? It can't be easy, being a young man with nothing to do.'

'Maybe.'

'Does he have any mates, or interests?'

'He has one mate: Jamie O'Donnel. The only interests they both have are drinking and horse racing.'

'Jamie O'Donnel?'

'Yeah … he moved onto the camp about a month ago. I don't know much about him.'

'Is he by himself, Orla?'

'No, he lives with an older brother and their da; they seem nice enough.'

'Is the camp getting bigger?'

'People come and go all the time.'

Taylor didn't want to spook her with too many questions. So he changed tack: 'So, what did you want to talk about?'

'I was thinking about your offer of going sailing.'

'Ah, yes.'

'It's still on, I assume?'

'Most definitely.'

'Then I'd like to take you up on the offer, and would be pleased to meet your parents.'

CHAPTER TWENTY-SIX

Michael Mullen was racking his brains for an excuse to go into town that night. He had promised Maureen he would go for dinner at her house and she was getting rid of her father for the evening. Then it dawned on him: McCann was upstairs and the rest of the men were – as usual – gathered around the television. Michael put a plate of sandwiches down on the table in front of the television and sat on a dining chair.

'When I was in town the other day I noticed a few good-looking pubs, you know …' he said to no one in particular. At first they said nothing, so he continued: 'And I'm sure I saw a leaflet advertising a dance at the hall.' They all became interested.

'Really?'

'When? Tonight?'

'Yep, I'm sure that's what it said.'

'They'll be girls there.' Mickey Kelly rubbed his hands.

'Plenty of booze, too,' said Andy McDowell, slapping Mickey on the back.

'Right, leave this to me, boys.' Mickey was thinking hard.

When McCann came back down the stairs he couldn't believe his eyes. 'Now what the feck is going on?'

The television was off and Michael and Andy were in the kitchen having a wash, while Mickey was standing in front of a mirror combing his hair and Sean O'Brean was putting on his shoes. The crushed-velvet jacket he wore was too small for him.

McCann spoke again: 'Mickey, what the feck?' He held out his hands.

'We're going into town.'

'Oh no you're not!' McCann became enraged, pushing over a chair, and moved towards Mickey.

'I wouldn't do that if I were you.'

It was said in such a way that McCann stopped in his tracks. The rest of the gang were now standing behind him, and as he turned he knew they meant business.

McCann tried to reason with them. 'Guys, come on … the whole fecking world is looking for us. If we get caught they'll kill us for sure.'

'We're not spending another night in this godforsaken house. If Gallymore can go out, then so can we.' Mickey was in no mood to argue.

'Nobody knows we're here, McCann. It's a small town in the middle of fecking nowhere. Even if we *are* seen, who will know who we are?' Andy said, putting on his shirt.

Sean O'Brean stood up from his chair. 'This isn't what we signed up for, hiding in this fecking house like rats. We need to be out there fighting for the cause, killing them English bastards. We might as well be dead, stuck in here.'

McCann's whole body began to slump. 'So you're all in agreement, then?'

'Yep.' They all said at once.

'Feck it ... if – just *if* – we get away with this and we don't get recognised in town.' He paused for a moment. 'Do not, I repeat, do *not* speak a word of this to Gallymore.'

Dooley's bar was particularly quiet for a Tuesday night. Andy noticed that the barmaid had a very low-cut shirt on, her assets not being appreciated by the two old guys sat at the bar. The only other person in the bar was sat in the corner reading a newspaper with half a pint of Guinness on the table in front of him that had dust floating on top. An hour later the jukebox was playing louder than it had ever been played and the balls were rattling on the pool table. Bets were being placed on the winner and darts were being thrown into the board – and in the case of McCann, into the wall. Michael Mullen slid out the door unnoticed. Andy stood at the bar, his eyes transfixed by the barmaid's chest.

'We've not seen you boys in here before …' she said.

Andy didn't divert his stare. 'Yeah, we're new to the area.'

'So, what brings you all to this backwater of a town?'

'We're … uh … doing some renovations to the farm up the road.'

'I thought that had been empty for a while now. Does someone actually live there?'

'No, they're on holiday at the moment. We're getting it ready for them when they come back.' Someone down the other end of the bar wanted serving, and Andy was upset when the barmaid went to serve him.

Sean came to stand next to Andy and whispered in his ear: 'She's very sociable.'

'First woman I've spoken to in weeks.'

'She probably just fancies you, Andy.'

'Oh, I really hope so.' They both had broad smiles on their faces. The barmaid came back. Sean kicked Andy in the foot.

'I was told there's some sort of dance going on in town tonight?'

'Whoever told you that? Hasn't been a dance in this town for years, honey.'

The lying bastard. Andy looked round the bar but couldn't see Michael.

McCann had finished his pint and was putting his glass down on the bar. 'Get the pints in, Sean, there's a good lad.'

'You've cheered up.'

'Well, we're here now.'

Sean dutifully bought another round. The noise level in the bar got higher as the night went on. An hour later they were drinking whisky along with their pints.

'You ought to 'ave got into that barmaid's knickers by now. She's hasn't taken her eyes off you,' Sean stammered to Andy.

The 'closed' sign was up and the door locked, but the lights were still on in the store. He knocked on the door. Maureen appeared from behind the counter and looked excited when she saw him through the glass panel.

'I didn't think you were coming.'

'I had a lot to do today.'

'That's OK, you're here now. The stew I made is on a low simmer, it'll be fine. Come on in, I'll show you upstairs.'

The lights went out in the store.

The inside of the bar was filling up with cigarette smoke. The two old guys sitting at the bar got up and left.

'Where the feck is he?' McCann looked round the bar. 'Andy, where the feck is Michael?'

'Why ask me? I'm not his keeper.' He looked round the bar anyway.

'Check the loos!' McCann shouted at Mickey.

The guy in the corner folded his newspaper and walked out the door.

'Last orders, please, last orders! Sorry, boys, playtime's over!' the barmaid shouted from behind the bar. She leaned beneath the bar and turned the volume down on the remote control of the jukebox. Andy dashed to the bar and bought another round. 'You don't have to rush, honey, my bar is always open for you.'

'Let me get rid of these clowns and I'll keep you company.' He reached out and squeezed her hand.

McCann had gathered the others at a table under the dartboard. Andy carried the tray of drinks over.

'What's the plan?' he said as he sat down.

'Did anyone see him leave?' Anxiously, McCann moved his pint closer to him. The others just shook their heads. 'Fecking useless,' he said quietly. He noticed the barmaid looking over at them.

'Something must have happened to him; he wouldn't just wander off.' Mickey played with a bar mat.

McCann gave him a hard stare. 'Obviously, you buffoon.'

'So, what's the plan?' Andy asked again.

'I don't know … I haven't got one.' McCann studied the wall.

'Maybe we should go look for him,' Sean added.

'And just where would you suggest we start?' McCann said. 'Just be quiet for a minute, let me think ...' Five minutes passed quickly, and now as they reflected they all became anxious. All of them except Andy.

Eventually, Mickey spoke: 'She's going to kick us out in a minute.'

Andy leaned back in his chair. 'Let's go to the local Garda and report him missing.'

'I'm going to break your nose.' McCann tensed up.

Andy smiled. 'OK, just joking! But seriously, you lot go back to the farmhouse and I'll stay here in case he comes back.'

McCann actually thought that was a good idea, but didn't like to leave another team member on his own. 'Right, we'll check round the local and all of you will go back to the farm. This place is closing, so he won't come back here.'

'He might not know what time the pub shuts, or be in a confused state. You know how thick he is,' Andy tried to convince McCann.

'No; I can't risk losing another man. We're all going back.' McCann had made his decision.

'Nobody will take me down, McCann. I can hold my own against any man.'

'It might not be just one man, Andy. We're are all sticking together.'

'You're an arsehole, McCann. You're going to get us all killed.'

'If I do then I'll take responsibility for it.'

'But we'll all be dead,' piped up a puzzled Mickey.

'Shut the feck up.' McCann finished his drink.

The gang moved to the door and Andy went to the bar.

'The bar is shut, Andy.' McCann opened the door.

'I'm coming, I'm coming.' He spoke with his eyes back on the barmaid's chest. 'Sorry, babe, urgent business. It breaks my heart but I've got to go.'

'I'm sorry to hear that; I was planning on having some fun.'

'So was I … I'll be back soon, though.'

'Don't be too long.' The barmaid blew him a kiss.

Andy breathed a big sigh as he left the bar. *Fecking McCann, fecking Michael!*

Outside, the streets were quiet. The main roads were lit with the glare from the street lights, but the side streets and alleys behind the buildings were not lit.

McCann signalled to Sean and Mickey. 'You two go to the other side of the street and move down with us. Concentrate on the alleys, lads, and keep your ears open.'

McCann and the team moved stealthily down the street with their guns drawn. For an hour they searched. Eventually McCann told Sean to go and get the van.

Back in the farmhouse, the whisky was being poured into tumblers.

'We'd better take it easy, lads,' McCann warned.

Andy drank his tumbler and poured another. 'If he's been caught, they'll interrogate him, and that means we're not safe here, McCann.'

'Let's just stay alert.'

Michael Mullen walked up the drive quietly. He took a deep breath and opened the front door to the farmhouse. He felt the butt of a gun smash his nose, and the acrid taste of blood hit the back of his mouth straight away. He felt his arms being forced behind his back and he could do nothing to stop it. Something hard hit him behind the knees and he fell to the floor. He registered the first punch to his face but not the second.

'Where?' was the only thing he heard as his head began to clear. He knew he was lying flat somewhere, then realised his cheek was on the carpet. His head hurt like mad and fireworks were going off behind his eyes. He tried to move but decided to stay still for a while.

'Been ...' was the next recognisable word he heard. He was still unable to speak, his jaw not responding to his brain's commands. All went quiet again and he felt peace as the pain subsided.

When he came to he could smell something putrid but familiar close to his nose.

'Where the feck have you been, laddie?' He recognised the voice, and when he opened his eyes McCann's face was just a few inches away from his. Michael swallowed hard; his mouth was dry and there was something stuck in the back of his throat. After the second swallow it moved slightly and disappeared into his gullet.

'I was going to tell you, boss.'

'Let him have some water, McCann,' Mickey pleaded.

'Water? Let him have some water? I'll drown the bastard!' McCann raised his gun over Michael's head.

'Stop!' Andy grabbed McCann's wrist, the gun falling to the floor. 'He's had enough … get him up, sit him on the sofa. We'll get the story from him. At least he's safe.' Then, as an afterthought he asked: 'Michael, are we safe?'

Michael nodded his head painfully slowly.

The next day McCann heard a noise from the gate at the bottom of the drive.

'Sean,' he called out, waving his gun at the window. The others drew their guns immediately. Sean moved the blind slightly and looked out the window. A white van drove up the drive and parked in front of the house. Sean slowly let the blind go and moved to the side of the door.

'White van,' he said.

They heard doors opening and slamming and a shuffle of boxes on the porch.

Then there was a knock on the door.

McCann spoke loudly. 'Yeah?'

'Delivery for you, sir,' came the reply from the other side of the door.

McCann thought for a moment, then opened the door slightly to look outside. 'Help this guy get unloaded, boys, it's OK.'

The boxes were marked 'Fertiliser', 'Lime,' 'Electrical goods' and 'Chemicals: this way up'. One was marked in red 'Fragile: medical supplies'.

'Get everything inside.' McCann signed for the goods and the van drove off.

'This, my friends, is the start of our fight back.'

CHAPTER TWENTY-SEVEN

Taylor's father Mathew sat on the bank and admired the new varnish on his wooden seat. He unbuttoned his shirt slightly and leaned back against the hull of his yacht. He reached into his bag and pulled out the cheese and onion sandwich which his wife had lovingly made for his lunch. He felt the heat of the sun warm his whole body and his thoughts went to his son. Mathew woke a few minutes later and was embarrassed he had fallen asleep in the afternoon. He checked the mooring ropes and made his way home. Elli asked him how he was as he entered the house.

'I'm fine ... the sun was so hot I fell asleep after my lunch.'

'Did you get everything done you wanted?' she enquired.

'Yes. The yacht is looking her best and is ready to go.'

'Well that's good, because I've just had a call from Benjamin: he's coming home tomorrow ... and guess what?'

Mathew could see his wife was excited. 'Well, he'll want to go sailing, of course.'

'That's not all: he's bringing a young lady with him.' She rubbed her hands and smiled at her husband.

'Oh, right. Who is she, do we know? When did this happen?'

'Well, all he said was that he'd met her a few weeks ago and that he'd like to take her sailing.'

'And is that it?'

'Yes. He was of course in a rush, but I'm sure she's just lovely.' She stroked her husband's cheek. 'Now, wash your hands – I'm about to make some supper.'

Taylor packed his weekend bag and left his contact number with the quartermaster on board *Covert* then made his way to the main gate of HMS *Neptune*. He jumped into a cab and asked the driver to stop at the peace camp. The driver seemed surprised as he drove off.

She was standing by the roadside as the cab pulled up, and the smile on her face when she saw him was infectious. Taylor noticed how wonderful she looked in a tight pair of jeans and a warm jumper. She waved quickly as he jumped out.

'Hi … you OK?'

'Yes I'm fine, thanks.'

'Ready to go?'

'I am.'

Mrs Brodie came out of the caravan and approached her daughter. Orla turned and walked to her and they hugged.

'You have a good time, my love.'

'I will, Mam.'

Mrs Brodie loosened her grip on Orla. 'And you look after my daughter, young man.'

'I will, Mrs Brodie.'

Orla jumped into the back of the cab; Taylor put her bag in the boot and climbed in beside her. Orla waved back at her mother until she could no longer see her.

The time went quickly as they talked most of the journey. Soon the train was pulling into Crewe station, and Taylor saw his father waiting on the platform.

'Dad, how are you?'

'I'm good, Son. Glad to see you.' Taylor's father turned to the young woman beside his son. 'And this is?'

'Dad, let me introduce you to Orla.'

'Orla, what a lovely name; I'm very pleased to meet you, young lady.' Mathew Taylor bent down for her bag. 'I'll take that for you. Come on, let's get you home. I managed to get a space right outside the station on the forecourt.' Mathew strode away quickly towards the stairway leading up to the front entrance. Mathew loaded the baggage into the rear of the car and Taylor opened the door for Orla.

'Would it be possible to stop on the way, Ben? I'd like to buy some flowers for your mother.'

'Sure, no problem, I'll tell Dad to stop.'

Mathew had a million questions to ask Orla but didn't want to bombard her so soon. 'How long are you home for, Son?'

'Just the weekend, Dad; we'll be going back late on Sunday.'

'Have you got any plans?'

'I'd really like to take Orla sailing tomorrow.'

'Sure thing – the boat's all ready to go and the forecast is good.' Then he turned to Orla. 'Have you sailed before, Orla?'

'No, Mister Taylor, this will be my first time.'

'Oh, please call me Mathew. My wife's name is Elizabeth but she likes to be called Elli.'

They turned left after passing the hospital and drove through the Cheshire countryside. Orla spoke just after they crossed a little humpback bridge over the canal.

'It's very beautiful here. You're very lucky.'

'The town was built round the rock-salt works … in fact, the flash we'll be sailing on tomorrow is a collapsed mine.' Ben smiled at her, and Orla squeezed his hand. The conversation was gentle for the rest of the journey. Orla felt right at ease.

When they got to the house, Taylor's mother was waiting by the front door. 'Come here you!' She gave Taylor a huge hug.

'This is Orla, Mum.' Ben introduced his friend when his mother eventually released her grip on him.

Elli smiled at Orla, and then gave her a big hug too. 'You're very welcome, my dear. I hope Benjamin's been looking after you. How was your trip? Come on, let's get you all inside, I don't know why we're stood outside. I'll put the kettle on and we can have a good chat.' She put her arm around Orla's shoulders and they walked into the house.

'I guess that leaves us to get the bags, then,' Taylor laughed as he put his arm round his father's shoulders.

Orla was shown round the house by Elli. 'I've prepared the spare bedroom for you, my love.' Elli opened the door to a huge bedroom. 'I hope you'll be comfortable in here; we don't use it that often.'

'Wow, it's huge!' she exclaimed. It's bigger than the caravan I live in.' Orla wowed at everything in the room, especially the king-size bed.

'There's fresh towels in the en suite, and if you need anything just let me know.'

While Elli continued giving Orla the grand tour, Ben and his father caught up in the garden.

'Your mother seems to like Orla, Ben.'

'Yeah, I thought she would. Orla seems settled, too. She hasn't been away from the peace camp for a while. She's coping with these new surroundings and meeting you and Mum really well. Thanks for making her so welcome.'

'It's the least we could do. Have you done any checks on her?'

'No, not on her, Dad, but I believe Tim is looking at her family's history.'

'How is he? Have you had chance to talk?'

'Yes. He came into the base and we had a chat. He's got an idea that a splinter group from the IRA are up to something. Maybe at the base. So I said I would keep my eyes and ears open.'

'Well, if you need any help with anything, don't hesitate to ask.'

'Sure will.'

Elli and Orla joined them in the garden.

'Here you are!' Mathew smiled at his wife. 'Surely the house isn't that big?'

'Us girls had things to discuss, I'll thank you.' Elli took his hand, and Orla surprised Taylor by taking his hand too. He smiled at her.

'Everything OK?'

'You have a wonderful house, Ben.'

'Thank you,' he said, squeezing her fingers gently.

After dinner, Taylor's mother suggested he take Orla for a drive.

'Delamere Forest is nice this time of year; the colours up there are wonderful, and there are plenty of walks.' Then Taylor's father had an idea.

'If you do go to Delamere, go through Whitegate and past Oulton Park. Are you into motor racing, Orla?' Matthew asked her.

'Not really,' she said with a shy smile.

Elli gave her husband a smirk. 'He's got no idea,' she said to Taylor.

An hour later, Taylor and Orla were walking hand in hand through Delamere forest.

'This will have to be a short walk: we'll lose the light soon, the sun is falling fast behind the trees.'

'It's a lovely part of the country to live in, Ben. I've never been to Cheshire before.'

'I'm from Manchester originally, but my father came here for work.'

'Your parents are so nice; they've both made me feel at home.'

'Are you still glad you came?'

'More than ever, thank you.' She stopped walking and Taylor faced her. Orla took hold of his other hand. 'You're a nice man, Benjamin Taylor, even if you *are* a nuclear submariner.'

Taylor smiled at her. 'Don't spoil it.' He gave her a kiss on the cheek and they continued walking.

Next morning, Taylor woke up early and after showering went downstairs, where he heard his mother in the kitchen.

'Hi, Mum, did you sleep well?'

'Morning my lovely.' She gave him a hug. 'Yes, I slept well, thank you, even though your father snores like an ox.'

'How is he?'

'He's good at the moment, I think ... because I can't be sure: he doesn't give much away.'

'And how do *you* feel? Are you getting out much?'

'Yes, thank you. The garden keeps me busy and I have a new friend called Laura from the flower-arranging course I went on. We go shopping and have started to visit garden centres. There's a new one open out towards Church Minshull; they have a lovely lunch menu.'

'Oh good, I'm pleased. Can I help with anything here?' Taylor wanted to help his mother with making breakfast before the others got up.

'Course you can, my love; there's some unsliced bread in that cupboard that needs cutting, if you like.'

Taylor knew the routine. He took the bread knife from a draw and placed a wooden chopping block on the work surface. Elli had her back to him as she whisked eggs.

'Orla seems a very nice young lady, Benjamin.'

He knew she was fishing. 'Yes, she's very pleasant to be with.'

'I suppose it's too early for you to know if she's the one?'

'Yes, Mum, I've only known her a few weeks.'

'OK, I know, I'm not interfering … but you don't meet many girls, do you? You know, in your job.'

'Well that's true, but I'm going to take things slowly and if she is the one, then so be it. A good solid foundation is the making of any strong building.'

'That's very true, my love.' Elli gave him a quick eyebrow raise.

The house came alive as first Taylor's father then Orla came down for breakfast. Taylor loved his mother's breakfasts, they were so varied and healthy. After more conversation about the weather, gardening and past sailing trips along the southern coast of England, Orla turned to Elli.

'Can I help with the washing up of these pots, Elli?'

'No, certainly not, my love. You're my guest. Perhaps when you come next time,' she said, teasing Taylor.

Orla and Taylor gave each other a knowing look.

'Right, then, time to go sailing. Orla, you up for it?'

'I think so, but you'll have to show me the ropes, if you don't mind the pun.' Orla went upstairs and put on a bright summer dress that came down to her knees, and then joined them in garden.

'You look absolutely gorgeous my dear,' said Elli. She turned to her husband, who was pruning a rose bush. 'Doesn't she, Mathew?'

'She looks stunning,' he replied, stopping what he was doing. Taylor emerged into the garden wearing shorts and a t-shirt and carrying a small bag.

'Right, I'm ready,' said Taylor, catching the car keys his father threw to him. 'Thanks, Dad.' He gave his mum a kiss on the cheek. 'See you later.'

Taylor parked the car at his father's space by the yacht.

'She's beautiful,' Orla said before even getting out of the car.

'Wait till you see the interior – my dad's a perfectionist. She sails almost by herself,' he added. They climbed on the yacht via the shrouds holding up the main mast and Taylor opened the cabin saloon hatch.

'Put your bag down there, Orla. I'll get the sails ready and we can slip from the berth.'

'It looks like the weather is going to be nice,' Orla said with a smile, but Taylor noticed her nervousness.

'I'll show you where everything is and how it works before we leave the mooring. Don't worry, we're not going racing, take everything slowly. Like I said – she almost sails herself.' Taylor introduced Orla to the yacht, showing her the ropes she would need to control the sails. She was a fast learner. She watched Taylor as he carried out the pre-engine checks, started the engine, disconnected the gearbox and put on a few revs to get some charge into the batteries. He then showed Orla around the yacht. Moments later, with Taylor at the helm, Orla let the last mooring line go and they sailed off up the flash.

'The first thing you need to learn is how to helm.' Taylor was at the helm and Orla sat next to him in the cockpit. 'Come closer and put your hands on the tiller.'

Orla shuffled close to Taylor so their legs were touching. 'Feel how she catches the wind? Move the tiller slightly and you can almost let go. See: the sails are now balancing each other.'

Orla felt the power of the breeze as the sails filled, and it excited her. 'This is wonderful. Why have I not done this before?' she wondered.

Taylor shrugged and prepared to go about. 'OK, slightly tricky bit: you turn the boat, putting the bow through the wind, and keep going till she's facing down the flash. I'll tell you when … and Orla?'

'Yes, Ben?'

Taylor could see she was concentrating very hard. 'Do it slowly; I'll sort the sails out.' Taylor asked her to ready about.

'Yep,' came her unsure reply.

'Turn, lee-ho.'

Orla moved the tiller slowly and the yacht began to turn. She watched Taylor run around pulling on sheets; winches buzzed as he pulled and secured the ropes. And all of a sudden, without her knowing what had happened, they were sailing again in the opposite direction.

'Wow, this is exciting!' she shouted.

Ben noticed her hair flying over her shoulders, and the wind blew her dress upwards to reveal smooth thighs and a very slender waist. The yacht suddenly lurched and Taylor was flung across the deck. He scrambled to his feet and quickly grabbed the tiller with Orla still holding on to it.

'Too far, gorgeous.' He helped her pull the tiller back and the boat was under control again.

Orla saw what he had done and realised the fault, but mostly realised that he had called her gorgeous.

They sailed up and down the flash and perfected the turning of the boat.

Then Taylor showed her the different points of sailing; downwind with the wind behind them and beam reaches with the wind coming from the side of the yacht. Taylor turned the yacht into the wind; it heeled over and picked up speed, the weight of the keel keeping it upright. He turned the yacht further into the wind and the sails were close-hauled, now heeling right over. Taylor instructed Orla to move across to the windward rail to assist the balancing of the yacht.

'This is very exciting,' Orla shouted. Taylor noticed the broad smile on her face.

'You can make sailing as hard or as easy as you wish, Orla. It's different when you're racing, of course: you have to keep the yacht right on the edge.'

'Do you enjoy racing, Ben?'

'Yeah, my Dad and I used to do it a lot; not so much now he's getting on a bit. I also like doing this, though: just cruising up and down. It gives you a chance to see more on the banks and even in the water. It can be very relaxing.'

'I don't feel very relaxed,' she said with a smile.

'Don't worry, you'll get the hang of it.' He smiled back at her and their gazes stayed locked on each other for a long time.

They sailed right to the top of the flash, almost until they went aground on the muddy bottom, then turned. Taylor sat next to Orla at the helm and put his arm around her. She snuggled into him. They sat like this until the echo sounder bleeped and the water was shallow again.

'Why do they call it a "flash", Ben?'

'Because it's not a natural lake, and is mostly used for sailing on.'

'Oh … because of the collapsed salt mine?'

'Ah, you were paying attention, then.'

'I was just taking it all in; it's so beautiful here.'

'Shall we stop for lunch?'

'Yeah, sure … where?'

'Right here ...' Taylor left the helm to Orla. Let the sheets fly free. The yacht stopped in the water, the noise from the flapping sails disrupting the tranquillity from a moment ago. He then moved onto the fore-deck and let the anchor go. It plashed into the water, the chain and rope clanging on the metal plate protecting the deck. Orla sat and watched in amazement: he was so agile.

'Boy, it's so hot today,' he said, wiping his brow on the back of his hand.

She was about to say 'It's all that running around you've been doing,' when he removed his shirt and threw it into the cockpit. It landed at Orla's feet. Her heart began to beat so fast it nearly jumped out of her chest. She watched the muscles in his arms and chest flex as he pulled down the sails. Orla wiped her brow with the back of her hand. With the anchor now firmly holding the yacht, they descended into the cabin.

'You sit down. I'll prepare lunch.' He gestured to the long couch-like bench seat that ran down the starboard side of the cabin. Orla slid behind the beech wood table onto the light blue cushions. Taylor busied himself in the small galley preparing the ham, cheese and fresh bread they had bought from the marina chandlery. He finished the plates with salad and slid in beside Orla on the cushion.

'This looks amazing, thank you.'

'No problem. I thought it might be what we wanted on a hot day like today.'

Orla tasted the food and felt the warmth of his body as he sat near to her. 'What's it like at sea, Ben?'

'Oh, it's a great feeling. As soon as you can after leaving harbour, switch the stinkpot of an engine off; feel the boat heel under you as the wind picks up and the sails fill. Settle the boat down on her course and all is quiet ... you feel free. Look over your shoulder to catch the last glimpse of land disappear, and you're on your own. Your senses tune into nature; any change in wind strength or direction you pick up straight away. Check the sky for the coming weather, your body rolls with the waves and it all mixes in the pot and becomes one. Before you know it the light begins to fade; switch on your navigation lights and watch the sun sink into the watery horizon. One by one the stars come out, until you're in complete darkness and the sky is covered with millions of shimmering jewels. All you hear is the slapping of the bow wave and the cockpit has a red hew from the compass light. Everything is soft and rhythmic; it's hard to stay awake.'

Orla put down her knife and fork and turned to face him. Taylor stopped eating and looked at her. Her eyes locked into his and he felt time slow down. He reached his hand out towards her face and stroked her hair. Orla responded, leaning her face into his hand and wrapping her arms around his neck. She slowly pulled him closer, her slightly parted lips reaching out for his.

Finally their mouths met. Her fingers felt the muscles in his back tighten and Taylor pressed his lips firmly into hers. Orla moved one of her hands round to the front of his body and caressed his chest and stomach. Taylor ran his fingers through her hair and down the nape of her neck, slowly sliding the zip down on the back of her dress. Their mouths now open, they kissed feverishly. Taylor removed the straps from her shoulders and let the dress fall to the deck. He pushed her gently down on the cushion and removed the rest of his clothes.

CHAPTER TWENTY-EIGHT

Gallymore drove to the village, parked the car in the small central car park and telephoned for a taxi. He was travelling light and carried only a small overnight bag. The taxi arrived moments later and sped off in the direction of the airport, the driver having no idea of just how dangerous the passenger in the back was.

'Thank feck he's gone. Gallymore's a real psycho. I thought he was going to blow a fuse.' Andy jumped into his favourite chair.

'You don't know just how lucky you are to be alive!' McCann pointed his finger at Michael.

'Sorry, boss.'

'Sorry doesn't cut it, Michael. You could have got us all shot. When are you lot going to realise this is serious shit we're in, here. If we're lucky they'll shoot us. First they'll take off your kneecaps and hang them on the fecking fence out there.' McCann began pacing the room.

'Right, let's calm down!' shouted Sean from the couch.

McCann kicked the television and sent it off its stand.

'No, not the fecking TV!' Andy leaped from his chair and carefully inspected the screen.

McCann went upstairs, muttering more obscenities.

Andy slowly put the television back on its stand. 'We'd better check this,' he said to himself.

'All mad … all fecking mad …' uttered Mickey, shaking his head. 'This place is driving us all mad. McCann, get down here!' he shouted up the stairs.

All the others stood in silence at his outburst; even Andy stopped playing with the television as they waited to see what would happen next. McCann came down the stairs.

'What are we doing here? How long do we have to stay in this dump?' Mickey was staring crazily at McCann. 'Is Gallymore preparing another attack?'

McCann moved slowly over to the couch, rubbed his head and sat down heavily. 'Get me a drink will you, Michael?' Now calm again, he started thinking. 'OK, here's the deal: Gallymore has been to Libya and secured some funds for us – don't ask me how much, I don't know myself, you know how he is. All I know is, it's a large amount. Now he's going to America to buy some … again, all I know is it's going to be good for the cause. We, in the meantime, must get on and prepare these explosives so on his return we're ready to go into action.'

'And when is he coming back?' asked Mickey.

'He's got to do a recky first. So if he sees an opening it'll take a week. Or, if it's going to be difficult … blahdy-blah, it will be longer.'

'So in the meantime we stay here.' Andy pushed his index fingers into the arms of his chair.

'Exactly.' McCann spoke right back at him.

'Then let's go downtown; you lot can have a drink and I'll bone that barmaid in the pub.'

McCann drew his .38 calibre revolver, pointed it at Andy's head and pulled back the hammer.

'Not even funny,' Andy said slowly. He raised his hands, slowly slid off his chair and crawled across the floor to the television.

Gallymore flew with a false passport in economy class from Dublin to Paris. He then went by coach to Amsterdam, where he continued his journey first class with KLM using a second false passport, on his way to Los Angeles. During the flight he planned his next seven days, and thought through the general steps he would take, the more intimate details he would have to do once he was there. He had told McCann he would be away for one week but knew it might take longer. He also knew that without him there, McCann would not be able to control the four men back at the farm, and knew eventually they would be found – it was inevitable. They were expendable; he had no feelings for them. They would die for a good cause. Thirteen hours later he landed at Los Angeles International Airport. He told the immigration man he was there for a holiday, and after the usual suspicious look, the man passed him through. The address Gaddafi had given him as he left the desert camp took him to the outskirts of Los Angeles. Thankfully the taxi driver knew exactly where it was.
'The stink from this place sends me nauseous … people have petitioned to get it closed down but I guess someone is making a lot of money here.' The driver complained throughout the trip. Gallymore hardly spoke.

He was dropped off outside what looked like a huge chemical plant, with large steel tanks and pipework running from towers high in the sky to outhouses and buildings. The taxi driver was right: someone had invested a lot of money here. Gallymore entered what he imagined to be the main building; inside he found a secretary in a small office. She beamed a smile at him as he spoke.

'Sorry to disturb you … I'm looking for a Chris.' All he had was a name. The secretary took him to another slightly larger office.

'Come in, I'm Chris.'

'The name's Gallymore.'

'Take a seat. So, what can I do for you, Mister Gallymore?'

'I was given your address by a mutual colleague in Libya. Our friend said you might be able to help me.' Gallymore took an instant dislike to this man.

'Well, firstly, I don't know anyone in … where did you say? Libya?' He sat back in his chair with a smug grin on his face.

Gallymore noticed a distinct, pungent odour coming through an open window. He decided to take a different tack. 'Maybe I have the wrong address?' Gallymore handed him the piece of paper Gaddafi had given him.

Chris looked at it and threw it nonchalantly on his desk. 'Sorry you've come all this way for nothing, Mister Gallymore.' Another grin, displaying perfectly straight, white teeth.

'Well, that's a shame; because if you were the right man that I was looking for, I could make your bank account a lot heavier.'

Gallymore saw Chris's left eye flicker and realised he had found his weakness. 'What is it you make here, Chris?' Gallymore smiled back and watched Chris trying to think quickly.

'We're a pioneering chemical plant. We primarily prepare the raw materials ethylene and propylene to make monomers for the manufacture of plastics.

Alongside this and as a subsidiary operation, we use chemicals to make ammonia. Have you heard of the Haber process?' Gallymore shook his head. 'Well, it's a process of using hydrogen and nitrogen to make ammonia. This we then use to make fertiliser and cleaning products. Our best clients are the pool-cleaning companies.'

Gallymore realised he was getting a well-rehearsed spiel, probably used against all the protesters this idiot would have come across. He had had enough of the crap.

'I'm a leader of an army of soldiers trying to free Ireland from the torment of political, cultural and religious dictatorship.' He stared directly into Chris's eyes. 'Colonel Gaddafi is a good friend of mine and would be upset if you weren't helpful to my cause.' Gallymore watched as this outburst startled Chris. He decided to press on. 'What I need is a chemical munition that can be detonated from a long distance, or perhaps on a timer.' The room fell silent.

Chris scratched his head, the smile gone. 'To make what you require would be an easy process, but unfortunately it's not something I can do for you. If you had come to me directly I would have considered it, but for Gaddafi, there's no chance.'

'Why is that?'

'In my opinion Gaddafi is on his way out, and if you had any sense you wouldn't have anything to do with him. When he goes down he'll take a lot of people with him and I don't plan on being in that number.

The Americans know a lot more about his whereabouts and his movements than they're letting on to the national and international news media. They have agents deep within his organisation and are moments away from taking him down. I have severed all ties with him and his people. Do yourself a favour and stay well clear of him.'

'And no amount of money would change your mind?'

'That's right.'

Gallymore left without saying goodbye.

A taxi drove him down Interstate 5 at a steady fifty-file miles per hour, and an hour later it pulled up outside the Holiday Inn on Rosecrans Street. He checked in, went to his room and immediately fell asleep. When Gallymore awoke, he opened the window slightly for some fresh air. The blast of heat from outside made him close it again. Although the room was air-conditioned, it wasn't long before he had to open the little fridge that had been filled to the brim with drinks. He wanted something stronger but for now a cool glass of Coke would have to do. He settled down in a chair and spread a detailed map of San Diego in front of him. He had half-emptied the fridge before the germination of a plan came to him.

Gallymore slipped on a light jacket and stepped from the cool hotel into the searing heat of the street.

He turned left and walked down Rosecrans for five minutes, stopping now and then to peer into shop windows and check if he was being followed. Half an hour later he was glad to walk into the cool bar. The barmaid was a sweet little thing who seemed genuinely glad to serve him. It wasn't long before two men joined him at the bar.

'Gallymore?' one of them enquired. He wore a bandana and looked like he had just stepped off a motorcycle. The other was in similar attire except for the bandana, but had a moustache that nauseated Gallymore. He checked them out before answering.

'Guys … pleased to make your acquaintance.' He shook both their hands. 'Get you a drink?'

'Sure.' They both looked thirsty.

The sweet little thing came over. 'My name is Pam, can I get you three a pitcher?' she asked with a smile, placing napkins in front of them.

They just nodded.

'Shall we move to a table?' Gallymore said.

All three men moved from the bar.

'It's great to meet you, sir. We've been supporting the cause for some years now,' said Bandana.

'Raised a shitload of money, too,' added Moustache.

Gallymore showed no interested in the two bikers' history. He leaned back in his chair. 'So, what can you tell me about the University of San Diego Health at La Jolla?'

'We both studied there.'

Yeah, and I went to Oxford, thought Gallymore.

'What do you want know, Mister Gallymore?'

'Everything. General layout? What security they have? Any passes that I'll need? That sort of thing ...'

'OK, so you want entry, yeah?'

These guys are going to be hard work. Why do I always have to deal with fecking idiots? Gallymore gritted his teeth.

'It's a good bet that at some stage I will want to gain access, yes.' He moved his eyes from one man to the other to gauge their reaction. 'And depending if they have what I want, I'll need access out of hours as well.'

'OK, can be done, can be done ...' Bandana was obviously the leader of this duo. 'What is it you're looking for, Mister Gallymore?'

'I've been reliably informed that they carry out tests on viruses, and at the moment are conducting trials with a particular virus call Ebola.'

'Ah, I see. Well, there we have a problem. You see, we were in a different department and have no knowledge of the uh … science laboratory section.'

'Know anyone who does?' Gallymore was drinking his beer faster than he usually did.

The two bikers looked at each other for a while, thinking.

'Actually, there's a friend of ours whose girlfriend works in the lab. Maybe he would know?'

'Is he a member of our club?'

'No, but he's cool, man.'

'Can you take me to him? I'd sure like to meet him, and soon. I don't have a lot of time over here, you know; got to get back and fight.' He made a fist.

'Yeah, no problem. We'll take you right now. Buck has a spare helmet.' Gallymore nearly choked on his beer but managed to hide is emotion. *Buck!* Gallymore climbed on the back of the Harley-Davidson and they sped off. After a short trip up 94 they pulled into a driveway somewhere in La Mesa. Buck kicked down the stand and Gallymore jumped off. He was introduced to spectacled young man called Stefan. Gallymore put on a posh voice.

'Hello, Stefan, my name is Gallymore. I'm from Oxford University in England and I was wondering if your girlfriend – or you, for that matter – could talk a while about the Ebola virus. You see, I'm preparing a thesis on rare diseases and need all the help I can get.'

'We'll, it's a long way to come, but sure, no problem; my girlfriend isn't here at the moment but she's worked at the UC San Diego for four years now. She's involved at the moment in a very delicate project, looking into the symptoms of Ebola, and through that she hopes to find a cure – or at least, a vaccine that will slow the process. D'you know, it's a very contagious virus that destroys human organs.' Gallymore nodded. 'She's been working with other countries to establish its origin and I think she said it's from Zaire in Africa.'

'You seem to know a lot about it?'

'Yeah, she tells me everything.'

'What part of the university does she … sorry, what's your girlfriends name, Stefan?'

'Julie.'

'Julie, right. What part of the university does Julie actually work in, Stefan?'

'Well, as I said, she's worked there for some time, and they move her about quite a lot, but right now she's in a special area on the campus called ... now what is it ... the Altman Clinical and Translational Research Institute, at the moment supporting the Infectious Virus Unit. Yeah, that's it: IVU.'

Gallymore looked at the two bikers and raised his eyebrows. They nodded back.

'And presumably the security is quite tight in the IVU?' asked Gallymore.

'Oh, yes. The whole campus is. Julie's always complaining about the time it takes to clear through the guards and sensors ... people checking her handbag and body searches. It probably only takes a few minutes but she's always complaining.'

'What about passes? Does she have a special pass to get in?'

'Two, actually. She forgot one once when she changed her coveralls and had to come all the way home to get it. She was fuming ... that was *not* a good day, I'll tell you ...'

'Is this her here?' Gallymore picked up a framed photograph off the table.

'Sure is; that was taken a month ago when we went to Disneyland.'

Gallymore told him he'd been a great help and had all the information he wanted. He thanked him for his time and said his goodbyes to Stefan.

Back at his hotel on Rosencrans, Gallymore climbed off the Harley and signalled the bikers to switch off. Once the roar of the engines had subsided he addressed them:

'I need detailed drawings of the university, especially the Altman Clinic and IVU. I need …' He thought for a moment. 'Can you get me two passes to clear the security guards, and I'll need one of those lab coats.' And as an afterthought: 'Oh, and a pair of those clear-glass, thick-rimmed spectacles.'

'Sure thing, boss, leave it to us.' The three men talked for a while longer about Irish history and then Gallymore grew tired of them. They said they would be in touch soon. The two men flashed up the bikes and roared out of the parking lot.

Fecking idiots, he thought.

CHAPTER TWENTY-NINE

The atmosphere in the room was heavy; all four men were smoking long cigarettes. The tall man with a scar on his face spoke first.

'Frank is back from Mullingar, I spoke to him last night,' he told his smartly dressed colleague.

'I hope he had something interesting to say. I'm getting a lot of grief for this little fiasco.'

'He found this big guy, a stranger buying food from the village store, quite easily. He goes there every couple of days … he's also buying for more than one person. Frank followed him back to a farmhouse just outside the town. He monitored the house for a week. The mailman is coming and going normally, some large deliveries have been arriving, but it's only the big guy who goes to the store. There are, however, five men in total staying there. They're very sloppy, though: he had no problem in photographing them through the windows.' He placed a spread of photographs across the table. The smartly dressed man looked at each one in turn before passing them around the table.

'Who are we looking at here?' he asked the scarred man.

'They're all small-time crooks, apart from this one here: he's Shamus McCann.'

'Shamus … I grew up with his father.'

'He splintered about the same time as Gallymore, and has probably become Gallymore's right-hand man.'

'Is there any sign of Gallymore?'

'No, he's nowhere to be seen.'

The smartly dressed man thumped the photographs onto the table. 'Bastard, where is he?' The room became quiet for a long period while he thought. 'Who are these clowns?' He pointed at the photographs in front of him.

'Michael Kelly, from Belfast ... done a bit of driving for us about five years ago. Michael Mullen, also from Belfast ... had a safe house for us in the early seventies. Sean O'Brean ... I'm not sure where he was born but he held an arms store for us before it was raided by the British Army, and he spent three years in HM Prison Maze, NI. The last one is Andy McDowell, and I've got nothing on him at all.'

'Was Frank seen?'

'No. They're so sloppy, boss, it was an easy surveillance for him. Even followed them to a pub in town.'

There followed another period of quiet, this time longer than the first. The smartly dressed man stood up and paced the room.

'So, there can be no mistake, it's them?'

'None whatsoever.'

'What mail are they getting?'

The scarred man became nervous and fidgeted in his seat. His face went slightly pink, which made his scar more prominent.

'Frank only got back last night; I didn't ask him about it. I didn't think it was important.'

'Don't worry. This is what I want you to do. Get me more info on these scumbags. I want to know what mail is going into that house, and most important ... most important, do you hear me ... I don't want them to know we're onto them.'

He picked up the photographs from the table. 'If you see Gallymore, let me know straight away.'

'OK, boss, leave it to me.'

CHAPTER THIRTY

Orla woke from a deep sleep. She could smell his aftershave. Her head was on Taylor's shoulder and she was surprised how long she had slept.

'Where are we?' She raised her head and looked out the window.

'Carlisle. The train's just splitting; it doesn't usually take too long.' He was talking from a long time of experience travelling this journey. 'We should be in Glasgow Central before 9 p.m. and we can jump in a taxi; I won't make you walk again all the way to Queen Street.'

'I don't mind, it was quite nice to stretch my legs.'

'Well, we don't have a lot of time to spare before the last train leaves for Helensburgh, and I promised your mum I would get you home tonight.'

'I was hoping we might stay in a hotel tonight.' Orla put her arm on Taylor's chest and looked deeply into his eyes. She saw the panic start to rise and his cheeks redden slightly. 'It's OK, don't panic, I'm only joking.' She patted him on the chest. *Damn it! Oh God, what am I saying, if he'd asked me, I would have said yes straight away. Perhaps Liam was right. Am I desperate?*

They held hands tightly as they departed the train at Glasgow. They crossed quickly to Glasgow Queen Street and jumped on the last train to Helensburgh. They were now both feeling tired, the conversation was on when they would go sailing again. He said he had seen a poster advertising sailing on Loch Lomond, so they agreed to investigate.

Taylor's mind shifted to America, and he hoped all went well so he could get back to her.

The train stopped at Helensburgh; Taylor and Orla stepped out into the cold night air huddled together. They walked past all the noisy bars and Taylor was happy to get a taxi without being noticed by any of his crewmates. They sped away towards the base in relief, and suddenly Taylor felt the need to be with her.

'Did you have a nice time?'

'It was great, Ben; I can't remember when I enjoyed myself so much.'

'So, we're going sailing when I get back from America?'

'Yes, I would love to.'

The taxi pulled up to the kerb at the peace camp. They ran across the road after Taylor let the taxi go.

'How are you getting back from here?' she asked him.

'I'll walk, it's not far.'

'I would love to invite you inside but I think my mam will be asleep by now.'

'That's OK, I've got a lot to do before tomorrow.' Taylor held her close, and when she smiled up at him he squeezed her tightly. They held each other not talking for a long time, until finally Taylor loosened his grip and kissed her full on the lips. She kissed him back, passionately. The kiss ended when they heard a noise from inside the caravan and a light come on.

'I'd better go in,' she said, trembling.

'I'll see you soon.'

'You better had. I know where you live!' She smiled and moved towards the caravan.

'Orla,' he said quietly. She turned to face him. Taylor didn't say anything; he just looked at her and smiled, and she knowingly smiled back. Then he turned and walked thoughtfully back to the naval base.

Taylor slept fitfully in his cabin and woke early. Tim was waiting for Taylor when he came down to the foyer.

'Tadpole, I didn't expect to see you.'

'You're going to San Diego today; I wanted to see you before you went.'

Taylor ushered him towards the bar. 'I was heading down to the boat; come in here, I'll get us some coffee.' The sun shone through the large windows of the empty bar, casting shards of light over the tables. Taylor went behind the counter. Moments later he appeared with two cups of coffee. Tim was seated near one of the windows, and Taylor noticed he looked agitated. A steward came through the door carrying bar towels and cleaning cloths. Taylor asked him to give them a minute.

'Sure thing, Chief.' He left the room and headed back to the office.

Tim was staring out the window, at nothing in particular. 'We have a good rapport, you and I, wouldn't you say?' Tim's eyes came back into the room but he didn't look at Taylor.

'I have a good respect for all you "leathernecks." ' Taylor took a sip from his cup.

'Almost like I can read your mind ...' There was a pause. Both men now looked at each other.

'Although,' Taylor continued, 'since the course, I'm not sure what you've been up to.'

'But you still trust me?'

'With my life.' It was now Taylor's turn to look anxious. There was a short pause as Tim looked directly at Taylor.

'You know I've had some arguments with my father, and it became clear to me at an early age that he was trying to manipulate me, steer me down the same route he had taken in the Army.'

'To become an officer, you mean.'

'Yes, but more than that: it was almost like a controlling thing. He wanted to start his life again, correct all the mistakes he had made ... he wanted me to be the younger version of him.'

'And when did you realise this?'

'In my early teens, I suppose. As soon as I came home from school he was on my case. Analysing my day, telling me what I should have done, what I should have said ... who I should be talking to, and who not to talk to.'

'And that's why you joined the Navy, I know …'

'I joined the Navy because I knew it would upset him. Break the hold he had on me. If I had joined the Army he would have had me watched, pulled strings to get me where he wanted to me to be – where *he* wanted to be.'

'And was it the right decision?'

'That's the big question.'

'You definitely chose the more difficult route for yourself. Most people would love to have a father that could get them to high places fast without too much effort.'

'That's exactly it, Ben. I want to do it myself. I don't want other people making my decisions for me. I want to make my own mistakes … well, not … you know what I mean.'

'It's a difficult life we lead in any of the services, Tadpole. We have to make not only difficult decisions in a military sense but decisions that affect our home life, our other life. Sometimes it's like choosing between family and the job: which comes first? And we have to block out one of them … you can't have both, not in our line of work. We're on the front line, my friend, and you have to deal with it.' Taylor drew a deep breath. 'Do you want another coffee?'

Tim didn't answer straight away. 'Uh, yeah, go on then.'

Taylor disappeared around the counter again for a few minutes. When he came back Tim looked more at ease; his facial expression had become more composed.

'Now, tell me more about the Intelligence Corps.' Taylor placed the hot coffee in front of his friend.

'It's like we don't exist – not in the real world anyway. Collecting, processing and collating information just to gain the upper hand … trying to be constantly one step ahead of the enemy. We're at war. Most of the time we work alone and we can't tell anyone, can't discuss things with … well, people like you. And I like our talks – it gives a different perspective, someone with other than your own outlook on things.'

'It doesn't involve shooting people or getting your hands dirty?'

'No, that's left to people like the SAS or the Special Boat Service.'

'I think you've turned down the wrong road, buddy. You may want to consider a U-turn, get yourself back on track.' Taylor changed the subject drastically. 'When was the last time you went home?'

Tim shrugged his shoulders and fidgeted in his seat.

'I'll bet your mum will be pleased to see you.'

Tim sat for a while and looked out the window. 'Maybe, after I've sorted this IRA thing out.' Tim scratched his head and rubbed his eyes.

'Where are we with that?' Taylor probed.

'Well, just between you and me, I can tell you that our friend in charge of the splinter group, Gallymore, has been to see Gaddafi. We're not sure if it's money, guns or explosives he's after, but whatever it is, it's big.'

'I see.' Taylor shuffled in his chair. 'What else?'

'That's it, the trail has gone cold again … but I still need your help.'

'*Semper fidelis*,' Taylor said as he shook his friend's hand.

CHAPTER THIRTY-ONE

The RAF air station at Brize Norton in Oxfordshire was characteristically sparse with passengers but bustling with cargo and supplies being dispatched to UK military bases around the world. The three-man team from HMS/M *Covert* did not have to wait long in the departure lounge before walking onto the USAF Boeing C-17 Globemaster on its way back home.

While flying over the Atlantic the commanding officer handed Taylor a small folder. Inside he found information on the Point Loma US submarine base. The first thing Taylor noticed was that all the pages were in colour and very professionally presented; it must have cost a small fortune to have these printed. Taylor then turned his attention to the details and read the print on the elaborate pages: 'Welcome to the Navy's finest submarine base. Located in beautiful sunny San Diego, California, at the mouth of San Diego Harbour ...' Taylor thought right then that he had joined the wrong Navy. It went on to list all the different commands, squadrons and training that are stationed at the base. All in glossy brochure format. Taylor glanced across at his CO, who was smiling at him.

'Pretty impressive isn't it?'

Taylor raised his eyebrows and carried on reading. 'The base comprises 316 acres of beautiful but rugged coastline, although the main facilities are located on approximately 30 acres of relatively flat land.'

Other sheets of paper contained information on how to get to the base – if arriving by air, personnel vehicle or by bus. A whole page was devoted to important and useful telephone numbers. Finally, it listed 'things to see and do while in San Diego', along with maps of the base and San Diego City. *All in all*, he thought, *a pretty impressive package.* Taylor slept for most of the remainder of the flight.

They landed at Miramar Marine Corps Air Station in San Diego and were met by an extremely well-groomed American sailor who came straight over, saluted all three of them while he approached and saluted again every time he was spoken to. The captain of HMS/M *Covert*, Commander Peter Coleman, put him at ease and promptly stopped him from saluting. The sailor eventually calmed down and they left the airport in what can only be described as a large vehicle. Taylor sat in the front with the young sailor and began chatting. His name was Steven, and he was from New York. Taylor explained to him that he was a senior rate and not a commissioned officer, and therefore did not warrant a salute. Taylor thought he saw a blush, and hoped he had not embarrassed the young sailor too much.

They drove for a short while down Pacific Coast Highway and turned onto Barnett Avenue, which becomes Lytton Street. At an intersection, Steven turned onto Rosecrans Street and eventually pulled up outside the Holiday Inn hotel. Three different rooms had been booked for them. After unpacking, they met in the bar.

'Tomorrow morning we'll be picked up outside the hotel at 0800 hours.

We'll be taken to the base, which is only five miles down this road.' Commander Coleman went through the programme, which Taylor and Lieutenant Alistair Duncan both had a copy of in front of them. 'Tomorrow we're all due to meet the base commanding officer first, then we'll split. Alistair, you'll come with me to meet the base technical facilities officer, while Ben you go straight to the Diving Section. It's very unlikely that we'll all finish at the same time, although I don't envisage us working too late. Therefore, I propose we meet up here for our evening meal tomorrow at 1900 hours to discuss how the day unfolded. This will probably mean that you'll have to make your own way back here tomorrow, Ben – will you be OK?'

'I'll be fine, boss,'

'Good, that's that settled then. Alistair, go and get the drinks in.'

Lieutenant Duncan went to the bar without questioning his commanding officer. When the diving officer was out of earshot, Peter Coleman leaned over to Taylor.

'You have to keep these young officers in their place, you know.' The Peter Coleman seemed to grow physically as he sat back in his chair and looked around the bar.

The next day they met in the entrance foyer after breakfast. The heat was almost overpowering: it dried the back of Taylor's throat as soon as he walked through the main door and breathed in the outside air. Inside the hotel lobby the air conditioning had kept the temperature cool, so Taylor wasn't quite ready for the difference in temperature, and it seemed very strange to walk from cool air inside into warm air outside. The official car took the three of them the few miles from the hotel to the naval base at Point Loma. The sentries at the main gate saluted the car as they passed through. The driver deposited Commander Coleman and Lieutenant Duncan outside the main office building, saluting them as they left the car. The US base commander greeted Commander Coleman, whom he had met before at a dinner at Admiralty House in London. Commander Coleman introduced him to his two colleagues and apologised for Chief Taylor's departure to the Diving Section.

Taylor jumped back into the car outside and was driven slowly through the massive naval base to the Diving Section. It was difficult to take in the vastness of this base. Walking was not an option here – you needed transport everywhere you went. The driver saluted him as he left the car.

Taylor thought about telling him he didn't warrant a salute, but decided it would take too long, and the Americans would salute him anyway. He found himself standing outside a huge building with double roller doors for its front. Also out front where displays of the explosive ordinance that the team had obviously disposed of. Newly painted torpedo and shell cases, there were airdropped shells from aircraft of all nations. Taylor was puzzled as he recognised a Russian-made two-hundred-pound blast bomb. He walked through a small door at the side and was glad to get out of the heat.

The interior reminded him of an aircraft hangar. Pipes were strewn around the walls, ending at workbenches that housed diving sets, and three heavy vehicles where parked in the centre of the floor. At the far end of the building there was a large tank with glass windows spaced around the outside, allowing a view inside. A shadow caught Taylor's eye.

'Hi there, can I help?'

The voice came from Taylor's side: a small man had appeared from nowhere. He was looking at Taylor's uniform and lapel badges, and Taylor deduced that he didn't know what or whom he was looking at.

'Hello, my name is Ben – Ben Taylor.' Taylor held out his hand, and it was received with a firm grip from the other man.

'Pleased to meet you, uh, Mister Taylor. I'm sorry, sir, I'm not familiar with your rank.'

'Then it's me who should apologise. 'I'm Chief Petty Officer Taylor from the Royal Navy. I'm also an underwater ordinance clearance diver, for which I hold the rank of First Class. I'm here to see Chief Master Diver Speed.' Taylor was careful to get his wording of the rank correct in this new environment, wanting to make a good impression.

'Ah, yes. I'm sorry. Glad to meet you, Chief, I was told you'd be arriving sometime today, but you caught me off guard. I'm Petty Officer Paine, but everyone calls me Sid. Very pleased to meet you, Chief,' he repeated, then held out his hand. Taylor shook his firm grip. 'Come, I'll take you to his office.'

Taylor held off relaxing formal names until he got to know Sid. He followed him up a flight of stairs and along a corridor. Sid knocked on a solid oak door with Chief Master Diver Speed's name on a brass plate, under which there was another brass plate that read 'San Diego Diving Team'. Sid was summoned to enter and he walked in.

'Master Diver, I've charged the main banks of air, and the recompression chamber has been tested with no faults found.' Taylor followed him into the large office. 'And I found Chief Petty Officer Taylor from the Royal Navy, who I believe you're expecting.' Sid smiled at Taylor. 'I'll catch up with you later, buddy.'

Taylor raised his eyebrows and then smiled at Sid.

Chief Speed came from behind his large desk with a huge smile on his face and held out his hand ready to shake Taylor's.

'On behalf of all the diving team here, I welcome you to San Diego and the United States.' He stood well over six feet and had two patches of hair on either side of his head, which Taylor deduced was all that remained of what must have been once a full head of shocking red hair. He also sported an abundance of freckles dotted round his face and neck and even the back of his two enormous hands. He shook Taylor's hand. 'Please, have a seat.' He ushered Taylor to a comfortable leather chair in front of his desk. 'Can I offer you anything?'

Taylor shook his head. 'I'm fine, thank you; not long had my breakfast, Chief.'

The two men made themselves comfortable.

'Well, let me introduce myself. I'm Chief Master Diver Speed, but most people call me "Speedy". I've been a diver for over thirty-two years and seen action in Guatemala, Suez and most of the Pacific, and been here in San Diego for ... gosh, it must be around nine years now ... and it's probably going to be my last job.'

'This is quite an impressive office, Chief.' Taylor looked at all the diving memorabilia that was hanging on the walls and displayed around the room.

'Please, call me "Speedy", we're quite a relaxed diving team here. My boss is Lieutenant Commander "Butch" DuPont; he's a great guy. His office is down the hall, I'll introduce you later. He had a lot to do with the early stages of development of the DSRV[10] for submarine escape. Which, if you didn't already know, is docked just five hundred yards from the section, and can be attached to a nuclear submarine and transported anywhere in the world. I'll get one of the team to show you round if you want.'

'I'd be very interested in taking a look at it. Obviously I was instructed on its use during my initial submarine training, but it would be very useful to see it up close.'

'Sure, no problem; but the main reason you're here is for the update on the rebreather set we have. So we'd better get that done first. I've organised the next two days for you to spend time learning about it: tomorrow will be in the work shop; we'll go through preparation and maintenance, and then on to assembly and pre-dive tests ... then hopefully on the second day

---

[10] Deep Sea Rescue Vessel.

you can have a dive in it, if that's OK with you?'

'That's fine with me, Speedy; it'll be a pleasure to dive in such warm, clear water. Oh, and my name is Ben.'

'OK, Ben, if you're sure you don't need anything else?' Taylor shook his head. 'Then let me show you round our little establishment.'

When Speedy stood up, Taylor noticed how cleanly pressed his uniform was. You could have cut your finger on the sharp creases in his trousers, and his shirt had more badges sewn into it than a Boy Scout. Speedy seemed to take great delight in showing off his "toys" to the Englishman. The layout of the Diving Section had been well thought out, with easy access to all areas. Everything was big, as expected. The compressors were hidden and well insulated out the back, which made the maintenance prep rooms quiet and clean. The garage housed what seemed to be a vehicle for every occasion. Two large roller doors opened to reveal the habitable recompression chambers, with easy access to locate and secure the smaller transportable chambers onto them. Everything was provided for, and in a lot of cases a backup was in place. No expense had been spared, and Taylor felt a little envious – back in the UK, everything had a budget, and guidelines were set in stone with no extra money available for niceties. *The 'make do' attitude of the British is still the normal way we work*, Taylor thought.

The tour stopped at around 1200 hours and Speedy drove Taylor to lunch in a V8 Dodge flatbed that would be too wide for most British roads. The dining hall was busy.

High ceilings were covered with slow-moving large-bladed fans. Senior unlisted male and female ranks ate in the same hall. Speedy and Taylor chose burgers from the self-service counter and sat in a small booth. Taylor would have preferred tea but chose the safe option of coffee.

'This afternoon I'll show you round the base before we head back to the office to meet the CO.' Taylor was happy for Speedy to take control; he was too engrossed in absorbing all the information and different aspects of this base. When they climbed back into the Dodge, the temperature outside was soaring.

'Wow, now it's getting hot!' Taylor exclaimed.

'Yeah ... it'll reach the high nineties before the day's out,' Speedy replied with a smile, and turned on the air-con.

'Speedy, tell me how it all started – what's the history of this base?'

'The history of Point Loma goes way back. Native Americans lived here over seven thousand years ago. The Spanish built a fort here in the late 1790s because the peninsula formed a natural guard to the bay. It was covered with smooth stones originally and these were used as ballast on wooden sailing ships, and so it got its name of "Ballast Point".

In the mid-1850s the southern part was taken over by the Army and given the name 'Fort Rosecrans' after General Rosecrans.

The Navy took over the fort in 1959. It took a while for the submarine support facilities to be built, and around the late sixties/early seventies it became home to Submarine Group 5, Sub Squadron 3,

Submarine Development Group 1, Submarine Squadron 11 and also the submarine training facility. Defence cuts and budgeting in 1998 consolidated the base into what it is now: Naval Base Point Loma.' Speedy was clearly happy giving this history lesson as he slowly drove around the base pointing things out. 'It's now home to Commander 3rd Fleet, Space and Naval Warfare Systems, the Fleet Anti-Submarine Warfare Training Centre and the Fleet Intelligence Training Centre Pacific. And there we have the Fleet Combat Training Centre Pacific, Comsubron 11, Comsubdevron 11, Comsubdevron 5 ...' Taylor had no idea what the abbreviations stood for but let him carry on. '... Military Sealift Command and Submarine Training Centre Pacific.' Speedy went quiet as he drove down to one of the waterfront quay areas. 'There are six submarines and the floating dock. Over there is the DSRV unit; that will be moved alongside soon, after undergoing some updates. I believe you now have the NATO ring that will allow us to couple onto your submarines?' Speedy asked.

'Yes we have, and not too soon. Every new option of escaping from a stricken submarine is a big bonus in my book.'

'And just up there is our very own Diving Section, which you've already seen. The enlisted men's club is over there, and our mess is on the other side of that building there, which houses the Navy's Substance Abuse and Rehabilitation Department.

Unfortunately a part of life wherever you go these days. Although I think it's not as big a deal in the UK as it is over here?'

'Well, some people wouldn't agree with you. There are some areas where it's more common than others, but certainly not as big a problem in the Armed Services as you have. Maybe due to the amount of people we have ...' Taylor changed the subject. 'Obviously, San Diego is a Spanish name?'

'The Spanish were trading here from Mexico and the Orient, and in 1602 a Spanish trader called Sebastian Vizcaino renamed it in honour of San Diego de Alcala, who was a Franciscan lay brother.'

'And just how big is this base?'

'Total area covers about three hundred and sixteen acres ... but most of the buildings are on the flat bit, about thirty acres.' Speedy drove on. 'This area here is designated for recreation. We have the fitness centre, library, swimming pool, all types of sports fields ... All the facilities are open to servicemen and their families – even the local civilians are encouraged to come and use them, and we hold tournaments and competitions here at all skill levels. You can get tickets to museums, cinemas, art galleries, movie studios, amusement parks and biking trails in San Diego, and there are even bus trips to Los Angeles. Car hire and motor home hire is reserved for service personnel.'

'Sounds like a great place to be stationed – you want for nothing.'

'Oh it is, I love it here. You can be in Mexico in minutes and up in the mountains the next. The best thing is the sailing, though: I have a yacht in the harbour at Coronado.' Taylor was truly impressed. 'Right that's the whistle-stop tour of the base; let's get you back to meet the boss.'

Speedy drove back to the Diving Section and parked in the hangar garage.

Lieutenant Commander 'Butch' DuPont stood up immediately when Taylor entered his office. He was another tall man, over six feet tall, with a lean athletic body, but unlike Speedy he had a full head of dark hair. His face showed the marks of stress and his eyes were sunken, made to look even darker by the prominent brows. He shook Taylor's hand firmly.

'Pleased to meet you, Chief; come in, sit down. Let's talk. I'm sure the master diver has given you a tour by now and told you how we work. Please call me "Butch", by the way – unless we're in the company of other officers, then I'm afraid we'll have to go all formal. Are you OK with that? I know some senior rates prefer to keep it formal all the time.'

'That's fine with me, sir.' Taylor threw caution to the wind: 'My name is Ben.'

'We don't stand on ceremony round here, I find it helps to be relaxed, and as long as the job gets done and no one oversteps the mark, we get along just fine.'

Taylor thought that it wouldn't be a good idea to overstep the mark with this man.

'Now, can I get you anything, Ben?' Butch enquired as he sat back down in his leather chair behind a huge desk.

'Coffee would be nice, thank you, Butch.'

'Sure thing.' DuPont pressed an intercom button on his desk and ordered two coffees from somewhere. 'Now, tell me all about yourself, and lay it on thick: I want to be impressed.'

Taylor went through his RN history and explained what he wanted to gain from his visit to San Diego. He thought a little smoke-blowing wouldn't hurt, and told Butch he'd already seen a lot of good ideas that he planned to instigate when back in the UK.

'Well, what you've seen so far is just the tip – tomorrow we can fulfil one of your goals by asking you to dive with one of our guys to inspect the seabed before we move the DSRV into a berth off the Section here.' Butch stood up quickly and looked out the window. When Taylor joined him he pointed to a vacant jetty not far from the Diving Section. 'A simple dive, just to make sure there are no large objects on the seabed there that could cause damage to the DSRV should we sit it on the bottom.'

'What depth have you got there, Butch?'

'I'll detail one of the guys to show you round the set with the new modification and pre-dive check it. So you'll be going in on a rising tide by late morning, which will give you a depth of around forty feet, but Speedy will measure it accurately before you go in.'

Taylor noticed that Butch was becoming slightly more agitated and was beginning to shuffle papers into order on his desk.

'Well, thank you, Butch. What time do we start?'

'Uh ...' He seemed distracted by something. 'The best thing to do is ... I think I'll call Sid up here and he can arrange everything you need for tomorrow. Sorry, I've an important meeting with the experimental people in ten minutes, I'd love to spend more time with you but it's something I can't get out of.'

'That's all right by me, I understand. You must have a very demanding job to do here.'

'I have many hats to wear, that's for sure. OK then, I'll spend more time with you tomorrow on the dive site.'

The two men stood and shook hands again, and Butch followed Taylor to the door. Outside stood a sailor in a pristine black well-pressed tracksuit emblazoned with the San Diego Diving Team emblem on the left breast. Taylor recognised the smiling face of Sid.

'Right then, I'll leave you in the capable hands of Petty Officer Paine here; and I'll see you in the morning.' Butch smiled and shook Taylor's hand again.

'Right, Chief, if you'd like to follow me ...' Sid started to walk along the corridor.

Taylor stopped him and smiled. 'Sid, please – call me Ben.'

Sid smiled back. 'Awesome, Ben, now you're getting the hang of it.'

They walked down to the huge garage and across to a door marked 'Maintenance'. Inside, a much smaller air conditioned room, made the environment comfortable. As Taylor expected, long benches ran down all four walls. Taylor recognised the test gauges for setting flow rates on reducers and the manometers hung on the walls above the benches. Everything was arranged in an orderly fashion and everything had been immaculately cleaned, from the rubber mats on the floor to the fluorescent lighting on the ceiling. Sid grabbed two rebreather sets from the racks where they had been hung to dry from the last time they were washed off with fresh water. Full-length rubber suits hung next to the sets. Freshwater hoses hung above the racks; they were used to remove the salt from the rubber and prevent corrosion. Large drains in the floor took all the salty water away to a tank outside.

'The large tanks outside collect the drains from here?'

'Yes, they do.'

'Why not just dump it into the harbour?' asked Taylor.

'We would have the environment people complaining at us if we did.'

Sid began to arrange the ancillaries needed to make the set usable underwater: a reducer, the canister containing soda lime for absorbing the carbon dioxide, hoses for vital oxygen to flow down and a bag of weights to make the diver less buoyant and able to sink without struggling to leave the surface of the water. Sid went on to show Taylor the new modification.

'As you know, Ben, soda lime is used to absorb the CO_2 that the diver as breathed out. When preparing the soda canisters, extreme care is taken to check for leaks. What we've made is a device to stop the diver breathing contaminated oxygen. This device stops the diver from getting what we call a "cocktail". If seawater enters the counterlung then the diver can breathe in not only the fumes but, if it continues to flood, the wet soda lime mixture too, which will burn everything it comes in touch with –

the mouth, lips, tongue and throat; it burns like acid. The diver would probably be dead before it reached his lungs. This simple device like a completely separate double counterlung stops the soda lime coming into contact with the diver's breathing supply.'

'Crickey ... so simple.'

'Yeah ... you ever had one?'

'What, a cocktail? No! Come close, though ... I heard the gurgling sound of the water coming through the soda lime and was able to surface before I breathed it in.'

'Lucky – sometimes you get no notice. It just happens. I've not had one either, but I've seen the effects after someone has breathed it in and believe me, it's not nice. So, that's the sets ready for tomorrow ... all we need now is a dry suit for you.' Sid waved his hand at the line of rubber suits hanging from a rail. 'Our suits are marked with our names, so just find one unmarked that fits and we're ready to go.'

Taylor checked the size stamped on the front of the 'dry bags' and asked Sid: 'What do you normally wear underneath the bag, Sid? I have a thick undersuit called a "woolly bear" in the UK, but I'd cook in it with these water temperatures.'

'I wear tracksuit bottoms and a t-shirt.' The door opened to the maintenance room. 'Ah, here he is.' Another man wearing an identical tracksuit to Sid's entered the room and came across to meet them. He was a lot shorter than Taylor and stocky with no neck – his head joined straight onto his shoulders. 'Ben, this is Roy; he'll be with us tomorrow.'

'Hi, Roy – Ben Taylor, Royal Navy.'

'Hi, Ben, I'll be the standby diver tomorrow, but I doubt very much that you'll need me.'

'Thanks, mate. Visibility will certainly be better than the UK,' Taylor said with a smile.

Both US divers suddenly seemed to have the same question, but it was Sid who asked it first: 'What is it like to have no visibility at all? How do you cope?'

'I had to dive in the Thames in London once – I'll not bore you with the details, but I took down a bag of visibility with me.'

'What? What's a bag of visibility?' The two divers were intrigued.

'Well, a bag of vis is a plastic bag ... the size is determined by the job and what you can manage to carry. You fill it with fresh water on the surface then take it down with you, and the diver can see quite clearly through it.'

'Really? Does it work?'

'Sure it does. Press the bag against the object you want to look at, and bingo, clear as a bell.'

'Wow! We'll have to try it.' Sid smacked Roy on the arm.

'I wonder if Speedy knows about a bag of vis?' Roy was excited at this opportunity to get one over on the boss.

Then Sid checked his watch and turned to Roy. 'Listen, buddy, what about showing Ben here the watering hole?'

'Yeah, can do.'

Then Sid faced Taylor. 'OK, it's four o'clock, nothing else for us to do here. Would you like a cold one?'

'Explain?' Taylor was confused.

'We'll show you our local watering hole and you can meet some more of the team. They'll probably be in there.' He nodded at Roy.

'Yeah, it's like our second office. It's a submariners' bar really but the diving team has taken over it now, and if you ever want to find someone, that's the place they'll be.'

'Where is it?' Taylor asked his new friends.

'It's the nearest bar to the base. Out of the main gate, it's the first bar you come to on Rosecrans.'

'I've a meeting with the skipper in the hotel around six o'clock, but right now I could do with a cool drink.'

'Oh, the beer is cold all right, not like the warm stuff you drink.' Roy was already gathering up his hold-all.

'I'll just check with Speedy that all is done for tomorrow and I'll meet you outside.' Sid went upstairs to find Speedy, and Taylor followed Roy outside.

Taylor, Sid and Roy walked into the 'divers' bar.' Skylights provided light, and with the windows open a cool breeze blew around the room. The walls were plastered with pictures of submarines from all nations.

Cap tallies and memorabilia from different ships and submarines belonging to US and other navies from around the world were displayed above and behind the bar-serving area. A jukebox played country music, which could be heard above the noise of the twenty or so people sat at tables drinking.

'Is it always this busy?' asked Taylor.

'This is nothing yet. It'll fill up soon. Grab a table, Roy. I'll get the beer in. Ben, what do you want to drink?'

'I'll have what you're drinking, thank you.'

Sid went to the bar while Roy and Taylor found a table.

'This is where we catch up on all the scuttlebutt,' Roy explained.

'Scuttlebutt?' Taylor repeated quizzically.

'Yeah, rumours, gossip – you know ...'

Roy began a barrage of questions about the Royal Navy and its diving practices. Sid came back from the bar with a large pitcher of beer and three glasses. The three men filled their glasses and the questions continued. A bus from the base pulled up outside and half a dozen sailors entered the bar.

'Here we go, filling up now.' Roy looked a little smug.

'What time does it stay open to?'

'It stays open until Pam gets bored,' replied Roy.

'Pam runs the show all by herself, but it'll stay open until around midnight,' added Sid.

The three men chatted until the pitcher was empty.

'Right, I'll get you guys another beer, but I must be getting off,' Ben announced. 'I've got to debrief the skipper at dinner tonight.' The two men nodded. Taylor picked up the empty pitcher. 'What beer am I filling this with?' he enquired. Suddenly, an ear-splitting dive claxon from a submarine went off: 'Ah-ooh-ah, ah-ooh-ah.'

The bar went quiet and Pam shouted from behind the bar: 'No swearing, gentlemen, or you'll be out.' Pam was wagging a finger at a pair at the end of the bar.

'Crickey! That gets the message across.' Taylor held his ears.

'Pam had it installed to keep some kind of order in here,' Roy laughed.

'So, what is this?' Taylor held up the pitcher.

'Just ask Pam, she knows which one we have.'

Taylor walked to the bar and Pam came straight over.

'Well, where have you sprung from?'

'Oh, I'm just learning all about the naval base from my new friends over there.' Taylor pointed at the table. 'Can I have a refill, please?'

'Wow! Nobody has said "please" to me in a long while, sweetie. Is that a British accent?' She smiled and Taylor noticed her cat-like green eyes tighten into slits.

'It certainly is.' He smiled back.

Pam continued to fill the pitcher but shouted out over the bar. 'Hey, you two bubble-heads didn't tell me you were bringing this handsome chap into my bar today.' Sid and Roy waved at her.

'If I'd have known, I'd have put some make-up on and done my hair.' Taylor noticed two little dimples begin to show in her cheeks as she smiled. She placed the beer in front of Taylor. 'It's on me, honey.'

'Thank you, Pam.' He gave her his best smile and walked back to the table.

'Here you go, guys. What time do we start in the morning?'

'You're staying at the Holiday Inn down the road, aren't you?'

Taylor nodded.

'Then I'll pick you up at seven thirty.' Sid filled his glass.

'Oh, you don't have to, Sid, I can—'

'Nah, I'll be driving past there anyway, so it'll be no trouble.'

'That's very kind, Sid. I'll be outside.' Taylor said his goodbyes, and as he opened the door to leave he looked back at the bar. Pam stopped serving a customer and gave him a huge smile. Taylor couldn't hear her but read her lips: 'You come back soon.' He smiled and left.

At the hotel, Taylor washed and changed before going down to the dining room. His DO was sitting at a table writing in a small notebook.

'Good evening, boss,' Taylor said.

'Good evening. How was your day?'

'Very good, thank you. Is the Peter joining us?'

'He'll be down in a moment. Can I get you a drink?'

'No thanks, I've already had some with the divers from the section. I'll have a coffee after we've eaten.'

Commander Coleman came down from his room and joined his two subordinates at the table.

'Hi, chaps ... have you ordered yet?' he asked.

'No, Peter, we thought we would wait for you,' replied Alistair.

'Well, good. How are you, Ben?'

'Good, Peter, thank you. I've had a very interesting day.'

'Great, you can tell me all about it in a moment. First things first: let's order.'

The three men examined the menu and the waiter took their order. Taylor began to inform his Commanding Officer of the day's events.

'The CO is a really busy man ... seems to take a lot on his shoulders, even though he has a good man in Speedy. He doesn't like to delegate and prefers to do things by himself. Speedy on the other hand is laid back and quite content to let his superior carry on, leaving him with an easy life; probably because he's ready for retirement. Unless of course that's the way things are done in this country. The Section runs very casually and everything seems to get done.' Taylor went on to explain the modifications on the diving set to both his DO and CO. 'Tomorrow I'm being picked up at seven thirty and the day will be spent with a dive in the new set, followed by a tour of the DSRV.'

Commander Coleman thanked Taylor and then the conversation turned to the local food and the hot weather.

The next morning at seven thirty Taylor watched Sid skid to a halt in a gas-guzzling Cadillac outside the hotel.

'Hey buddy, climb in.' Sid leaned across and threw open the door. 'D'ya like my wheels? Don't know if it would pass a smog test but I picked this baby up really cheap from the Navy Exchange on the base.'

'It's as big as a bus!' Taylor exclaimed.

'You could easily get all your diving gear in here,' he said, looking round the huge interior. 'It would appear you can almost anything from the PX?'

'You certainly can. You should get yourself up there and check it out.' Sid explained that if he ever got caught without transport he should just jump on a bus, as they go round and round the base. 'Just stop one and hop on.'

'What time did you leave the bar last night?'

'Not long after you left actually ... it got a bit rowdy.' Sid drove slowly down Rosecrans towards the base. He chatted as he drove. 'We also do a lot for local charities and bring disadvantaged children into the base to use the facilities. We have a lot of things like barbecues as well.'

They waved their ID cards at the main gate staff and soon pulled up outside the Diving Section. The big roller door at the front of the building was open. Roy was inside holding a US Navy tracksuit, which he handed to Taylor.

'For you, buddy.'

'Well, thank you very much.' Taylor shook Roy's hand. They went to the back of the garage and into the personal locker room. A wet suit was also supplied for Taylor, and he soon changed into diving gear.

'Gus has gone down to the dive site already; he'll set things up for us,' Sid said. 'Roy is standby diver and you'll be going in with me. We'll get everything ready and Speedy will be down with the boss when we're ready.'

A large purpose-built pickup truck was loaded with gear and the three men headed off.

There was a small hill to go down before they got to the jetty. From the top, Taylor got a view of the entire harbour. The first thing he noticed was the colour of the sea. It was the most beautiful deep blue in the foreground, transforming into a lighter blue as his eye moved towards the horizon. The sky mingled into the blueness of the sea, its identity being given away only by the occasional white whiff of a cloud. There was no wind and the sea was flat and calm. White jetties jutted out into the sea of blue at different angles and were dotted with the usual cranes and bland buildings that housed workshops and offices. Ships of all shapes and sizes where tied up in no particular order, and there were few empty spaces. Taylor was introduced to Gus, another member of the team; he too was wearing a smart USN tracksuit, and he laid out the diving sets and safety lines on the jetty. A black people carrier pulled up and Speedy jumped out followed by the boss, 'Butch' DuPont. There were handshakes all round, and then Speedy mustered the whole group into a huddle for a brief on the dive.

'The ship that carries the DSRV piggyback is moving across from her normal berth to this one so she can receive a new generator. This jetty is easier to get to from the main road, so access and the use of a crane will make life easier for the engineers. The generator is arriving first thing tomorrow from Fort Lauderdale by truck. What I'd like you divers to do, Ben and Sid, is to check the jetty for ant damage, making sure that the last ship to dock here didn't decide to take any part with it when it left. Look for major structural defects or damage and things sticking out. When you've OK'ed that area, drop down to the seabed; we're on the rising tide by the movement of the last ship. The DSRV vessel will be very close to the seabed at low water, so we don't want her sitting on anything sharp and possibly causing damage to the hull. The weather is good – you won't experience any tidal flow down there, so take as long as you like, especially you, Ben: get a good feel for that new set. Sid, keep a good eye on him, we wouldn't want to lose our first diver in this harbour, especially one so distinguished and from our closest ally. Does anybody have any questions?' Nobody answered. 'OK then, gentlemen, let's go diving.'

Taylor and Sid were helped on with their diving sets by Gus and Roy. Once ready for the water they were given a final check-over by Speedy.

'OK, let's get this show on the road. Flag Alpha is flying, tide and time wait for no man, in you go.' Speedy checked his watch and both divers jumped into the water. Warm water filled Taylor's wet suit. Both divers had their sets checked for any signs of bubbles and leaks by Roy on the surface and Speedy gave the order to dive. He checked his watch again. The visibility was excellent. Taylor wasn't used to this luxury, he was amazed at the different colours he could see. He checked around three hundred and sixty degrees, made sure he could see his buddy and swam to the jetty. Back in the UK he would have to be inches away to see it, but here he swam a few feet away and carried out the check. The sun's rays beamed down through the water and lit up the jetty for him. Taylor used his bypass oxygen supply to give himself more O_2 and flush through his set. The jetty area was checked clear; Sid swam over and gave the signal to dive to the seabed. Taylor signalled back and followed. Looking away from the jetty, Taylor could see the gentle slope of the sand stretching away from him into the blueness until it eventually faded into a blur. He equalised his eardrums. The seabed was a lovely beach with small plants dotted around. He stopped for a moment to take in the different colours they were displaying. Small sea urchins showed their tentacles as he swam by. He proceeded down the slope slowly, checking intently around him as he went. There were no signs of any rocks or obstacles, large or small. He then swam back up the slope, zigzagging as he went, keeping Sid in the corner of his eye. Taylor came across small piles of broken shells where something had been eaten by something else further up the food chain. The slope levelled out and Taylor was faced by the dark area under the jetty. Sid came over and stopped Taylor. He signalled for him to stop and wait. Taylor signalled back and watched Sid slowly ascend up to the surface. He could see Sid on the surface obviously communicating to Speedy. Taylor was slightly confused as to why he had been told to wait on the bottom. Sid came slowly back down and signalled Taylor to follow him under the jetty. The jetty blocked out all the sun's rays and formed a black shadow. Taylor had to wait a moment for his eyes to adjust to the darkness. Visibility under here was reduced to a couple of feet, and the temperature was drastically reduced. Large concrete slabs lay strewn around and the seabed was rough gravel. Lots more broken shells and what looked like fish bones lay in piles. Sid had moved off behind one of the pylons holding up the jetty and was out of Taylor's view for a moment.

Taylor saw something move in front of him and stopped dead in the water. He was face to face with a large, fierce-looking fish. Both Taylor and the fish remained motionless in the water, just feet apart, eyeing each other curiously. Taylor had never seen a fish with such an intimidating appearance; he had no idea what it was. It turned slowly, presenting Taylor with a broadside view. He could see the long, slender, muscular body covered in small scales, approximately six feet in length. Taylor glanced to find Sid but couldn't see him. He decided to back away slowly and the fish turned quickly to face him again. *This is the reason for the fish bones under here*, Taylor thought.

He moved back slightly and the fish opened its mouth wide to reveal sharp fang-like teeth. Taylor thought about removing his knife, which was strapped to his leg. A dark shadow fell over Taylor; the fish darted towards him at tremendous speed and disappeared over his shoulder. Taylor looked up and saw Sid hovering above him with a huge smile on his face. He signalled for Taylor to follow him out from under the jetty. Taylor nervously complied, looking for any signs of the fish.

Gus had rigged a temporary ladder for the divers to get out of the water, and Taylor could hear Sid laughing as soon as his face mask was removed.

'What the fuck was that?' exclaimed Taylor.

The whole of the surface crew were now in hysterics.

Eventually Speedy regained some order and explained: 'You've just met Big Barry. He's a great barracuda ... harmless enough.'

'It didn't look harmless to me!' Taylor was not happy.

The Americans saw his mood and quickly went about their business.

Sid went to Taylor. 'Sorry, Ben, you weren't in any danger, it was just something I thought you should see. I'll get the beers in later.' Sid held out his hand. Taylor thought about it for a while and shook it. 'But you should have seen your face.'

Taylor put him in a playful headlock and both men laughed.

Speedy was given a debrief on the dive and he asked Taylor how the set was.

'No flow restriction, it was easy to take a breath, and the O_2 was cool and tasted sweet. Buoyancy was easily controlled, all valves within reach, and it felt good.' Lieutenant Commander DuPont called the group to attention. Each man sprung up statue-like. Commander Coleman and Lieutenant Duncan came marching down the jetty.

'As you were, men.' Taylor's captain shook the hands of Lieutenant Commander DuPont and Master Diver Speed. Then he spoke to Taylor.

'How was it?'

'Marvellous, sir, no problems at all.'

'Good. I'll expect a written report as soon as you can.' He turned and left with Butch. Taylor helped the divers pack up and load the vehicles and they drove back to the Diving Section.

After lunch Sid drove Taylor to the DSRV berth.

'Have you forgiven me yet?'

'Just biding my time, mate, waiting for an opportunity ... don't worry, I'll get you back.'

Both men laughed. They pulled up outside a large building across from which was berthed an unusual ship.

'Let me tell you a little more about the DSRV. Forgive me if I go over what you already know, Ben.'

'No problem, Sid, you just carry on; I'm certain you know more than me.'

'The DSRV performs rescue operations on submerged, disabled submarines. Not only on US submarines but our allies' subs as well.
It can be deployed quickly and transported by truck, aircraft, or ship, or by another specially configured submarine.' Taylor followed Sid onto the jetty. 'Once on site it works in conjunction with the "mother ship" or "mother submarine". It's deployed from the "mother" and carries out a sonar sweep, locates the damaged sub and attaches itself to the escape hatch. It needs a NATO adaptor ring to attach to your hatches unfortunately, because of the difference in the hatch configuration. Without that, it's a no go.
Communication is by underwater sound-powered telephone 185. Once a seal has been made, both hatches can be opened and it can embark twenty-four personnel for transfer to the mother vessel. It also has a hydraulic arm with a combined gripper and cable cutter, which it can use to clear any debris from the hatch. The gripper, by the way, can lift a thousand pounds in weight!'

'Was it developed for any particular reason or incident?'

'Yes: it was developed as a direct result of a tragic accident involving USS *Thresher* in 1963. She went down with all lives lost. At the time, submarine operating depths greatly exceeded the capabilities of rescue vessels. So, the Deep Submergence Systems Project along with Lockheed Missiles and Space Company were challenged to produce a deep diving rescue vessel that could cope with these extreme depths. It took them a while but in 1970 the first one rolled off the production line.'

'How deep can it go, Sid?'

'It has a displacement of thirty-eight tonnes, has a speed of four knots and can dive to a depth of five thousand feet, or one thousand five hundred and twenty-four metres.' Sid held out his hand before him. 'Here we are, then, the USS *Avalon*.' Taylor followed Sid up the gangway. 'When on a rescue mission it has two pilots and two rescue crew on board. It's powered by electric motors with a single shaft; it also has four thrusters to help it manoeuvre. It's forty-nine feet long and has a beam of eight feet.' The two men conducted a detailed tour of the DSRV and mother vessel.

CHAPTER THIRTY-TWO

Gallymore woke early ... he lay on his bed and thought over his change of plan from the night before. After a shower he tucked the .38 Saturday night special into his trouser pocket and headed for the hire car in the car park. In La Mesa the traffic was occasional and he had no problem parking outside Stefan's house. The sun was rising and already he knew it was going to be a hot one. The morning air smelled sweeter up here and the temperature was a few degrees cooler than down in the town. Gallymore watched the house for signs of movement but the curtains were still drawn. He checked he had the right address, the one the two bikers had taken him to the day before, and confident he was right, settled back in the rising heat. The rental car had no air conditioning, so he wound down the window and cursed.

At seven thirty the curtains were opened; and at eight o'clock a young woman, smartly dressed, came out of the house and got into the brown Ford Pinto parked on the drive. Gallymore started the engine and followed the Pinto. She drove carefully through the morning traffic and parked in an unmarked bay outside the UC San Diego Health campus. He watched her go inside and waited. After an hour had passed and she had not reappeared, he figured he had time to spare. Gallymore drove to the airport and booked a flight to Cancun in Mexico; he left the return date open.

At half past four Gallymore parked to give himself a clear view of the entrance to the campus.

He sat back, tried to find a rock station on the radio and gave up after hearing only love songs and country music.

At 5.15 p.m. the little brown Ford Pinto pulled off campus and headed towards La Mesa. Gallymore followed her into the parking lot of a 7-Eleven and realised he needed a drink. Inside the store he opened the refrigerator door and pulled out a Coke while watching the young lady fill a small basket with fresh fruit and milk. He beat her to the checkout and waited in the car again for her to appear. The Pinto drove straight home and Gallymore waited for her to get settled before checking the gun and exiting his car.

When Stefan opened the door, Gallymore's expression was demur. 'Hi, Stefan, sorry to disturb you – can I have a quick word? It won't take long.'

Stefan stepped outside and closed the door quietly behind him. 'Listen, I got into a lot of trouble telling you about Julie and where she works yesterday. She wasn't impressed when I told her about you last night. I'm in a lot of trouble, so whatever it is you want now, I'm very sorry but I can't help you.'

Gallymore couldn't help himself: a smile appeared on his face. His big hands grabbed Stefan round the neck and he squeezed.

'Listen, you little fucker, I haven't got time to play games with you anymore.' He glared into Stefan's eyes and watched him start to choke. 'Now, inside.' Gallymore pushed him through the door.

'Who is it, Stef?'' called a meek voice from the kitchen. When there was no reply the young woman walked into the living room, wiping her hands on a towel. When she saw Gallymore with his hands on Stefan, she stopped in horror.

'Come and join us, Julie ... we need to get better acquainted.' Gallymore shoved Stefan on the couch. 'Sit! Both of you.'

Stefan began to protest, but Gallymore shut him up quickly. Julie joined her boyfriend on the couch and he grabbed her hand.

'Sweet.' Gallymore produced the gun from his pocket and moved to the open fireplace. 'Let's have a chat about what it is you actual do at the IVU, Julie.'

Julie took a little more prompting but eventually started to open up to Gallymore. After he had heard what he wanted, Gallymore stopped her. He thought a while, and then he spoke.

'Now, here's what's going to happen ...'

An hour later the brown Pinto backed from the drive in La Mesa. The only thing Julie had going through her mind were the words of Gallymore: 'All you need to do is stay calm and Stefan will be all right.' Her hands were shaking on the steering wheel. *These things don't happen in real life*, she told herself. *Why us?* She drove to the campus like the thousands of times she had done before, but this time she was terrified. When she drove through the first security check her face was not lit with her usual smile. Julie parked in her normal spot and switched off the engine. She couldn't remember any of the roads she had just driven through to get here. *Like I was on autopilot ... it's just a blank.* Her thoughts turned to Stefan and him being tied up in the same house as that madman. She headed for the next security check.

'Hi, Julie, what are you doing back in?' The security guard came from behind his desk.

'I've forgotten my notes ... I need to take them home and sort a few things out before tomorrow.' She reached for one of her passes that hung from a chain round her neck.

'Oh, no need for that. I know who you are. I do need to check your bag though, sorry.' Julie held her bag open for the man to peer inside. 'That's fine ... don't stay up too late.' He smiled and waved her through. Once inside, she walked down the normally busy corridor, listening to her footsteps echoing in the unnatural quietness. She passed through a fire door with a blank expression and carried on walking to the laboratory section marked 'INFECTIOUS VIRUS UNIT. AUTHORIZED PERSONNEL ONLY'. Julie removed the chain from her neck and selected a tag before swiping it along the scanner at the side of the door. Nothing happened. Her heart rate, which was already high, quickened even more. She swiped the tag again and waited; nothing happened. She turned to see if anyone was watching but the corridors were quiet this time of night. *Why is it not working?* She found herself fumbling with the chain and selected a different tag. She swiped it down the scanner and a light came on above the door before a loud click could be heard. Julie pushed the handle down and swung the door open. Quickly dashing inside she shut the door behind her and leaned against it, breathing hard. Julie closed her eyes. *What am I doing?* She stayed leaning on the inside of the laboratory door for what seemed like an age, trying to gather her thoughts.

Eventually she opened her eyes and moved away. The lights inside the IVU laboratory room had come on as soon as the door was opened; the motion sensors in the ceiling would keep them on.

Julie focused on the rows of glass-fronted refrigerated cabinets along the far wall. She knew exactly where the Ebola virus was kept but instead turned her attention to the small metal locker at the back of the laboratory. She found herself thinking again of Stefan and moved to the desk in the middle of the room. She removed a set of keys from her bag and unlocked a drawer. Pulling open the draw she removed a set of keys and then went to stand in front of the small cabinet. Julie took a deep breath. She grimaced when one of the hinges creaked as she opened the door. Inside the cabinet the glass vials where numbered, not named. *How would he know if I didn't take the right ones? I could give him water with a dye in it*, she thought, her mind frantic. *This is my job on the line, all those years of hard work. Maybe they'll understand: he has my boyfriend. I can't be too long, he knows how long it takes to get here and back to the house. He's threatened to kill Stefan.* Julie formed a vision in her head of Stefan lying on the carpet with thick red blood oozing from a gaping bullet hole in his chest, Gallymore standing over him laughing. *It would be my fault; I would have caused his death.*

Julie carefully chose two vials and put them in her bag. She locked the cabinet and put the keys back in the drawer. Then she locked it and put those keys back in her bag.

She crossed over to the door and pulled it open. It would lock as the strong spring closed it behind her and inside the lights would go off. She walked in a daze down the corridor, thinking she must get to the fresh air before she passed out.

Through the fire door, she could hear music playing quietly in the distance. Her legs turned to jelly as she approached the security guard. His head lifted from the magazine he was reading. He smiled as she approached and turned the volume on his little transistor radio down low. A frown replaced the smile on his face.

'Is everything OK, miss? You don't look too well.'

Julie felt tears welling up inside. *Run to the guard, throw your arms round him and tell him everything.* A song came into her head, a song being played on the radio, a song she knew.

'I'm fine,' she said. 'Hope I'm not coming down with anything.'

'You're maybe working too many late nights, miss. Don't burn the candle at both ends, it's not good for you. Goodnight.' He began reading the magazine on the desk in front of him again. Julie heard someone reply goodnight. Her legs carried her to the door and she didn't look back. The Pinto stayed on I8 and thirty minutes later Julie was parked outside her house in La Mesa. The house looked normal. Julie stood trembling by the front door, frightened to open it. The vision of Stefan came back into her head. Suddenly the front door opened and Gallymore beckoned her to come in. She saw Stefan tied up on the floor and ran to him, throwing her arms round him and sobbing uncontrollably.

'Did you get it?' she heard Gallymore ask from behind her. 'Did you get it?' Louder this time.

She pointed to her bag, which she had dropped on the floor beside her.

Gallymore picked it up and took out the two vials. 'And this is definitely the right stuff?'

'You're a monster, get out of our house!' she screamed, all her emotions flooding out. 'Untie my boyfriend, now!'

Gallymore knew he had the right stuff. He raised the .38 and shot her in the forehead, calmly altered his aim slightly, and shot Stefan behind the ear.

Before Gallymore left the States he had one more thing to do.

CHAPTER THIRTY-THREE

Taylor was getting used to the heat, almost enjoying it. Commander Coleman had informed him that they had another three days to get everything they needed before heading back to Faslane. Speedy had organised a tour and possibly a dive with the improved JIM suit that the San Diego diving team had at Point Loma. When Taylor arrived at the Diving Section, Sid was there to greet him.

'We keep the JIM suit in its own area, back here.' Sid took him to the back of the Diving Section. 'What do you know about this suit, Ben?'

Taylor was glad he had done his homework. 'The suit is named after the man who first test-dived in it, Jim Garrett. Tests were carried out at HMS *Vernon* in Portsmouth and HMS *Portland* in Dorset. On successful completion of the tests, deep dives were carried out on board the Royal Naval salvage ship *Reclaim*. They've always had problems with the joints, though: leaking water and pinching the skin of the diver inside. The diver's oxygen is fed through an umbilical but he has a backup emergency supply in external tanks on the rear of the suit. Comms is also through the umbilical. The JIM suit has been replaced by a new SAM suit.' Taylor was looking round the new suit held upright in its stand.

'UMEL[11] made us a suit and we updated it massively at the Space and Naval Warfare Systems. Modifications include a new acrylic that has replaced the Plexiglas dome on the head. Oil-sealed joints

---

[11] Marine Equipment Limited.

have been replaced by silicon-based seals. Comms is now through water on the advanced 185 system. The glass-reinforced plastic torso is now made of carbon fibre, and of course we've made the soda lime scrubbers more efficient.' Sid pointed out the improvements as he went round the suit. The two men didn't notice that Speedy had quietly entered the Section and was standing behind them.

'Sorry guys, can I interrupt you?' Speedy's face was solemn and his whole body demeanour was sombre. Taylor and Sid realised something was wrong. They stood up straight in front of the Master Diver. 'Ben, the boss would like a word in his office.' Taylor hadn't seen this serious side of Speedy before.

'Sure,' he said to Speedy, then to Sid: 'I'll catch up with you later, mate.'

Sid looked confused.

Speedy walked with Taylor up the stairs, knocked on the door and ushered him into the office. Speedy didn't follow him in. Taylor was surprised to see Commander Coleman standing by the window. Both men did not smile.

'Ben, come in, close the door buddy, take a seat.' DuPont went behind the desk and sat upright in his chair. Taylor sat in front of the desk. Taylor's commander officer turned from the window and faced him.

'Ben, I have bad news. Every morning I talk to the duty officer in charge of the 3rd Submarine Squadron back in Faslane. I give him an update on our progress and he fills me in with latest reports. He gave me some really grave news, news that was a great shock to me.'

Taylor's CO began to pace. Taylor didn't know what to think. Commander Coleman stopped pacing. 'The last thing he reported to me was a personal message from your family. In fact, it was from your mother. Ben, there's no easy way to say this ... he reported that your father has passed away.'

Taylor went into instant denial. 'No, sir, you must have the wrong message. It's just not possible. He's fit and well. I was with him just a few days ago.'

The room fell silent for a while. Coleman spoke again.

'Your mother told him that your father had a massive heart attack. It has shocked everyone. Ben, I'm making plans to send you home. As soon as I have a flight for you, I'll get you on it.' The room fell silent again. 'Take the rest of the day off.' Coleman nodded to DuPont, who nodded back. Commander Coleman continued: 'Pack your things and I'll contact you when I have your flight details.'

Sid gave Taylor a lift back to the hotel. It was a quiet journey. Back at the hotel Taylor could only think of his father. He kept himself busy by packing his clothes, ready to depart. He then concentrated on writing up his reports for the captain. He received a telephone call in reception informing him that he would be flying home at 10 a.m. the following morning. At 6 p.m. the phone in his room rang again.

'Hello, Sid, what are you—?' He was interrupted.

'I'm in the foyer, can you come down?'

'I've just got out of the shower, buddy. Go in the bar, I'll meet you in there.' Taylor quickly dressed and went down to the bar.

'What's up, mate?'

'I couldn't leave you by yourself with the bad news you just received, buddy, so I've come to take you down the divers'.

'But I have stuff to do before I go home tomorrow.'

'Plenty of time for that. Come on, Roy and Gus are waiting.'

Taylor followed Sid out of the hotel and jumped into his Cadillac. 'You don't have to do this, you know – I'm fine, really.'

'I know, but I'm your friend and you need me right now.'

Taylor shook his head.

When they entered the bar there was a loud cheer. The bar was full. All the diving team from San Diego were in there, cheering as Taylor walked through the door.

Pam came from behind the bar. 'Ben, I'm so sorry.'

Taylor told her thank you and she held his hand tightly before giving him a hug. Taylor felt her firm breasts press against his chest as she squeezed him.

'Come on, you look like you need a drink.'

The jukebox in the corner had been switched off; the ambient noise came from people talking. Taylor sat between Roy and Sid at the bar. The drinks flowed freely.

One of the sailors stood by the door, dropped his drink and the glass smashed on the floor. 'Ah-ooh-ah, ah-ooh-ah.' The noise of the submarine dive claxon nearly made Taylor drop his own drink.

The bar went quiet for a second as the sailor sheepishly came to the bar.

'Sorry, Pam.'

Pam handed the sailor a mop, dustpan and brush.

Taylor was deep in thought but the glass smashing brought him back. 'For someone so small she certainly packs a lot of weight around here,' he said to his two companions.

'You don't want to get barred from this bar!' said Roy.

'The thought of getting barred from here is not worth thinking about.' Sid held up his glass to Pam. 'Come on, there's a booth free over there.' Sid stood up and moved from the bar.

'I'll get another round in, chaps ... I'll bring it over.' Taylor reached into his pocket and took out his wallet to check how many dollars he had left.

'I thought I recognised an English accent?' The man slid onto the seat next to Taylor.

'And that's an Irish one if I'm not mistaken?'

'Sure is.' Gallymore thought about giving him a false name, but why bother. 'Name's Gallymore, pleased to meet you.' He held out his hand and shook Taylor's. 'I've seen your photograph somewhere. Did you rescue a girl from a cave or something? I seem to remember reading it in the paper back home.' Before Taylor could answer he continued: 'You're a fucking hero mate ... come on, let me buy you a drink.'

'That's OK, buddy. I'm in a round, but thank you anyway.'

'What brings you over here, then?' Gallymore enquired.

Taylor suddenly became very wary. 'I'm just enjoying the sun, kicking back, you know ...'

'You've certainly made a lot of friends?'

Taylor nodded his answer. 'Look, uh, I'm buying, can I get you one?'

Gallymore drained his glass. 'You're a good guy, erh ...what's your name again?'

'Taylor.'

'Taylor, yes. Thanks, I'll have a Jameson. I remember now: Royal Navy isn't it?'

Taylor again nodded his answer. 'And what brings you over here?' Taylor asked.

'I'm over here mixing business with pleasure.'

Taylor was relieved when Pam came over and served him.

'There you go, Mister Gallymore, hope you enjoy your time in San Diego.' Taylor put the whisky in front of the Irishman, smiled and walked away. He then sat back down at the table with his friends.

'Thought you'd got lost.' Roy reached for his drink.

'Let's have a team photo,' cried Sid suddenly. He reached into his jacket pocket and produced a small camera. Then, to one of the sailors who was standing by the jukebox: 'Buddy, can you take a team photo of us?' He handed the camera to the man and turned back to his friends. 'Here, stand up, we need the bar in the background.' He shouted behind the bar: 'Pam, get in the photo! Yeah! That's it. Awesome.' They posed for the camera and moments later were sat back down enjoying another glass of beer.

Every sailor who left the bar came over and shook Taylor's hand. Most of them bought him a beer and said they were sorry for his loss. The conversation at the table died down and Taylor found himself looking at submarine pictures on the walls. He tried to pick out the British ones. Then his thoughts turned to Orla. He had a strong urge to be with her.

'Guys, I'm sorry but I'm going to have to leave.' Taylor didn't see Sid signal to Pam. 'Ah-ooh-ah, ah-ooh-ah,' the claxon blared from the behind the bar.

'Man trying to leave here!' shouted Sid.

'Not on my watch,' added Roy.

Pam hurried over with another pitcher of beer. 'Here you go, sailor; I'll look after you.'

'I'll bet you will,' Roy said quietly.

The light from outside filled the room as the door opened and in walked two women dressed in US Navy uniform. The first was of medium build and the second very large and rotund, making the first look small.

'Never date a woman who eats more than you do,' Roy said randomly. The two men sat at the table looked at Roy with furrowed brows, then laughed.

The two women removed their hats, spoke to Pam and approached the table.

'Would you three handsome boys like to go to a barbecue?'

'Well, we sure would,' Roy replied instantly.

'Where is it?' asked Sid.

'Down on Mission Beach ... we have transport waiting.' The large one was doing all the talking.

'Well, we haven't eaten yet.' Roy smiled.

Before Taylor knew what was happening, he was in a minibus on the way to a barbecue. Inside the minibus was very hot; Taylor was glad of the breeze coming through the open windows.

'How far is it?' asked Taylor.

'We're here,' Roy said excitedly.

'Now you're in for a view. This is just want you want to take you're mind off things.' Sid touched Taylor's arm and pointed ahead. The minibus turned round a corner to reveal a magnificent white sandy beach stretching as far as the eye could see. The sea was a beautiful turquoise colour disrupted only at the edges by small flashes of white as the waves broke on the sand. The barbecue was set up by a rocky outcrop, and a volleyball net had been put up too. Music played from a ghetto blaster and the smell of food cooking wafted into the minibus as the wheels slid to a halt on the sand and the doors opened.

'Here we are,' the large woman said. Sid and Roy man-hugged most of the sailors at the barbecue and Taylor recognised faces from the divers' bar. Beer cans were opened from the cooler and thrust into their hands. Girls were dancing while the men stood round chatting.

'Come on, Ben, I'll introduce you to some more of our friends.' Sid took hold of Taylor's arm.

Taylor went along with them. The sun was getting close to the horizon when someone tapped Taylor on the back. As he turned round he had a shock.

'Hi,' she said.

Taylor's reactions surprised him. He threw his arms around her and gave her a huge hug, holding on tightly for what seemed an age. When they pulled away her smile filled her whole face. Taylor couldn't hold himself back and kissed her lightly on the lips.

'Oh, I'm sorry.' He began to flush as he apologised.

'That's OK, I didn't mind at all. In fact, it was quite nice,' she said, putting him at ease. They stood facing each for a moment, Taylor looking deep into her green eyes and her into his.

Eventually she asked: 'Can we get some food? I'm starving.' Taylor smiled and they walked to the fire.

'How ... what are you doing here?'

'I phoned a friend, she's looking after the bar. I told you I would look after you, and here I am. I knew those two bozos would be off chasing those two chicks who brought you here, so I came to make sure you weren't left alone.'

'You're an amazing woman, Pam. Thank you.'

After they made themselves some burgers, Pam said: 'Shall we walk? The sun's about to set, it would be a shame to miss it.'

They walked along the beach; Pam slid off her shoes and let the warm sand filter between her toes.

'I love doing this. It's been a while ... I should do it more often.'

Taylor knew he should not be doing this but the alcohol was taking over.

'I suppose working in a bar like yours can take over your whole life. This place is a paradise. This beach, with the city as a backdrop ... it's amazing.'

They finished their food and walked on. Pam slid her hand into his.

'Come on, the dunes up here are wonderful.'

She pulled him up the beach and soon they were out of view from the rest of the beach. She lay down on the warm sand and Taylor lay down by her side. She placed her hand on his stomach. He wanted a brief respite from the pain he was feeling. Taylor leaned over and kissed her full on the lips. She let her hand slip down to his waist and unbuckled his belt.

CHAPTER THIRTY-FOUR

McCann came downstairs and stopped at the bottom. He looked around the living room and made a decision.

'Right, you lot, nobody is to use the upstairs sink in the bathroom.' The gang of men knew McCann was an expert bomb-maker and realised he had 'fixed' the upstairs sink.

Andy wanted to know what he had done.

McCann explained: 'There's a steel ball in the drain under the sink; turn on the water and it gets flushed down to the U-bend, where it'll come into contact with another steel ball, causing an electrical contact to the det, which will blow the fuck out of the glycerine glycol, potassium and permanganate of potash.'

'That'll blow your fucking legs off!' exclaimed Michael.

'Exactly,' agreed McCann. 'Oh, and don't switch the hall light on. The lamp has been injected with sulphur dioxide and mercury. It'll blow when the filament gets hot.'

'Blinded.' Michael smiled. 'Nice.'

Andy shook his head. 'Is there anything else you've forgotten to tell us about?'

'Actually, yes: there's a bit of magnesium sulphate in there too. I'm the only one doing anything to protect us.'

'Trying to kill us all, you mean. There's just one fault with your protection plan.'

'And that is?'

'Your protection is in here, and the war will come from out there.' Andy pointed to the door.

'That's something I want you guys to sort out. I've done my bit.' McCann went into the kitchen. 'Mickey, is there any tea going?'

Mickey nodded his head. 'Sure.'

A car followed by two unmarked vans drove through the town. In the passenger seat of the car sat Frank.

'Not far to go. We'll pull up before we get to the farmhouse.'

The night sky was cloudy and dark; it looked like rain. Before they had set out, Frank had given the IRA team a full briefing on just who they were after, where they were and why there could be no one left alive when they left. The car pulled off the road and its headlights were switched off. The first van went past and parked on the other side of the entrance to the farmhouse. The second van pulled in behind the car. All was quiet as the men walked gingerly up the drive, guns in hands. Frank signalled them to spread out. Some of the team moved to the back of the house.

'Right, let's get this over with.'

Four hand grenades flew through the air and smashed through the downstairs windows. Before they could explode, four more flew through the windows upstairs. When the explosion came, the ground-floor windows blew out, spewing glass high into the air. Shortly after the upstairs windows showered glass down from the sky. Inside, the grenades going off had stunned everyone.

Glass and furniture debris flew round the room hitting anything in its way. Confused and deafened, the men inside stumbled around to make sense of what had happened. Before they could, the door had opened and muffled sounds of gunfire could be heard.

Mickey Kelly appeared in the doorway of the kitchen; he gazed in astonishment at the carnage and smoke that was the living room. He thought he heard another blast and felt his stomach being ripped out. The other two blasts he didn't hear as his head left his body.

McCann lay stunned on the floor, his brain trying desperately to take control of his body. His ears filled his head with a high-pitched ringing; he couldn't make any sense of the cacophony of noise around him. He couldn't see either: his eyes stinging with the smoke streamed with tears as they tried instinctively to clear the invasive material from them. His body went into convulsions as he tried to gulp in fresh air ... then he thought he heard a voice, far away and unrecognisable. The voice was repeating something. McCann focused on the voice.

'Where is …?'

He felt his body being dragged from the floor; he was now kneeling. His head was pulled back and the voice was inches away from his face. The smell of garlic was strong and it helped him focus. He couldn't turn his head as someone had hold of it.

'Where's Gallymore?'

Now McCann knew who they were looking for, and he guessed they were IRA.

'We're not interested in you morons; tell us where he is and you can go.'

Yeah, right, McCann thought, *none of us are getting out of here alive.*

Garlic Breath moved away and McCann's head was released. He still found it hard to breathe; the smoke had burned his throat.

He looked quickly around the room: Mickey was dead in the kitchen doorway ... Andy had a face but the back of his head was missing; he lay on the floor in front of his favourite chair ... Sean was kneeling by the television, blood flowing from the large cut in his scalp ... and Michael was alive but lying on his back holding his stomach; McCann noticed blood oozing through his fingers.

Garlic Breath was obviously in charge. 'Someone needs to tell me where the feck Gallymore is, and I need to know now!' He was getting very agitated.

Michael foolishly spoke up. 'We don't know, he comes and goes as he pleases.'

Garlic Breath shot him in the head.

'Wrong answer.' He turned to McCann. 'You're McCann, aren't you?'

McCann kept quiet.

'Keep a close eye on them, I've got to take a piss.' Garlic Breath moved to the bottom of the stairs. 'When I come back down, you two had better be a lot more chatty.' He disappeared up the stairs.

McCann's brain was working at last. He would have to move quickly – there would only be one chance. He slid his fingers inside his boot, removed the fixed-blade knife from inside and prayed. He listened intently upstairs to try and predict Garlic Breath's movements.

He heard the toilet flush and prepared himself, but was still startled by the huge explosion, followed quickly by a scream that he thought could only be made by a wild animal.

McCann thrust the knife into the man who stood behind him and didn't look to see where he had stabbed him. He tried to stand and run at the same time but stumbled; he wanted to go out the rear door but realised he wouldn't make it. Knowing what was waiting for him if he stayed, and without any consideration for his safety, he quickly decided on the window and crashed through it into the garden. A bullet narrowly missed his head, which spurred him on. He wanted to jump over the hedge but ran straight into it as another bullet hit the ground between his legs. The last thing he heard was a shotgun being fired inside the house.

CHAPTER THIRTY-FIVE

The unobtrusive sound of the travel alarm clock roused Taylor slowly from a deep sleep. It took a moment for him to realise that he was in his bed at the Holiday Inn. The clock at his side showed 7 a.m. He slowly lifted his head from the pillow, gently eased his body from the bed and strolled gingerly to the shower. He dressed in civilian clothing and went down to breakfast.

'Morning, Ben, are you ready to go?' Commander Coleman was tucking into a plate of eggs and bacon.

'Yes, Peter, thank you.' Taylor sat down and poured some coffee.

'Heard you had a … a few drinks yesterday.' Alistair Duncan forked a pancake dripping with syrup into his mouth.

Coleman scowled at his fellow officer. 'How are you feeling?' he asked, not moving his eyes from Duncan.

'I'll be fine, Peter. Nothing a cup of coffee won't sort out.'

'Good man. Probably best to get some food inside you, too. I can recommend the eggs.' Coleman smiled at Taylor. 'I've arranged a car to pick you up at 0830 outside; I've got to go into the base, so I'll leave Alistair here to give you a hand.'

'That's not necessary, Peter, but thank you. I have a couple of things to sort out before I go, and I'll need to see some people before I leave. When will you be travelling home?'

Taylor topped up his coffee, gesturing to the others whether they needed topping up too.

'Oh, we'll be finished in a couple of days from now.' Coleman moved his coffee cup nearer to Taylor. 'When you land at Brize, go to the station; there will be a ticket waiting for you. When you get home, do what you have to and then phone the boat and let me know …' Coleman moved his cup back and took a drink.

'Thank you, Peter; as soon as I have things arranged, I'll let you know.'

'Give my condolences to your mother and family. Now, gentlemen, you will have to excuse me.'

Taylor went back to his room, finished packing and went back down to the bar. He drank from a cold water bottle from the refrigerator and thought about what he had done the night before. *I've never felt that alone before. I'm a long way from my family ... goodness knows what my mother is feeling right now. I have to get home quick. Being with Pam was a moment of weakness ... I was vulnerable, and the drink didn't help. Still, it was no excuse.* Moments later he walked from the hotel towards the divers' bar. The sun was already heating the sidewalk.

Local people were out watering their gardens and said hello as he passed. *Just another day*, he thought. Taylor stood outside the divers' bar. What was he going to say to her? Sorry, it was just a moment of passion? What? He knew she wouldn't be there but he had to make sure. Try to apologise somehow. Tell her it hadn't meant anything. He checked the door again and peered through the window.

No number ... I don't even know her surname.
Taylor checked his watch and walked back to hotel.
The hotel receptionist saw him enter and called him
over.

'An envelope for you, sir.' She handed him a
small envelope. Taylor looked at it quickly: just his
name handwritten on the front. He slipped it into his
jacket pocket and went to phone the Diving Section.

'Sid ... hi, mate. Sorry I didn't get to see you
before I leave but the transport is ready to go now. I
wanted to thank you for all your help and being a
good friend.'

'Well it's been very nice to meet you as well,
and who knows, maybe I'll get to visit you in
England one day.'

'I hope so, buddy, I really do.'

'OK, take care, I wish you luck.'

'Sid ... will you do one other thing for me?'

'Sure ... I'll tell her for you.' Sid made a mental
note to speak to Pam.

Taylor was somewhat relieved to get on the
plane. His thoughts gradually left San Diego ... and
the Pam incident. His mind wandered back home. He
thought about his mother, if she was coping?

What was he going to say to Orla? How would
he explain what he had done? How could he have
been such a fool? His mind in turmoil, he closed his
eyes.

*Maybe Tadpole was right: spending all that
time confined in a submarine can't be good for you.
You'd certainly become institutionalised quicker than
anywhere else, even prison. Maybe it's time to settle
down and have some children.*

Is this a good time to leave submarines? Even leave the Royal Navy? Start a new life at home near my family, instead of trying to block them out of my mind while I'm away? There's not much you can do for them if something goes wrong, it's better not knowing sometimes.

Would I be able to cope with civilian life? Mundane, regularly doing the same thing ... is that what they call leading a normal life? Being with your family is normal; living, eating, sleeping and working together in a tight-knit group, relying on and helping each other in difficult times. Taylor forced his eyes open and focused on the cargo net slung on the aeroplane's fuselage. *Fucking get a grip, man!*

Taylor was proud of the way his mother had handled the last seven days. She'd had most things organised by the time he'd arrived home from San Diego. Thankfully, friends and relations were turning up in drips and drabs and not all at once. There was, however, a constant stream of people knocking at the door giving condolences. The only time Elli had shown any emotion was at the actual funeral, where she'd begun to shake and then had flooded with tears Taylor held her tight as Matthew's coffin was lowered into the ground. The headstone she'd chosen was black marble and the inscription read: 'MATTHEW TAYLOR. DEARLY LOVED – DEARLY MISSED. UNTIL WE MEET AGAIN.'

Taylor was helping his mother prepare lunch in the kitchen when there was a knock at the door.

'I'll go, sweetheart, you carry on here.' Elli washed her hands and went to the door.

Moments later Taylor heard her talking to a man after inviting him in. Voices could be heard in the living room.

'Ben, it's a gentleman to see you. It's a policeman.'

Taylor stopped what he was doing and washed his hands.

'I'll make some tea.' Elli said, looking worried.

'A policeman to see me? Don't worry, Mum, it's probably nothing. I've done nothing wrong.' Taylor held his mother's hand. Elli just nodded. Taylor went into the living room. The policeman was sat on the couch; he had removed his helmet and was running his fingers round the rim.

'Hi, I'm Ben Taylor.'

'Hello Mister Taylor, I'm PC Jones, sorry to disturb you sir. I have some bad news I'm afraid, especially at this difficult time. Did the funeral go OK?'

'Uh, yes, thank you ... we're just trying to get back to a routine, but it's very difficult.'

'Well sir, I'm afraid I have the daunting task of making things even more difficult.'

The policeman was obviously having difficulty in explaining what it is he came to say. Taylor decided to help him out. 'Sometimes you just have to come out with it.'

Elli entered the room with a tray of tea and biscuits. 'Now, how can we help you, PC Jones?' she said with a smile.

'I have a travel permit for you, Mister Taylor. We received a phone call from your captain this morning and unfortunately, sir, you're to return to your ship as soon as possible.' The policeman's radio began to crackle. He turned a small knob and the crackle went away. 'The warrant it made out for today, sir. I'm not sure what the reason for the recall is but it must be important.'

Taylor looked at his mother; she was pouring tea into a cup.

'I see ... well, I'll make a call to the boat and find out what the excitement is about.'

The policeman took the cup Elli was handing to him.

'Would you like a biscuit?' she asked.

Taylor went to the phone in the hall. Ten minutes later he came back into the living room.

'Thank you very much for the warrant.' He took the piece of paper from the officer and signed his receipt.

The policeman apologised for the intrusion, said his goodbyes and left Taylor with his mother.

'It would appear that Argentina has invaded a British island called South Georgia near to the Falklands in the South Atlantic, mother. The surface fleet have already left Portsmouth. I have to go back to Faslane today.'

'Well, I'm sure that the fleet will sort it. They won't need submarines, will they?'

'Probably not, Mum, but we must be ready. It's probably another one of those "just in case" scenarios.'

Taylor went upstairs to pack. When he came down half an hour later, his mother was watching the television.

'HMS *Hermes* and *Invincible* are leaving Portsmouth harbour as we speak.' The camera panned round from the reporter and focused on the crowds of people who lined the walls of the harbour and stood on the shore and cheered as the ships manoeuvred out.

'What's happening, Mum?' Taylor asked.

'Well you're right, the fleet is leaving now for the South Atlantic.'

'Are you OK?'

'Sure ... when will you have to leave?'

'Almost right away. I've ordered a taxi to take me to the station. Will you be all right?'

'I'm going to be fine, love. Don't worry about me. Laura is coming over to sit with me for a while. What will you be required to do, Ben?'

'I don't know yet, Mum ... it's all a bit sketchy. I'll know more when I get back to the boat.'

'Telephone me as soon as you get back. Let me know what's happening.'

'As soon as I know, you'll know.'

Taylor set off again on the train from Crewe, a journey he knew every mile of. As he stared out the window, his thoughts turned to trying to put all this mess into some order. *I'd really like to talk to someone right now. Dad would be the obvious choice but I suppose I'm going to have to get used to making my own decisions.* Taylor went to the buffet car and bought coffee; he felt like something stronger but thought he'd better keep a clear head. He passed through Glasgow with the usual ease and soon arrived in Helensburgh. There was a queue at the taxi rank.

Taylor jumped in with some other sailors he didn't know but who were willing to share. The driver talked continuously on the way back to the base.

'All day I've been ferrying sailors back to the base. I'm having to do a second shift because we're all busy, we haven't got enough cars on the road to keep up. It's all one-way traffic, though – nobody is going from the base to the town. As soon as we've dropped off, it's back to town to pick another fare up. I suppose you guys will be going to sea for a while?'

Nobody answered him.

Taylor entered the base and went straight to the submarine. He looked up to the sky: rain clouds were gathering above the hills on the far side of the loch and the light was fading. Taylor noticed all the hatches were open, which was unusual, and crew and dockside workers were loading and moving stores. The dockside cranes were busy moving cargo nets of wooden crates above his head. The quartermaster greeted him on the casing as he crossed the gangway.

'Hi, Chief ... wow, it's all gone crazy round here. We're "storing for war" at the moment. Be careful when you go down, all is not as it should be: some of the ladders have been removed and part of the deck is up on the main accommodation.'

A large truck pulled up on the dockside and the driver got out and started to cross the gangway. The QM went to check his pass. There was a queue of people trying to climb out of the main access hatch.

Taylor went to the conning tower and climbed down into the submarine. The accommodation ladder had been removed and lay on the deck in the control room. Taylor climbed down the side using a seawater valve for his foothold and walked across a plank that had replaced the decking at the bottom. He threw his bag onto his bunk and popped his head into the senior rates' mess. The mess was unusually full; the noise level was high with everyone talking. Taylor got the gist of the conversation straight away. Speculation and worry seemed to be the main topic and Taylor left them to it. He climbed back up to the control room. This too was packed to the rafters and he had to squeeze past men in white overalls to get to the captain's cabin. The captain greeted him warmly and sat him down on the bunk.

'I'd offer you a tea or coffee but it just isn't going to happen right now – I can't even get one myself. How is everything at home?'

Taylor thanked him for asking and reassured him all was well.

'You're probably wondering what's going on, Ben.'

'Well, it's not often you see the dockyard working this late, sir.' He smiled.

'Indeed.' The captain smiled back. 'Well here it is. The Argentinians have taken control of an island in the South Atlantic called South Georgia. They're making moves to take over the larger group of islands called the Falklands Isles. Intel informs us that the harbour in Buenos Aries is a hive of activity. The prime minister hasn't been hanging around; two carriers have already left Portsmouth and HMS *Fearless* is leaving tomorrow with more troops on board than we can think of. *Courageous* is ahead of us and will be sailing as soon as she's stored for war. We've been ordered to store for war and will stand by at immediate notice to sail.'

There was a loud bang from within the conning tower.

'Excuse me a moment, Ben.' The captain left the cabin and moments later returned. He was shaking his head. 'They're pulling my boat apart!'

Taylor could see he was stressing about the work going on.

'Who's coordinating all the work, sir?'

'The first lieutenant has his finger on the pulse ... I hope!'

'Sir, I've never heard of the Falklands. Where exactly is it?'

The captain pulled out a chart and showed Taylor where the islands were positioned in the South Atlantic and their closeness to Argentina.

'How long will it take us to get there?'

'Our top speed underwater is around thirty knots, and if we have to surface then that's reduced to around twenty. So realistically we're looking at an average speed of maybe twenty knots. The navigator is checking the relative charts at the moment and plotting the course, but from my initial examination I predict around fourteen days, maybe a little less. Everything is happening quickly, and as you can see it's very hectic. It's taking me all my time to oversee that everything is being done as it should be and on time. I've sent most of the crew inboard to prepare to leave, as it's not safe to have everybody inboard while this work is carried out.'

'What's happening on the main accommodation deck, sir?'

'As you know, the submarine can stay at sea indefinitely – we make our own water and fresh air and the reactor can supply us with power for years. The two main factors that limit our time at sea is the morale of the crew and, most importantly, food. Food will run out long before the crew goes mad. So some bright spark as come up with the idea that when we store for war, the fridges will be filled to the brim and dry stores like tins of beans, potatoes and veg will be laid on the floor of the accommodation deck and a false deck put down on top. This obviously means the deck will be around six inches higher. The cox'n and leading chef are working with the dockyard to get that done.'

There was a knock at the door and the first lieutenant popped his head round the curtain. 'Sorry to disturb you, sir; the tunnel will be shut for thirty minutes while we conduct a primary reactor water sample.'

'OK, Number One. Access will be over the casing, though?'

'Yes sir, all the hatches are open.'

'Very good; make sure lifelines are rigged on the upper casing and make the relevant main broadcast warnings, will you?'

'Will do, sir.' The first lieutenant left the doorway.

The captain turned back to Taylor. 'Now where was I? Oh yes ... the other concern I have is we normally have riders and trainees bedding down on the vacant torpedo racks in the fore-ends; there won't be any vacant racks. We have the capability to carry twenty-four torpedoes, and Flag Officer Submarines wants us to carry thirty; so extra racks are being installed in the lower section of the torpedo compartment. This means we can't take every one with us. The crew will have to be reduced. We won't have the luxury of a one-in-four watch, Ben ... this will have to be cut to one-in-three, and in some cases one-in-two: six hours on watch, six hours off.'

'That's going to be a tough decision to make, sir. Who goes and who stays?'

'Yes, not a decision I'm looking forward to having to make. So unfortunately, the first thing I'd like you to do is inform young Mister Thompson he won't be coming with us. Make sure he understands the reason why;

I don't want him having some sort of mental reaction to the news, as I believe he'll be a good submariner. His kit will have to be taken inboard, and he is to report to Engineering Section at E11 in the dockyard, where he is to remain until our return.'

'Leave it to me, sir, I'll make sure he's looked after. Is there anything happening back aft in the machinery spaces?'

'Compared with the rest of the submarine, not a lot – all outstanding maintenance is being carried out; that's were Thompson is now. Oh, there is another thing I would like you do: we're to receive the NATO adaptor ring for the DSRV and escape tower; can you make sure it is fitted and secured properly? The uh ... MEO will give you the exact time of its arrival.

Ben, I don't want any noise shorts transmitting from it, the Argentinians have good sonar equipment.'

'Aye aye, sir, leave that to me. Did everything thing go OK in San Diego, sir?'

'Yes, thanks, it went well ... although this little episode will put things on the back burner for a while.'

'Is there anything else I can help with, sir?'

'Yes: the diving officer will require some help with stores. We'll be taking extra diving equipment with us as well. God knows how we're going to adjust the trim with all this extra weight ... but that's my problem. Do you have anything for me?'

'No sir.'

'Very well then, that is all. God be with us.'

Taylor left the captain and went up through the conning tower to the casing. It was now completely dark, and dockyard workers were assembling the torpedo loading rails above the for'd hatch. Boxes and crates were beginning to pile up on the casing, ready to be taken below. Two quartermasters were now on watch at the gangway, both with SMGs. Taylor continued aft to find Martin.

Gallymore turned off Sherbrooke Avenue and looked around before entering the Sherbrooke Castle Hotel in Glasgow. He ordered a pint and sat by the window, watching people going by outside. He turned his attention to the occupants of the bar and watched them carefully. Nobody seemed to be paying any attention to him. Satisfied he was not being followed he finished his pint and left the hotel, heading towards

Queen Street station.

Orla needed to go into Helensburgh for fresh milk and vegetables. Liam was also going into town, and they sat next to each other on the bus. Orla knew Liam would be going to the pub, but he was acting strange.

'Why are you so quiet?' she probed.

'No reason,' he snapped.

Orla suspected he was up to no good but didn't want to get involved. When the bus stopped in Helensburgh, Orla watched Liam go into the Buccaneer, a bar he didn't usually frequent.

It was very quiet inside, with just one man drinking at the end of the bar. The windows were small and high up on the wall; nobody walking passed could see in, and it was permanently dark inside. Liam sat at the opposite end of the bar, away from the other drinker.

Gallymore walked out of Helensburgh station, crossed the road and entered the Buccaneer bar. He saw the man he was looking for and moved beside him.

'Hey, arsehole.'

Liam turned round and smiled at his friend. 'What fucking time do you call this?'

'Nice to see you as well.' Gallymore ordered two pints. 'Let's move somewhere a little more private.' They moved to the farthest table away from the bar.

'What a fucking dive this is. No jukebox, not even a dartboard,' Liam complained.

Gallymore looked round the place. 'That's why I suggested meeting in here: sailors don't use this bar and only a handful of local people come in.'

They both took a long drink from their pints.

'It's good to see you, mate ... what's been happening? Why did you want to see me?' Liam was genuinely excited. 'It's so fucking dead round here ... I'm going out of my mind.'

'Well that's about to change, Liam. Are you still living in that caravan with your mum?'

Liam looked down at the table. 'Uh, yeah. But it's a great cover, nobody suspects a thing.'

'Good.'

'So, what's happening? I thought you'd forgotten about me.'

'I've just been out of the country for a while and came back to find out the team has been taken out. McCann managed to get away, so I need to speak to him. Have you any solid contacts in the submarine base?'

'No, not really, but it's mayhem there at the moment. They're preparing to go to war. So they're taking on extra staff at the dockyard to get the subs ready in time.'

'Can you get in?'

'I would think so; they're advertising everywhere for extra workers.' Liam thought for a while. 'I know the supervisor in the car pool garage; I'm pretty sure if I asked him he could get me a job.'

The two men sat drinking in silence for a while.

It was Liam who broke the silence. 'What is it you want me to do?'

'It needs to happen quickly.'

'Well, like I said: they're desperate for help. So I could probably start straight away.'

There was another long silence.

This time it was Gallymore who spoke first. 'I have something that I'd like you to put on board one of the submarines. It needs to go into the drinking water supply ... better still, in the freshwater tank.'

'So it's not explosive, then?'

'No, nothing like that ... though just as deadly.' He smiled at Liam.

'Great! At last some action.' Liam rubbed his hands together. 'What is it? And more to the point, how much money will I get?'

'You don't need to know what it is. Get the drinks in and I'll fill you in on the details.'

A bright ray of light streamed into the bar as the door opened and in walked a young woman. She saw Liam at the bar and went over to him.

'Orla, what the fuck are you doing in here?'

'I could ask the same about you!'

Liam looked at Gallymore; Orla followed his gaze. Gallymore smiled at her; she did not smile back.

'What is it you want?' he snapped at her. 'What are you doing following me around?'

'I'm not following you, Liam. I haven't got enough money to get home, can you lend me a couple of quid?'

Liam quickly checked his pockets and gave her three pounds. 'Will that be enough?'

'Yeah, sure. Thanks, see ya.' Orla walked out of the bar not saying another word.

Liam took the beer back to the table.

'Sorry about that.'

'She's cute.'

'Fucking nuisance, that's what she is,' Liam said picking up his pint.

Gallymore took a long drink from his pint and they began to talk again.

'This is a stand-alone job, just between me and you.' Gallymore pushed a small wooden box across the table. 'Inside are two glass vials; it's up to you how you get them on board. Make sure you do. Break the two vials into the water system and leave immediately. Don't make me come back here looking for you.' Gallymore left the bar, crossed the road and entered the train station.

CHAPTER THIRTY-SIX

Orla took a small plant pot from underneath the caravan, shook the earth off it and wiped it clean with a cloth. She crouched down and looked at the small area of earth she had cleared of grass the year before and stabbed the trowel into the soil. She dug out a small hole and forced the fragile plant into it. The sun was high in the sky and the air was unexpectedly warm for this time of year. All the same, Orla wore the shawl her mother had made for her.

Liam came from around the van holding a large board. 'What do you think of me new placard, sis?' He held it high so Orla had a good view: 'BAN CORPORAL PUNISHMENT IN REPUBLICAN SCHOOLS.'

'I agree with you, Liam, but we're supposed to be campaigning against nuclear power. You're such an idiot.' She picked up a small stone and hurled it at her brother. 'Leave.'

Liam dodged the stone and went inside the caravan. His mother was stood peeling potatoes by the sink.

'What's wrong with Orla, Mam? She's got a right hump on.'

'You really don't know, do you?' His mother shook her head in disbelief. Liam went into his bedroom. Mrs Brodie wiped her hands and went outside. She sat down in the folding chair close to Orla.

'He's got to be very busy at the moment, Orla.' Orla didn't reply and busied herself with the soil. 'He'll come to see you when he can. If I'm any judge of character he'll be trying his hardest to get away.'

Orla looked at her mother. 'I know. I hate him being in the Navy; why couldn't he be a greengrocer or a doctor, or anything except …' Orla lay back on the grass; she looked up at the sky, clenched her fists and kicked her legs. 'Why would anyone want to invade a small island in the middle of nowhere?' Her legs were now still as she regained some control. 'It's on the other side of the world! It's beyond me. It's probably going to take forever to get there ... God knows what's in store for them when they arrive, and who knows how many of them will come home again.' A tear fell from her cheek and landed on a petal of the small flower she had just planted.

'He knows where you are, my love; just give him time, he'll be here.'

Taylor had an hour before the low-loader was arriving with the NATO adaptor ring. From the hectic control room, he made a phone call to his friend Tim. Taylor was surprised to hear that Tim was now (temporarily, at least) stationed in HMS *Neptune* at Faslane. He arranged to meet him that evening. Then he made a pipe for MEM[12] Thompson to go to the senior rates' mess. Taylor left the control room and climbed and squeezed his way through the submarine to the senior rates' mess. There were two other people in the mess, so when Martin arrived Taylor took him into the bunk space for privacy.

'How are you, Martin?' Taylor noticed how tired he looked.

---

[12] Marine Engineering Mechanic.

'Everything is just so ... exciting! I love the closeness and team spirit that is building. Learning about the boat, how it works, is just what I thought it would be. It's hard work, long hours and not too much sleep, but I'm getting there.'

'Are you managing to get anything done with all this work that's going on?'

'No, there are too many people on board, it's difficult just to move about at the moment.'

'And you know why all this work is being done?'

'Oh yes.'

'So how do you feel about that?'

'Well, it's a bit daunting, I'm not sure if I'm ready. It's OK going to sea for a normal cruise but to go to war, well to be honest it's a bit scary.'

'Well, I can hopefully put your mind at ease. As you know we don't take a full crew into a war zone – there just isn't enough room. And this in no way reflects on your ability to do the job – in fact, the captain said to me just a while ago that he thinks you'll make a good submariner, so that's something to consider. I've come up with an idea to make the most of this unfortunate situation and improve your skills and knowledge of engineering at the same time. How does some leave sound? You haven't been home for a while I think?'

'No I haven't.'

Taylor noticed by the look on his face that Martin was a bit confused. 'Don't worry, it's all good. I've arranged for you to go on leave for a couple of weeks and when you return, you're to report to the Engineering Section here in Faslane.

The boss over there is a good friend of mine, Warrant Officer Dave Winslow. He knows everything there is to know about submarine propulsion machinery, so while you're there, learn everything you can.'

'So I'm not sailing with you?'

'Erm, no, Martin. Sorry ... there just isn't the room. We'll be carrying a full load of torpedoes'

Martin smiled and breathed a sigh of relief.

'Are you OK with that?' Taylor was surprised but pleased at his reaction.

'Yeah, that's fine with me ... I must admit I was starting to worry about going south. Going on leave as well, that's great. How long will I be working at the Engineering Section?'

'We don't know how long we'll be down there for, or if we're even going yet, but it will be until we get back. The cox'n will have all the details and travel warrants for you. There are three things I want you to do for me.'

'Sure, Chief, anything.' Martin was pleased to help.

'OK, first thing: find somewhere to make a coffee for the captain and take it to him. Second: get all your kit off the boat and take it to your cabin inboard.' Martin was nodding his head. 'And thirdly: choose you moment to approach the cox'n about getting your documents – like everybody he's really busy right now so don't upset him, he's doing us a big favour.'

'Not a problem ... and Chief?'

'Yeah?'

'Thanks again for all your help.'

'My pleasure; don't let me down with Winslow ... now get out of here.' Taylor patted him on the back as he left the bunk space. He stayed behind for moment leaning on his bunk; he felt tired. Wiping his face with his hands he sighed deeply and left the bunk space.

The NATO adaptor ring was delivered on time and Taylor saw to its correct stowage. Taylor asked the QM to move the wooden peg opposite his name to the ashore position and went inboard to eat first, before meeting with Tim. Taylor went to the second floor of the administration building and found the office that Tim had told him he would be in.

'How long have you been in here?' he asked his friend when he saw him sat by the window. 'Nice view, mate.' Taylor admired.

'They eventually agreed with me about the people at that peace camp, so they decided it would be better to have me here on a more permanent position. Now that this thing with the Argies has started it's a good job I am. The dockyard is taking on extra workers, and they're not being vetted as they normally would be. There isn't the time. We don't know who's being given a pass to come through those gates. It's mayhem, Ben. How are things with you, buddy? I'm really sorry to hear about your dad ... how's your mum holding up?'

'She's being strong, mate; it doesn't help me being here. There's never a good time to go to war, but this is particularly bad. So, what have you been doing?'

Tim Sherwin made a mental note to send Taylor's mother some flowers and a letter; he then realised Taylor wanted to change the subject.

'I've actually been over to Ireland and it certainly opened my eyes. I thought I knew what was going on but it's far worse.'

'In what way?' Taylor sat down in a comfortable armchair.

'Well, I witnessed a young boy who couldn't have been older than fifteen throwing his weight around on grown men. The only reason he got away with it was because of his older brother, who was a known psychopath. These kids are being groomed from an early age and they don't know the difference between right and wrong; they do as their parents tell them. Having said that, not all the Irish hate us – some actually want us there and believe we're doing a good job at stopping violence. I talked with a man who fought at the Somme in the British Army and he wanted the IRA demilitarised ... but he was in a minority. It's been going on now for so long, the black and white lines have become blurred, making it easier to cross from one side to the other. The whole thing is on a knife-edge; it's like a tinderbox and it won't take much to spark it off. We have to tread very carefully or the whole thing will flare up in our faces. It's already come over to the UK mainland, but I think it will get a lot worse.'

'And you think the IRA has something to do with the peace camp?'

'I certainly do. I believe the IRA have already infiltrated that camp.'

'Tadpole, I ...' Taylor looked directly into his eyes. He decided it was probably a good time to tell him. 'I have met a young lady.'

Tim stared at his friend in silence for a moment. 'Well that's good news, mate ... best I've heard for a while. Do yourself a favour: marry her and get out of submarines.'

'Well, I've only just met her. Though in fact, she did go home with me.'

'What! When did all this happen?' Tim stood up and moved round his desk.

'Before I went to San Diego.'

'You're a dark horse. Oh, wait a minute – is she Irish?'

'Yes, she is actually.'

'And just how much do you know about this woman?'

'I know enough, Tadpole. I can trust her, I know I can.'

'You've just told me you only just met her. But hey – I'm not saying she's the enemy. As I said, not all the Irish hate us. When can I meet her?'

'What for, so you can interrogate her?'

'Well, tell me all about her, then.' Tim seemed genuinely interested.

'What would be the point of that – in an hour you'll know more than I do.' Taylor smiled at his friend.

'I'll just be doing my job, Ben. What's her name?' Taylor gave him her name. Tim wrote it down on a notepad. 'I hope it works out for you Ben, I really do.' Tim made two cups of coffee and sat back down behind his desk.

The two men talked about San Diego, Taylor concentrating on the details of the improvements being made to the diving equipment.

'They have a huge base to work from, Tadpole, four times the size of this place, and it seems like money is not a problem. If someone gets a good idea they're positively encouraged to see it through. They're given help to enhance their ideas, whereas we don't have the money or the time to improve. They all seem to be happy, relaxed. They have the right proportion of time at work and time off to do want they want and recuperate. Whereas we work all the time. It's a constant struggle to maintain what we have, never mind improve. We're stagnant and no development is undergoing to advance us in preparation for the future.'

'So, what are you planning? A transfer?'

'No way – I'd miss all this stress. Besides, I can't stand the lingo.''

'Well, I think things are being improved, but you just don't see it.'

'Well that's what I'm talking about, Tadpole; these research and improvement centres are manned by so-called experts that're blinkered and restricted in their ideas. What we need is a system put in place to throw open any ideas to the masses. It's the man at the coalface that will know how to improve stuff; they use it every day, so they should be involved in the process, not a spotty-nosed kid fresh from university.'

'I don't know what went on over there, Ben, but seems it really got to you.'

'Well ...' Taylor stood up and looked out the window. 'There's a lot going on in my head at the moment.'

'I'm sure there is, buddy. Just take it one step at a time. Put it into boxes, or the big picture will turn your mind into Swish cheese.'

Taylor settled back down into his comfortable chair and drank his coffee. 'So, what's happening with our splinter group?'

'As far as I know they're still at large. The IRA have told us that the search is narrowing and it won't be long before they're caught.'

'You've actually been speaking to the IRA?'

'Well, not me personally, but certain elements of the Intelligence Corps have. The "enemy of my enemy is my friend" and all that.'

'Nothing to worry about, then?' Taylor raised his eyebrows. 'Can we believe the intel, after all? It's their problem and they'll want to sort it themselves.'

'We'll make a spy of you yet! I think we can ...'

Taylor wasn't so sure. 'Oh, check this out ...' He reached into his pocket and handed Tim the envelope that the receptionist had given him at the Holiday Inn in San Diego.

Tim opened the envelope and inspected the photograph inside.

'A nice-looking bar ... is this the diving team?'

'Yeah ... this is where they hang out after work. The inside of the "divers' bar" ... we had some wild times in there, boy, I'll tell you.'

Tim studied the picture in detail. 'Seems to get pretty full ... nice barmaid, too.'

Taylor quickly changed the subject. 'Good luck in your new office, buddy – I've got to go.'

'Would you be going ashore by any chance?'

'I thought I might just go for a walk.'

'Right on! Give her my regards.'

They shook hands and gave each other a quick hug.

'Let me know if I can do anything at home?'

Taylor assured him things were good at home, but before he left his friend to carry on his work he pointed out the window. 'Love that view, man.'

'Yeah, not bad is it?' Tim stopped Taylor at the door and threw him a set of keys.

'What are these for?' Taylor looked at the keys.

'Take my car; it's in the car park outside. Under the big tree.'

'Your own?' Taylor asked.

'No, it's from the car pool ... another perk.'

Taylor thanked him and went back to his cabin for his coat, before finding the car and leaving the base. The sun had now set but the main gate was still busy with people coming and going like it was day. He pulled up at the side of the road by the peace camp and walked to Orla's caravan. The lights were on but the curtains were pulled, stopping him seeing inside. He knocked on the door and was greeted by a huge smile on Orla's face as she opened the door. She stepped outside and gave him a long hug. Taylor hugged her back and felt all the stress flow from him. While she was still in his arms, Taylor apologised.

'I'm so sorry, Orla; I've been so busy. I wish you had a telephone here.' She kissed him passionately.

They eventually went inside. He said hello and apologised to Mrs Brodie. Liam was sat watching the television but just grunted. Taylor asked Orla if she wanted to go for a drive. Half an hour later Taylor parked on the banks of Loch Lomond. After he locked the doors Taylor held Orla's hand as they walked along the shore.

'I can't tell you how relaxed you make me feel.'

'I feel the same way.' She squeezed his hand.

They walked for a while not talking. Taylor thought about telling Orla what had happened with Pam, but now was not the time. Eventually Taylor told her about the death of his father. She became very upset and hugged him again. With tears in her eyes she kissed him softly on the lips.

'This isn't going to be an easy relationship, is it?' She sniffed and wiped her nose on a handkerchief.

'That's an understatement,' he replied with a smile.

'But I do want to continue.'

'So do I, Orla. In fact, I'm having thoughts about coming out of submarines.'

'What, leaving the Navy?'

'Well, not straight away, but maybe asking for a job shoreside, until I can decide on my future.'

'Are the submarines getting involved in this conflict with Argentina?'

'I'm afraid so.'

They stopped for a while and listened to the ripple of the waves breaking on the shore while they looked at the stars.

'Will you be going?'

'We're on standby, so we might be called to go anytime.'

She faced him and asked if he was scared.

'No. We have a great crew. The boats are the best in the world. But …'

'But what?' She asked.

'Well, I've trained and trained all my life for this moment: this is the real thing. But with everything that's been going on lately, it doesn't feel right.'

Orla thought for a moment. She kissed him again and said: 'Right, here's what you do. You show them Argies what you're made of. Do whatever it takes to make you stop thinking of me and concentrate on what you have to do on board. You're a good man, Ben; get this war over and come back to me as quickly as you can.' Orla smiled again. 'Then we sort all the other stuff out, as it comes.'

Taylor was shocked again at how tough this girl was. 'Shooting straight from the hip, I like it. I don't suppose we have the time to mess about, so ... you're right, let's get on with it.'

'You know where I'll be,' she added. 'Now, let's enjoy our walk.'

The next day Taylor was entering the red security area. There was an unusual amount of people waiting to get in – Taylor had to queue along with the dockyard workers. Then out of the corner of his eye he thought he noticed someone resembling Liam crossing the road to the car pool garage. The man disappeared into the building. He couldn't be sure.

CHAPTER THIRTY-SEVEN

'So now we must demonstrate even more. They're bound to be sending nuclear submarines from this base to join the task force and we must try to stop them.' Mrs Brodie stood with her hands on her hips outside the caravan; she was facing the majority of the other peace camp occupants. We'll need more placards and banners; and I think we need to take this protest nearer to the base.'

Two men stepped forward. 'Yeah! Let's protest at the main gate, block it off.'

The assembled crowd became more animated. The two men were now in full control, whipping the crowd into wild excitement.

Mrs Brodie went inside. 'What are you up too?' she asked Liam.

'Nothing,' he replied sharply.

'Well, unless it has escaped your notice, we're arranging a protest out here. You know: what we came here to do. I suggest you get out there and help.'

'I'm not protesting, Mam; don't want to be part of it.' He sat watching the television.

'What! Then why are you here?' She switched the television off and stood in front of it.

'I have a job in the base, Mam; I don't want to be seen protesting against my employer.'

'When did this happen?'

'They're desperate for people at the moment ... the money is good. Anyway, you're always telling me to get a job.'

'Well I never. You will never cease to amaze me, Liam.' Mrs Brodie sat in her chair, pondering her son. 'Where's your sister?' Liam pointed to her bedroom. Mrs Brodie shook her head. She struggled to get up from the chair, knocked gently on the bedroom door and went in.

Orla lay awake on her bed.

'Are you bothering to help us with this protest?' When her daughter didn't reply, Mrs Brodie sat on Orla's bed. 'I understand that things have changed since you met this man, Orla, but don't forget why we came here, what we're trying to stop.'

'I don't know, Mam, I'm confused.'

'Remember when we first decided to come here ... the reasons we came and what we wanted to achieve. We discussed it for a long time, Orla.'

'I know, Mam.'

'Even though you have feelings for this man, you can't let him change your own views ... what you stand for ... your principles. You are who you are. Have you thought that might be the thing he likes about you?' They sat in silence for a moment. 'You won't be hurting him if you protest – passively – against killing people and destroying the planet.' Mrs Brodie sighed heavily and left her daughter to think it over.

She stormed through the living room. 'Your sister is in love with Mister Taylor, Liam. We have a double reason to stop these sailor boys going to war.'

Tim Sherwin sat behind his desk in his office with the telephone receiver pressed to his ear.

'O-R-L-A – yes, that's right. Brodie. Yeah ... I need all the information you can get me. Oh, and I need a photograph sent over. Thanks mate, I'll speak to you soon.' He replaced the receiver in its cradle and picked it up again to order some flowers.

Taylor had one leg on the ladder and the other on a valve casing. He was halfway down the ladder on the port side of the engine room. With the reactor shut down and no steam in the system, the engine room was surprisingly cold, the cool air flowing through the submarine from the unusual amount of hatches open. Taylor was repairing a leaky steam valve by replacing damaged graphite gland packing on the valve spindle, his thoughts not on the job he was doing.

Mrs Brodie helped Orla with her banner and they mingled with the crowd that had assembled on the roadway outside the peace camp. The sun had come out today, the warm air drifting up the side of the hills on the far side of the loch. Orla folded the banner and put it under her arm. The procession moved off and she followed along, her thoughts elsewhere. She removed her shawl as they reached the barrier at the naval base and wondered where Taylor was at this moment. The crowd began to chant and shout their protests. Someone tapped her on the shoulder; Orla turned and was faced by a man in a green uniform.

He introduced himself. 'Hi there, my name is Tim, Tim Sherwin. I'm on the security team here at the base ... could I have a quick word?'

Sherwin held out his hand. Orla shook it gently. She followed him to the side of the road. The chanting and cheering from the crowd became louder.

Sherwin moved his head closer to hers. 'I'm sorry, it's going to be difficult to hear ourselves speak here – will you follow me?'

Orla nodded.

Sherwin ducked under the barrier. A soldier raised the barrel of his rifle – Sherwin held up a pass and the rifle barrel went back down.

Orla had secretly always wanted to get inside this base. *Whoever this man is, he must be pretty important.* She looked over her shoulder but her mother was nowhere to be seen. They walked to the administration building and Sherwin held the door open for her. They took the lift to the second floor. Orla was impressed by the view from his office window.

'Can I get you something to drink?' he politely asked. She shook her head. He ushered her to a comfortable chair.

'What's all this about?' Orla crossed her legs and folded her arms.

'I'm new to this job and I was wondering if you could help me with a few things?'

'Why me?'

Sherwin avoided her question. 'I was wondering if you would be kind enough to fill me in on some missing details I have about the peace camp.'

'What details?' Orla cast her eyes round the room.

'I'm not asking you to spy for me. All I'd like to know is how many people live in the peace camp. Who they are, where they're from, et cetera.

My predecessor started to compile a list but it was never completed, possibly because so many people come and go so often. It's something that needs to be kept on top of – it could benefit us both.' Tim looked at her closely and saw the raw beauty that Taylor must have seen. 'What I'd like to know are the names and how many families are actually living together. I can get this information from the mail listings and some off the council records, but that's not how I work. It would be a lot easier to have someone I can formulate a mutual trust with ... a go-between. It's not the more permanent families that live there I'm concerned with, it's the single men and women who come to the camp that I'd be most interested in. The families won't be disturbed; in fact, it's your God-given right to protest. You probably won't believe me but I too hate these submarines. I have a very good friend whom I'm constantly trying to get to leave them and re-join the real world.'

'So all you want is names and numbers?'

'Pretty much, yeah. Maybe on rare occasions I'll require a little extra information, but yes – names and numbers to start with.'

'I would have to give this some serious thought.' Orla's eyes drifted to his desk. There was a photograph on top of white envelope lying on his jotting pad. She couldn't see it properly as it was facing him. She dismissed it. 'If I did decide to help you, how is this going to work? I wouldn't want you showing up at the camp every five minutes.'

'No need to worry, I can get you a visitor's pass that will allow you to come into the base whenever you want. It'll only give you access to the administration building,
but it would provide you some anonymity and prevent any unnecessary bad blood with your neighbours.' Tim could see she was thinking hard. 'How about that coffee? I know I could use one ...'

'Yes, that would be nice. Thank you, Mister Sherwin.'

'Please, call me Tim.' He walked over to a small table by the wall. 'I'm sorry, I only have one cup here ... I'll get another from the galley, it won't take me a minute.'

Orla nodded and Tim left the office. Her eyes began to drift round the office ... the carpet was new and the chair she sat in was comfortable. The décor was plain but not depressing. The desk was wooden and also new; it was kept reasonably neat for a man's, and had all the usual things on it: computer, telephone, writing pads and pens ... but she realised there were no pictures of a wife or children. There was, however, the photograph lying on the white envelope ... she twisted her head to see it more clearly. The shock hit her like a lightning bolt. Orla reached across and took hold of the photograph.

There was no doubt it was Ben Taylor. *Why would he have a photograph of Ben on his desk?* She studied it closely. Ben was in a bar surrounded by other men; they were all smiling; Orla looked at each one individually, and then behind them she saw a man sitting at the bar. She frowned; the man at the bar looked familiar, but she couldn't remember where she knew him from. Orla heard footsteps coming down the corridor and replaced the photograph on Tim's desk.

'Sorry about that, I don't get many visitors. How do you take your coffee?'

'Just a little milk, thank you.' Orla took a deep breath. 'If we're going to work together, we need to be honest with each other, right?'

'Of course.' Tim looked slightly puzzled.

'This sailor that you're trying to persuade to come out of submarines, what's his name?'

'Ah ... how did you know?'

'You shouldn't leave photographs lying around.'

'I've known Ben for some time ... we were on a diving course together.'

'Do you know about him and me?'

'Uh, yes ... he did mention that he had been seeing you.'

'So has my relationship with him got anything to do with this meeting?'

'No, ma'am, I've been honest with you: all I want is the information about the peace camp.'

'Come on, Tim: you wanted to check me out, didn't you?'

'OK, I admit ... I was curious about you. But I assure you it was only because he's my friend.' Sherwin sat back down and continued. 'You're a smart lady. I hope you two make it. He really is a great guy, he deserves a break. Do you know he just lost his father?'

'Yes, I do. I think it has affected him more than he would admit. Why do you think he's so stubborn about leaving submarines?'

'Well, he believes he's making a difference.'

'I don't understand why we need nuclear power.' Orla placed her head in her hands. She began to tremble slightly.

'The need for nuclear energy is actually simple. The UK needs a nuclear programme because we face energy shortages. Oil and gas supplies at the moment can't be relied upon. There are risks with any power supplying plants. Combine it with solar and wind power and just hopefully we can have a sustainable energy source. Now, with regard to nuclear warheads, if we didn't have them as a deterrent, then some fanatic would use them against us. The genie is already out of the bottle, so we have to have them. Nobody in their right mind would want to use them, but there are some people who are not in their right mind ... and it's these people we're concerned about protecting ourselves from.'

'You know, I think you're right,' she gradually agreed.

'But that doesn't mean I want my friend wasting his life in a steel can.'

'You're a good friend, Tim.'

'Well, I'm trying to be.'

'OK, sign me up. I'll be your spy.' She smiled.

Gallymore was back in Glasgow. He spoke into the telephone quietly.

'How did they find us?' Gallymore asked McCann, purposely not mentioning his name.

'I don't know, I can only guess someone grassed.'

'OK ... we have to meet. Where are you?'
Gallymore arranged to meet with McCann.

CHAPTER THIRTY-EIGHT

He liked Scotland. He liked the open spaces. He liked
the people, especially the way they kept themselves to
themselves. He especially liked the way a man could
lose himself in the rugged countryside. He even liked
the rain. The sky darkened as he drove through
Stirling. Gallymore saw the sign for 'Crieff' and
decided to stop there to buy a sandwich and check he
wasn't being followed. Nobody was following him on
the road but Gallymore noticed a helicopter flying
round the hilltops. He made a mental note to keep an
eye on it. He was vastly exceeding the speed limit as
he drove past Inverness on the A9, and continued
north to Fortrose. Gallymore had arranged to meet
'the Fisherman' in the Whiskey Bar at an inn called
The Anderson on Union Street off Cathedral Square.
Even though he would make the pre-arranged time
easily, he drove the car hard. He liked driving fast. He
would meet McCann at the same place later that
evening.

Gallymore parked the car in Cathedral Square.
He walked over to the old inn and found the Whiskey
Bar – a snug little place separated from the main
dining area. The cigarette smoke in there hurt his
eyes. Gallymore needed a drink. He bought two large
glasses of scotch and a pint of Guinness, and then
took a seat near the window so he could see the whole
of the bar. Gallymore felt at ease as he took his first
sip, and glanced at the old man sat at the bar with his
dejected-looking dog lying at the foot of his stool. His
thoughts went to Liam and the submarine: he
wondered when it would happen.

When The Fisherman walked in, Gallymore pushed a glass of scotch across the table and the man sat down.

Gallymore's escape plan was faultless. The Fisherman had been paid well. He had asked no difficult questions, just how many men and where to take him. Once Gallymore was in Holland he would stay low and live the life for a while. Nobody would know who he was or would even care. He would let the English chase their tails for a while, and then he would go and see his old friend Gaddafi. A young couple entered the bar; the dog raised its head begrudgingly and looked at the man and woman, before resting it back on his front paws. Gallymore smiled as he heard the dog sigh. The man bought two drinks and sat next to the woman at a table near the door. Gallymore thought he recognised the woman, who wore a green flannel open-neck blouse. He heard them speak in a Scottish dialect about how the English had raised the price of Scottish petrol again. Gallymore glanced out the window just in time to see a man in jeans and a jumper take a photograph of his car parked in Cathedral Square.

The bar steadily began to fill up as people drifted in after eating lunch in the dining room. Gallymore couldn't get the girl out of his mind. He couldn't place where he knew her from. The more he had to drink, the more it worried him. He swore to himself as he watched two men standing at the bar talking; they both wore dark suits and would pass as businessmen. Gallymore wondered where they worked and why they were here, in this fishing village. One of them glanced at him, and when

Gallymore glanced back he quickly turned away.

Gallymore turned around to look out the window and saw it had begun to rain heavily. He also noticed a man under a tree on the opposite side of the road.

He thanked The Fisherman again and watched as he left the bar. Gallymore stood up slowly and staggered slightly to the bar with his empty glass. The dog yelped loudly as he stood on its paw; its owner pushed Gallymore, warning him to watch what he was doing. Gallymore fell into the two men in business suits; he instantly recognised the feel of the gun under the man's arm.

'Sorry, sorry,' he apologised to everyone. He offered to buy the man with the dog a wee dram of whisky, who accepted the offer straight away. Gallymore set his pint down on the table by the window and left the Whiskey Bar, heading towards the toilets inside the main part of the inn. Once there, he desperately looked for a way out. He knew he didn't have much time, but it was obvious that an escape through here was impossible: small windows and bars everywhere blocked his exit. Gallymore went back into the bar and sat down. He waved the barman over and asked him what room number was above the bar, as he was a light sleeper. Gallymore had no intention of staying overnight.

'Number 7, sir.'

Gallymore thanked him. He knew he was safe while he stayed in this public place. He had no idea how many there were in here, not to mention outside. Gallymore headed off once more towards the toilets, but this time he stopped at the reception desk.

'Do you have a key for Number 7? I've left mine in the room.' The helpful receptionist gave him the spare key. Gallymore ran up the stairs two at a time and quickly opened the door of the room.

The man on the bed reading a book didn't have time to speak: Gallymore hit him in his throat so hard, with his open hand like a karate chop, that blood immediately began to pool on the sheets beneath him. The man's eyes bulged out of his head and his hands shook for a few moments, before he lay perfectly still. Gallymore hadn't stopped to watch the man die. He ran into the bathroom, placed the plug in the bath and turned on both taps full. He then did the same with the washbasin. After wedging a towel under the bathroom door, he left the room and closed the door to Number 7 quietly. He went down to the inn's toilets and was washing his hands when one of the suited men came in.

'Sorry about earlier, mate.'

'That's OK, don't worry about it.' Gallymore went back into the bar, sat back down at the table by the window and waited.

As more people lit cigarettes the room became even smokier. Standing up and turning to face the window, Gallymore raised the bottom half of the sash window, leaving a gap of about a foot. Luckily it stayed open by itself. The old man at the bar gave him puzzled look.

'Just letting a little smoke out.'

'Do what ya want to, mate,' came the gruff reply.

Gallymore noticed the swelling in the ceiling. It looked like a burn blister forming on skin, high above his head. By the time Gallymore had finished another pint the blister grew to a grotesque size. It now had warts growing on it. Gallymore couldn't resist a smile. He prepared himself.

When the ceiling collapsed, even Gallymore was surprised at the amount of water and debris that fell down. The noise was deafening as glasses and bottles were knocked over. A woman screamed and the dog ran out through the door. Tables and chairs piled themselves into corners as the water washed them from the centre of the room.

'He's gone out the window,' someone shouted.

Gallymore didn't move; he was lying in at least two inches of water, squashed into an alcove. He had knocked the window open further with his elbow as he'd slid under the table. He'd then crawled into this dark corner of the room, and was fortunate to be covered by a table and two chairs that the water had tossed onto him. He decided to stay there not moving a muscle. He heard people splashing through the water as they rushed out of the bar. He heard shouting far off but couldn't make out what was being said. The room became quieter ... then he recognised the barman's voice.

'We had better get clear of this mess, Mister McGregor. God knows what will come down next. The fire brigade will be here soon. Are you injured?'

'Where's my dog gone?'

'He went outside ... come on, we'll find him.'

The silence was broken only by the water now dripping through the hole in the ceiling.

Gallymore decided it was time to leave. He pushed the table slowly away from him and stood up. He couldn't believe his eyes: the bar was a complete mess. A proud smile came across his face.

Gallymore walked soaking wet from the bar and climbed the stairs to the accommodation part of the inn once more. He then walked along the second-floor corridor where he had noticed the sign for the fire exit. The outside steps led him down to a small courtyard behind the Inn. From there he crossed the road unseen and hid in the bushes. There was a lot of activity in front of the Inn. Cathedral Square was crowded with onlookers. The emergency services were turning up with their sirens wailing. All this confusion made it easy for him to slip away. He decided to enter the ruined cathedral in the centre of the square, and wait until dark before making his escape from Fortrose.

Inside the dilapidated building Gallymore found a dark corner and, feeling drowsy, decided to make himself comfortable and take a rest. His eyes had just closed when he felt the strong arm around his neck and the searing heat in his back. He tried to struggle but the arm held him fast. The hot feeling in his back was replaced with the taste of frothy blood in his mouth, and he knew the knife had penetrated his lung.

'Who ...' Gallymore felt all his strength being sapped away quickly. The arm loosened slightly and at last he saw the face of his killer. 'McCann! You bastard. I knew I couldn't trust you.' Gallymore slumped over on the cold stone floor of the cathedral.

'Don't move!' a loud voice suddenly boomed from behind McCann.

Kneeling over Gallymore, he raised his hands and turned slowly. Maybe the man in the black suit pointing the gun at him hadn't seen the knife still in McCann's hand.

He moved the knife into the throwing position and quickly let fly. It hit the gunman in the middle of his chest. As he fell to the floor, standing behind him was the second suited man. McCann didn't hear the shot from his gun. The bullet hit him in the temple and he fell forward not breathing. From his prostrate position, Gallymore had watched the second suited man shoot McCann, and shakily aimed his own gun at the man's torso. He pulled the trigger three times. He didn't stay around to see if the man had been killed; Gallymore was approaching unconsciousness and quickly crawled out of the building and into a bush. The ground underneath him gave way and he felt himself fall for a while, his body rolling down a bank. When he came to he was lying in a ditch, water running over his waist. He passed out again.

Liam drove the pool car onto the dockside, and after locking it ran up the gangway. He was stopped by the quartermaster.

Liam spoke quickly. 'I'm in rush, mate, I have a car to deliver to the admiral's house straight away ... in fact, I'm late already. I need your navigating officer to sign for these keys or I can't leave the car.' Liam pointed to the car and jangled the keys in front of the QM.

'You'll find him in the wardroom: down the ladder, turn left at the bottom, the wardroom is a few paces down on the left.'

'Thanks, mate.' Liam quickly descended the main access ladder. He walked casually through the crowded control room,
climbed down the accommodation ladder and banged his head on the light fitting as he walked on the raised false deck. There was a group of people looking at drawings outside the radio shack; Liam had to squeeze past them. He passed the galley serving hatch and descended the ladder to the bathroom flat. Behind the ladder he climbed down another smaller ladder into the cramped auxiliary machinery space. He took a deep breath, crouching above the freshwater tank. The inspection hatch was easy to remove. Liam quickly broke the glass vials and replaced the hatch. A few minutes later he thanked the QM as he walked off the submarine.

   Your navigator has changed his mind, he said to himself.

CHAPTER THIRTY-NINE

The preparations for *Covert* to go to war continued. Taylor had finished his tasks for the day and had been called to the captain's cabin.

'Come in, Ben ... how's it going?'

'We're ready to go in the machinery spaces, sir,' he replied enthusiastically.

'Good. I'm just putting the final crew list together. It's been easier than I thought.' The captain pulled a small stool from beside his desk. 'Please, sit.' Taylor squatted on the wobbly stool beside his captain in the small cabin. 'I've had a confidential message from Flag Officer Submarines ... so, the normal security protocols have to be applied.' The captain picked up a buff file from his desk, opened it and read from the contents. 'To all captains Submarine Squadron 3, Her Majesty's Fleet Submarine *Courageous* is to set sail at 2000 hours this evening and proceed south to the Falkland Islands.' He closed the file and placed it on his desk. 'So, she's on her way ... which means we're next in line. We must be ready in all respects to go at immediate notice; let's crank it up.'

'Will she go direct to the Falklands, sir?'

'No, she'll spend a day in Gibraltar, taking on some top-secret radio encryption equipment, and then she'll be heading directly to the Southern Ocean.'

Taylor raised his eyebrows. 'I was planning on double-checking the diving equipment.'

'Will you ask the first lieutenant to come and see me?' The captain said finally.

Taylor left the captain and went in search of the Jimmy. He found him on the casing.

'What idiot has ordered these?!' The first lieutenant was reading the label on a box: 'Eight-millimetre cinema film … *Two-Lane Blacktop* … *Rambo*… Clint Eastwood … Get this stuff back on the truck, there's no room for them on board this submarine.' He turned to the QM. 'Make sure all the eight-millimetre cinema projectors get removed and stored inboard; they're not to come to sea with us.' He then mumbled to himself. 'As if we're going to have time to sit around watching movies ...'

Taylor chose his moment. 'Excuse me, sir, the captain would like to see you in his cabin.'

'OK, thanks Chief.' The first lieutenant finished signing for another load of food supplies and disappeared down the access ladder.

Taylor had arranged to meet with Orla at the main gate at six o'clock; he checked his watch. The QM was busy helping supplies being loaded so he pegged himself out on the list board and ran to his cabin inboard. After a shower he walked to the main gate, where he saw Orla waiting inside the barrier.

'Orla, I'm so glad to see you, you look amazing.' He gave her a tight hug and a peck on the cheek. The security guard watched them but didn't speak. 'How have you managed to get through security?'

'I have my own pass now,' she boasted.

'But ... how?' Taylor looked at the pass that hung around her neck.

'It's all thanks to your friend Tim. Shall we get a coffee?' As they walked to the senior rates' mess, Orla told him all about her meeting with Tim Sherwin. In the mess they sat in the bar and Taylor made two cups of coffee.

'It's cold tonight, that wind is biting.' Taylor placed the coffee on the table and sat next to Orla.

She held his hand. 'Have there been any developments?' she asked him.

'Preparations are still going ahead – the Argentinians won't back down. Everything is being done from the government here down to the officials on the Falklands. But as you can imagine, communications with the islanders is sketchy and reports are vague and intermittent.' Taylor couldn't tell her *Courageous* was sailing in about an hour's time.

'What is it all about, Ben? Why have they done this?'

'I don't know, Orla ... only the bureaucrats who preside in Buenos Aires can answer that question.'

And you don't know if you'll be going yet?'

'No, we don't know. *Covert* is at a moment's notice to sail.'

'Have you spoken to your mam?'

'I spoke to her yesterday; she's fine, trying to get some normality back in her life.'

'I wish I could go and see her.' Orla squeezed his hand.

'Would you really?'

'Yes, of course I would.'

'It's a long way to go. Would you like me to ask her if she'd like for you to spend some time with her?'

'Yes, do it. If you're going to leave me, I'd like very much to be with your mother.'

In his mind Taylor went through the process of getting tickets and travel arrangements. 'What's my friend Tadpole been up to? Tell me about the pass.'

'I'm his representative in the peace camp.'

'His spy, you mean.'

'No, he just wants to know the comings and goings of people.'

Taylor made a mental note to have a word with his friend. Then the two of them were startled by the noise outside. Sirens sounded on the dockside and ships' horns blasted from the support vessels docked at the quay. All the tugs sounded their horns too and the roar of people shouting could be heard when Taylor opened the window.

'What's going on down there?' Orla was mystified.

'It'll be *Courageou*s going out,' said Taylor glumly. He stood and walked to the window. Taylor stared into the darkness, he could just make out the black cigar shaped outline of a submarine gliding down the loch. Orla looked at him without speaking. They both knew what this meant. Then she asked.

'Is *Covert* ready to sail?'

'Pretty much ... what isn't ready will be made good now. I'd better take you home. Things won't be the same around here for a while.' Taylor walked with Orla through security, the noise of sirens and commotion now abating.

He held her hand as they walked through the still night air down the road to the peace camp. A few people began walking the other way, carrying banners and posters over their shoulders; they said hello begrudgingly when they saw Orla with Taylor. The couple walked on in silence, thinking. As they neared the caravans, Orla stopped Taylor. She smiled, put her arm around his waist and pulled him closer.

'You're lucky to have Tim as a friend; he has your best interests at heart.'

'I'll speak to my mother this evening.'

They kissed passionately for a long time before Taylor eventually said he must be getting back. Orla reluctantly released her grip on him. She watched him go until he disappeared into the darkness down the road to the base. She turned quickly, flung open the door of the caravan and flew inside. Seeing her brother sat in his chair she hit him hard on the head, hurting her hand badly in the process. Then she ran crying into her bedroom. Liam held his head and looked at his mother, bemused.

Taylor stopped on the road at a gap in the trees and watched the dark shadow of the submarine slip silently down the loch. He wondered when he would see her again and whispered: 'Good luck, Godspeed.'

When he arrived on board, the submarine was still in chaos. Taylor informed the QM that he would be sleeping on board tonight. The QM moved the peg by his name to the on-board hole. Taylor went down to his mess. When he entered he was met by a barrage of questions.

'Have you seen this? *Courageous* has set sail. We're next.'

The other senior rates were in loud conversation and seemed to be disagreeing about most things.

'Seen what?' he enquired. A piece of official-looking headed paper was thrust at him. Taylor read it: 'Below is a comprehensive list of crew members that are to make themselves ready to go to sea at immediate notice.' Taylor checked for his name. 'So, what's wrong with that?' he asked the man who had given him the paper.

'What's wrong with it?!' the man shouted. 'Half the fucking crew are missing from that list! How on earth does the old man expect us to manage?'

Taylor didn't answer the man, but just handed the paper back to him. The conversations went on. Taylor suddenly felt the urge to be alone and left the mess. Outside he was met by an anxious junior torpedo man.

'Chief, Chief! You've got to see this!' He beckoned Taylor to follow him. They went into the for'd torpedo compartment. The torpedo man pointed. Taylor saw two men dressed in camouflage uniform unloading their kit. He walked over as they pulled two parachutes from their kit bags, and figured they must be Special Forces.

Taylor approached them with his hand out. 'Hi ... Chief Taylor ... are you guys travelling with us?' They didn't speak but shook his hand. Taylor noticed the two SIG Sauer handguns on the deck by their kit. 'Well, as you can see, there are no bunks in here ...'

'That's OK, Chief, we'll be fine: we've brought our own.' Taylor shook their hands again.

'It looks like you guys are self-sufficient, but if you need anything, just ask a member of the crew.'

Taylor left them to it. He found the torpedo man at the door.

'Let them know where they can make tea, Chris, and where the heads and bathroom are, will you? And oh – better let the cox'n know that they have weapons with them.' Taylor patted him on the shoulder.

'Whatever next?' he muttered.

Taylor went back up to the control room to make a shore telephone call to his mother.

The next day the submarine was surprisingly quiet. People had thinned and there wasn't as much noise.

Taylor had gone inboard for breakfast, and to his surprise he was joined by Tim.

'You do get out of that office, then?' Taylor gestured for his friend to join him. 'What's happening?' he asked.

'One dead guy up at a place called Fortrose. MI5 followed a man they thought was the number two in our splinter group, a man called McCann; it turned out he was meeting Gallymore, and after a shoot-out McCann was shot dead.'

'And Gallymore?'

'They don't know. He was badly injured; they think he was stabbed, but found no body.' Tim ate his full breakfast with gusto. 'I haven't eaten for a while, please excuse me.'

'Go right ahead.' Taylor couldn't concentrate on what Tim was telling him: his thoughts were on preparing to go to sea ... although he had done it thousands of times before, this time it was different.

Taylor left Tim in the dining hall and went on board *Covert*. He checked his kit; he had all his usual things for a sea voyage, but had decided on taking a few extra luxuries like chocolate, batteries for his Walkman cassette player and plenty of unscented soap and shampoo. He hadn't been back on board long before the captain came on the main tannoy system.

'Do you hear there, this is the captain speaking. I've just received notice from Flag Officer SM3; it reads: To the captain HMS/M *Covert*.

Once final checks on storing for war are complete, proceed to sea immediately. Gentlemen, we are going to war.

This is what we've been training for. It's time to put those skills we've honed to the test. Anybody not on the crew list must leave the submarine immediately. We will be carrying out intense exercising and drills on our way south. The Safeguard Rule is now in force. All heads of departments will muster in the wardroom in five minutes' time. That is all.'

Taylor knew one of the last things to be removed would be the telephone lines, but he still ran to the control room.

'Tadpole, it's me: we're going, I won't have time to tell Orla ... will you let her know? I couldn't ...' The phone line went dead as it was unplugged from the gangway.

CHAPTER FORTY

Orla felt a certain pride in showing her pass to the
security guard and walking into the submarine base
by herself. She went straight to Tim's office.

'He's gone, hasn't he?'

'Yes, I'm afraid he has. He spoke to me briefly
on the phone yesterday. He didn't have time to see
you – they were ordered to sail straight away. He
asked me to say sorry and he … well, you know.'

Orla sat in a chair with an empty feeling in her
stomach. She wanted to scream and cry at the same
time. Her eyes began to fill with tears. Tim handed
her a tissue and sat close beside her.

'*Covert* is one of the best submarines in the
fleet, and Ben Taylor is the best submariner in
Covert,' he said softly.

Orla didn't answer. She blew her nose and sat
back in the chair. 'Why did I have to meet a sailor?'
She wiped her mouth with a fresh tissue. 'And a
dedicated one, at that.'

Tim put his arm around her shoulders and gave
her a hug. 'Submarines are far safer than being on a
surface ship.'

'That doesn't help, Tim.'

'Sorry, I was just trying …' Then he had a
better thought. 'What's been happening at the peace
camp? Any newcomers?'

'No, it's all quiet. Well, not quiet, as people are
protesting more each day now that this stupid war has
started. But there have been no newcomers and
nobody has left.'

'Has anybody new been hanging around the camp, or have you seen anybody from the camp talking to strangers?' Tim let her think. 'Has anyone been acting differently or going to different places?' He let her think again.

Orla thought about the other families at the camp and what had been happening ... then she suddenly thought about Liam. The bar she had found him in, one he doesn't normally frequent ... the stranger she had seen him with. It hit her like a thunderbolt. She stood up, grabbed the photograph on his desk and stared at the man pictured at the bar in San Diego.

'It's him!' she shouted. Tim came over to her and looked at the picture. Orla pointed at the man sat at the bar. 'This man here was in the Buccaneer in Helensburgh with my brother Liam.' Tim took the photograph from her and went to his desk.

'You sure about this?'

'Oh yes, I'd remember that face.' Orla told Tim the story of that day.

'Why would this man be in San Diego and then appear in Helensburgh?' He picked up the phone.

Orla had no idea who he was on the phone to, but he'd been on quite some time. She decided to make some more tea. As she put the cups down on Tim's desk his fax machine burst into life.

When he hung up she asked: 'Who was that?'

'We're in well over our heads here, and your brother is in big trouble, Orla. That was my boss in London and he thinks this is Gallymore – he's leading a group of splinter terrorists who split from the IRA a few months ago.

My boss is on the phone now to MI6.' Tim put his hand to his mouth and stared at the photo.

'You're kidding me? And Liam's involved?' She was sat on the edge of her chair.

'Orla, will you be kind enough to tell me about Liam? I need to know his history, your history, everything – from where he was born to the school he went to, everything.'

Orla had been talking for over twenty minutes when the fax machine began to burr into life. She was still talking as Tim went to it and removed paper reports. His face went ashen as he flopped in his chair reading the print. Orla stopped talking. The fax machine made a churning noise and more paper spilled out of it. Orla went over to the machine and gathered up the reports, giving them to Tim as he read intently. He hadn't finished them all when he put the pile of papers down on his desk.

'We're in big trouble!'

'What is it? Who are they from?'

'I asked my boss to fax through all news bulletins and police involvement in anything big around the time Gallymore and Ben where in San Diego together.' Tim picked up the sheets again from his desk. He read out loud: 'There was a large explosion at a chemical plant on the outskirts of Los Angeles ... a lot of people killed in the blast and subsequent fire ... toxic fumes spread over a mile and a half ... parts of Los Angeles were evacuated.'

Then from another: 'Virus stolen from San Diego University … two people killed, possibly held hostage ... police appealing for witnesses.'

Tim put the papers down and sat quietly for a moment, his eyes narrowing. Orla sat and watched him.

'Does Liam have access into the base?'

Orla didn't answer straight away; she hesitated for a moment as she tried to imagine the ramifications this could have. Then reality dawned. The true severity of the situation struck home. Her hand went to her mouth and she began to shake.

'Orla, does Liam have access to the base?!' Tim repeated louder.

'He took a job ... to help out in the car pool,' she eventually said very quietly.

'Fuck me. When did he start?' Tim asked as he again picked up the telephone. 'Car pool manager, please.' He was put on hold. Tim Sherwin put the receiver down after talking to the car pool manager. He sat down in the chair behind his desk. 'I'm going to have to talk to the admiral. Orla, would you be a good girl and make some coffee?' He started to make some notes on a writing pad. Orla made a pot of coffee. He continued to write while they talked through the events, making a chronological list of what had happened to report to the admiral.

When he had finished he turned to Orla. 'Orla, I'm sorry but you're going to have to leave. I'll contact the admiral and sort out where we're going from here.' He paused as he watched her frown. 'Don't worry, I'll keep you informed.'

'What will happen to Liam?'

'Don't mention anything to him: we don't want to spook him. We need to keep him around and we'll need to speak to him.

We have to find out exactly what it is he's done.
Right, I'm off to see the admiral.'

Orla left him to it, and walked out of the base
with her mind racing, trying to figure out what Liam
had been up to. It took her a while to get home as she
walked slowly along the road. When she approached
the caravan at the peace camp she could hear Liam
coughing violently inside.

'You can go in now, Sergeant.'

The Wren assistant to the admiral opened the
door for him and Tim Sherwin entered the admiral's
office. Sherwin was glad he'd written the notes to
present to the admiral: he didn't want to miss
anything out. Admiral Johnson was in charge of all
the submarines in the 3rd Squadron Base at Faslane.
He had had the title Flag Officer Submarines for three
years. While Tim was still reading his report the
Admiral straightened his tunic and paced his office
floor, then picked up the phone to the Wren in the
other office.

'Janet, I need to talk to the base commander,
will you ask him to come over, it's very urgent.' He
replaced the receiver. 'We need to get this Liam
Brodie in for some serious questioning. What
submarines COULD he have had access to? Including
the ones that have sailed. The base must be brought to
the highest state of security – I want all non-essential
personnel OFF this base. As if we hadn't got enough
to contend with!'

'Sir, MI6 have been alerted that this man
Gallymore has been seen in San Diego and they've

sent me two news bulletins that happened while he was in California.' Tim Sherwin handed the admiral two faxes.

After reading them quickly the admiral sat back in his chair and removed his glasses. 'So, what you're saying is, this lunatic has either a chemical weapon from the plant in Los Angeles or a virus of some sort stolen from San Diego University? I'll also want a full Hazmat team on the base – I don't care where they come from but I want the best ... that probably means the Army.' The admiral was interrupted by the intercom on his desk.

'Admiral, sir, I'm sorry to disturb you ...'

The Admiral walked to his desk and pressed a button. 'Go ahead, Janet.'

'Sir, the chief yeoman has an urgent dispatch he thinks you need to see right away. I've told him you're busy but he insists.'

'Very well, let him in.' The chief yeoman from the signals office came in and handed the admiral a signal pad.

After reading the signal the admiral turned to Sergeant Sherwin. 'We have a submarine missing!'

The submarine base at Faslane had been put on its highest security alert. No longer was there just a barrier at the main gate: the large iron side gates had been closed. Every vehicle and person entering and leaving was subject to close inspection and the correct authorisation papers had to be in their possession. The amount of armed Royal Marine guards had been doubled alongside the normal military police presence. The road outside the base had armed Marines patrolling along its length. The admiral had ordered the base to be closed tighter than a drum. Military vehicles ran along the road from Helensburgh to the base throughout the day and night and helicopters flew overhead.

Orla Brodie watched the commotion from the window of her caravan, while Liam coughed violently from inside his bedroom.

Admiral Johnson had convened a meeting with the highest-ranking officers from all three services, as well as MI6 and Sergeant Tim Sherwin.

'Gentlemen thank you for coming. We have a serious problem on our hands.' The admiral addressed the meeting with a weighty demeanour. 'Before we start I would like to give a Bravo Zulu to Sergeant Sherwin for bringing relevant information to my notice, although I wish he had come sooner.' The admiral removed his cap, leaned on the table in front of him and gave a long sigh. 'That said we have a few issues to address, the first and most important one being the fact we have a missing submarine off the coast of Gibraltar.

Courageous missed her last report time and has not been heard from since 1900 hours yesterday. This puts her almost fourteen hours overdue. SUBMISS instructions have been passed to all NATO and worldwide navies allied to the UK. SUBSUNK operating protocols and instructions are ready to be released. We have asked the United States Deep Sea Rescue Vessel to be put on standby. I will need a specialist team to fly out to Gibraltar and liaise with the Gib diving team to help with the search. May I suggest, Sergeant Sherwin, that as you are a qualified diver yourself, you can organise that.' The admiral looked at Sherwin, who nodded his head. The admiral added: 'Come and see me after and we'll discuss it.' He then continued: 'We currently have one other submarine at sea, HMS/M *Covert*, and it would appear that all is well on board as her report times have been kept. She is the most suitable and has the capability to search with her advanced sonar for her sister submarine, but unfortunately she cannot be diverted to help because she has orders from the PM to head directly south for the Falklands.' The admiral rubbed his head. 'Now, we have a scumbag in the peace camp who needs to be brought in for questioning, ASAP. Commander, will you get on with that straight away?' the admiral said turning to the base commander.

'Certainly, sir.' The base commander stood up, placed his cap on his head and walked swiftly to the door. The admiral remained silent for a moment after the commander had left the room. Then he scanned the room with his eyes as he spoke:

'Gentlemen, we have two Polaris submarines and two other hunter-killer submarines alongside in this base; I do not want anything to happen to them, do I make myself clear?' There was a loud acknowledgement from the meeting. The admiral replaced his cap and strode from the room purposefully.

His aid and steward joined him at the door and followed behind closely back to his office.

Once they were inside, the admiral let loose: 'Why oh *why* has this happened to me? How did this man get into the base anyway?! I know we're short-staffed but to cut corners on security is ludicrous!' The admiral started to pace the floor. His aid didn't know what to do; it was too early to pour a drink.

'Admiral, can I get you something? A hot drink, perhaps?'

'No, no ... what I need are some answers. If anything has happened to those submariners, the prime minister will be all over this like a rash, and I'm going to be the one she comes to for answers. I need something stronger than a hot drink, Chief.' The admiral walked to his desk and pressed the intercom. 'Janet, get hold of Sergeant Sherwin and ask him to come to my office as soon as he can, will you?'

'I'm looking at him now, sir, he's sat in my office ... I'll send him straight in.' The steward excused himself and collided with Sherwin coming in through the door.

'Sorry, Sergeant,' he said ruefully.

Sherwin smiled and entered the office he was now familiar with.

'Come in, Sergeant, close the door ... sit down and make yourself comfortable.'

The admiral had regained his composure. Before Sherwin had sat down the admiral was firing questions. 'Who else knows about this man Gallymore?'

Sherwin sat down in the chair tentatively. 'Well, sir, my boss Colonel Leonard and whoever he has informed at MI6. There's also this girl, Orla Brodie, the sister of Liam at the peace camp ... and the only other person is Chief Petty Officer Taylor.'

The admiral paused for a moment. 'Who is Chief Petty Officer Taylor? What is his involvement here?'

Tim Sherwin told the admiral how they'd met and the diving course they'd done together. He then went on to inform the admiral about Taylor's relationship with Orla.

'Can we trust him?' the admiral enquired.

'Without a doubt, sir. I would trust him with my life.'

'And this girl?'

'I would say so. She reported the fact that she saw her brother Liam with this man Gallymore in a pub in Helensburgh. This is what tied it all together for me: it was that sighting that convinced me to come and see you, sir. She wouldn't have landed her brother in it like that if she was involved.'

'No, I suppose not ... but they're a sneaky lot this IRA.' The admiral had now sat down behind his desk. 'Liam Brodie is being brought in for questioning as we speak. I'd like you to bring this young lady in for a chat with me. In this office.

Let's see if she has anything else to share with us. Where is this Taylor person right now? I'd like to speak to him as well.'

Sherwin grimaced and closed his eyes for a second. 'We might have a slight problem there, sir – he's on board *Covert*, heading south at maximum speed.'

The general alarm had sounded for an exercise flood in the motor room. Taylor banged his head on a valve cover as he ran along the accommodation deck – a valve that would normally be a lot higher, but due to extra food tins the deck had been raised by six inches. By the time he was in the engine room blood was oozing down his cheek. He wiped it with a rag.

'Who is on watch with you, Stewart?' Taylor spoke to the man stood watching the main turbines.

'Tam, Chief; he's helping with the flooding in the motor room. I haven't seen these temperatures so hot, everything is cooking down here. If the old man continues pushing the boat and the crew like this, we'll be fucked before we even get to the Falklands.'

'He's pushing hard, that's for sure. What depth are we at?'

'Eight hundred feet at the moment, but it keeps changing .. and we're altering course a lot as well. I don't know who's driving this bucket!'

'It's not the Argentinians the skipper is worried about at the moment, Stewart. We'll sort them out when we get there. Right now he's worrying about the Russians: they'll have heard about the conflict and will be searching this area with a fine-tooth comb looking for us. It's a great opportunity for them to see how we really work.'

'Sounds like every fucker is out to get us.'

Taylor ruffled Stewart's hair. 'Everybody wants to beat the best, eh!' He smiled.

When the exercise was over and the flooding stopped, Taylor went forward to the accommodation deck, where he heard a commotion from down in the bathroom flat. Taylor stopped the chef as he came out of the galley.

'What's going on down there, Chef?'
The chef began to laugh and shake his head but regained control long enough to speak: 'Snipz ... you know, the guy who used to be a barber before he joined up?' Taylor didn't know but nodded anyway. 'Went for a shit when we were shallow ... sub went deep, pressure came on ... Snipz couldn't get the fucking door open – it jammed and he couldn't get out of the cubicle.' The chef laughed louder. 'The toilet pan had a blowback and he was covered. Had to stay like that until the sub came back up.' The chef laughed again. 'Never heard nothing like it.'

'So what's happening now?'

'Snipz has been thrown in the shower and the Jimmy's having all the doors removed – no privacy anymore on this boat.' Then the chef went serious and asked: 'Chief, is there anything we can do about these bags of gash in the can crusher? We won't be able to get in there soon and they're beginning to smell.'

'I'm sure the captain is aware of the situation. That can crusher makes a racket when that piston crushes the can; make sure you get permission from the control room before it's used – it'll be detected from miles away by sonar.

He'll be waiting for an opportunity to ditch all the rubbish when he's sure we're in deep water and there's nobody around to recover it. A lot can be read from another boat's rubbish. What we must make sure of is that the sacks are doubly heavy with crushed cans so they sink to the bottom.'

Country music started to play from the junior rates' mess.

'There are a few music tapes in there that I'd like to crush.'

'I'll bet there is, but we don't want to start upsetting your mates so early in the voyage – things will get difficult enough. So, what have we for supper?'

'That's another thing I'm not sure of. The range and oven have both been on; then we go to action stations and they get turned off again. With all these exercises going on it's difficult to prepare anything hot; the crew won't survive for long on sandwiches.'

'Do the best you can, buddy, it's going to get worse.' The general alarm sounded for an exercise fire in the torpedo compartment.

'Here we go again!' cried the chef.

Alongside the general exercises of fires, floods and casualties, the captain went through mechanical breakdowns and loss of electrical supply along with atmosphere and ship's ventilation problems. Systems were cross-connected, power was rerouted and makeshift fans and pumps were placed at strategic points around the submarine. When he was satisfied with the ship's company's performance he switched to tactical routines. He exercised finding and attacking other submarines and surface ships, including navigation and sonar evaluation. High-speed avoidance manoeuvres made sure that everything was lashed down and stowed away; some of the crew sustained minor injuries. Taylor was looking forward to climbing into his bunk after a long stint on watch in the engine room, when he was called to the captain's cabin.

'Ben, I've received a top-secret message from Flag Officer Scotland and Northern Ireland, and it makes very interesting reading. You'd better sit down, this might take some time.' He ushered Taylor to a stool. 'I suppose I'd better start at the beginning.' The captain gave Taylor a stern look. 'From FOSNI to commanding officer HMS/M *Covert*: it has been brought to my attention that a possible terrorist threat has been carried out at the submarine base at Faslane Scotland. A hazardous chemical or viral type of substance may have been placed on your submarine while alongside and likely places are the water supply or ventilation system. Recommend you surface and purge all atmosphere immediately and drain all water tanks, flushing with fresh. Also advise a thorough inspection of all compartments and tanks for vials or virus containers. Full Hazardous Material Standard Operating Procedures and extreme caution to be used if found. More details to follow.' Captain Coleman placed the document on his desk slowly. 'I wanted you to know, Ben, for security reasons. Keep your eyes open.'

Ben instantly thought of Tim.

'OK,' The Captain continued. 'When the helicopter arrives we can exercise emergency surface and dive procedures.'

'Sir, what helicopter? FOSNI doesn't mention a helicopter.'

'Not in this signal. I've been in communication with him directly and we've come to believe that if the virus was on board *Covert*, it would have taken effect by now, but we have to be sure. So, as a precaution, Hazmat SOPs must be carried out.

Now, he also informs me that we have a SUBMISS alert running at the moment. *Courageous* has gone missing near Gibraltar. We are to rendezvous with a helicopter, which your relief will be coming in on, and you'll be taken to Gibraltar, where you, with your knowledge of this class of submarine along with diving know-how, will assist and advise the search team. God knows what you're getting into, Ben, but be careful.'

'How long have I got to pack?'

'Half an hour.' The captain held out his hand. 'Our paths are to part, so it would seem; let's hope we meet up again soon.'

Taylor stood and shook the captain's hand.

The captain brought the submarine to periscope depth and briefed his team in the control room. 'It's very dark up top, cloud cover is full; the sea state is not perfect, though – moderate to rough, and unfortunately we can't wait for it to improve.' The captain turned to the engineer on the systems console.

'Go ahead and raise the ALN comms mast; the helo will contact us when it's overhead. Radar and sonar, keep a close watch for unwanted guests. This operation must run smoothly – I don't want to spend any more time on the roof than is necessary. Our main aim here is to remain undetected ... and having said that, let's not rush it either – the last thing we need is a man in the water. The first lieutenant will now give a safety brief.' The captain stood back and the first lieutenant stepped forward.

The submarine's deck began to alter its angle slightly, the first signs for the crew that the boat was heading for the roof. For those members who became sea-sick, this was their worst nightmare.

'Submarines don't have a keel and roll on wet grass. You'd better grab hold of something,' the on-watch torpedo man told the Special Ops soldier in the fore-ends.

The experienced crew knew that moving about the submarine would be a whole lot more difficult. The hull was a smooth, sleek shape below the surface, but on the surface it wasn't stable: the large conning tower sticking up from the centre of the deck acted like a sail, swaying and rolling the boat from side to side.

In the control room the deck party readied themselves. The captain moved the periscope through three hundred and sixty degrees checking the surface was clear, the order to crash-dive on the tip of his tongue. Once he was sure no ship was bearing down on them he relaxed slightly. 'Open the hatch Number One, up you go. Down periscope. Trim the submarine for surface running, Chief.' He ordered the systems console operator: 'Two degrees down on the stern planes, keep the nose up.'

The cold air from the open hatch filled the control room quickly. Crewmen reached for their jumpers as they sat at their controls.

The deck crew scrambled up the ladder wearing heavy foul-weather gear and hazardous-duty lifejackets, torches burning brightly strapped to their heads. Guardrails were rigged quickly and lifelines clipped on. The first lieutenant checked the sky for the helicopter but saw only blackness; the rain hurting his eyes. The noise of the sea blocking out any rotor engine noise, salt spray flew over the heaving deck. Taylor waited in the control. From nowhere, bright lights lit up the sky and the helicopter appeared overhead.

'OK, Ben: up you go ... good luck!' The captain shook his hand.

'Good luck to you, sir, keep safe.' Taylor climbed the ladder to the deck. The deck crew had the cage attached by winch to the helicopter in hand; Ben climbed straight in and he immediately felt the cage swing free from the submarine. He was now spinning above the sea and watched the deck crew start to disappear back down the ladder into the safety of the submarine. He was winched to the helicopter and hands grabbed the cage and pulled him in through the door. The pilot plotted a course for Gibraltar.

CHAPTER FORTY-TWO

The sun was rising from the sea and warming the Barbary macaque monkeys eating the constant supply of fruit supplied by tourists on the Rock. The helicopter landed on the short air strip by the crossing from Gibraltar to Spain. Taylor took a cab through the narrow streets to the dockyard and went directly to the operations room.

'My name is Chief Taylor. I'm not sure who it is I'm here to see as I was brought straight here from my submarine *Covert* last night.' He spoke to a young Wren officer.

'The lieutenant commander is expecting you, Chief. Although he is very busy at the moment – would you mind waiting?' She pointed to a long seat along the far wall.

'What is the lieutenant commander's name, please?'

'Lieutenant Commander Paulsdon. He's in charge of all operations here on the Rock.' Taylor sat on the seat. The Wren stood up, walked to a large printing machine by the door and gathered some papers. 'He's busy at the moment preparing ships to go south, and we're expecting more to arrive soon.'

'Who's in charge of the diving team at the moment?' Taylor asked.

She pointed her finger at the door at the other end of the office. 'He is.' She sat back down at her desk. 'There's a warrant officer over at the actual Diving Section. He runs things on a day-to-day basis, but Lieutenant Commander Paulsdon is in overall charge.'

Taylor thought he noticed some admiration in her voice. They sat in silence for fifteen minutes, before the Wren asked him if he wanted a cup of tea.

'I would love a cup, thanks – white, no sugar. Do you know how long the lieutenant commander is going to be?'

She shook her head and went to make the tea. When she came back she handed him a mug.

'You're just going to have to wait, Chief ... he'll get to you when he's able to.'

Taylor drank his tea and felt refreshed. He stood and walked to the window. The scene on the dockside was mayhem. Overhead cranes swung loads onto ships and vehicles charged along the old roads ... men where dashing from ship to shore to ship ... small boats sped around the harbour causing wash from their bow to break on the sides of the Royal Navy warships.

Taylor turned to the Wren officer. 'Excuse me, ma'am, but I have an important search to start. Would you give my apologies to the lieutenant commander, I'm going to see the warrant officer over at the Diving Section and see if I can get things started.'

'But you have to wait. The lieutenant commander wants to see you. He won't be happy if you're not here …'

Taylor walked out the door, leaving her with a startled look on her face. By the time he got to the Diving Section he was perspiring – the sun was now high in the sky, although it hadn't yet reached its maximum intensity. He stepped through the large doors into the garage. Two empty boat trailers stood in the middle.

Taylor called out but no one answered. There was a staircase at the back. Taylor climbed the steps and walked along a lengthy passage on the first floor. He called out again and this time heard a faint voice from one of the offices further down the corridor.

'Warrant Officer Bailey?' Taylor got his name from the brass plaque on the door.

'Yes, come in!' came the reply.

When Taylor entered, he found the warrant officer with a quizzical look on his face. Large furrows criss-crossed his forehead, and his nearly completely bald head sat on a stocky body.

'Can I help you?'

'Sorry to disturb you, sir – I'm Chief Taylor from the submarine *Covert*.' The quizzical look stayed on the WO Bailey's face. Taylor realised Bailey didn't know who he was or why he was there. He didn't wait to be asked to sit but made himself comfortable in a chair. 'There's a SUBMISS out for HMS *Courageous*. She's missing somewhere off Gibraltar and I've been asked to locate her.' Taylor told him the full story. 'So you see, sir, I need to borrow a dive boat with sonar equipment, and I'll need some of your team to help.'

'I've not been told of any SUBMISS since this war started with Argentina ... but some messages haven't been coming down to us from the ops room ... the base has gone haywire, it's chaotic. The whole team are out now carrying out underwater searches for explosives on every ship in the harbour. I don't have any divers to let you have.'

'What about a boat?'

'The team are using the harbour launch for their searches at the moment, but we do have a larger sea-going boat.

'Does it have sonar?'

'Yes ... but I'll need to get approval from the boss.'

'Do what you have to, sir, but I'll need that boat. Does it have its own crew?'

'Yes, it has a civilian crew, but you'll still need to get some divers. I'm not being difficult, Chief, but we're stretched to the limit already, preparing ships to go to war. The task you've been set will be very difficult – if not impossible – until things start to quieten down and get back to some sort of normality. Our resources are limited here: our normal duties are to search the hulls of warships and carry out small underwater maintenance procedures. Anything large or technical, we have to call in a specialist team from the UK. Right now with this added exertion of preparation for war, everyone is working flat out. My team have been on the go for two days working through the night and on call twenty-four hours a day, ready to go at a moment's notice.'

'I realise things are extremely busy at the moment and God knows how long it will continue, but I really need your help to find this submarine, sir.'

The warrant officer stood and walked to the window. 'Chief, come and look out here.'

Taylor didn't need to look out the window. 'I know how hard everyone is working out there, I was nearly run over by a lorry and I lost count of how many pushbikes I had to jump out of the way of on my way over here. All I'm asking is to set me up with the ability to search for this submarine and I'll run the rest by myself.'

'I'll help you as much as I can, but I don't know how helpful the ops lieutenant commander will be.'

'What do you mean?'

'He's a bit of a stickler for rules: he's in line for his other half-ring and wants to become a commander badly ... promotion is the only thing on his mind right now.'

'Well this is a perfect situation for him to shine and show his superiors that he can step up to the mark.'

'That's how you and I would see it, but he only sees stumbling blocks.'

Taylor joined his new ally at the window. 'Well, he's obviously under a lot of stress at the moment. I'm not saying lie or hide things from him, and I'm not one for cutting corners, especially where people's lives are at stake ... but let's keep the communication with him to a minimum. Obviously you'll have to get approval for certain things and that I understand – I wouldn't want you to put your head on the chopping block ... but I would appreciate moving fast with this.'

Both men moved back into the air-conditioned office as the sun was too hot by the window.

'OK, the dive boat I can let you have.' Bailey rubbed his chin. 'The captain's name is Pedro – you'll find him on board. He'll show you around and explain the workings. Permission must be obtained from the ops room before you leave the dockside. All boat movement is scrutinised and recorded, but Pedro will sort that out for you, he knows the routine.

All aspects of leaving harbour and getting you to the dive site will be sorted by Pedro and his crew; but you'll still need divers.'

'Does the boat have a recompression chamber on board?'

'No, the nearest one is here in the Section.'

'I'd like to see it as soon as I can.'

'Sure thing, I'll take you down now and introduce you to Pedro.' WO Bailey opened a drawer in his desk, took out a portable VHF radio and clipped it to his belt.

As they walked down to the dive boat Taylor talked about walking out of the lieutenant commander's office. 'I was air-lifted off my submarine in the middle of the night only to spend my time waiting in his office. I don't think he realised just how important this search is. If those men are still alive then we need to find them quickly. Finding the submarine is just the start of the operation – then we have to raise the sub or get the crew off. We could be looking at losing a hundred lives if we don't move fast.'

'The boss won't be pleased you left his office before he saw you. But I do understand why you did it. You can start searching straight away with just the dive boat crew, and when you find it I'll try and get you divers. It's the best I can offer.'

'Thank you, sir.'

'And leave the boss to me – I'll do my best to keep him off your back.'

They walked across the gangplank onto the dive boat. WO Bailey introduced him to Pedro, who was in the galley.

'What's cooking, Chef?'

'Chef? You cheeky man.' The bearded, well-built man spoke in broken English.

'Hi, Pedro, good to see you ... is everything OK?'

'Everything is fine, with me and boat. I look after her for you and she's ready to go.'

Taylor expected the firm grip of the skipper as they shook hands. He was dressed shabbily and had a distinct odour about him. When he smiled he showed gaps in his teeth at the side of his mouth.

Bailey, realising that Taylor might have his doubts about this man, said: 'Don't be misled by his appearance, Ben: he's a good man, and an even better skipper. He knows the seas around here like the back of his hand. If anyone can find your submarine, he will.'

'Finding submarine? Tell more. Come, I show you around.' The skipper smiled and put his arm round Taylor's shoulders.

'I'll leave you to it, Ben ... I'd better get back to the office and inform the boss that he's just lost his dive boat for a while.' Bailey smiled.

'Good luck, sir.' Taylor smiled back.

'You call me Pedro, I am the only permanent crew member of dive boat. There used to be more crew but cutbacks.' He wagged his finger in the air. 'I am captain and chief engineer, although I have good mechanic who has learned well; he look after things down below. Three deck hands, who manage ropes and anchor us at dive site when we need; all good men, with plenty experience—'

'I noticed you have a large derrick on the deck up for'd,' Taylor interrupted.

'Yes, fully operational, but not big enough to pick up submarine I'm afraid. The boat is forty-foot ex-fishing trawler, converted to diving tender twelve years ago. She has twin Paxman diesel engines with plenty power. The fish hold has been turned into changing room and houses the compressors, drying room and maintenance benches. The charging hoses come up onto deck from the compressors below and all charging is done up here in the open air for safety. All diving equipment is down in the hold with the diving suits. The divers from the Section look after that side.'

'Tell me more about the sonar, Pedro.'

'Well, best place to do that is up on the bridge, so we go up there.' Taylor followed the big man up the steep ladder to the bridge. 'Is smaller version of MK2006 sonar but only has active facility. I think one of the divers found it in a mine sweeper that was being dismantled, and the dockyard fitted it for us. It works really well. We also have very good MK776 echo sounder.' Pedro continued to show Taylor the rest of the bridge. 'Navigation and chart table here at back and steering and speed is controlled from here at front.

'Perfect ... this will be perfect. How long will it take to get her ready for sea?'

'We keep her ready for always; heaters keep engines warm. So, get permission from ops room, unplug shore power connection and throw off ropes ... bam, we're on our way.'

'Good.' Taylor looked out the bridge window at the fore-deck, deep in thought. 'OK, Pedro, make the boat ready for sea. I'll be back shortly after I've spoken with Mister Bailey.' Then as an afterthought: 'Oh – can I take one of your local charts up to his office with me?'

'Sure can ...' Pedro opened a large drawer and removed a chart for him.

Taylor ran off the dive boat.

WO Bailey was sat at his desk. 'What do you think of the dive boat – will it do?'

'Perfect, sir.' Taylor stood by the door.

'Call me Bill; I think we're going to get to know each other quite well.'

Taylor laid the chart on his desk. 'Your ops room will have been sent the lat and long of the last position known on the *Courageous*; I'd like to mark it on this chart and use it as a starting point for my search.' WO Bailey picked up the phone. 'I'd also like to make a request to FOSM in Faslane for a Sergeant Tim Sherwin to join me here.' Bailey held up his thumb. 'Oh, and ask him to bring any spare divers with him.'

Bailey smiled and put his thumb up again. He wrote down some figures on a pad in front of him. A few minutes later he put down the phone.

'Right, a request has been sent for Sherwin and spare divers. The Wren over there is very efficient, but when he'll arrive is another thing. Let's transfer these figures to the chart.' He picked up the pad and stood over the chart.

Ten minutes later, Taylor was running back on board the dive boat. He could hear the engines running and felt the vibrations through his feet. The skipper was on the bridge wing and shouted down.

'We ready to go, admiral?'

Taylor smiled at the new rank given him by Pedro.

'Let's go, skipper.'

'Loose that brow, boys, let go the mooring lines.'

The crew immediately pulled on board the brow from the jetty and set about loosening the mooring lines. As soon as they were removed the dive boat started to slip away from the jetty.

Taylor joined Pedro on the bridge. 'Where are we going, admiral?'

Taylor placed the chart on the navigation table. 'Here.' He put his finger on the chart.

Pedro looked over his shoulder as he steered the boat. 'OK ...' He thought for a moment. 'Yah, I got it.' He pushed the throttle open and the boat sped out of the harbour. 'Tidal range here around Gibraltar is not much – this due to volume of water not being able to move in and out of Mediterranean easy through narrow gap between Spain and Africa. It can reach maximum of around four feet but at the moment we are on neap tides and it's around one to two feet. I take accurate depth with echo sounder when we get to the site. Which will be in about fifty minutes.'

'Thanks, Pedro.' Taylor drew a pencil line from the harbour to the position on the chart where he wanted to start the search. 'Fancy a brew?' He asked.

'I never say no to offer, admiral,' he smiled.

When Taylor returned from the galley with the coffee he stood by the side of Pedro as he steered a straight course.

'Can you take helm for moment? I just want to check something on chart.'

Taylor took the helm and Pedro walked to the chart table. 'Do you want us to anchor when we get there?'

'Not necessary, Pedro, we can go straight into the search if that's OK with you.'

'Perfect.' Pedro walked over to the sonar screen and reached down beneath it. 'Let's get this *chiquita* warmed up eh?'

Pedro took the helm again and Taylor started to draw a grid system on the chart around the marked point the *Courageous* was last heard from.

'Where are you from, Pedro? How did you end up with a cushy job like this?' Taylor asked as he drew on the chart.

'I'm from Algeciras, just across border, and I started working in dockyard as apprentice twenty-one years ago now. This job become available when the last man retired and I apply and get it. It is good lifestyle now – I am own boss and left to do what I want, pretty much. As long as boat kept clean and working, they leave me alone to get on with it.'

'You're a lucky man, to have a job you like doing.'

'That I know, and I don't abuse it. I want to work here for as long as I can.'

After another mug of coffee they arrived at the search site. Taylor moved from the chart table to the sonar screen.

Pedro was relieved on the helm by a crew member and he went to the chart table to conduct the search. They passed up and down a square search grid transferred from the chart to the sea by expert boat handling. The first box revealed nothing on the seabed that could resemble a submarine.

'It's going to give us a good signal back on the screen, being so large and all metal.' Taylor adjusted the resonance of the sonar slightly for a better picture. 'Once this box is cleared we can move straight to the next one, just south of here.' The dive boat continued searching slowly and meticulously. When an area was searched and cleared, Pedro cross-hatched the area on the chart with his pencil. Now there were four boxes north, south, east and west around the initial mark on the chart and nothing had been found. Seven hours later they were still searching, with the sun now beginning to dip towards the horizon.

Pedro turned to Taylor: 'We better call it a day, admiral. The men will have to get home. Overtime not paid and we working late, now.' He watched Taylor staring at the screen.

Taylor eventually looked up and rubbed his eyes. 'Yeah, sure. We'll have to extend the search area ... maybe check the lat and long and amend the initial mark. Can we start as early as possible tomorrow?'

'We be ready at eight in the morning.' Pedro took the helm, and before they left the area a large orange buoy was dropped into the sea to clearly mark the area. The skipper then headed back to port. Taylor sat in the chair by the sonar screen. He rubbed his forehead and suddenly felt very tired.

By the time the dive boat docked, the Diving Section was locked up and no one was around. Taylor said goodnight and thanked the crew before he walked slowly to the senior rates' mess. He ate a large plate of lamb stew before falling asleep fully clothed on his bed. In the morning he showered quickly before heading down to the jetty. He boarded the dive boat at 0715 hours and went straight to the galley. He could smell coffee.

'Hey admiral, how are you today?' Pedro smiled as he began to open tins of potatoes, carrots and stewing-meat chunks. He poured them into a large pot on the stove and added water. 'This is lunch ... the crew love "pot mess", as they call it. The divers teach us the recipe; it's really good.' He began to stir it with a large wooden spoon. 'Oh, warrant officer wants to see you before we go anywhere.'

Taylor left Pedro to the cooking and walked to the Diving Section. WO Bailey was drinking coffee too.

'Ben, come in ... would you like a coffee?'

'Thanks, Bill, yes I would. Pedro said you wanted to see me?'

'How did it go yesterday?'

'The crew were very professional but the search didn't go well. We're going out again as soon as the crew are on board.'

'Well, hold your horses for a while longer. Your friend Sherwin is arriving at 10 a.m., I thought you might want to meet him at the airport. You can borrow a Land Rover from the garage.'

Taylor told Pedro to delay departure and headed for the airport in an old Land Rover. He watched as the aeroplane turned quickly, rounding the Rock and avoiding Spanish air space. He was surprised at how fast it stopped on the short runway. Tim was through customs in no time and they hugged outside the main building.

'Hi, buddy, what's been happening?'

'I'll fill you in on the way to the dive boat. Do you have any divers with you?'

Three young men walked from the main building carrying large canvas bags.

'Just these bozos,' Tim said, pointing at the men. 'They don't know what they've let themselves in for but they volunteered.' He laughed.

'Climb in, guys,' Taylor shouted to them.

They threw their gear in the back and climbed in through the rear door. Taylor showed them around the dive boat as they made their way out of the harbour, and the makeshift team hung rubber suits in the drying room. Then they set about preparing and checking the diving gear. Taylor and Tim where on the bridge.

'This is where we searched yesterday, Tadpole, so I thought we would try further out in the channel.' He pointed to a spot on the chart. 'We'll do the same box searches out here.'

'Sounds good ... show me how this sonar works, will you? I've not used one before.'

Taylor showed Tim the controls for the sonar and explained as best he could what the submarine would look like on screen. They both watched the screen showing a picture of the seabed as the boat moved slowly through the search box. Tim shouted every now and then when something showed, but Taylor shook his head on every occasion: 'No, mate, too small' or 'wrong shape.'

At around 1300 hours they stopped for pot mess. Two crew members were left on the bridge while the rest of the crew and the diving team were in the galley. They sat in silence for a long time before Tim eventually spoke.

'Don't worry, pal, we will find them.' Tim looked at Taylor solemnly. Taylor didn't look up. Then Tim turned to Pedro. 'This is quite good.' Everybody agreed, and Pedro smiled proudly.

Taylor went out on deck and Tim followed him. They stood at the stern looking at the water.

'What's your plan when we do find them, mate?' Tim asked his friend quietly.

Taylor thought for a moment. 'We'll secure a line to the submarine; I'll dive and try to communicate with the crew inside.'

'How will you do that?'

'Knocking on the pressure hull with a hammer will do to start with. Then I'll try and gain access through one of the escape towers.'

'That could be dangerous if there's a virus on board.'

'I'll be breathing from a diving set. Keeping the mask on will protect me.' Taylor turned to face the boat.

Tim looked at his friend. 'Tell me how you operate the escape tower hatch.'

Taylor went through the routine for opening the hatch.

Tim drew a deep breath. 'What are the chances of finding them alive, Ben?'

There was a long silence as Taylor faced his friend. 'Come on, let's get back to work,' Taylor ordered.

Moments later Taylor and Tim where back on the bridge. The search continued at a snail's pace and Tim was becoming anxious.

'This is too slow – can't we speed it up?'

'No, mate, we have to be thorough – we can't waste time going back over the grid we've already searched, it would take us twice as long.'

Both men's eyes were becoming blurred, and rubbing did not help. At 1600 hours Pedro was thinking about ending another day when a large shape appeared on the sonar screen. Tim shouted out. Taylor moved his head closer to the screen.

'That's it! That's a submarine!' Taylor shouted.

Some of the diving team who were sat in the galley heard the commotion and ran up to the bridge.

'OK, let's get a diver ready,' Taylor ordered one of the young divers. 'The first thing we need to do is get a sturdy line attached to that sub. Pedro, can you hold us in this position?'

'No problem. Weather is good, no wind and the tide is slight. Our position in channel is safe, very little traffic. I get up-to-date weather forecast.' He smiled.

The diving team sprang into action and started to move equipment onto the deck.

CHAPTER FORTY-THREE

Before Taylor left the bridge he checked the echo sounder and read the depth to be a hundred and eight feet. He then turned it off.

'I raise Flag Alpha for you, admiral,' Pedro assured him.

'Thanks, Pedro. You'd better radio the ops room and let them know we've found a contact; I'll confirm it when we're sure. The depth is a hundred and eight feet on the echo sounder but we'll check it on our sounding line ... I'm sure your instruments are calibrated accurately but I must check it.'

'No offence taken,' Pedro said as he walked onto the bridge wing.

Taylor went down on deck. 'Right, men, listen in.' He gathered the team around him. 'First off, check the depth with the sounding line.' One of the young men threw over a depth-marked line. Taylor continued. 'Launch the inflatable boat; we'll use a metal weighted shot to position a line right on the sub with a big LL float on the end. I'll check its position on the sonar. Then tie the boat off at the base of the ladder, we'll use it for the standby safety diver and if needed to recover and remove the diver's gear before getting him up the ladder and onto the deck.'

'The depth is a hundred and four feet, Chief,' reported the young man.

Taylor thanked him, converted it to metres in his head and turned to one of the other divers. 'Dave, you'll dive using an air set; take down a strong line, go down the shot line and locate the submarine. Don't hang around down there, you have seventeen

minutes' bottom time
before you'll need to decompress, so your one and only job is to tie onto the submarine and come straight back up. A good place to tie on would be the hand rail going around the conning tower, but if you can't find it, tie on to anything that's fixed to the sub.' Then he turned to one of the other young divers. 'You'll be safety standby diver. Right, let's go.'

The divers went straight to work.

Taylor turned to Tim. 'I'll supervise this first dive and then you supervise for my dive. Will you prepare two sets of forty–sixty gas mixture sets, buddy?'

'Sure will. How are we going to communicate, Ben?'

'The divers will be wearing lifelines, so we'll use standard pull signals.'

Twenty minutes later the divers were ready.

Taylor shouted down to the diver in the water. 'Diver has no leaks; leave surface!' He pressed the button on the stopwatch dangling from a string around his neck.

Pedro came onto the deck. 'I have updated weather report, Ben: doesn't look good. Strong winds coming from west, which means maybe we get big rollers coming in from Atlantic.'

'Thanks, Pedro.' Taylor checked his stopwatch. 'Come on, Dave, get a move on.'

Tim came up from the hold in a rubber diving dry suit; he was carrying two diving sets.

Pedro was intrigued. 'I see these diving sets before but I don't know anything about them.'

'Ask away ...' Tim put the sets down carefully on the deck.

'How deep you go in one of this?'

'Well, that's not an easy question to answer. The maximum safe depth of any mixture is determined by the partial pressure of the oxygen. Oxygen becomes toxic when it reaches around two bar absolute, but it can depend on the physique of the diver himself.'

'What's the difference between this set and air?'

'This set uses a mixture of oxygen and nitrogen. This particular set is forty per cent oxygen and sixty per cent nitrogen. By using a gas mixture instead of air, the time spent decompressing is reduced because less nitrogen is absorbed into the body. Less time decompressing means more time for the diver on the seabed.'

'How long will this give Ben at bottom?'

'His bottom time will be increased to twenty minutes, from seventeen minutes.'

'What if he goes over that time?'

'No drama – we'll lower a lazy shot over the side and he's trained to stop at the shot until the good book tells us he's decompressed.'

'Oh really?'

'Yeah ... basically, say he's on the bottom for twenty-one minutes ... he'll stop at three metres for five minutes until the small nitrogen bubbles have come out of solution, called "fizzing off", and then he can come up to surface safely.'

One of the young divers shouted: 'Diver left the bottom and is coming up!'

Taylor checked his stopwatch. 'Fourteen minutes ... that's good ... bring him up at the correct rate of accent.'

Once the diver was on the surface and he'd reported he was well, they dragged him out into the rubber inflatable boat. He removed his face mask.

'Line is on, Chief ... secured to the conning tower rail.'

Taylor gripped his fist and went down into the hold to put on his diving suit. 'Pedro, inform the ops room we have her,' he shouted as he climbed down the ladder.

Just minutes later he was back up on deck.

'OK, pull up the shot line that's not needed any more and might get in the way. Tie on two floats to the line on the submarine – we don't want to lose that. Someone get me a hammer. Tadpole, help get this set on, will you?' Tim came across and helped his friend get dressed. Taylor tied on his own lifeline.

'You be careful down there, buddy.'

'What could go wrong? I know you'll come and save me.' Taylor jumped into the water. He was checked for leaks and Tim shouted for him to leave surface.

Taylor felt the pressure coming on his suit as he descended. He blew against his nose clip and equalised the pressure on either side of his eardrums. The visibility was amazing: he could soon make out the shape of the submarine on the bottom.

Taylor made a note of the orientation and how she was lying on the seabed – it looked as if she'd just settled on it. He moved along the casing until he was just above the control room and hit it hard three times with the hammer. He waited and listened ... then hit it three times again. There was no reply. He moved aft and positioned himself above the manoeuvring room, where he hit the casing again

three times and waited. He repeated the procedure, but again there was no answer. Taylor moved to the aft escape tower and pulled the emergency handle; a small handle popped up and he wound it open. The hatch started to open slowly. He untied his lifeline and re-tied it to the top of the escape hatch. When he was able, he slipped inside and began to close the hatch. It was dark inside the escape tower and Taylor switched on the torch that was strapped to his leg. He opened the drain down valve and immediately the tower began to empty. Taylor felt the weight coming back onto his body.

When the tower was empty he unclipped the lower hatch and let it hang onto its hinge as he climbed down into the motor room, being careful to not to knock his diving set. When he was standing on the motor room deck plates he had to close the escape tower hatch to get past it to the entrance. Taylor was surprised to find no watch-keeper. He removed his fins so he could walk easier but kept his face mask on. Taylor walked out of the motor room and into the stores passage above the engine room. He moved quickly to the manoeuvring room.

The sight that met him made him feel nauseous and he was nearly sick in his mask. Every watch-keeping station was manned, but the crew were dead. They had died in their seats. Taylor could see no injuries on them; it seemed as if they'd fallen asleep.

He looked around the panels and checked the readings on the gauges and dials. He noticed that three Dowty warnings were showing red and the rest were yellow. None of them were green, as they should be. He walked slowly to the tunnel over the reactor compartment.

Meanwhile on the dive boat Tim Sherwin was asking the young diver who held Taylor's lifeline if he could feel him moving.

'No, Sergeant, he has definitely stopped moving. I can feel resistance but he's not moving.'

Tim checked the stopwatch. 'He's been down there for twenty-four minutes.' Tim checked the lifeline himself. He gave it a tug and realised it was tied off. 'He's gone inside,' he said to no one in particular. 'Right, get me dressed!' he shouted.

'But who's supervising?'

'You are.' He passed the stopwatch to the young diver. Tim was dressed in no time and jumped into the water. He didn't test for leaks and left the surface, heading down Taylor's lifeline.

Taylor pressed the hydraulic lever down on the tunnel aft door and it opened slowly.

Tim saw the lifeline tied to the escape tower and began opening the hatch.

Taylor turned and looked back through the manoeuvring room and wondered what he would find in the control room.

Tim slid into the tower and closed the upper hatch.

Taylor entered the tunnel and moved the lever, watching the door close slowly.

Tim struggled to move in the cramped conditions he was unaccustomed to. He strained to reach the drain valve and exerted all his energy to open it. He was now draining the seawater from the escape tower into the motor room bilge. As the level of water in the bilge hit the high-level switch, the fourth Dowty alarm in the manoeuvring room changed from yellow to red, initiating containment and shutting off the

hydraulics to the tunnel doors. The reactor scrammed and the ventilation went off.

CHAPTER FORTY-FOUR

The American fast attack submarine USS *Seawolf* (SSN-21) received an immediate execute signal from her home base. She glided effortlessly and quietly out of Groton and past the Harbour Light lighthouse. Her captain watched the street lights of nearby Pequot Avenue disappear as she slipped out without being noticed into the Long Island Sound. Now the three-hundred-and-fifty-three-feet-long, nine-thousand-one-hundred-and-thirty-seven-ton nuclear-propelled submarine had received a change of orders. Her captain read the message to his first lieutenant.

'Looks like the Limeys have got themselves a bit o' trouble in the Med. We've to meet up with *Potomac* carrying the DSRV, transfer it across to us and proceed to these coordinates at flank speed. Apparently the weather's too bad in the Atlantic for her to make more than ten knots. Once we've dived we'll be there in no time. Sounds like a bad one, Merv ... this is a SUBMISS priority message.' The captain grimaced at his Number One and slapped the message into his hand before saying, 'Come to my cabin.'

As the two men left the control room he ordered the helmsman to alter course. The helmsman on USS *Seawolf* altered course as she headed for her rendezvous with USS *Potomac*.

Taylor immediately knew something horrible had just happened. He'd heard the hydraulic valves close with a slight bang. He reached down and pushed the handle to open the door ... nothing happened.

Taylor looked through the small round window in the door and saw Tim coming to the door on the other side.

He picked up the black microphone. Taylor kept his face mask on but spat out his mouthpiece. 'Tadpole, pick up the mic by the door.' He watched as Tim looked for the microphone. When he had found it and had it in his hand, Taylor pressed the button on his mic. 'Keep your face mask on. What are you doing here?'

'I thought you were in trouble, and wanted to help.'

Taylor shook his head. 'We've fucked up big style, mate. I'm now trapped in here. Hydraulics to the door are off and it can't be opened.'

'How do we get them back on?' Tim was breathing heavily from his diving set.

'Calm down, buddy, you'll use all your gas supply.'

'Tell me how I can get the hydraulics back onto this door.'

'You can't ...' Taylor took a long pause. 'The containment valves are shut off and can only be reset from the manoeuvring room and the control room. After seeing the dead watch-keepers in manoeuvring, I'm guessing the men in the control room are in a similar way.'

The two men looked at each other through the small window.

'What about I go back out and come in again through the for'rd escape hatch.'

'You don't have enough dive time, buddy.'

'Then I've killed you, haven't I?'

'We had to try and do something.' Now Tim was shaking his head. Taylor continued. 'What we need to do now is get you off this boat.'

'Right from the start we've not had much help with this job.'

'Things have been against us, that's for sure. Now, go back to the escape tower, get off this boat and raise mayhem from that dive boat. Get some help on the surface, Tadpole. I don't know how long I can stay alive in here but maybe there's something they can do topside.'

'I can't leave you, Ben.'

'You must, Tadpole: you're the only person who can help me now. I can communicate with you on the 183 underwater comms from in here.'

Both men thought for a while.

Taylor became agitated. 'Go!' he shouted.

Tim looked at his friend through the window and felt sick.

Taylor calmed himself. 'Go on Tadpole, get yourself off this death trap.' There was another long pause. 'If you go there's a slight chance that something can be done; if you die then there's no hope.'

'OK, I'm going ...' Tim said, resigned.

'Tadpole, look after Orla for me.' Taylor replaced the microphone and sat on the deck.

Tim walked back towards the escape tower.

Lieutenant Commander Paulsdon threw the paperweight across the room and cracked the glass of a picture hanging on the wall. He grabbed his cap from the hat stand and charged out the office.

'I'm going out on the launch – will you take all my calls and inform them that I will get back to them as soon as I can. There's been an accident on the dive boat.' He continued out of the building.

The crew of the launch saluted the ops officer as he jumped on board, and the launch sped off towards the dive boat. It came alongside the dive boat and Lieutenant Commander Paulsdon climbed up onto the deck. He had never seen such a shambles. He ordered the launch back to the Diving Section.

'Get Warrant Officer Bailey out here as quickly as you can. What a mess!' He shouted for Pedro. 'And where is Sergeant Sherwin now?' he demanded.

'He's in the hold, sir.'

The lieutenant commander stormed down the ladder. Tim Sherwin was sat on a diving hamper wearing just his undersuit. He was staring at the floor. He didn't move when the officer came down.

'You, young man, are in a whole world of trouble.'

Tim stayed sat down and didn't look up.

'Do you understand?'

Tim tried to control his emotions.

'This man Taylor has been a pain ever since he arrived.'

'My friend is trapped in a bloody submarine at the bottom of the sea. What happens to me isn't important.' He stood up and faced the officer. 'With all due respect, sir, the submarine needed to be found; with this bloody war starting he wasn't receiving the help he needed. What I'd like to do now is save his life ... and sir – I need your help.'

Lieutenant Commander Paulsdon walked over to the sergeant. He put his hand on his shoulder. 'Then you had better tell me just how much trouble he's in.' He pulled another hamper close and sat down.

WO Bailey jumped off the launch. Lieutenant Commander Paulsdon and Tim were now in the galley of the diving boat and the WO joined them there.

'Ah, Bill, come in, sit down.'

The three men began to discuss how they could get Taylor out of that compartment.

'We could use cutting equipment to go through the door,' suggested Bailey.

'It would take too long, Ben would be out of gas before we could even get the gear down to the sub,' answered Tim.

'What's keeping the submarine on the bottom?' asked Bailey.

'The ballast tanks will be flooded with water,' answered the lieutenant commander.

'So if we could pump air into them we could raise the whole submarine?'

'Wouldn't we need people on board to open the valves and vents?' added Tim.

'I think it's quite clear we need an expert,' said Bailey.

'And that would be Ben,' Tim said quickly.

'Do we have communications to him?' asked the lieutenant commander.

'There's a battery-operated 183 underwater telephone system in both escape compartments and the tunnel. The control room has a 185 system.' Tim remembered this from talking to Taylor.

'Right, then, that's our start. You two get some comms with the tunnel; I'll talk to Flag Officer Submarines in Scotland and see what he comes up with.' The lieutenant commander donned his cap. 'And I had better contact his next of kin,' he added to himself.

'Sir, before you go: Taylor has a girl … she's important in his life right now. It's going to get rough for him down there. It might be beneficial to him if she were out here.'

'I'll do what I can.' The lieutenant commander headed for the launch.

Ben lay on the floor of the tunnel. He had exhausted his thoughts on escaping. He went through the systems of valves and bypasses, searching for a system line-up that would open the containment valves and free the hydraulic oil that would allow him to open the door. He had worked through routines as far back as his first week at HMS *Dolphin*, where he had begun his submarine schooling many years ago. He started to become confused and anxious and his breathing increased. Taylor calmed himself and took control of his body. He began thinking again.

The containment valves are kept shut by hydraulic fluid locked against the valves, keeping it shut. He began to feel excited – he was getting an idea that might just work. *All I have to do is cut the pipe, release the hydraulic fluid and bingo: the valve would open …*

But his idea was quickly dashed. *Great idea, Ben. What are you going to cut the pipe with? Idiot, it's impossible.* His breathing became difficult.

Taylor realised he was running out of gas in his diving set. *Well, here goes nothing.* He removed his face mask. The air tasted sweeter and his breathing was now easier. He drew in long, full breaths. Ben found himself laying out his diving equipment for a fast dress. When he realised what he was doing he lost his temper and threw the diving cylinder across the tunnel.

After the initial impact on a pipe the cylinder jammed itself under a stainless-steel ventilation cowling. Ben started pacing the tunnel, his thoughts erratic. He thought of his mother and how she would cope with a second tragedy in such a short time. Then Orla came to his mind, her face solemn and tearful. Then he was thinking of Tim. Had he got out? And had he made it safely to the surface and the dive boat? Was it possible that someone could have survived in the for'd part of the submarine? Ben opened the stainless-steel box that housed the 183 underwater telephone. *If they had,* he thought to himself, *surely they would be in the for'd escape compartment.* He switched it on.

'For'd 183 this is Tunnel 183, over.' He waited. *Maybe they could get to the control room and reset these damn containment valves.* 'For'd 183 this is Tunnel 183, over.' Still no answer. Taylor anxiously tried the control room. 'Control Room 185 this is Tunnel 183, over.' Without him realising, Taylor's voice began to rise in volume until he was almost shouting.

He listened intently in between his calls for any response, but none came. Taylor stopped broadcasting. The microphone hung limp at his side. He leaned on a pipe and sighed heavily.

The voice blasted out throughout the tunnel. It was so loud Taylor instinctively flinched and banged his elbow on a valve, sending a searing pain up his arm all the way to his shoulder. The conflict of emotion was almost overwhelming. The joy of hearing someone answer him had shocked him into silence, yet the pain in his arm made him want to scream. Then it came again.

Taylor had no idea who it was or where it was coming from. It was so loud it came from all around him, filling the tunnel. Taylor fumbled with the microphone.

'Station calling the tunnel, I hear you very loud but distorted, over.' Taylor waited, his heart pounding.

On the dive boat, Bailey altered the power rating. 'Tunnel this is Dive Boat. How do you read me now, over?'

A smile came over Taylor's face. 'Loud and clear. Who's this, over?'

'This is Bill Bailey. How are things down there, over?'

'Well I've got myself in a bit of a pickle this time, Bill. I've been racking my brains trying to think of a way out of this compartment but nothing is working, over.'

'Well be assured, buddy, we're working on it. The boss has contacted all the bigwigs and they'll come up with an answer. Don't worry, buddy, we'll get you out, over'

'Did Tim arrive back on the surface? Is he well, over?'

'He did, Ben, he's up here and well. He gave us a good description of what's happening. Sorry, Ben, I have to ask if you've managed to assess for'd? Are there any survivors, over?'

'I've tried the 183 and the 185 but no answer, over.'

'You've obviously taken off your mask – what's the air like, over?'

'Sweet as a nut at the moment. The ventilation is off, so I don't know how much air I have left in here, over.'

'OK, hang on in there for a moment, Ben ... we'll get someone to work that out. I'll get back to you soon. Bailey out.' Bailey put down the microphone.

Lieutenant Commander Paulsdon drafted a long signal to be dispatched immediately to all high-ranking officers concerned. It would include Gibraltar on the UK mainland, the Chiefs of Staff Committee, the foreign secretary and of course the prime minister. In the signal he asked for advice on rescue and how to proceed. He also wanted to know the position and ETA of the DSRV. And he included a request for transportation of Orla.

CHAPTER FORTY-FIVE

At the submarine base in San Diego, Lieutenant Commander DuPont had received a signal from the Military Sealift Command. He looked at the clock on the wall: it was 1900 hours. He knew his master diver would still be at his desk, and walked briskly to his office.

'Speedy, I received this signal just moments ago, I thought you'd want to hear it. I'll miss out all the boring bits.' Then he added: 'You'd better prepare yourself for some bad news I'm afraid.' He raised the paper in front of him and began to read from it. 'To … the Royal Navy has issued a SUMBISS operation off Gibraltar … DSRV mobilised and en route at flank speed … Submarine located but crew appear to have perished…' Then he paused and lowered the paper. 'Chief Petty Officer Diver Taylor trapped on board in tunnel compartment above the reactor.'

The two men stood looking at each other trying to process what they knew to be an impossible situation.

'Is there anything we can do, sir?' Speedy felt his legs go weak.

'The Royal Navy are running the show, Speedy. They'll ask us if they need us. The only thing we can do is pray the DSRV gets there in time.' Then he added: 'You'd better let the team know first thing in the morning.'

'Will do, sir.' Speedy put away the reports he was working on and locked his office. Morning could not wait, he checked his Rolex and headed for the car park.

The 'diver's bar' went quiet as the master diver entered. It was the first time he had ever stepped foot inside.

'I was hoping I would find you lot in here,' he said solemnly to his team.

A small flotilla of vessels had arrived at the area of sea above the stricken submarine, which was now becoming crowded with ships of varying descriptions. Four large anchors now secured a wooden floating platform above the submarine and more lines had been connected to various parts of the boat on the seabed. Compressors and electrical generators were strewn over the platform and diving equipment lay in an orderly fashion along the middle of it. WO Bailey and Sergeant Tim Sherwin were taking charge and organising the rescue site. They were as yet not sure of the way ahead but were trying to prepare for the decision that would eventually come from the experts.

Inside Number 10 Downing Street the Chiefs of Staff Committee were convening for the third time in two days. The top-ranking officers from the three Armed Forces branches, as well as MI5, MI6, the Metropolitan Police and the head of Customs and Excise, sat in silence reading confidential report files as they waited for the prime minister. When she entered she was carrying a large report and sat down immediately.

'I'll get straight to the point, gentlemen: I know you're busy but yet another crisis has raised its ugly head.'

She opened the large file she had placed on the table. 'It would appear, as you can see from the reports in front of you, that not only do we have a crisis down in the South Atlantic to deal with, but there is another one brewing a lot closer to home. A splinter group from the IRA has taken possession of a virus, and its leader ...' the PM put on a pair of spectacles and read from the file, '... a man called Gallymore .... has somehow managed to get it on board one of our finest submarines, which was on its way to the Falklands and is now crippled on the seabed off Gibraltar. This virus is a mixture of Ebola and snake venom, stolen by Gallymore from a university in San Diego, California. Now, before we decide how to deal with this incident, I have some questions.' The PM removed her spectacles and leaned back in her chair. 'I do not want to hear excuses or long drawn-out explanations, gentlemen – give me the facts. Now ... how did this virus get into the country?'

The head of Customs and Excise shuffled in his chair. 'The virus was carried in a glass vial, ma'am, totally undetectable to any scanner or x-ray machine at our entrance terminals.'

'How do we know it was carried in a glass vial?' The PM tapped her pen on the table.

The First Sea Lord now spoke: 'We ascertained that the virus was put on board the submarine by a dockyard worker who had been employed to help with the urgency of preparations for war at the Faslane base. This person was apprehended at the peace camp outside the base and subsequent interrogation proved he had put the virus carried in a glass vial into the water tanks on board.'

'What do we know about this person?'

'He is a sleeper for the IRA and has not been active for some time, but he was in the right place at the right time for this splinter group to wake up and utilise. While we had him in custody it became apparent that he was extremely unwell, and after consulting with medical experts he was transferred to our Defence Science and Technology Laboratory at Porton Down in Wiltshire for further examination. We have since heard from Porton Down that it is unlikely he will live.'

There was silence in the room as they all contemplated what this meant. Then the PM spoke again.

'Is there any chance this virus could have spread and become a problem to the public?'

'It's very doubtful. The perpetrator was contained and isolated as soon as we knew he was ill. The Ebola in the virus can only be contracted through bodily fluids and open wounds. However, we're not sure about the snake venom ... I'm waiting for a full report from Porton Down.'

'Well, I've not heard of snake venom being airborne. However, let me know the results of that report as soon as you get them.' The PM opened the floor to the men in front of her: 'OK, your thoughts: how are we going to sort this out?'

The First Sea Lord started: 'The report we have from the submarine is that the crew in the aft section have definitely passed away, and although we've not been able to gain access to the forward half of the submarine, no communication has been established and therefore in all probability there are no survivors on board. Cause of death has not been established as yet ...

but as we have the confession from the terrorist, we must assume that the virus did indeed spread through the water system and completed its work. Due to the nature of the water supply on board being an internal system, we can safely assume that the virus is contained on board and at present presents no problem in terms of contamination elsewhere.'

'So, what are you suggesting – we leave it where it is?'

'What I'm saying is, it will present us with a huge problem trying to retrieve this submarine and contain any possible spread of this terrible virus. We have an incredible logistical dilemma to sort out, what with the conflict against Argentina. It will tie up a huge amount of resources and personnel to rescue this submarine at the moment. It is going nowhere and does not present an immediate threat; the immediate threat is getting our Armed Forces south to protect our people and British territory from invasion.'

'Well, we must make a decision quickly on this, gentlemen ... has anyone else got a solution?'

The PM looked at the shaking heads one by one around the table.

'OK. My decision is to abort all rescue attempts and remove all but one marker line from the submarine. We will leave it as a war grave and assign a local coastal ship to protect the area from prying eyes.' The prime minister sighed heavily and closed the file on the table. 'Does anyone disagree?'

Again, there were shaking heads around the table.

'Let's keep this under our hats until this crisis is over, gentlemen. I do not want the press getting hold of this before they have to.'

As the admiral was leaving the room, the prime minister stopped the First Sea Lord. 'George, make sure as few people know about this as possible ... and start thinking about how we can retrieve that submarine when the time comes.'

The admiral nodded.

Orla followed the man out of the security building at the submarine base. He drove her to the medical block, where he told her he would wait. She entered the sickbay and asked for Nurse Callahan at the reception. The nurse was paged and soon appeared.

'Hi, my name is Orla ... I was told to come and see you by the base commander.'

'Ah, yes, come with me, Miss Brodie, we're all ready for you.' Orla followed her into a private room. 'Please sit on the bed and remove your shirt, Miss Brodie: I need to get at your arm.'

Orla complied and waited for the needle. 'When will I know the results of the blood test?'

'It won't take long ... you can wait in the foyer and I'll bring the results out to you. Does the commander want a copy?'

'Well, if you're going to give a copy to me, I'll make sure he sees it.'

The nurse took some blood from her arm. 'The lab is two floors up – I'll take it there now. You can get dressed again and wait outside for me. The foyer is by the reception area.'

Fifteen minutes later Orla slid back into the waiting car. She was carrying a large brown envelope. When she was back at the security office she entered the office of the base commander. She handed him the envelope.

'I don't know who you are, Miss Brodie, but this is highly irregular ... however, I have my orders. You're lucky there are a lot of flights to Gibraltar.' He opened the envelope and read the report. 'And it would seem you don't have the virus. So, you're ready to go.' He handed the report back to her.

Ben Taylor had broken off a thin, rectangular stainless-steel 'tally' plate with the number of the valve stamped on it from one of the valves. He was using it to try and undo screws that fastened another larger plate. His plan was to then use the larger plate to break a pipe, and then use that to break the hydraulic pipe. He knew it wouldn't work but it kept him occupied. He wished the guys at the surface would contact him.

The train journey south was boring. Orla wanted to sleep but couldn't. She tried reading but couldn't concentrate. She had asked the commander if she could have a car, but he had laughed. 'We have a war to fight, Miss Brodie.' Orla knew the commander didn't like her. She didn't care much for him either. Orla thought of Ben, and wished she was with him. She watched the scenery fly past outside the train window but her thoughts were on Ben. She had taken the train from Glasgow to Wolverhampton and eventually arrived at Oxford. She struggled with her luggage through the station and hailed a cab outside to take her to RAF Brize Norton.

Lieutenant Commander Paulsdon read the encrypted signal and asked his secretary to contact WO Bailey.

He slouched in his chair and pondered over how he was going to impart this information to his second-in-command.

Orla sat near the rear of the small Boeing aircraft. Most people sat by themselves, as the plane was only half-full, with some passengers in civilian clothing and some in highly pressed and spotlessly clean uniform. She felt intimidated and out of place ... and very alone. She must have snoozed during the three-hour flight, because she was surprised to hear the captain announce they would be landing in five minutes. Her heart began to race. She peered out the small window but could only see sky. The plane tilted rapidly and now she could only see the sea. She decided to close her eyes.

Bill Bailey walked into the office, and when he saw the demeanour and look on his boss's face, he instantly knew bad news was coming.

'Come in, Bill, take a seat.'

Bailey's mind began to race. *Confirmed bad news coming – he hasn't called me Bill since the last Christmas party in the wardroom*, WO Bailey thought. *Is it my family? Or are they sending me to the Falklands?* He sat bolt upright in a chair.

Lieutenant Commander Paulsdon decided to come straight out with it – there was no point in trying to gloss over this. 'Signal from Whitehall, Bill: they've pulled the plug on the rescue of that submarine.'

He remained quiet for a moment to let the news sink in.

'It's too dangerous at this time to risk contamination from the virus. We are to disengage all lines except one and mark it as a war grave.' He paused again. 'Then when things quieten down we will continue the … uh … well, they'll let us know.'

WO Bailey was stunned. He sat in silence not believing what he had just heard. 'How could they?' His eyes pierced into the lieutenant commander's. 'There is a man still alive down there!' His forehead was now furrowed and his mouth pressed into a grim line.

'Bill, it's not my decision, don't get angry with me.'

'But sir, you don't seem very upset about this. There is a sailor – a British military person – trapped, and we're going to leave him, abandon him. I've never heard of such … ludicrous … sir, this is murder!'

'This is no such thing!' Both men were now very agitated. 'All our resources are being stretched to the limit; we cannot risk thousands of lives just to save one man. I'm getting signals from around the world asking for support. "Can we have this?" "Can we have that?" The harbour is nearly full and I have to say who comes and goes.'

'Well let me tell you something right now: I'm not doing your dirty work for you – if you want to stop this rescue, you're the one who will have to go out there and tell the men to stop. I'm not killing that chief petty officer!'

'That chief petty officer was dead as soon as he entered that submarine. I have a meeting with the colonel from the Royal Marines in fifteen minutes.'

The lieutenant commander walked from behind his desk, took his cap from the stand and played with the rim. 'Bill, the decision has come from the Chiefs of Staff Committee in London.' He nearly dropped his cap. 'Pull the plug. That's an order.' He placed his cap on his head and left WO Bailey in his office.

The small Boeing aircraft rapidly decelerated on the reclaimed land that formed the runway. The plane vibrated violently as it braked hard nearing the end of the runway. Orla found herself trembling as she gripped the arms of her chair. Eventually, the shaking having stopped, the aeroplane slowed and she released her grip as the plane came to standstill outside the terminal. Orla sat in her chair trying to control her breathing as the other passengers hustled to get their gear together in preparation to leave.

'Is everything all right, Miss Brodie?' asked one of the cabin crew with a genuine smile.

'Yes, everything is fine.' Orla couldn't believe she was in Gibraltar. As the door of the aircraft swung open the heat came in and surrounded her, engulfing her whole body and holding her tightly. It initially took her breath away. She waited in her seat until everyone else had got off the plane.

She wished Ben was there to meet her; she wanted desperately to be with him. Orla collected her hand luggage and walked to the door. As she stepped through into the night air she looked down the stairs to the tarmac ... and then her eyes came up slowly. The view stopped her in her tracks. The lights of the terminal led her eyes to the coloured lights of the town beyond. These lights in turn led her eyes still upward to the base of the Rock.

Orla could make out different shapes and colours as her gazed continued to move up – dark patches then light areas of chalk. Eventually she stood with her mouth open at the lights on the summit, and beyond that a million stars that took her eyes on and on into infinity. She managed somehow to tear them away from this magnificent view, only to find her gaze pulled towards the silver rays of the moon shimmering on the sea and the silhouettes of ships at anchor in the sound. A tear ran down Orla's cheek. She had never imagined a place could be so beautiful.

'Is this your first time here?'

Without looking, Orla replied to the voice behind her. 'This is my first time on an aeroplane.' She turned to find the pilot standing behind her.

'Are you sure you're OK?' he asked, seeing the tear running down her cheek.

'Yes.' Orla wiped her cheek. 'I'm fine, thank you for asking. I just wish I was here under better circumstances.'

'Then may I have the privilege of showing you around the rest of this jewel of a Rock?'

'I'm being met, actually. I'm here to see my …'
Orla struggled to find the right words. What was Ben?
Her boyfriend? Surely he was more than that.

'How thoughtless of me – I should have known
a lovely girl like yourself would be meeting with
someone. Please except my apologies. I didn't mean
to offend.'

'No offence taken. Would you be kind enough
to show me where I collect the rest of my baggage?'

'Yes of course, this way.' He escorted Orla
across the tarmac and into a large building. Inside, the
pilot apologised for the air conditioning not working.
'In fact, I can't remember when it was last working.'
He spoke as they approached a small carousel with
bags already trundling round on it. 'Well here we are,
then.' He turned and stood close to Orla.

'Thank you for a lovely first flight, Captain.
And thank you for your help here.'

The pilot took hold of Orla's hand and kissed
the back gently. 'The pleasure has been all mine.'

Orla wanted to pull her hand away and slap the
amorous pilot. Something stopped her. She wasn't
acting as she normally would.

Orla put her bags on a trolley and walked out
into the warm night air. Tim was leaning on the front
wing of a Land Rover, staring up at the starry sky.
When Orla saw him she couldn't control herself. She
left the trolley and ran to him, throwing her arms
around him.

'Oh Tim, it's so good to see a friendly face!'
They held each other close for a long while. When
her arms began to ache she let go. 'How is he?' she
asked slowly, peering deep into his eyes.

'I'll tell you all about it on the way.' The trolley was moving slowly away down a slope. 'Rescue that trolley before it runs in front of a plane.'

They drove slowly through the narrow streets of the town.

'What a beautiful place this is ... I've never seen such incredible charm. Even the Rock is alluring.' Orla avoided looking at Tim and stared out the side window.

'It's even better in the sunshine. Takes on a different character.' Tim braked and brought the vehicle to a stop, as directed by the English-looking police officer who had stepped into the road and was now waving traffic from a side street. He waved Tim on. As they approached the dockyard Tim pulled off the road and switched off the engine.

Orla knew that Ben was in a very difficult situation. 'What do you know? The commander at Faslane told me that a submarine was stuck on the seabed and Ben was trapped on board somehow ... but I don't know exactly how.' Orla now looked at Tim. 'Can't he just swim out?'

Tim shuffled in his seat and looked seriously at Orla. 'It's not that simple ...' He told her the news she was dreading to hear.

They sat, looking at the lights flickering high up on the Rock and far out to sea. Orla thought of Ben all by himself, trapped in that submarine, and she felt the anger billowing up inside her. The silence was broken by the two-way radio that was screwed under the dashboard.

'Tim? Come in, Tim ... where are you?' Tim recognised Bailey's voice.

Tim unclipped the microphone. 'On the road, outside the dockyard,' Tim told Bailey.

'Come to the ops room, buddy, I have some … bad news.'

Orla spoke in a subdued tone. 'More bad news?'

'I'm on my way.' Tim started the engine.

The outer office of the ops room was empty. This time of night the office was usually closed but the door to the lieutenant commander's office was open and the light was on. Tim and Orla went straight through. Bailey was sat in the large chair with his feet on the desk.

'Why aren't you on the dive boat, Bill?'

'No point,' he said decisively. 'Take a seat.' When Bailey saw Orla he stood up.

'This is Orla … Orla Brodie.'

Bailey had guessed who she was; he tried to smile but his features didn't change. He nodded slightly.

'So, what's happened?' Tim asked while he took a seat next to Orla.

Bailey twiddled a pen between his fingers.

'Bill …?' Tim nudged.

'The prime minister and the Joint Chiefs have pulled the plug on the rescue.' He threw the pen at the wall. 'The bastards say they can't waste time or resources to recover what could "possibly be a deadly virus" and "risk contamination on a wider scale".'

'There must be some mistake. They wouldn't just leave a man down there. The bodies of the crew need to be brought up!'

'They're going to mark it as a war grave and recover the whole submarine after this goddam war is over.' Bailey sat down down again.

'And when will that be?' Tim thumped the arm of his chair.

'It's no use, Tim.' Bailey rubbed his forehead. 'They've made their decision and that's that.'

'So we just sit here and let Ben die?' Tim stood up.

Orla felt a tear run down her cheek. The room fell silent. Tim sat back down despondently.

'There's nothing we can do,' Bailey said eventually; he was looking at Orla. She had begun to shiver.

'Orla, are you OK? Tim ...' He nodded his head towards Orla.

Tim looked at her and realised she hadn't said a word since coming into the office. He tried to put his arm around her but she pulled away and shrugged him off.

'Are you OK?' Tim asked her.

'I'm fine.' She spoke looking at the floor. 'It's Ben we should be worried for.'

Both men looked at each other.

'Orla, you must understand ...' Bailey searched for the right words. 'The Joint Chiefs have to make their decision based on saving as many lives as they can. They have to be ...' Bailey stopped when he realised he wasn't helping.

Tim continued. 'At times like these they have to make difficult decisions.'

'Sounds like you two are defending their decision to kill the man I love.'

'The hell no,' Tim disagreed. 'But I wouldn't want their job ...'

'It's getting late ...' sighed Bailey. 'We ought to tell the surface crew to stand down.'

'Someone needs to let Ben know,' Tim finally said.

'I'll do it,' Orla said, looking determined.

CHAPTER FORTY-SIX

'We have communications with him in the tunnel through an underwater telephone system. Press the microphone to speak and release to listen. It's a good idea to say "over" when you've finished speaking and want him to reply. When the total conversation has finished we normally say "out" ... but none of this is absolutely necessary,' Tim explained to Orla as they bounced out of the harbour in the launch.

The full height of the Rock could now be seen from the sea. Orla felt her stomach rumble and realised she had not eaten since leaving home. The motion of the launch over the small waves made her feel nauseous. The lights of small vessels showed ahead and soon they were alongside the dive boat. Bailey climbed onto the boat first and held his hand down for Orla to grab hold off. Tim helped her with the first difficult step onto the rickety ladder. Once on board, Bailey went to talk to the men while Tim took Orla to the tiny radio shack.

'I'll contact him first then hand him over to you,' said Tim while settling onto the seat in front of the radio.

Orla nodded her head and tried to gather her thoughts.

'Tunnel, this is Dive Boat, over.' There was no answer. Tim tried again. 'Ben, this is Tim, over.'

'Hey, buddy ...' The voice coming through the small speaker on the panel was slow and quiet. Orla recognised Ben's voice immediately.

'How are you, pal, over?' Tim enquired.

'Could kill for a drink of water, matey. How are things progressing up there? Got any good ideas?'

'Well, one good idea I had was to let you speak to Orla, over.' The speaker went quiet. Tim could envisage Ben trying to think how he could possibly speak to Orla. 'She's right here, pal. I had her flown over from Brize today. OK, I'll hand over to her now; speak to you soon, pal, keep your chin up.' Tim stood up from the stool and Orla trembled as she sat down and picked up the mic. 'I'll leave you to it.'

Orla watched Tim walk away across the deck. She found herself staring at the microphone in her hand. Then the speaker burst into life. She heard Ben's voice.

'I've lost all track of time.'

'It's nearly eleven o'clock at night,' she said, before she burst into tears uncontrollably. She controlled the tears and regained some composure. 'I suppose you've had quite a long day … you must be very tired.'

'I've had better…'

She managed a smile. 'The pilot of the aeroplane tried it on with me as we were getting off, but I put him in his place.'

'I'll bet you did.'

'How have you got yourself trapped, Ben?'

'Basically, I'm in what they call the "tunnel"; it runs over the top of the reactor compartment and the hydraulics has been cut off to the doors.'

'And you can't get it back?'

'No, sweetheart, it's a safety feature.'

'I spoke to your mam yesterday ... she's obviously very worried.'

'Typical of the RAF.'

Orla was confused. 'What is?'

'The pilot ... typical of the RAF.'

'Oh, right.' There was a pause, then Taylor came back.

'Thanks for talking to my mother.' Taylor voice was slurred.

Orla keyed the mic' 'The security men came to the caravan and arrested Liam. They took him to the base at first – you know, to interview him. Then they realised he wasn't well and they took him to some specialist hospital in England. He's very ill.'

'When I get home, I'm going to help my father more, especially on his yacht. He struggles with the work, I know that ...' Taylor was now mumbling deliriously.

Orla began to sob quietly 'Ben, I'm pregnant.' Orla felt relieved she had told him. There was a long pause as she waited for a reply.

'I'm really happy. That's amazing news.' Taylor seemed to recover from his delirium. 'There is something I wanted to talk to you about, but now is not the time.' Another short pause before he continued. 'We should get married.'

'Is that a proposal?'

'I'll ask you properly when I get out of here. Do we know if the baby is a boy or a girl?'

'Not sure. I don't want to know.'

'Orla, what are you going to do? Will you move back to Ireland?'

'No, I want to stay near to your mam. She's been very kind. My mam and I will move down to Cheshire and be near her. She's looking forward to becoming a nan.'

'Remember when we first met?'

'I do ... you wouldn't get me down a hole in the ground again.'

'You looked pretty frightened.'

'Frightened? I was terrified.'

'If it's a boy I'd like to call him Calum.' Taylor lay on his back on the floor of the tunnel. 'I've always been under decompression rules when near to Ben Nevis. I would love to go to the summit.'

'Ben, I love you.'

'I love you more,' he said softly.

'Don't give up, Ben. Even if the people in power have given in, we will not. There must be a way to get you off. Tim Sherwin is a good man.' Orla felt panic begin. She struggled to hear his voice. 'If it's a boy I'd like to call him Calum.'

She realised he was rambling. She felt herself trembling and tears were now flooding down her face. 'Ben, I'm going now. Don't give up, hold on down there. I love you.'

Ben Taylor said 'I love you more', but Orla didn't hear him.

EPILOGUE

The war with Argentina ended swiftly with the taking back of the Falkland Islands, both Argentina and the United Kingdom suffering heavy losses of life. With the majority of the warships back in UK home waters, HMS *Reclaim*, the Royal Navy's deep diving and submarine rescue, along with the United States Undersea Rescue Command from San Diego, lifted HMS/M *Courageous* from the seabed off Gibraltar and transported the submarine to a remote sea loch in Scotland, where a decontamination team slowly cleared the boat of the bodies and the submarine was decommissioned.

Orla Brodie moved with her mother to be near to Mrs Taylor in Cheshire. Orla's baby boy was born seven pounds four ounces and she named him Calum. Tim Sherwin visits her regularly.

Lieutenant Commander Paulsdon was awarded his next half-ring and became a Commander for his efforts during the Falklands conflict.

Printed in Poland
by Amazon Fulfillment
Poland Sp. z o.o., Wrocław